PRAISE FOR

The God of Animals

"Aryn Kyle's stunning debut is a wry and moving look at a disappearing
way of life. [A] powerfully understated, ruefully funny novel."
—*Vogue*

"Involving and accomplished, Aryn Kyle's debut delivers all
the fun of the books about horses that you loved as a kid—but with the
added weight and seriousness of a novel for grown-ups."
—Francine Prose, *People*

"A beautiful first novel. [Alice is] close cousin to the little girls in
To Kill a Mockingbird and *The Member of the Wedding*."
—*The Washington Post*

"An awesome debut. To write about such wild country,
such beautiful land, and to know the people living in it,
is a writer's dream. Kyle makes it seem easy."
—*The Globe and Mail* (Toronto)

"*The God of Animals* is a moving tale of loss and love. [It's] an admirable
debut by a writer who holds the promise of one day becoming one of the
more significant names in the American literary landscape."
—*The Denver Post*

More Praise for Aryn Kyle and
The God of Animals

"[Aryn Kyle] is a seamless storyteller. . . . It will be wonderful to watch her write more and more subtle fiction and to relax into the arms of her own competence."

—*Los Angeles Times*

"Kyle has a lovely new voice, one that will most certainly be added to the landscape of talented American writers."

—*The Globe and Mail* (Toronto)

"Aryn Kyle is one of those handful of first-time novelists whose arrival trumpets what might be a major talent. . . . It's an impressive debut."

—*The Star-Ledger* (Newark)

"Kyle's obvious and delightfully unpostmodern pleasure in the old-school art of storytelling is sure to make converts of all but the most jaded readers."

—*Elle*

"Gorgeous, cinematic prose."

—*The Charlotte Observer*

"Kyle is pitch perfect. . . . She creates a strong narrative pulse around these characters, capable of surprising Alice and us."

—*The Plain Dealer* (Cleveland)

"Impressive . . . fresh, realistic, and sometimes heartbreaking."

—*Great Falls Tribune* (Montana)

"A compelling book with complex characters you'll grow to love."

—*Columbia Missourian*

"Kyle's debut tracks the complicated, often punitive business of love . . . [and she] delivers the story in graceful, translucent prose."

—*Kirkus Reviews*

"A very impressive debut. Kyle's prose is graceful and mature, and her themes are subtly stitched into the story. . . . A powerful tale from a writer with real promise."

—*Booklist*

"Horses and lost love propel this confident debut novel. . . . The coupling of female adolescence with the stark West produces its share of harsh truths."

—*Publishers Weekly*

"Kyle's novel . . . brims with confidence and assuredness atypical of a debut. . . . [She] keeps the reader glued to the story. Highly recommended."

—*Library Journal*

"No novel in recent memory has captured the West so well. Kyle is an absolute discovery, her book a perfect read."

—Andrew Sean Greer, author of
The Confessions of Max Tivoli

"Aryn Kyle's *The God of Animals* is a moving, beautifully crafted novel about families, horses, love, death, class in America, and serious weather. Narrated by a twelve-year-old girl, it still contains a full adult measure of betrayal and desire and complex joy, and has a terrifying momentum by the end. It's a wonderful book."

—Maile Meloy, author of
Liars and Saints and *A Family Daughter*

"Aryn Kyle is one of those rare writers who thoroughly understands both horses and people. Her characters are complex, compelling, and real. . . . They'll break your heart—and heal it again."

—Sy Montgomery, author of
The Good Good Pig and *Journey of the Pink Dolphins*

The God of Animals

A Novel

ARYN KYLE

Scribner

NEW YORK   LONDON   TORONTO   SYDNEY

SCRIBNER
A Division of Simon & Schuster, Inc.
1230 Avenue of the Americas
New York, NY 10020

Copyright © 2007 by Aryn Kyle

First Scribner trade paperback edition March 2008

Chapter 1 originally appeared as "Foaling Season" in *The Atlantic Monthly*, May 2004.

"Sonnets to Orpheus" copyright © 1982 by Stephen Mitchell, from *The Selected
Poetry of Rainer Maria Rilke* by Rainer Maria Rilke, translated by Stephen Mitchell.
Used by permission of Random House, Inc.

"Do-Re-Mi" and "So Long, Farewell" by Richard Rodgers and Oscar Hammerstein II.
Copyright © 1959, 1960 by Richard Rodgers and Oscar Hammerstein II. Copyright
Renewed. WILLIAMSON MUSIC owner of publication and allied rights throughout the
world. International Copyright Secured. All Rights Reserved. Used by Permission.

SCRIBNER and design are trademarks of Macmillan Library Reference USA, Inc.,
used under license by Simon & Schuster, the publisher of this work.

For information about special discounts for bulk purchases,
please contact Simon & Schuster Special Sales at
1-800-456-6798 or business@simonandschuster.com.

Designed by Kyoko Watanabe
Text set in Garamond 3

Manufactured in the United States of America

1   3   5   7   9   10   8   6   4   2

Library of Congress Cataloging-in-Publication Data

Kyle, Aryn.
The god of animals : a novel / Aryn Kyle
p. cm.
1. Ranches—Fiction. 2. Colorado—Fiction. I. Title.

PS3611.Y55G63 2007
813'.6—dc22
2006050605

ISBN-13: 978-1-4165-3324-5
ISBN-10: 1-4165-3324-9
ISBN-13: 978-1-4165-3325-2 (pbk)
ISBN-10: 1-4165-3325-7 (pbk)

for my mother

The God of Animals

one

Six months before Polly Cain drowned in the canal, my sister, Nona, ran off and married a cowboy. My father said there was a time when he would have been able to stop her, and I wasn't sure if he meant a time in our lives when she would have listened to him, or a time in history when the Desert Valley Sheriff's Posse would have been allowed to chase after her with torches and drag her back to our house by her yellow hair. My father had been a member of the sheriff's posse since before I was born, and he said that the group was pretty much the same as the Masons, except without the virgin sacrifices. They paid dues, rode their horses in parades, and directed traffic at the rodeo where my sister met her cowboy. Only once in a great while were they called upon for a task of real importance, like clearing a fallen tree from a hunting trail, or pulling a dead girl out of the canal.

Polly Cain disappeared on a Wednesday afternoon, and at first people were talking kidnapping. An eleven-year-old girl was too young to be a runaway, so they figured someone must have snatched her. But then they found her backpack on the dirt road that ran alongside the canal, and soon they called my father. For the two days that the sheriff's posse dragged the canal, they traded in their white tuxedo shirts and black felt Stetsons for rubber waders that came up to their armpits, and they walked shoulder to shoulder through the brown water. I passed them on my way home from school. It was only April, but already the mayflies were starting to hatch off the water, and I watched my father swat them away from his face. I waved and called to him from the side of the canal, but he clenched his jaw and didn't look at me.

"We found that girl today," he said when he came home the next afternoon. I was making Kool-Aid in a plastic pitcher, and he stuck his finger in and then licked it. "Tangled in one of the grates."

"Is she dead?" I asked and he stared at me.

"You stay away from that canal when you're walking home, Alice," he said.

"Will there be a funeral?" I pictured myself like a woman in the movies, standing beside the grave in a black dress and thick sunglasses, too sad to cry.

"What do you care?"

"We were partners in shop class. We were making a lantern." The truth was that Polly had been making the lantern while I watched. She had been a good sport about the whole thing and let me hold it when our teacher, Mr. McClusky, walked by, so that he would think I was doing some of the work.

"I don't have time to take you to a funeral, Alice," my father said, and he put his hand on the top of my head. "There's just too much work around here. I've already lost two days."

I nodded and stirred the Kool-Aid with a wooden spoon. There was always too much work. My father owned a stable. Between posse meetings he gave riding lessons and bred and raised horses, which he sold to people who fed them apple slices by hand and called them "baby." In the mornings my father and I fed the horses while it was still dark, and I would walk to school shaking hay from my hair and clothing, scratching at the pieces that had fallen down the front of my shirt. In the afternoons we cleaned the stalls and groomed and exercised the horses. It was foaling season and my father didn't like to leave the barn even for a minute, in case one of our mares went into labor. It was just as well. I didn't have a black dress.

"You've been a trouper, kid," he said. "When your sister comes back, things will calm down."

He always did this—talked about how my sister would come home and everything would be the way it was. For a while I'd wondered if he might be right. It had all happened so fast. Nona met Jerry on a Sunday, and on Thursday she packed four boxes and a backpack and went off in his pickup truck. Jerry rode broncs on the rodeo circuit and married my sister at a courthouse in Kansas. My father said that Jerry would break his spine riding broncs, and Nona would spend the rest of her life pushing him around in a wheelchair and holding a cup for him to drool into. She wasn't the marrying kind, my father said. She wouldn't be satisfied to spend her life on the outside of an arena, cheering for someone else.

But the months had passed, and Nona's letters were still filled with smiley faces and exclamation points. Compared with the horse-show circuit, she wrote, rodeos were a dream. She and Jerry ate steak for dinner and slept in motels, which was a big step up from horse shows, where we ate granola bars and drank soda pop and slept in the stalls with the horses so that no one could steal them during the night.

Her letters were always addressed to me. They opened with "Baby Alice," and closed with "Give my love to Mom and Dad." I would leave the letters on the counter for my father to read, which he hardly ever did, and after a few days I would go up to my mother's room and read the letters aloud to her.

My mother had spent nearly my whole life in her bedroom. Nona said that before we came along, our mother had been a star in horse shows, had won left and right, and even had her picture in the paper. She said that one day, when I was still a baby, our mother had handed me to her, said she was tired, and gone upstairs to rest. She never came back down. My father moved into the guest bedroom so as not to disrupt her, and we were careful to take our shoes off when we walked past her room. She didn't make much of a fuss. She didn't call for extra blankets or crushed ice or quiet. She just stayed in bed with the curtains drawn and watched television without the sound. It was easy to forget she was there.

I would sit on her bed and read Nona's letters to her by the blue light of the TV screen, and she would pat my leg and say, "Real nice. It sounds real nice, doesn't it, Alice?"

I would breathe through my mouth to filter the sour, damp scent of her yellow skin and oily hair. My mother made me say the name of the town each letter had come from, and what I thought it looked like. I pictured the rodeo towns as dry, dusty places with dirty motels and lines of fast-food restaurants, but I tried to be inventive: McCook, Nebraska, had chestnut trees lining every street; Marion, Illinois, had purple sunsets; and Sikeston, Missouri, had a park with a pond in the middle where people could feed ducks. When I couldn't think anymore, I would say that I had to go to the bathroom or that I had to help my father in the barn, and I would creep out of her bedroom and shut the door behind me.

After Nona left, my father said, we were lucky to get Sheila Altman. She lived on the other side of Desert Valley and went to a new school with computers and air-conditioning. Sheila Altman had blue eyes and a soft voice. She said "If I might" and "Would you mind," and never forgot to say "please" and "thank you." I wanted to rip her baby-fine hair out in tufts. When her mother drove her to our house, Sheila would rush into the stable to kiss the horses and feed them carrots she had brought from home. Mrs. Altman would get out of the car with her camera and checkbook and watch her daughter scramble into the barn. "Well, Mr. Winston," she would say, "you've got your work cut out for you today."

Mrs. Altman had told my father that for the past few years she had spent thousands of dollars to send Sheila to equestrian camp, where for one week she got to care for a horse as if it were her own, feeding it, grooming it, and cleaning its stall. My father had jokingly said that he would let Sheila clean his stalls for half that, but when Mrs. Altman gasped and said, "Really?" he didn't falter.

"For *this* girl?" he said. "Absolutely." After that Mrs. Altman drove Sheila across the valley every day after school and paid my father to let her groom our horses and muck out our stalls. While Sheila was there, my father was chipper and lighthearted. He told her what a hard worker she was and said he didn't know how we had managed without her. After she was gone, he would rub my back and say, "You give that girl anything she wants, Alice. Talk nice to her. Sheila Altman is our meal ticket. And she doesn't have attitude like your sister."

My father had always said that Nona had a wicked tongue and an ungrateful heart, but he usually smiled when he said it. She threw fits like nobody's business. When she was thirsty, she shrieked. When she was hot, she cried. And when she was mad at my father, her face would get so tight and rigid that it looked like it might split apart right between her eyes.

My father was being kind when he said I didn't have the temperament for showing, because what he meant was that I didn't have the talent. I couldn't remember to smile and keep my heels down and my toes in and my elbows tight and my back straight all at the same time. When I focused on smiling, I dropped my reins, and when I thought about sitting up straight, my feet slipped out of the stirrups. My father said that he needed me more outside the ring anyway, but I saw how it was. We had a reputation to maintain and a livelihood to earn. In the end, I wasn't good for business.

But Nona was good enough for both of us. She smiled and laughed and winked at the judges. Outside the ring she would let little girls from the stands sit on her horse. While she showed them how to hold the reins and where to put their feet, she would aim her voice at their parents and say, "You're a natural!" Then she would flash her smile at the mother and say, "My daddy gives lessons. You all should come out sometime."

Yellow Cap was the last horse my father bought for her. He was a palomino—the flashiest, biggest, most beautiful animal in the ring. The first time I saw him, I thought he would kill my sister for sure, but Nona mounted him easily. She jiggled the reins and said, "There's my boy." Yellow Cap's neck arched, and his body tucked, and they rode around the arena like they were under a spotlight. My father watched from the sidelines with prospective clients and said, "That horse would walk on water if she asked him to."

The day after Polly was pulled from the canal, we didn't have shop class. Instead, the whole sixth grade was taken into the gymnasium and invited to pray if we wanted to. Then we were told to go home and talk with our parents about what we were feeling.

When I got home, Mrs. Altman and my father were gathered around Sheila, who was wearing my sister's show clothes.

"I don't know," Mrs. Altman was saying. "I'm not sure about the color."

"I was just thinking that," my father told her. "I was just thinking the same thing about the color."

"She looks better in red." Mrs. Altman made a circular motion with her finger, and Sheila gave me a shy smile as she turned around to let her mother see the back.

"We have a red shirt," my father said. "Alice, go up to Nona's room and get the red shirt." Sheila stared down at the pavement, and I dropped my backpack and went into the house.

I had to pick my way between piles of ribbons and trophies to get to the closet, and when I opened it, Nona's smell was gone from the clothes. I pushed my face into the different fabrics, trying to find a trace of her, the sweet, powdery scent of her deodorant, the fruity smell of her lotion, but there was nothing.

My mother's door was open a crack when I passed it, with the red shirt still on its hanger.

"Alice, is that you?"

I creaked the door open and braced myself against the wave of stale air. My mother was propped up on three pillows, and the TV light flickered across her face. I arranged my feet in the doorway, careful not to let them cross the line where the hallway carpet changed into the bedroom carpet.

"Be my good girl and close the window." She tossed her pale hand limply at the wrist and sighed. "Those little white bugs are coming in. I'm afraid they'll bite me in my sleep."

"Mayflies don't bite, Mom," I said, but I crossed the room to close the window.

"I hate them," she said. "Filthy things. Off that horrible water."

In the glow of the TV the mayflies looked gray and sickly, and I tried to fan them out the window. I could feel my mother's stare on the back of my neck. "Would you like to stay and tell me what you learned in school today?" She patted the bed beside her.

I held up the red shirt. "I have to take this to Dad."

She blinked at me for a second and then looked back at the television. "Better hurry, then."

Sheila really did look much better in red, and my father sold Nona's shirt to Mrs. Altman for twice what he had paid for it.

In shop class I didn't know what to do with the half-finished lantern. I was afraid to weld, and I didn't think I could tape the pieces together. But the boys couldn't get enough of welding, and several of them bid for the chance to finish the lantern for me. In the end I accepted an offer of three dollars and a Pepsi, and then watched while they pieced my lantern together.

Mr. McClusky told me that it would be a nice gesture to give the lantern to Polly's mother, and after school I practiced what I might say when I rang Polly's doorbell. I had barely known Polly and had never met her mother, but such a heartfelt gesture would probably make her cry. Maybe she would ask me to stay and visit. She would make me tea and feed me gingersnaps while she ran her fingers through my hair. "Come back anytime," she would say. "Stay the night if you want."

But while I was practicing the right way to make my gesture, I noticed the places on the lantern where I had smudged the paint by touching it to see if it was dry. Polly's mother probably had rooms full of perfect things Polly had made over the years: neatly sewn beanbags from home ec, symmetrical clay pencil holders from art, the kinds of things that when I made them always came out crooked or lumpy. Giving her a crummy lantern would only confuse her. Instead of taking it to Polly's house, I wrapped the lantern in notebook paper and put it in my backpack. I walked home along the canal, sipping my Pepsi and wishing I had let the boys paint my lantern too.

My father was sitting in front of the barn, polishing Nona's show saddle, when I got home. His face was red, and the skin around his lips looked tight and drawn. "Your mother's been crying all day," he said when he saw me. "Where have you been?"

"At school, like I always am."

"Don't use a tone with me."

I stared at my feet.

"Now you go upstairs and be sweet to your mother. Tell her how much you love her. Make her feel special. Then come back and help me. There's a million things to do. I'm sick of doing all the work around here."

I looked at him. Nona wasn't coming back. Not ever. "Maybe Sheila Altman can do it when she gets here."

My father stood up then, and he seemed bigger than any human being had ever been. For a second I thought he might hit me, and I tried to gauge the distance to the house. I might be able to outrun him. But then he put his hands up to his face, and his shoulders sagged. "Please, Alice," he said through his fingers. "Please."

Upstairs, my mother's face was streaked and strands of her hair clung to the damp patches on her cheeks.

"Why are you crying, Mom?" I asked from the doorway. I meant for it to sound sweet, but it came out tired. "Are you sick?"

She let out a cry when she saw me. "Come here to me." Every part of my body went stiff, but I thought of my father with his face in his hands, and I held my breath as I crossed the room to her. She pulled me into the bed with her and pressed my head against her shoulder.

"He sent you up here, didn't he? I've been a nuisance today."

"Dad's worried about you," I told her.

Her hair fell across my face and I tried to lift my head to breathe. "I used to be able to make him smile," she whispered. "He used to look at me like I was a movie star. Do you believe that?" She sighed and straightened herself. Then she bit her lip and looked down at her hands. "She was smart," she said quietly. "Smart to leave when she did."

I didn't know what to say.

"She would have been used up here. She would be old fast, and used up. And now she gets to travel to new places and meet new people." She turned her head away from me.

Her nightgown was wrinkled, and in the light of the television her skin looked dull and heavy. "I made you something," I told her. "In school."

"You did?" Her mouth opened and she touched her hand to her chest. "Really truly?"

I rummaged in my backpack. "It's a lantern," I said. "See? You put a candle here and then you can hang it and it will light your room."

My mother gasped as I handed it to her. She touched her fingers along the welded edges and paint-smeared center. "You made this? For me?"

"Uh-huh."

"Oh, baby," she said, and hugged me. "You and I will take care of each other, won't we?"

I stood up and backed to the door. "I have to go help in the barn now. Dad said."

Outside, Mrs. Altman was writing a check to my father. When I came up beside him, he raised his eyebrows at me, and I nodded. "She's fine," I said, and he sighed.

"Who?" Mrs. Altman asked with a bright smile. "Mrs. Winston?" My father and I glanced at each other. "I'd love to meet her."

"My wife keeps to herself," my father said awkwardly, his eyes on the check.

"She's sick," I added and they both looked at me.

"With what?" Mrs. Altman glanced at my father.

"She has an allergy to the sun," I said. "And to fresh air." My father opened his mouth slightly.

"How awful!" Mrs. Altman said. "What happens to her?"

"Her head gets big," I said. They both stared. "And she gets hives. And fevers. And sometimes she faints." My father nudged me.

Mrs. Altman clasped her hands. "That's dreadful," she said. "The poor thing!"

After she handed over the check and followed her daughter into the barn, my father gave me a searching look. "You're a wicked lying fiend, Alice Winston," he said. But he smiled when he said it.

Sheila Altman helped us clear the show horses out of the barn to make room for the broodmares, who got to live indoors when they birthed. While we brought the pregnant mares in from the pasture, Sheila squealed and clapped her hands.

"I can't wait for the babies!" she said to me.

Our broodmares had simple names like Misty, Lucy, Ginger, and Sally. They were slow and quiet, with long heads, matted manes, and misshapen stomachs. Sheila put her hands on the mares' barrel stomachs and said she could feel the foals moving inside.

"It kicked!" she told me. "I swear I felt it kick."

After she left, I took Cap from his pen and tried to brush the snarls from his mane and tail. My father watched. As I pulled the loose hair from the brush and let it fall on the ground, he cleared his throat.

"Mrs. Altman wants to buy Cap for Sheila," he said.

My fingertips went cold, and I pretended to clean more hair from the brush. "He's too much horse for her."

My father picked an invisible piece of lint off his shirt. "You want to show this year?"

I stared at him.

"Then keep your opinions to yourself."

Polly Cain's funeral was to begin at five o'clock on a Thursday afternoon, at the cemetery across from the waterslide. When I got home from school, I practiced looking sad and remorseful in the mirror. Maybe my father would change his mind and take me, and then Polly's mother would pick me out of the crowd as someone who had been close to Polly. I would walk slowly up to her and let her pull me against her body. As I stared at myself in the mirror, I imagined the afternoons I would spend sitting with Polly's mother at her kitchen table, with photo albums spread before us. She would point out pictures of Polly in Halloween costumes and at piano recitals. "See?" she would say. "See how much you look like her?" I would lean my head against her shoulder, and her hair would smell like strawberries and lemons. I would tell her how much I missed Polly, how nothing would ever be the same now that she was gone, and she would kiss my eyelids and fingers and cry into the palms of my hands. "She was my best friend in the world," I would say. And maybe it wouldn't be a real lie. No one could prove she wasn't my best friend. She was dead, after all.

But before I could persuade my father to take me, our mare Lucy gave birth to the first new foal of the year, and I knew that I would not be at the cemetery to pay my last respects. I helped my father wrap Lucy's tail with an Ace bandage so that the foal wouldn't get tangled in it. We moved around the mare on our knees, clearing the sawdust away from her legs to keep it from clogging the foal's nostrils. The foal came out, thin and wet, breaking the fetal sac open with its weak white hooves.

"It's a colt," my father said, grinning. "Look at him." I pressed myself across the colt's body to keep him still while my father cut the umbilical cord, and then we watched him try to stand on his tiny, pointed feet.

My father cupped the back of my head in his hand. "You did good, Alice," he said. "You're a pro." We waited in the stall doorway until the colt was balanced on his trembling legs. For a second it felt as if we had made something happen.

When we heard the Altmans' minivan pull up in the driveway, my father closed his eyes and said, "Christ, I don't have the energy for this today."

Mrs. Altman got out of the car and began examining the grille. "There are tiny white insects all over the place," she told us. "Their little corpses are stuck all over my car."

My father shook his head at me and then walked over to look. "Mayflies," he announced. "They hatch off the canals. We found about a hundred of them stuck in that girl's hair when we pulled her out of the water."

Mrs. Altman had taken a towel from the backseat and was trying to wipe the front of her car. "Down the road it almost looks like it's snowing there are so many of them." She looked at me and stopped. "My God, Alice. What's happened?"

I glanced down and saw that my T-shirt was stained with blood where I had leaned across the colt.

"We got our first foal this afternoon," my father said, gesturing at the barn.

"I can't believe we missed it," Sheila wailed. "You should have called us!"

My father turned to me and rolled his eyes. "We'll have plenty more," he said.

Sheila and her mother crowded around Lucy's stall and began clicking and cooing at the foal. Lucy bared her teeth and flattened her ears. My father nudged Sheila away. "Let's give them a while to adjust," he said. "The mothers are a little protective at first."

"I can't believe I forgot my camera today," Mrs. Altman said. "What a day to forget."

"We might get another tonight," I said. "They sometimes come right on top of each other."

"Mom, can I stay—please?" Sheila clasped her hands against her chest and rose up on her toes. "If you wouldn't mind, that is," she added, glancing at my father.

In my head I tried to will my father to say no, but he didn't look at me. "She can stay the night," he told Mrs. Altman. "Alice and I will be up all night checking on the mares anyway."

"Oh, please, Mom?" Sheila begged. "It will be like a slumber party."

Mrs. Altman adjusted the fold of her collar. "Tomorrow is a school day, but for something like this—this is a life lesson, and I think that's more important. You'll get to see the miracle of birth. It's the most beautiful thing in the world, isn't it, Alice?"

I wanted to tell her about the blood and the smell and the sound a mare made when her flesh began to rip around the opening for the foal. I wanted to tell her about our bay mare a few years back, whose uterus had come out when she birthed and hung behind her like a sack of jelly. I wanted to tell her that the bay had screamed a human scream but stood, trembling, to let the foal nurse. I wanted her to know that when the vet had come to put the mare down, Nona covered my eyes, but I could hear the bones crack when she hit the ground. The foal had cried out in its watery whinny for three whole days afterward. But I smiled and said, "Yes. Beautiful."

Mrs. Altman left us money to order pizza and said that she would pick Sheila up in the morning. As she got into her minivan, she asked me if Sheila could borrow clothes so that she wouldn't bloody up her nice ones. I thought about Polly's funeral, just starting across town. Her mother would have taken a seat already. People would be parking their cars and nodding to one another solemnly as they walked across the grass. I had never been to a funeral, but I imagined that everyone would come quietly, dignified and respectful in smart black dresses and stiff suits. They would sit rigid against the pain, but they would yield to it as the funeral progressed. Their bodies would soften and then lean into one another, arms circling waists and shoulders, fingers interlacing, as she was lowered into the ground.

We ate our pizza on paper napkins and played gin rummy in the tack room. We took turns walking through the barn to check on the mares, and at two in the morning Sheila came back at a run. "Ginger's lying down!" she shrieked. "She's sweating really bad."

"Here we go," my father said, and we trooped behind him through the barn. My father tossed me an Ace bandage and pointed to Ginger's tail. I knelt behind her and saw that her tail was already wet with clots of blood and mucus. Her muscles rippled across her body, and her back legs pushed into the sawdust.

"You're gonna get kicked," Sheila whispered into her fingers.

"She can't kick if she's lying down, dummy," I told her. My father pinched the back of my arm. "I mean, it's okay." I pulled the wet strands of Ginger's tail into the bandage and closed it with a safety pin.

Sheila took a step back and whispered, "Hurry, Alice."

My father knelt beside Ginger's head with his hands on her neck. He stroked her mane and talked in a low voice. "That's my girl," he said. "Come on, sweetheart." Most of the time my father referred to the broodmares as bitches or nags, but while they were birthing he would click his tongue and whisper to them as if they were children. "That's it, love," he purred. "You're okay."

Sheila crept beside my father and began breathing loudly in short breaths, like women on television did when they were in labor.

"You talk to her," he told Sheila, and she leaned down to touch Ginger's muzzle. My father patted her shoulder and added, "Just be careful she doesn't throw her head and knock your teeth out."

I could hear the other horses pacing and pawing at the ground outside. The pens were rattling, and my father told me to go check them. Ginger began to moan, and Sheila backed out of the stall with her hands over her mouth. "I'll come with you," she whispered.

The show mares had gathered around the pasture fence and a

cloud of mayflies swarmed around them. The mares were lying on the ground, their eyes rolled back and their bodies foamed with sweat. They lifted their heads and brought them down hard on the grass while they groaned and snorted, their muscles twitching, their tails whipping at the ever-gathering insects.

"What's wrong with them?" Sheila said.

"They're trying to birth," I told her, and for a second I thought it could be true.

Her mouth trembled. "But they aren't pregnant."

"They get the smell," I said. "They get the smell of the new foals, and they try to birth." I glanced to see if she believed me. In less than a month the show mares would be back in the barn, clean and clipped and ready for the show season. By then Sheila could be bored with horses, could switch to piano or gymnastics or ice-skating. We could dress Sheila Altman in my sister's clothes and sell her my sister's horse, but what could she understand about the way things worked? Sheila Altman—what could she understand about wanting?

Sheila's face froze, and she covered her ears with her hands. I felt a wonderful nastiness rise inside myself. "Isn't it beautiful?"

Sheila shuddered and turned away. "I can't look at them," she said.

Along the driveway the geldings were stomping at the ground and ramming the gates of their pens with their chests. Their heads were wildly high, and the whites of their eyes caught the moonlight as the mayflies floated around them. Yellow Cap whinnied, and I ran to his pen while Sheila watched. "It's okay, Cap," I told him.

"He's freaking out," Sheila said nervously. "They're all freaking out."

"He's fine," I told her, and reached out to pet him, but he jumped and pulled away. "Come on, boy," I called, and unlatched the gate to go in with him.

As I slid the gate open, Cap reared up, and his shoulder hit me in the face, knocking me to the ground. I heard the metal gate clang against the pen, and the sound of Cap's hooves on the gravel as he ran toward the road.

"Stop him!" I called to Sheila, but she stared after him without moving. My hip and leg felt rubbery and weak when I stood up, and my hands were shaking as I steadied myself on the fence. "I have to go get him," I told her.

"Alice, your face is bleeding," she said. I could taste blood and dirt between my teeth, and I touched my hand to my mouth. I couldn't tell what was bleeding. My whole face felt numb.

"He could get hit by a car," I said.

"He went toward the canal. We should get your dad."

I pushed past her, and she grabbed my hand. "We could tell him that *I* let Cap out. He won't get mad at me, I don't think. Or we could get your mom." I looked at her. "It's night, so maybe she could come outside. Come on, Alice, you're bleeding bad. Let me come with you."

The only thing that could get me in more trouble than losing Cap was losing Sheila Altman. Her mouth puckered as if she was about to cry, and I shook my hand away from her. "I'll be right back, Sheila. Don't be a baby."

I ran until I thought my lungs were going to rise up into my mouth. I tripped twice along the side of the road. When I had to slow down, I called for Cap and clicked my tongue. My nose was running, and I walked to the sound of my breath heaving. I wiped my nose with the back of my hand and rubbed the raw sting in my elbow where I had scraped it when I tripped. The mayflies were floating in front of me and I waved my arms to push them away. Up ahead I could just make out where the canal water should have been, but there was a glimmering fog over it: the bugs were rising off the canal by the millions, their snowflake bodies and paper wings a blizzard over the water. I started along the dirt road but had gone only several feet when I had to stop and shield my eyes from the storm of insects.

I could feel my heart beating in my throat and ears. I couldn't make out the water, but I could feel its coolness all around, and I pulled myself as far to the side of the road as I could. I waved my hand, but the bugs swelled like a vapor. I pressed my lips together to keep them out of my mouth and shook my head as hard as I could. I felt my way along the side of the road, bending at the waist to grasp the weeds there with the tips of my fingers.

"Here, Cap! Here, boy!" My voice was high and raspy, and lost itself in the thick swarm of insects. I spun my arms in front of me, but the mayflies were catching in my nostrils and ears, and I had to stop to paw at my face. When I saw the outline of Cap's body through the frost of wings, I thought it might be a mirage, but I stumbled toward him with my arms stretched out.

I put my hands on his side, running them along his body until I came to his head. Yellow Cap was standing stock-still, his knees locked and his muscles twitching. His eyes were wide and his nostrils flared, snorting at the cloud of bugs. "There's my boy," I said, and he tossed his head, knocking me backward. I hadn't thought to bring a halter or a rope, so I tugged at his mane and ears to get him to follow me. But Cap's eyes were frozen with fear, and his legs were rigid on the ground. I couldn't see where we were on the road, and all around us I sensed the water that had killed Polly Cain. Maybe she had just tripped and fallen in. Maybe she had dropped something. I thought of the time I had accidentally inhaled in a swimming pool—the way the water stabbed pain into the backs of my eyes, made my body retch and heave. No houses were close by. No one would have heard her scream.

I kicked at Cap's leg, and he bristled. "Come on!" I shouted. "Come on, you stupid horse. Move!" I pulled as hard as I could. I twisted his ear between my fingers and wrapped my arms around his neck to pull, but my body hung useless from his in the swarm of white. I would never get him back. He would bolt into the water. His hooves would catch in the grates. His legs would snap. His lungs would fill. And I wouldn't be able to stop it. I wouldn't even be able to see it happen—only to hear it. "Please!" I screamed. "You stupid, stupid horse. Please!" I tried to pick up his front foot and move it a step forward, but I couldn't tell which way was safe.

When I heard my father's voice through the hum of insect wings, I thought I was imagining it. But then I heard it again. "Alice!"

"Dad, I'm here! I have him. We're here!"

"I can't see a goddamned thing!"

"Here!" I called again, choking back a wave of sobs.

His hand touched my shoulder. "Jesus Christ! What the hell are you doing?"

"Cap got out. I was afraid he'd get hit or lost or fall in the water."
My fingers were wound through his mane, and I twisted to get them
free.

My father pushed me hard and then caught me by the arm before
I fell. "I could kill you," he said. "I could kill you for being so stupid." I tried to pull away, but I stumbled in the white haze and
grasped the pocket of my father's pants to steady myself.

He took off his shirt and wrapped it around Cap's neck. He had
to pull hard, but Cap followed, and we tried to brush the insects away
from his eyes as we led him back to the road. My father went ahead,
holding my arm to guide me while I clicked my tongue to keep Cap
moving. The mayflies swirled around us like a warm, dry snowstorm,
and when I looked up, I could see them rising into the black sky.

When the insects thinned, and we found ourselves on pavement,
we stopped, breathless. My arm ached where my father was holding
me and when he saw me wince, he let go. I rubbed at my arm. "Sheila
shouldn't have told you," I said. "I was fine."

"Like hell," my father said, but his voice was quiet, and he loosened his grip to let Cap nibble at the weeds. He looked back over the
clouded water and shook his head.

I held up the palms of my hands and touched at the insects' delicate bodies, at their sheet-white wings, as they billowed up from the
canal. The petals of their wings brushed against my palms and evaporated into the darkness. In the moonlight my father's bare chest was
pale and smooth against the rough tan of his arms.

"What about the mares?" I asked. "Should you have left them?"

"Alice, horses birth all the time. If a person had to be there to
help them, they would have died out centuries ago."

We walked back along the road with Yellow Cap between us, his
head low like a dog's.

"Well, Sheila Altman got her money's worth tonight," my father
said finally.

"I hate her," I said. I didn't care anymore.

"I know you do." He smiled and pulled at Cap.

"I hate you giving her Nona's horse."

My father was quiet for a second. "This horse is worth a hell of a lot of money, Alice. More than you could even understand." He sighed. "If I sell him, I can afford to hire someone to help me out here."

I stopped. "You have Sheila," I told him, and he laughed. I touched Cap's neck. "You have me."

My father started walking again, faster, and I had to run to keep up. A car passed us on the road, and once it was in front of us, I saw the trail of mayflies behind it, their bodies sprinkling dead onto the pavement.

When we reached the driveway, my father stared up at the house. "There's a light on in your mother's room." He pointed and I looked. It was small, yellow. A candle. A cloud of mayflies hovered at the light, touching the glass of the window.

"It's the lantern I made her."

"You made her a lantern?"

"Sort of." Polly Cain's nimble fingers lay still beneath feet of dry, dusty earth. I only painted the lantern.

"Why did you do that?"

I looked up at the window. "She wanted something. That was all I had."

He ran his thumb along my lip and then wiped the blood from my face with the heel of his hand. "Why don't you go in to bed now?" I turned my face into his touch and let my chin rest in the cup of his palm. He smelled like sweat and hay and leather. "You're no good to me if you're all worn out. Get some sleep." He started toward the pens, tugging at the shirt around Cap's neck.

"I'm not tired," I told him. "Really. Not at all. I'll stay up."

Before he came out of the pen, he rubbed the spot between Cap's ears and patted his neck. The gate clanged shut, and as my father passed me, he shook his head. "Any other girl would go up to bed." He put his hand around my upper arm and squeezed. "You must be tougher than the rest of them."

My arm was still tender from where he had seized me at the canal, but I flexed my muscle to make it hard. I waited for him to say something, but Sheila Altman came thumping out of the barn waving her arms above her head. "She did it," she cried, jumping up and down. "Oh, my God. It's perfect. Come see, come see!"

The foal was small and wet like all the others, and we huddled together to see over the stall door. Under the weak, yellow barn light it lay with its spindly legs curled. The mare stood above it, eyes half closed as she lowered her head to take in her foal's scent. Outside, the sky was turning tinsel gray, and the air had a deeper chill. Pieces of hay and dust hazed the air around us, and we stood silent in the barn, smelling of blood and earth and night, and watched their heads draw together to touch for the first time.

two

I WAS SEVEN THE YEAR my father bought Cap for my sister. Two men with necks like tree trunks drove him all the way from Kentucky and when they backed him out of the trailer, Cap threw his head, nearly knocking them to the ground. Nona had been barely twelve, but she walked right up to him and held her hand out. The muscles across Cap's chest quivered and he stomped one foot, spraying my sister's legs with gravel. "Careful now," said one of the tree trunks, but Nona stood her ground.

After a minute, Cap lowered his head. The rest of us watched as Nona smoothed her hand up Cap's nose, clicking her tongue and twisting his forelock into a curlicue between his eyes. "There now," she'd said. "You're not so tough."

The moment that Yellow Cap became Sheila's was not nearly so memorable. Mrs. Altman handed my father a check and he handed her the registration papers. The horse never even left his pen. Afterward, my father took me out for cheeseburgers and told me it was going to be one hell of a year—he could feel it. He was smiling, bouncing his leg under the table. "Get dessert," he said through a mouthful of burger. "Anything you want."

My father said that soon our barn would be flooded with clients. Sheila's friends would come out to watch her ride. When they saw her, proud and graceful on her beautiful new horse, they would want lessons too, then beautiful horses of their own. And, my father added, they would be girls like Sheila. Rich girls. That made all the difference.

"Nona was getting bored with it, lazy." My father slurped on his empty soda, then reached across the table for mine. "But Sheila's so new. She's excited—*fierce.*"

Sheila Altman was new all right. And she was certainly excited— she jumped up and down more than anyone I'd ever known. But *fierce* belonged to girls like Nona who had been showing their whole lives, girls with set jaws and tight eyes and arms like knotted ropes. They slouched on their horses when they weren't in the ring and snuck cigarettes behind the announcer's booth during breaks. These were girls who had been thrown and stomped and dragged, girls who'd had horses fall beneath them or flip on top of them. By the time they were thirteen, they all had a story: a collarbone broken when a young horse bucked, a knee blown when a mare shied sideways into a fence post, a pelvis shattered when a horse had lain down and rolled, pinning the rider beneath. Sheila Altman had smooth skin and pink cheeks. No one was going to be impressed.

"What?" my father asked and raised one eyebrow, a warning more than a question.

"Nothing," I told him. "I just don't want dessert is all."

At school, the custodians cleaned out Polly's desk and scraped the stickers off her locker. The principal made an announcement over the loudspeakers, thanking the sixth-grade class for such overwhelming attendance at the funeral and told us that when the weather got a little warmer, the whole sixth grade would plant a tree in the courtyard as a memorial to Polly. Until then, he said, we should go on as we had, learning and laughing and turning our homework in on time— that was the way Polly would have wanted it.

In death, Polly Cain had become infinitely more popular than she ever was in life. Girls wore black to school, or navy if it was the best they could come up with. Everyone who had brushed against her in the hallway had a story to tell: She had let people borrow pencils during spelling tests and loaned quarters for the soda machine. In class, she always raised her hand before speaking, and once she had been seen picking up a piece of trash that was not her own. If Polly had ever sworn or tripped or called someone a nasty name, no one could remember it. Now she was dead and gone. The only explanation was that she had been generous, benevolent, and environmentally conscious—too good for this world.

The small circle of girls who had been friends with Polly became instant celebrities. In the days following the funeral, people hovered around them in the hallways, asking how they were doing and offering to help them make up assignments they had missed while they were working through their grief. Polly's friends were plain and quiet, unaccustomed to such attention. I watched them navigate through the hallways with their shoulders stooped and their heads down. In a slightly different world, I might have been one of them.

I picked up details of the funeral in bits and pieces. While I was washing my hands in the girls' room, I learned that Polly had been buried in a pink casket. Changing clothes for gym class, I heard two girls talking about a poem that had been read at the beginning of the service, and I pretended to work at a knot in the laces of my shoe while I listened. But it was in the lunch line that I found my greatest resource.

Under normal circumstances, Janice Reardon was the sort of person that other people avoided speaking with. Pale and moonfaced, with doughy shoulders and a crest of acne across her forehead, Janice routinely wore costumes to school on nontheme days and engaged in conversation with inanimate objects. Today Janice was wearing a plastic tiara and in between telling me the details of Polly's funeral, she paused to greet each item on her tray: "Hello, little fork. You're not very shiny today." But she had been to the funeral and I had not. So I smiled and nodded and pretended not to notice when she spoke to her silverware.

Janice told me that it was Polly's uncle who read the poem at the beginning of the service—the poem was about a flower. Polly's mother wore a green dress and carried a single white rose. As the sun set, a projector had shown pictures of Polly growing up while the sixth-grade choir sang "Candle in the Wind."

"It was devastating," Janice said. We stood together with our trays and she nodded toward an empty table. "Want to sit with me?"

Some of the plastic jewels had fallen off Janice's tiara and I could see the places where she had colored in the naked pocks with a red marker. I glanced over my shoulder to see if anyone was looking at us, but Janice only watched my face. "I haven't told you everything yet," she said. "I've practically scratched the surface is all."

I nodded and followed her to the table.

Polly had no sisters or brothers and her father had died when she was four. Janice smoothed her paper napkin across her lap while she repeated the stories she had heard at the funeral and described the pictures she had seen—Polly on Christmas morning with a red bow stuck to the top of her head, Polly on ice skates, Polly drinking chocolate milk out of a curly straw.

"Did her mother cry?" I asked and Janice paused with her hot dog midway to her mouth.

"Duh," she said. "It was her kid's funeral."

"What does she look like?" I asked and Janice shrugged.

"I don't know," she said. "Like a woman. Like anybody's mother."

I nodded, thinking of my own mother, who sometimes cried for no reason at all.

"Everyone cried," Janice went on. "When the funeral was over, I saw Mr. Delmar sitting inside his car. He was practically weeping."

Mr. Delmar taught seventh-grade English and I tried to picture what he looked like, tried to imagine a grown man alone inside his unmoving car, crying silently into his fingers. "Polly didn't even have Mr. Delmar," I said.

"She was on the tennis team," Janice told me. "Mr. Delmar's the coach."

"There's a tennis team?" Our school had one court, but weeds grew up between cracks in the pavement and there wasn't a net.

"It's more like a club," Janice said. "I don't think they meet that often."

"And Mr. Delmar was that upset?"

Janice opened her mouth to speak and I could see globs of partially chewed hot dog on her tongue. "He was *devastated.*"

I stared down at my tray without touching it. Even random teachers were falling to pieces, overcome by the prospect of a world without Polly. All those years Polly and I had walked the same road partway home, and I didn't even know she played tennis.

I let my eyes circle the cafeteria until I found the table where Polly used to eat her lunch, the empty chair she used to sit in. While Janice went on about the funeral, who had worn what and who had sat where, I watched Polly's friends sideways, hoping that in between nibbles of sandwich or sips of milk, they might look up and notice me. I wanted them to know that they weren't alone, that while I might not understand the full weight of their loss, I was willing to help shoulder it. Their group was one person short now. I could listen to their stories, let them talk through their pain. Three was a bad number when it came to girlfriends—everyone knew that. I could even out the balance.

"I have to go," I mumbled, and Janice's mouth froze in mid-sentence.

I took the long way around the cafeteria. As I approached their table, I thought I could feel the crowd parting on either side of me, the ghostly hand of Polly guiding me toward her friends. We would look into one another's eyes and all of us would feel the connection, the significance of our meeting. They would ask me to sit with them. They would ask me to stay. From that moment on, I would always be with them, guarding them from the prying questions of our classmates, filling the spaces that Polly had left empty.

But when I stopped in front of their table, all three of Polly's friends stared up at me with dead, glassy eyes and didn't say a word.

"I'm Alice," I told them.

"We know who you are," Sharon Hill said and poked a Tater Tot into a glob of ketchup. "What do you want?"

I shifted my tray from one hand to the other and tried to make my face open and honest, to let them see the sincerity of my feeling. "I just wanted to say how sorry I was—how sorry I *am*. I mean, I wanted to tell you how bad I feel about Polly, about her being dead."

Colleen Murphy rested her chin in her hand, and Abigail Wilson picked at one of her cuticles. I tried to think of anything I could say about Polly, a secret she had whispered while she was piecing our lantern together in shop, a funny story she had told, a particular talent, yet unrecognized, that might have shaped the course of her life had she stayed alive long enough to develop it. But in all those afternoons that we had spent side by side among tools and scraps of metal, Polly hadn't spoken except to read directions aloud or point out which piece went where. I backed away from their table and left the cafeteria alone.

Outside, Janice Reardon came up behind me and pinched my arm. "I saw you try and talk to them," she said.

"So?"

"You can't expect them to be nice, those girls," she said, quickening her pace to keep up with me. "They're *damaged*."

"I didn't expect anything," I told her. "I was just saying hi."

"They don't know anything anyway."

I stopped. Janice smiled and crooked a pudgy finger at me, drawing me close to hear her secret. "People have *seen* things," she whispered. "On the canal. White shadows over the water."

"Who?" I asked her. "Who's seen that?"

Janice pressed her mouth into a thin line and brought her fingers up in front of it, locking her lips with an invisible key before she threw it over her shoulder. This was the sort of thing you could expect from Janice Reardon. In fourth grade, she'd told everyone that the ghost of Karen Carpenter had come to her while she was having her tonsils removed and taken her on a tour of heaven. For weeks afterward, Janice had begged people to sit in a circle with her at recess, promising that if they held hands and sang "Close to You," Karen would return and show them all the things she had shown Janice.

"That's retarded," I said and Janice's face fell.

There was a rustling of footsteps behind us and when I looked over my shoulder, Abigail, Colleen, and Sharon were making their way out of the cafeteria. I took a step backward to show that Janice and I were not together.

Polly's friends passed us without lifting their eyes. When they were gone, Janice crossed her arms over her chest. "It isn't your fault," she said finally. "I mean, how could you understand? You weren't even at the funeral."

I walked home from school along the canal, watching sideways for the silky outline of a girl's face to appear on the surface, a whispering white shadow. But the water was flat and guiltless, a utility. Alongside, the gummy corpses of fallen mayflies floated through the grates and clung to weeds. This was the way things ended—in small, ugly pieces. People could cry or drown or eat lunch every day at a table all by themselves and the world couldn't care less. It just went right ahead with its business, pumping along like a human heart. There were no rules, no hints, no answers. There was only grief. But none of it belonged to me.

After the papers had been signed, the Altmans paid extra to have Cap's name stitched or stenciled onto everything they bought for him. The new halter had his name in gold across the nose and the matching blanket was monogrammed with the initials *YC*. Sheila used permanent marker to write *Yellow Cap* on all her grooming brushes and currycombs. Sometimes his name was underlined or followed by a series of exclamation points. Sometimes she drew stars around it.

"Alice, tell the truth," Sheila said as we were sweeping out the barn after school. "Isn't Cap the handsomest horse you've ever laid eyes on?"

"I guess so," I said.

"The smartest too," Sheila told me. "Whenever I walk up to his pen, he comes right to me, like he *knows* he's mine."

"He knows you feed him stuff he's not supposed to have," I said. From the tack room, my father coughed. "And he knows he's yours," I added.

Even though Sheila fed him apple cores and Oreos and crusts of sandwich that she saved from lunch, in the ring Cap was overpowering and she cowed to him. "You have to show him who's boss!" my father shouted during her lessons.

"I think Cap's just cranky today," she would say, grasping the saddle horn, or, "Maybe he's not feeling well."

At school our teachers told us not to make excuses for failure. But they only said this when something bad happened—someone's father getting sent to prison or a girl dying on her walk home. When Sheila's school was in the newspaper, it was for things like high test scores or a kid making it to the finals of the National Spelling Bee. It was unlikely that anyone had ever talked to Sheila Altman about failure.

Over the next couple of weeks, my father had the barn and all the pasture fences painted so that our entire property gleamed red and white. When that was finished, he had the truck and horse trailer repainted to match, cherry red with *Winston Stables* stenciled in white across both sides. "Take a look at these," he told me when I got home from school. Three new show saddles were set up in the tack room, each with engraved silver stirrups.

"Flashy," I said and he grinned. "Who's gonna use them?"

"The new clients!" he told me. "Wait and see, Alice. Everything out here's about to change."

But aside from a new coat of paint, nothing at the stable seemed much different than it had before. We moved the broodmares and new foals into the front pasture and when we brought the show horses back into the barn, Cap went into the first and largest stall, the one we had always kept him in. He still ate our hay and drank our water. He was still the best horse in the barn. The only real change was that he didn't belong to us.

Inside our house, the living room walls were lined with framed photos of Nona at horse shows, holding checks and ribbons and trophies. She was five and six and seven, riding horses I had no memory of, wearing clothes I'd seen on clients years after she'd outgrown them. In the more recent photos, Nona sat with her spine rigid atop Yellow Cap, shoulders squared, jaw set. All the blue ribbons and trophies were just garnish. The look Nona wore on her face was enough to let anyone know that she had won, that she was better than everyone else.

Clients came and went. They moved away or lost interest or found something else they liked better. Maybe Sheila Altman would be different. Maybe she would learn to ride like a dream, bringing in clients right and left. But right now, she rode like a sack of doorknobs. And if time and training were really all it took, if my father knew some sort of secret that could turn a regular girl into a champion, a secret he could give to anyone, it seemed that he would have given it to me.

At school, people were running out of things to say about Polly's life, so they began to pull apart the pieces of her death. Could a person really *fall into* the canal? No one remembered Polly being clumsy. No one remembered her liking to swim. And so the sixth grade thought back: Had Polly seemed sad or quiet or disconnected? Had she talked about loneliness? Had she lost weight? People stopped speaking to Polly's friends in delicate voices. Girls stomped up to them in the hallways, backing them into corners and demanding answers. What did they know that they weren't telling us? Why hadn't they *been there* for Polly? Why hadn't they seen the signs?

Just when it was about to turn into a bloodbath, Colleen Murphy slipped into the girls' room during a geography test and tried to end herself by gouging her fingernails into her wrists and throat. It didn't work very well. Tiny half-moon scratches puffed up on her neck and arms—she barely even drew blood. But it was enough to grind the whole thing to a stop.

Our principal made a second announcement. This time, he was neither grateful for our sympathy nor moved by our grief. He told us that there would be no more dressing in black or crying in hallways. If he heard one more word about Polly Cain, he would cancel the end-of-the-year trip to the water park and the sixth grade would spend the last day of school cleaning desks. It was time to move on, he said. Enough was enough.

"A girl tried to kill herself at school today," I told my father. "She dug her nails into her throat and wrists like this." I stuck my tongue out sideways and mimed clawing my fingers into my neck. "They called 911 and her parents came and they took her away in an ambulance."

My father was saddling Cap for Sheila's lesson, and he glanced at me sideways as he tightened the girth strap. "She sounds like an idiot."

I squatted down beside my father, pretending to watch him pick the dirt from the inside of Cap's hooves. "Have you ever been to a funeral?" I asked. Before he could answer, there was a rumbling over the gravel driveway and my father stood up, waving to Mrs. Altman and Sheila.

"Keep an eye on Sheila for a minute," he told me. "I need to talk to her mother."

Sheila climbed out of the car, waving a bag of baby carrots that she had brought for the new foals. I followed her to the front pasture, scuffing my feet through the gravel. The foals would be entirely uninterested in anything Sheila wanted to give them, but it didn't hurt to let her try. It was easier than having a conversation with her.

"Here, babies," she called as she climbed onto the fence. Across the pasture the broodmares raised their heads to gaze briefly at us before returning to the grass. The foals continued to wander around their mothers without acknowledging our presence. Sheila took a carrot from her bag and tossed it into the pasture, where it landed on the grass a few feet in front of us. "Babies!" she tried again, but none of them moved. Sheila's face fell. "They need names," she said. "I'm sure they'd come if we could call them by their names."

"They don't get names until we register them," I told her and glanced over my shoulder at my father. He was smiling as he leaned down into Mrs. Altman's open window, using his hands as he spoke.

"We could start thinking of names, at least," she said. "It will be that much easier when we have to register them." I raised my eyebrows at her. When had Sheila Altman become a *we*?

She pointed at one of the foals. "That one could be Brownie," she said. "And that one would make a good Rascal. He's so playful."

"You don't just *make up* names," I told her. "Part of the name comes from the sire." Sheila blinked at me. "The father," I explained. "Part of his name goes into the foal's name so that people know what the bloodlines are."

Sheila thought about this. "Who are their sires?"

"They all have the same one," I said. "Our stud Bart. He colicked last year and had to be put down."

"They're orphans," Sheila breathed and turned back to the foals. "Poor *babies*."

Bart had been a fixture for years. He had lived in the round pen next to the arena and my father had forbidden my sister and me to go near him. Studs were wild and unpredictable by nature, quick to kick or bite. Bart had been little more than a piece of equipment, and unless my father was breeding a mare, we had left him completely alone. "It isn't a big deal," I told her. "They never would have seen him anyway."

After Mrs. Altman left, I cleaned stalls alone while my father worked with Sheila in the arena. Show season was just around the corner and the once weekly riding lessons were now part of the daily routine. I kept waiting for my father to be struck dumb by my ability to get everything done by myself, to shake his head in amazement and ask what my secret was. Day after day, I forked fresh straw into every stall and used the hose to wash out the corners of the barn after I had swept. And day after day, my father said nothing.

At night, after all the work was done, I would sit on the floor of Nona's closet, holding her pink telephone on my lap. Nearly two months had passed since she last called home, and each evening I planned out what I would tell her when she did. I would tell her about the new foals and about Sheila Altman, who had bought Nona's horse but couldn't ride him. I would tell her about Polly Cain, who was dead, and Colleen Murphy, who wanted to be. I would tell her about the work I now did alone. "I'm running myself into the ground," I would say. "I'm getting old fast and used up."

School would be out soon. Maybe Nona would ask me to come visit, offer to buy me a bus ticket to wherever she was right now. Then I could explain how it would never work, how our father couldn't live without me even for a day. "I'm all he has now," I would tell her, and maybe saying the words out loud would be enough to make them true.

"What do we hear from our best girl?" my mother asked. Her eyes were closed, and until she spoke, I'd thought she was asleep.

"Nothing," I said. "She hasn't called."

Her forehead wrinkled. "We haven't gotten a letter?"

"Not in a while."

My mother opened her eyes and blinked at me as if she wasn't sure where I'd come from. "A long while?"

I thought back. "A few weeks, I guess."

"I wonder what that means."

I shifted my weight from one foot to the other in her doorway. "Dad told me to check if you needed anything," I said.

My mother patted the empty space of bed beside her. "Company?"

The curtains were drawn and the television flickered the room's only light, crawling shadows across the floor. I sat on the edge of my mother's bed, trying not to bounce her. "Are you hungry?" I asked. "Do you want me to fry you an egg?"

My mother twisted a cord of hair around one white finger and stared down at her bedspread. "Do you want to hear about my dream?"

A chilly sweat crept down the small of my back. "Okay."

"I was in a taxi," my mother told me. "Dressed in nice clothes— stockings and heels and a pretty dress. I had two baby kittens— teeny-tiny—inside my purse. But the taxi kept swerving and my purse kept sliding off my lap. Every time I opened it, the kittens were dead and I'd have to shake them like this." She raised her hands in fists and shook them in front of herself. "They were so little, like sticks of butter."

"What happened after you shook them?" I asked.

"They'd come back to life," she said. "But then I'd put them into my purse and they'd die again. I had to keep shaking them and every time it took a little bit longer. They were more and more dead each time I took them out." She dropped her fists into her lap and looked down at her empty hands. "What do you think it means?"

It sounded like a regular old dream to me. I didn't see why it had to mean anything. "Maybe you want to go somewhere," I suggested.

My mother twisted her mouth to one side. "No," she said. "That isn't it."

"Maybe you want a cat."

She sighed and slid her hand toward mine, brushing the tips of my fingers with the tips of hers. "I haven't seen much of your dad lately," she said. "I think maybe he's forgotten about me."

"He's really busy," I told her.

She nodded. "New foals."

"Have you seen them?" I asked and my mother's eyes narrowed.

"I don't want to see them," she said. "I don't even want to know their names." Her chest was rising and falling in quick, shallow breaths and her lower lip trembled.

"It's okay," I told her, trying to make my voice gentle. "You don't have to see them." I reached for her shoulder and she pulled away as if I'd burned her. I backed away from the bed. The walls were shrinking. The air was thin. I never said anything right.

"Your father says that one of them is the spitting image of our Bart," she said. "Is that true?"

After we had put Bart down, my father told my mother that he'd sold Bart to a rich man from the Midwest, that Bart was spending his golden years fat and happy on a farm in Nebraska. "One looks a little like him, I guess," I said.

"Your father wants me to see them," she said. "He wants to carry me downstairs and make me watch them through the window. And for what?" She gave me a hard look and I took another step backward. "So I can fall head over heels and he can sell them off to strangers." She bit her lip and the rims of her eyes swelled with tears.

"It's just business, Mom," I whispered. "He doesn't do it to be mean."

"I know that," she snapped. "Don't you think I know that?"

My mother used the cuffs of her nightgown to dab the corners of her eyes and I crossed to the window, folding back the curtain just enough to let a slip of light spill across the carpet. Outside, Sheila was standing in the center of the arena while my father rode Cap in a circle around her, demonstrating.

I pulled the curtain open wider and there, resting on the sill, was Polly Cain's lantern. I touched my fingers to its edge, brushing the back of my hand against the stubby candle my mother had wedged into the holder. A few days after the funeral, Mr. McClusky had asked me how it went when I took the lantern to Polly's mother.

Mr. McClusky was large and oafish, with hairy ears and a face like a gorilla. With the boys, he was loose and easy, slapping their backs, laughing at their jokes, and encouraging them to call him by the nickname "Booger." But with the girls, he seemed restless and awkward in his skin, edging backward as he spoke to us. Even as he asked about Polly's mother, how she was holding up and what she thought of the lantern her dead daughter had made in his class, his fingers twitched at his sides and he glanced over his shoulder as if someone else might be calling him. "She loved it," I told him. "She cried and cried." He hadn't spoken to me since.

Somewhere, Polly's mother was sitting in a house by herself. There was no husband, no other children. She cooked dinner and ate alone. She washed and dried her own dishes. She slept and woke and bathed and cried and all the while, the lantern sat in my mother's window. It didn't belong here. It didn't belong anywhere.

"You should get back to work," my mother said and my limbs jerked awake at the dismissal.

As I was closing the door, my mother said my name like a breath and I stopped. "What did he use to say?" she whispered. I inched the door back open.

"Who?"

"Your father," she said. "When Nona was little and would cry her heart out over a horse he sold away? I can't remember what he used to say to her."

From the doorway, my mother looked small and forgotten in her big bed, strange and lonely. It was something we had always done—my father, sister, and I—we tried to make things better, tried to make the world sound like a nicer place than it was. But my mind was itching with the need to get out of that room, and the true answer filled my head before I could make up a better one. "There isn't a horse that can't be replaced."

My mother laughed up at the ceiling. "Amen," she said.

There were two kinds of horses that my father would never sell: The broodmares were functional, they had a purpose, a job that they performed year after year. Besides, they were older, with dusty coats and creaking legs. No one would ever want to buy them. And then there were the geldings that my father kept in the back pasture. These were the horses that he picked up over the years at the sort of auctions he didn't talk about with clients.

The Kill Sales took place on the outskirts of town in dusty parking lots, attracting buyers who came with makeshift horse trailers held together by caulk and rope and duct tape. The horses had matted tails and manes, their legs and bellies crusted with dried mud, their coats patchy with malnourishment. My father would walk among the rusty pens, looking for the horses marked with an X of orange paint across their flanks—a sign to the buyer that they were damaged beyond repair, killers, good for nothing but rendering plants and schoolroom glue.

The horses were auctioned off by the pound and my father paid next to nothing for them, then brought them back home where he worked, rebuilding them like broken cars. With the show horses he trained, my father was often sharp and swift to punish. But with the Kills, he was gentle and patient, filled with quiet respect. *The Old Men,* he called them, and gave them names like Ace and Admiral, Chief and Charlie. He worked with them in the evenings, after all the clients had gone home. And though my sister and I often watched, we could never understand exactly what happened while he worked with them, what sort of understanding passed between them.

It took months, years sometimes, but when my father was finished, the Kill horses were solid, unshakable. Then he put them in our back pasture, where they grew fat, barrel bellies and walked on creaky, bowed legs.

"Why do we keep them around?" Nona used to ask. "They don't *do* anything."

"*Do* anything?" my father said. "They don't *do* anything? Look at old Ace. We don't have a more solid, steady horse in this whole barn than Ace. You could shoot a cannon off his head and he wouldn't even blink."

"That's because he's practically dead, Daddy. He's, like, a million years old."

But my father would not part with them. He told their stories to anyone who would pause to listen: Chief had been dragged behind a moving truck until his hooves were ground to stubs and had to be bandaged, cared for, regrown like endangered plants. Charlie had been starved to the point of madness, then left in the desert to die alone. Old Ace had been beaten with a hammer, his skull misshaped, his hindquarters stooped. My father said it was not the Old Men's age that made them so sturdy, so dependable. They had seen the depths of hell and they had come back. Nothing that happened from this point forward would ever spook them.

And so he put children on their backs, old people who had never been around horses, troops of Girl Scouts who came to us for one-time-only lessons to earn their patches. Other than that, my father left the Old Men alone. He kept them in the pasture that couldn't be seen from the road. When anyone asked, he said they were retired.

Ace was the first horse Sheila Altman had taken a lesson on, the horse that had convinced both her and her mother that she was a natural, gifted, ready to take the equine world by storm. All she needed was the perfect show horse to turn her into the perfect show girl.

Outside by the arena, I leaned against the fence and watched as Sheila finished out her daily lesson. She trotted Cap into the center of the ring and when my father told her to stop, Sheila yanked the reins all the way back to her shoulders, pulling Cap's chin into his chest and wrenching his mouth open. His body jerked and Sheila's legs swung back, her seat lifting out of the saddle as she tipped forward over the horn. "*Whoa,*" she said, but Cap had already stopped.

My father helped Sheila dismount and she wobbled on her ankles for a moment, then patted Cap's neck. "How did we look?" she asked. I gave her a thumbs-up.

When Sheila had taken her lessons on Ace, everything was smooth and easy. Like the other Old Men, Ace paid attention to my father, listened to his voice, watched his movements. When my father told a student to stop, Ace stopped. He was too old and creaky to move with any real speed. Riding him took no more skill than it would to ride a wooden rocking horse.

"I figured you would have had some friends out to visit by now," my father said to Sheila as they made their way out of the arena.

"Out here?" she asked.

"Sure," my father said. "Show off your new horse? Let people see what you've been up to?"

Sheila's ears blushed pink. "I thought I'd wait," she said. "I don't want people to see me ride until I'm *really* good."

My father's face twitched at one eye, but he kept smiling. In the tack room, the new show saddles were still on their stands, untouched since the day he'd bought them. "Well," he said. "We'll just keep working then."

After Sheila's mother had picked her up for the day, I helped my father carry buckets of grain out to the broodmares. He walked ahead of me, bouncing a bucket at the end of each arm. My shoulders ached and the metal handles pinched across the palms of my hands, but I hurried to keep up. "She's gonna get hurt," I told him.

"Everyone gets hurt," he said.

The mares crowded around us at the pasture gate and my father moved between them as they ate, trying to ease the foals into human contact while their mothers were preoccupied. "Look at the head on this one," he said to me and reached to pat the rump of Ginger's colt. He'll be worth some good dough." The foal whinnied and skittered sideways, avoiding my father's touch.

"What will Mrs. Altman say when the season starts and Sheila doesn't win?" I asked.

"These things take time," my father said and tried to run his hand down the length of a foal's spiky little mane before it could dart away. "Who goes out there and wins on their first try?"

"Nona did," I said.

"That was different," he told me.

"I know."

My father kicked at a fence post with the toe of his boot. "It'll be summer soon," he said. "I'll have more time to work with her."

A weight sank in my shoulders—summer. Sheila Altman would never go home.

My father nodded at the ground, convinced by his own thoughts. "It just takes time," he said again and scratched one of the mares behind her ear. She nipped sideways at him, baring her teeth between speckled lips. "Things don't change overnight, right?"

My father patted my head and I stood perfectly still, the only animal in the whole pasture that didn't flinch under his touch. "Hardly ever," I said.

In the end, it wasn't time or work that made things change. It was money. My father kept a drawer full of white envelopes in our living room, the outside of each scrawled in his cat-scratch handwriting—*heat, water, insurance, feed.* In the evenings, my father would sit at our dining room table with the envelopes spread in front of him, adding numbers on scraps of paper and cursing under his breath while I did my homework on the living room floor.

"Come here for a minute," he told me, using the hook of his foot to pull an empty chair beside him at the table. "I need your brain."

I sat down and my father handed me a scrap of paper. "I can't make the numbers come out right." He leaned back in his chair and closed his eyes, massaging his temples with his thumbs while I rewrote the figures on a different piece of paper, adding and subtracting as carefully as I could. Sweat prickled in the roots of my hair and I willed my brain to work right, now that it had been called upon to do something important.

"Is there enough?" my father asked when I set my pen down.

"No."

"Where the hell did it all go?" he asked.

Through the window, I could see the barn, slick and pretty with its new coat of paint, the truck and trailer gleaming under the floodlights. "I don't know."

My father had always said that he wasn't running the kind of stable that would take on boarders. We were a serious barn, he said. Our horses were champions. We would never push them into pens to make room for the pets of rich people. The sign at the end of our driveway had the name of our barn with three smaller signs dangling from chains beneath, listing the services we provided:

WINSTON STABLES

TRAINING

EQUITATION

BREEDING

With Bart dead, my father said it was high time we got rid of the third sign—we didn't want to be accused of false advertising. So he made a new sign: *Boarding.* "Compromise," he told me. "That's what business is all about. Sometimes you've gotta eat shit."

The first boarder was Patty Jo, whose husband had bought her a Thoroughbred for their anniversary. Patty Jo had shiny hair and dark eyelashes. She was small, only a few inches taller than me, and she wore a green suede jacket and pointy-toed shoes. When Patty Jo walked her horse into his stall, she looked at the ground and her nose crinkled. "Straw?"

"Is that a problem?" my father asked, bending at the knees to bring his head closer to hers.

Patty Jo tilted her tiny chin up to him. "Didn't I mention this on the phone?" She squinted, trying to remember. "I'm certain I did. Toy Boy just can't tolerate a straw floor. He simply *insists* on sawdust."

My father wet his lower lip with his tongue. "Does he now?" I could hear the control straining in the muscles of his throat, the contempt rising in his chest. But he smiled and said, "That shouldn't be a problem."

"Thank God," Patty Jo said. "I've had him all over town. People act like it's such a *chore* to change a few simple things."

"What happens if he doesn't have sawdust?" I asked.

Patty Jo dropped her voice. "He won't *do his business.*"

"I'll have sawdust in here by tomorrow," my father promised and Patty Jo flashed a mouthful of perfect white teeth at him. "It just costs a little more."

"Well, that's certainly not a problem," she said.

After she was gone, my father and I stood in the doorway of Toy Boy's stall, looking at his glossy mane and well-groomed coat. The horse stuck his head over the stall door and my father poked him in the nose with the point of his finger. "So you won't shit on the cheap stuff, huh?"

My father told me to remember my manners when Patty Jo was in the barn. "Please and thank you," he said. "You know, all that stuff. No spitting or swearing. We gotta look high-class."

I didn't spit or swear, but I nodded to show that I understood. "Is she gonna be out here all the time?" I asked.

"She'll be out here as much as she likes," my father told me. "And if we're lucky, she'll bring some friends."

It must have been luck then, because Patty Jo had lots of friends and within a couple of weeks, we had moved every one of our horses out of the barn to make room for theirs. My father spent his days welding small, square pens alongside the arena for our show horses and by the time I got home from school each afternoon, his face was beet red, his hair drenched with sweat.

"How long is this going to last?" I asked and my father lifted the hem of his T-shirt, wiping the sheen of sweat from his forehead.

"Once Sheila starts winning, we'll get some show clients," he promised. "Then we can send these women packing."

So everything depended on Sheila Altman. Until she proved herself a star, my father and I would do what we had to do. We would pay the bills. We would pretend to be high-class. This was compromise. This, I guessed, was business.

"Who's the little girl?" my mother asked. A letter had finally arrived from my sister and when I took it upstairs to my mother, I found her sitting in the window of her bedroom with her knees pulled to her chest beneath her nightgown.

"Her name's Sheila," I said, setting Nona's letter on the bedside table. "Her mom drops her off after school and picks her up when it gets dark."

Outside in the arena, Sheila was trying to make Cap weave through a line of orange cones, and my father ran alongside, calling instructions up to her. My mother opened her mouth and breathed a circle of fog onto the window. "Is she winning?" she asked.

The first local show of the year had been small. The horses were still shaggy in their winter coats and the girls were groggy, out of practice with early mornings and long days. Only four girls competed in Sheila's class, and though the other three looked bored and distracted while they waited outside the ring, Sheila had been animated, fanning her face with her hands while Mrs. Altman bustled around her, urging her to take sips from a water bottle and promising that she would be *just wonderful.* Inside the ring, Sheila had been flushed and clumsy in her new clothes, stiff on her new saddle. She came in fourth.

"Not yet," I said and my mother streaked the pad of her finger through the circle of breath on the window.

"She will, though," she said.

Ever since show season had started, my father had been singularly focused on Sheila. When she wasn't riding, they stood together in the barn, talking about technique and practice. If she didn't win, it wouldn't be for lack of other people wanting her to.

"Nona wrote," I said. "She's in Idaho." My mother nodded without turning away from the window. "She says they ate at a restaurant where the bread came baked in flowerpots."

My mother didn't answer and I started to leave. "Turn that off," she said and flicked her fingers toward the television. I clicked the knob and the room fell still. My mother tapped her index finger soundlessly against the window. "She's holding the reins too tight," she said in a voice so quiet I wasn't sure if it was meant for me. "Nona gave him his head."

The sun was setting when Sheila's lesson ended, and the orange sky lit the loose hairs of her ponytail like a halo as I passed her coming out of the arena. "I think he has trouble seeing at this time of day," she told me. "It gets so shadowy in late afternoon. Do you think Cap could have some sort of shadow blindness?"

I looked up at my mother's window, but it was empty. "I've heard of that," I said.

Sheila clicked her tongue to lead Cap into the barn and he jerked his head, nearly yanking her off her feet. "It's okay, boy," she said and patted his neck. "I'll be your eyes."

My father was still in the arena. "Good," he said when I walked up to the fence. "Help me with these." The orange cones were dented and knocked sideways, spread halfway across the ring.

"What happened out here?" I asked.

"Just doing a little pattern work," he said. My father bent to pick up a cone and I could see the sweat soaking down the back of his T-shirt. He reached his arm inside the cone and punched a dent out of it. "We still have a ways to go with patterns."

"You still have a ways to go with everything," I told him.

"We're gonna keep working," my father said. "She's gonna get better."

I kicked a cone upright. "What if she doesn't?"

My father gave me a sideways look, then held his arms out at the battlefield of fallen cones. "She has to."

When Mrs. Altman came to pick up Sheila, my father was leaning against the back porch, holding a can of soda to the back of his neck. She waved to him, then wobbled across the gravel driveway in her high heels, making her way into the barn. My father wiped the sweat from his forehead onto his shoulder, then started to follow her. Halfway across the driveway, he stopped behind Mrs. Altman's mini-van, staring at the back of it. A new bumper sticker in the rear window read, *I Brake for Palominos*.

"Well, that's good news," I said and my father looked at me. "When Cap bolts out of the arena and drags Sheila down the street, at least Mrs. Altman won't run them over in her car."

My father took a deep breath and I cringed, thinking he might yell at me for being a smart aleck, tell me how my negative attitude wasn't helping anyone. But instead, he closed his eyes and dropped his chin to his chest. "Sometimes," he said, "I just want to blow my fucking brains out."

On the last day of school, they handed out yearbooks at the water park. I had forgotten my swimsuit at home and when we got to the park, my social studies teacher offered to loan me a quarter for the pay phone. I could call my mother and ask her to bring my suit. I thanked her for the offer and explained how my mother was at work, in important meetings, and would never be able to get away. "Ah, well," she said, patting my shoulder. "There's always next year."

While my classmates swam, I sat against the chain-link fence with my yearbook open on my lap. My sister's yearbooks from the high school were thick and shiny with color pictures and her name in silver across the front. The middle school's were a disappointment by comparison, printed on a copy machine and held together with two staples in the center. The pictures were small and grainy, the print beneath so tiny that I had to squint to read it.

I had been sure there would be some mention of Polly Cain. The year before, a boy at Nona's school had been killed in a hunting accident and the last page of the high school's yearbook was dedicated to his memory, complete with pictures and a poem written by the dead boy's girlfriend. But the last page of the middle school's yearbook had a drawing of a panther in a football jersey—our school mascot— and a coupon for a free ice cream sandwich with the purchase of a hot lunch.

In the swimming pool, my classmates splashed and screamed, daring each other to jump off the high dive and doing cannonballs into the water. In the center, the sixth-grade cheerleaders took turns balancing on one another's shoulders. It was barely June, but already they glowed with suntans, whipping their wet hair over their shoulders and clapping their hands in unison as each member was lifted up to practice her part of the routine.

> *Hi my name's Kelly and I'm here to bet,*
> *I'm gonna run you over in my new Corvette!*

I thumbed backward through the pages of my yearbook, combing through the small print. But there was no poem, no promise, no Bible verse declaring that Polly Cain would live forever in the kingdom of heaven. They hadn't even printed her picture with our grade.

"Alice Winston." I snapped my yearbook shut and looked up to see Janice Reardon dripping wet in front of me. She held her towel in one hand and her yearbook in the other, the ends of her hair dribbling plops of water onto the cover. "Wanna sign mine?"

Before I could answer, Janice plucked my yearbook from my hands and dropped her own into my lap. She spread her towel on the grass and sat down beside me, stretching the milk-white sausages of her legs in front of herself. Her stomach tripled into rolls beneath her purple swimsuit as she leaned over my yearbook, and I looked away, embarrassed by her lack of self-awareness, her lack of shame.

I flipped through Janice's yearbook until I found my picture among the rows of others. The image was small and blurred and I leaned forward, trying to recognize the details of my face. I didn't wear glasses or pigtails or have a wide, toothy grin. Half the girls in my class had straight brown hair; I might have been anyone. But the picture had my name printed beneath, so I signed beside it and handed the book back to Janice.

"You can't just sign," she told me. "You have to write something *particular.* It's good manners."

In the center of the pool, the cheerleaders squealed as they dropped one girl into the water and lifted up another. Some of the boys sat along the edge, whistling through their teeth as they watched.

> *Hi my name's Rachel and you know I am*
> *Gonna run you over in my new Trans-am!*

Have a fun summer, I wrote above my signature. After she handed my yearbook back, Janice flopped down on her stomach and rested her chin on the back of her arm, staring out at the pool.

"My cousin's a cheerleader in Texas," she told me. "She stands on people's shoulders and gets tossed up in the air and does double back-flips."

"That's nice," I said.

"Our cheerleaders suck," Janice went on. "They don't even do cartwheels. Girls like us could easily be on the team."

I tried to look bored with the conversation, preoccupied. Except for that day in the lunchroom, I had never even spoken to Janice Reardon, never given her the slightest reason to think that I could stand her. We were not an *us.*

Janice rolled onto her side, shielding her face from the sun with one hand to look up at me. "I bet you didn't hear about Colleen," she said.

"Everyone heard about Colleen."

"No," she told me. "Not what happened in the bathroom. I mean, *after.*"

Colleen had not returned to school since the day she gouged herself in the girls' room. I had figured that her parents thought the stress was too much for her, and were letting her recover on the sofa, watching television and eating potato chips from the bag. "What happened?" I asked.

No one was sitting anywhere near us, but Janice sat up and cupped her mouth with her fingers to whisper into my ear. "Her parents sent her away," she said. "To a *center.*" She sat back on her heels, watching my face register this information.

"What sort of center?"

"Someplace in Arizona," she said. "For girls who try to . . . *you know.*" Janice dragged her thumb across her throat.

The sun was bright and warm, but a shiver crawled across my skin. The image of a building with white walls and no windows appeared in my mind, a place I hadn't known existed, a place where they sent girls who wanted to die. "She didn't try that hard," I said.

"It *was* sort of pathetic," Janice agreed. "I mean, she should have used a knife or scissors if she was really serious about it. But they sent her off anyway."

"How do you know that?"

Janice shrugged. "Sharon and Abigail told me."

"They talk to *you*?" I asked.

Janice narrowed her eyes. "All the time." She stood and bent forward, twisting her wet hair into a cord so that the water trickled onto the grass.

"I don't believe you," I said.

"Then don't."

The teachers were gathering around the pool, waving everyone out so that they would have time to change before the buses returned to take us back to school. In the water, my classmates groaned and whined, pleading for ten more minutes, then five, then two.

Janice touched my knee with her naked white toes and I looked up at her. "For your information," she said, "Sharon and Abigail are practically my best friends now. They need a shoulder to cry on and I've been there for them. They tell me everything."

I opened my yearbook, pretending to lose myself inside it so that she would see my lack of interest and go away. But Janice stood with her hands on her round hips, not moving.

"They talk about *her* sometimes," she whispered and I looked up. The sun was shining behind Janice's head, making me squint. But I couldn't lower my eyes, couldn't find the place inside myself that was able to pretend I didn't want to know what they said.

"If it makes you feel better," she told me, "Polly wasn't anything special. She was kind of boring."

Around the pool, my classmates were climbing out of the water, shaking their wet hair at one another as they headed toward the locker room. The spaces around Janice were beginning to blur and the ground felt uneven beneath me, loose and soggy. "You didn't even know her," I said.

"I have good intuition about people." Janice shrugged. "I'm psychic—I just *know* things."

I rose to join the class. "Then you know I'm not interested," I told her. "You know I don't care about any of this."

"I know it was your father," she said and I stopped. "I know he's the one who carried her out of the water."

My lungs heaved inside my chest, but I tried to smile, tried to roll my eyes. "And you know that because you're psychic?"

"No." Janice held my gaze, blank and unblinking. "I know that because my stepfather is on the posse and he told me."

Back at the school, my classmates stood in clusters, signing one another's yearbooks, exchanging phone numbers, promising to keep in touch even though everyone had gone to school together since kindergarten and no one's parents had plans to move.

After school I was supposed to hurry home to clean stalls and check on my mother. But I stood watching as people filed onto buses and climbed into their parents' cars. The minutes passed and the parking lot emptied. The year was over.

I made my way through the abandoned hallways of the school, shuffling my feet through scraps of loose-leaf paper and staring past the rows of empty lockers. In the fall, a whole new group of faces would fill the sixth grade, but they would be more or less the same. They would use the same textbooks and take the same tests. Years after we were gone, the school would probably still look the way it did now: The paint would still be peeling off the walls. The grass would still be patchy with thirst. People came and went. They were sent away or died or left of their own free will. Who they were, what they had said or done, it didn't matter. In the end, no one remembered anything.

It was probably just as well about the tree no one had planted for Polly. Trees that grew in the desert were crooked and skeletal, too weak for climbing, too thin for providing shade. In science, they had told us about places where time was recorded in rings of bark, and leaves painted whispering ceilings over mounds of damp earth. There were places where trees lived forever. But this was not one of them.

I stood in the seventh-grade wing and closed my eyes, trying to imagine myself three months later, three months older, starting a new grade at my old school. But when I closed my eyes, I saw my father, waist deep in the canal, water streaming from his arms as he carried Polly's lifeless body to the bank. Her skin would have been cold and slippery, her lips blue, her dark hair soaking brown water through the fabric of my father's T-shirt. And maybe he would have thought of me, how every day I walked that very same road beside that very same water. Maybe he would have imagined, as I had so many times, that it had been my backpack found next to the canal, my body tangled in a grate. Maybe he would have imagined his life without me. The day they'd found her, my father had touched her, lifted her, carried the dead, wet weight of her through the water to the edge. And then he'd come home to me. He'd never said a word about it.

And then I thought about the teacher, the man Janice Reardon had seen crying inside his car. Polly Cain had been no one special, just a girl. But he had wept for her. I crossed the hallway to the door marked *English.* Inside, the classroom looked like any other. The chalkboard was dusty and streaked with erasure lines, the desks gashed with years of student carvings. In the back corner, the teacher sat writing at his desk. "Mr. Delmar?" I asked.

He raised his eyes. "The one and only."

He was thin and wiry, with messy blond hair and a knobby Adam's apple. There was nothing at all special or interesting about him. And yet, I felt a flutter through my spine when he looked at me. I wanted him to know my name.

When I didn't speak, Mr. Delmar glanced over his shoulder at the clock behind him. "It's four-thirty," he said. "I figured everyone would have bolted by now."

"I'm Alice Winston?" I said finally, my voice weak and trembling in my throat. "From the sixth grade?"

He smiled and looked down at his desk. "Okay, Alice Winston from the sixth grade. What can I do for you?"

I didn't know how to answer. I wanted to ask if he had seen the yearbook, if he had thumbed through the pages to find that Polly's picture was not there. I wanted to know if he had heard about Colleen Murphy skewering herself in the bathroom or the sheriff's posse wading through the canal.

"I'm going to have you for advanced English next year?" I started. "And I thought maybe you had a list of books? So I could get a head start?"

Mr. Delmar sat back in his chair. "You're kidding," he said. "Really?"

I bit my lip. "Um, yeah?"

"Well, that's terrific." He drummed his fingers lightly on his desk. "Have a seat and I'll jot a few things down for you."

He started to write, and I balanced uneasily on the edge of a nearby desk. "What have you read so far that you've liked?" he asked.

A fire of panic rose into my ears as I tried to remember a book, any book. "Well," I said. "We read this one in class about a girl who goes blind. She has to get a dog and it's really hard for her to get used to being blind and having a dog."

He smiled. "I must have missed that one."

"It was okay," I said. "There was another one, about this boy who ran away from home and lived in a tree. I thought it was kind of stupid."

I looked around at his desk while he wrote. There were piles of loose paper, books and Post-it notes, a picture of a blond woman smiling in front of a waterfall. "You coach tennis, right?" I asked.

"That's right," he said. "Are you thinking about joining the team next year?"

"You knew Polly." The words came out in one short breath, moving through my lips before my brain could stop them.

Mr. Delmar stopped writing and looked at me. "Were you a friend of hers?"

Something had changed in his face. He looked older, calmer, sadder, and suddenly, I couldn't picture the way he had been a few moments before. Each of us had suffered over her—this was the real truth. Nothing else mattered. "She was my best friend," I said.

"I'm so sorry," he whispered. Mr. Delmar looked down at his hands and I could see the pen trembling in his fingers. The room was shrinking around me and I steadied myself on the edge of his desk, dizzy under the weight of what couldn't be taken back.

"This must have been a hard year for you," he said finally.

"It has."

"Lonely."

"Yes."

Mr. Delmar lifted his pen to his mouth, chewing at the end without looking at me. "You didn't really come here for a reading list."

"No," I told him. "I didn't."

He lifted his eyes and his gaze sliced straight through me. "She talked about me."

"Sometimes," I said.

"She never mentioned her friends," he told me. His voice was thick, his face flushed. He blinked several times and stared off to the side of me. "When she called me," he said, "she talked for hours. But she never really said anything." Mr. Delmar shook his head at his hands and I could feel the sadness tightening my lungs and filling my throat.

"She called you on the phone," I said.

"Yes."

And there it was: the past, alive and real and sitting at a desk in front of me. She had called him on the phone, had talked to him for hours. "She had a crush on you," I whispered.

"I know she did."

I looked down at the cluttered surface of his desk. I wanted to say something more, to tell him about Colleen's parents sending her away or Janice Reardon telling people that Polly's ghost hovered over the water. I wanted to say that it had become a circus to everyone else before they got bored with it, that he and I were the only two people on earth who understood the true pain of what had happened. But I could feel the air around me changing into something strained and fragile. Anything more would be too much.

"I'll take the list anyway," I told him. "Since you wrote it out and everything."

He smiled. "What a good sport you are."

I slipped the paper into my backpack and turned to go. "Alice Winston," he said, and I stopped. "You look like her."

In that moment, I felt the air between us thickening, the world around me melting away until there was no history, no future, no truth. "I know," I told him. "Everyone says so."

I ran home along the canal with my heart leaping. Every little part of myself was suddenly alive and tingling, my kneecaps and fingernails, the soles of my feet. The air hummed through my ears and my breath pounded inside my chest until I thought my rib cage might crack open under the pressure. Polly Cain had had a secret. And now I had one too.

three

THE BOARDERS CAME at all hours of the day, making it so that we could never entirely relax. Each of their horses was as picky about its surroundings as Toy Boy, and my father kept lists of instructions for each particular horse wadded in his pockets. Jaycee Sheridan said that her Arabian mare, Sierra, would only drink purified water. Bitsy Rowan taped up signs in the barn, requesting that no one use scented lotions, shampoos, or—above all—perfume, because her saddlebred, Heathcliff, had sensitive sinuses.

"Who *are* these women?" Sheila asked as we helped my father shovel a load of sawdust out of the back of his pickup truck. It was the third time in as many days that her lesson had been cut short so that Patty Jo and her friends could use the arena.

"Boarders," my father said, as if that explained it.

"Well," Sheila said, blowing her bangs off her forehead, "they're annoying."

"At least *your* horse gets to stay in the barn," I told her. Our own show horses paced tight circles in their new little pens, kicking up clouds of dust in the afternoon heat.

"The boarders are all right," my father said. "A little fussy, maybe. But we can handle fussy." Sheila nodded, showing that she was willing to put up with fussiness if he asked her to.

During the hottest part of the day, Sheila and I carried the hose around to the pens my father had welded beside the arena, filling water buckets and spraying the horses' backs to help cool them under the sun. The horses went still, closing their eyes and twitching the muscles in their backs beneath the water. "It won't be forever," I promised them.

"When?" Sheila asked. Around my father, she was upbeat and positive, not a complainer. But I could tell that she was getting tired of shoveling sawdust and carrying jugs of purified water, tired of cutting her lessons short.

"I'm not sure." There was no use putting pressure on her, no use telling her that the boarders would stay around until she started winning and bringing in show clients. "But it can't go on forever."

Sheila sighed. "Why do they even *have* such expensive horses if they never show them? What's the point?"

I had wondered that myself. The boarders came every day. But they didn't take riding lessons or show any interest in competition. They spent hours grooming and working their horses only to put them back in their stalls.

"And where are their husbands?" Sheila asked. "They never even talk about them."

"My dad says they're the kind of women who turn to horses when they're finished with men."

Sheila thought about this for a minute. "What does that mean?" she asked and I shrugged.

I wondered if Sheila was thinking about her own father. Every now and then, Mr. Altman would come out on a Saturday to watch Sheila ride, but he never stayed for long—he said the dust made him cough. And while he agreed that Yellow Cap was a looker, I hadn't seen him get within spitting distance of the horse. If one of the horses got too close to him, he would jump backward and yell, *"Whoa there!"*

Sheila leaned forward to take a sip from the hose, keeping her eyes on me as she waited for the answer. "I don't know," I said finally. "But we haven't seen a single one of their husbands and my dad says we never will."

"Well, I hope they go away *soon*," Sheila said, straightening to wipe her mouth with the back of her arm. "I'm getting really sick of that Bitsy woman sniffing at me all the time."

In the afternoons, the boarders came in twos and threes, carrying coolers filled with frozen grapes and thermoses of champagne and orange juice that they poured into paper cups. Jaycee bought a stereo for the barn and hired an electrician to hook up speakers so that she and her friends could listen to music while they groomed their horses. While Sheila and my father worked in the arena, I would clean stalls and listen to the conversations that filtered through the barn. As the hours passed and the thermoses emptied, their voices grew louder and their laughter rose in uncontrollable fits.

During those afternoons, I learned that pasta and potatoes made a person fat, that blow-drying hair made it coarse and brittle, that having more than one baby made women's stomachs droop like deflated tires.

"You're always working," Bitsy said while I was mucking out Heathcliff's stall. "Take a break. Come chat with us."

My father didn't like breaks. He said that resting only made it that much harder to start up again. But he also said that I was supposed to be polite and do whatever the boarders asked. So I sat on top of a cooler, nibbling on frozen grapes while they giggled into their paper cups and asked me questions.

"How old is your father?" Jaycee asked.

"Thirty-nine."

Bitsy whistled through her teeth. "He has really nice arms," she said.

"Is your mommy dead, honey?" Jaycee asked and my spine stiffened into wood.

"She's inside," I said.

"You should tell her to come out sometime," Patty Jo told me.

"She could have a little drinky with us," Bitsy added. "We'd love to get a look at her."

"She stays in bed most of the time," I told them and they shifted their eyes, exchanging a glance I couldn't translate.

"Is she ill?" Patty Jo asked.

I didn't know how to answer. Most of their husbands were doctors. They might know if I was lying. When I didn't say anything, Patty Jo cleared her throat and brushed her hands on her riding breeches. "Well," she said to the others. "Fiddle-dee-dee."

"I should get back to work," I told them and stood. "Thanks for the grapes."

After everyone had left for the day, my father carried a hose through the barn, refilling the horses' water. "Those women are making me nuts," he said.

"They're usually drunk," I told him.

"That explains some things," he said. He was standing in front of Sierra's stall and though there were jugs of purified water stacked beside it, my father filled her bin with hose water. "What's wrong?" he asked the mare as he squirted her with the hose. "You too good for this?"

Sierra tossed her head, trying to sidestep the spray, but my father followed her with the arch of water, cornering her in the stall. Sierra whinnied and stomped one foot, then lowered her head, cowering beneath the water. "No," my father said. "I didn't think so."

The second horse show was better attended than the first. By six-thirty in the morning, twenty trailers were already set up at the Posse Grounds. Sheila stood beside me, shivering in her sweatshirt while my father backed Cap out of the trailer and walked him toward the arena. We followed behind, breathing into our fingers to keep them warm.

The horses were still blanketed, their feet wrapped to keep them clean until the moment judging began. My father found an empty corner in the arena and hooked a lunge line to Cap's halter, feeding the rope and tapping a crop against his boot until Cap began to trot circles around him.

Sheila stood lock-kneed, chewing on the tip of her French braid as we watched from the fence. "*I* ought to be doing that," she said. All the other horses were being warmed up by their riders.

"He might yank you across the arena," I told her.

"I know," she said.

I felt a stirring of softness toward her and I touched the sleeve of her sweatshirt with my fingertips. "All these other kids have been doing this forever," I told her. Sheila nodded without looking at me.

Mrs. Altman came up behind us, holding her purse under her arm. "Are you cold?" she asked Sheila. "Would you like me to buy you a hot cocoa at the concession stand?"

Sheila didn't take her eyes off the ring. "I'll throw up," she said.

Mrs. Altman stood for a moment without speaking, then pulled her sweater tighter around her shoulders. "Alice?" she said and pointed toward the arena. "Why is this necessary?"

"It helps calm the horse down," I told her. "And it gets him used to the ring."

"Is that important?" Mrs. Altman asked. Sheila rolled her eyes.

"Horses are just like people," I said. "They get jumpy."

"Well," Mrs. Altman said, straightening. "I'm not sure I like the *whip.*"

Sheila took a deep breath and I stepped backward in case she really might throw up. "It's a *crop,* Mom," she said. "And Joe only uses it for the *noise.*"

I turned to look at her, trying to tell when my father had shifted from *Mr. Winston* into *Joe.* But Sheila's face was blank and frozen, staring out at the arena like it might swallow her whole.

The early morning crept by and the parking lot filled with horse trailers and motor homes. None of the big stables had entered riders in the first show, but that was to be expected. The first show was always unofficial, a practice round. None of the winnings counted toward the overall winnings at the end of the season. So none of the winners bothered with it. But they came out for the second show. We were set up next to Bud Pope, who ran the Pope Equestrian Center and came with eight students and two horse trailers. Bud wore a white button-down shirt and a black felt Stetson. "Got that trailer looking sharp, Joe," he said, and my father waved without smiling.

"What do you hear from that kid of yours?" Bud asked.

My father straightened. "She's fine, thanks."

The first class was beginning to gather near the ring, and mothers bustled around their daughters, sticking last-minute pins into hair, smearing rouge on cheeks, and wiping smudges off boots. Mrs. Altman hovered over Sheila, trying to be helpful. But she didn't know her way around a horse, couldn't lift a saddle by herself or figure out how to fasten the chin strap of Sheila's riding helmet. "There are some bleachers on the other side of the arena," I told her. "We can sit over there if you want."

"Oh," Mrs. Altman said and looked at Sheila, who wouldn't meet her eye. "I guess that would be okay."

Mrs. Altman bought me a hot cocoa and we climbed the bleachers as the smaller children circled their horses around the judge.

"Look how little," Mrs. Altman breathed as she watched. "Alice, is it safe for such small children to be on horses?" A young couple sitting near us glanced over and I smiled at them, hoping they weren't parents. This was not the way to win new clients.

"They only walk and trot," I told her. "They don't canter."

I didn't tell Mrs. Altman that my father had spent the weeks before the first show trying to figure out a way that Sheila could ride in the ten-and-under class. "If she was just *eleven,*" he kept saying.

"She's twelve," I told him. "And she isn't short for her age."

In a single day, there were over thirty different classes—different styles, different age groups, different criteria. Most of the riders had to race between their classes to change clothes or saddles or to get a drink of water. ("I'm in *sixteen* classes today," moaned Valerie Hayes, who was Bud Pope's student and one of the girls my sister used to sneak cigarettes with. "I might as well just fucking kill myself.") My father had only entered Sheila in two classes: English equitation and Western equitation. One was in the morning and the other was in the afternoon, so my father figured Sheila would have plenty of time to regroup in between. He had thought about entering Sheila only in the Western class. She was a little better at riding Western—the saddle horn made her feel more secure. But when he mentioned this to Sheila's mother, she had been confused. Mrs. Altman said that the only real differences between English and Western seemed to be the saddles and the outfits. Sheila already had both saddles and both outfits. It seemed like a waste if she didn't ride in both.

Sheila and the ten-to-thirteen group were lining up outside the arena and Mrs. Altman squeezed my arm. "There she is," she whispered. My father stood beside Yellow Cap, talking up to Sheila while she nodded her head and twisted the reins in her hands.

"What do you think your father's telling her?" Mrs. Altman asked and I squinted, trying to read his lips.

"He's probably telling her not to fall off," I said. Mrs. Altman's mouth froze in a circle of horror. "Or he's telling her to smile."

My father stepped back, and Sheila took a breath as she nudged Cap into the ring. She was followed by the Pope twins, Zach and Andy, who always slouched on their horses until the moment the judging began. "Look how many," Mrs. Altman said, counting the riders in Sheila's class. "Where did they all come from?"

My sister and I were never supposed to talk about other barns in front of our clients. I couldn't tell Mrs. Altman about Bud Pope and his army of students, or Diana Burns, who taught jumping and buggy riding and always carried a crop in her boot. Their students filed in after Sheila, and I looked down at my feet. "I'm not sure."

Zach and Andy Pope held their hands up at me as they passed by the bleachers and Andy crossed his eyes, then laughed.

"Friends?" Mrs. Altman asked. The Pope twins were loose and lanky, with shaggy haircuts and chapped lips that made them look like they'd been drinking fruit punch.

"No," I said and waved back at them.

The moment the gate closed, it was clear that Sheila didn't have a prayer. Gone were the fuzzy coats and sleepy eyes from the first show. Every boot was polished, every back straight. "How's she doing?" Mrs. Altman kept asking.

In the ring, Cap strained and Sheila tugged. Her elbows flapped at her sides and her feet swung back and forth in the stirrups. "Okay," I said.

On the far side of the arena, Cap came to a sudden stop and Sheila kicked him moving. "Oh no!" Mrs. Altman gasped. "What just happened?"

"Cap broke his gait," I told her. "The judge saw."

"That's bad?" she asked.

"It's not good."

The riders lined their horses up in the center of the arena and the judge walked down the row, picking the top six. Sheila's face was red and the corners of her mouth twitched downward, but she waited until the places were called and she was out of the ring before she started crying.

Mrs. Altman stood up. "I have to go to her."

My father was already at Cap's shoulder, looking up at Sheila as he talked to her. He held the reins in one hand and put the other on Sheila's knee, rubbing it in slow circles.

"She hardly ever cries," Mrs. Altman said without taking her eyes off Sheila. "I'm sure she wants me."

But when my father was done talking, Sheila lifted her chin and squared her shoulders. She said something I couldn't make out, and my father laughed with his whole body, tipping back on his heels. Then he patted her thigh and held up his hand to help her dismount. They walked back to the trailer without ever looking at us.

During the lunch break, I walked around the corner of our truck and collided into Valerie Hayes. "Jesus Christ," she said. "I've been look-ing for you."

Valerie was Nona's age, with red hair and skin so freckled that from a distance, she looked pink. Though she had always been around, I couldn't remember her ever noticing me before, and I glanced over my shoulder to see if someone was standing behind me.

"I have to change. Come with me." Valerie took me by the elbow, leading me toward Bud Pope's trailer. "I wanted to find you earlier," she said. "But I haven't had a single fucking minute today. Not a minute."

I followed Valerie into the back of the horse trailer, where she had her show clothes for the afternoon laid out on the back of a fold-ing chair. "We can talk while I do this," she said and closed the door behind us. It was dark and cool inside, the light shining through in paper-thin stripes. "Have you seen me out there?" Valerie asked as she pushed her boots off with her feet. "I've been out there, like, *all day.*"

"You're doing good," I told her, staring down at the floor as she shimmied out of her riding breeches. "Two blues and a red."

"Yeah," she said. "Now that Barbie's gone, right?" She wiggled her hips and through a bar of light I saw the purple lace of her underwear against her pumpkin-speckled skin.

"Seriously, though," Valerie said. "How's Nona? What do you hear?"

It felt like an important question and I wanted to have an important answer. In my mind, I flipped back through all of Nona's letters, searching for anything that might impress Valerie Hayes. "She's in Idaho," I said at last. "I mean, she was. I'm not sure where she is right now. She and Jerry. Her husband."

"Jesus," Valerie said. "I couldn't believe she went through with it."

"I know," I said.

"It was a total fucking *scandal*."

"It was?" I asked.

"You should have seen it," Valerie said. She stripped her shirt off in one quick motion and a slip of light shimmered across the pink of her stomach as she reached for another. "Everyone was like, *She got married?*"

"Everyone who?" I asked and Valerie cocked her head at me.

"Everyone at school."

Nona had never talked much about school. It seemed strange now to think of her having teachers and locker partners and conversations with people I had never met, people who saw her every day, just like I did. I watched Valerie Hayes fumble with the buttons of her shirt in the darkness and I wondered what else she knew about my sister, what sort of people they had been when they were alone together.

Valerie smoothed her hair with the palms of her hands and opened the back of the trailer, spilling light across the floor. "Anything new with you?" she asked.

"A girl at my school died," I said. "She drowned in the canal."

"Wow," Valerie said. "That's no fun." She stepped out of the trailer and held her arms out so that I could see her outfit in the light, her jeans hugging the narrow slip of her waist, her shirt buckling slightly around the swell of her breasts. "Wish me luck," she said.

I wanted to say that Nona was disappearing, that I couldn't quite remember the shape of her body, the shade of her skin. I wanted to tell Valerie that my sister didn't call us, that she barely wrote, that at night, I passed the hours of dark silence by imagining what was happening in her life, what was so exciting and important that she might forget all about us and leave us to navigate the world without her.

"Good luck," I said. But Valerie had already turned around the side of the horse trailer, gone before my words could reach her.

The second half of the day wasn't much different from the first. I sat with Mrs. Altman in the bleachers, trying to explain how things worked while she fanned herself with a program. Sheila didn't make any giant mistakes during her second class, but it wasn't enough to win her a ribbon. Zach and Andy Pope took first and second place, as they had in Sheila's first class. The winners filed out of the arena and Mrs. Altman and I walked down to the gate to stand with my father as Sheila came out behind them.

"Better," my father said and Sheila smiled.

Out of the corner of my eye, I saw Bud Pope leaning against the fence, watching us. When he walked by, he tipped his Stetson at Sheila. "Quite a horse," he said.

Sheila beamed. "His name's Yellow Cap," she said. "He's the best horse in the world."

"A horse for a princess." Bud winked at Sheila and my father's lips flattened into a line. "Hope you're getting everything out of him that you can."

"We're doing just fine, thanks," my father said.

"Let me know if you have any trouble," Bud told Sheila. "I might know a few tricks to help you out."

Bud walked away and Mrs. Altman looked over her shoulder at him. "That was awfully nice," she said.

Sheila changed out of her show clothes and we stood to the side while Mrs. Altman and my father discussed the cost of the following week's lessons. Sheila leaned back against the horse trailer and blew her bangs off her forehead. "Oh my God, I'm dying," she said. "What happens when it gets *really* hot?"

"You sweat more," I told her.

My father spoke quickly to Mrs. Altman, using his hands. A trickle of sweat crept behind my ear and I wiped it on my shoulder, letting my father's big sale fade into background noise—a little more time, a little more money, Sheila's great future of trophies and blue ribbons. Mrs. Altman opened her checkbook and started writing.

On the other side of the parking lot, Zach and Andy Pope were heading back from the concession stand, their arms filled with hot dogs and nachos. I leaned against the trailer and watched as Bud came up behind them, putting an arm around each of their shoulders and leaning forward to speak into their ears. When he was finished, the twins glanced at Sheila and me, then made a face like they smelled something rotten. Bud said something else, then pushed them in our direction. They waited until they were almost on top of us before they smiled.

"Hey, princess," Andy said to Sheila. "You were looking pretty good out there."

Sheila blushed at the ground. "Thanks," she said.

"How long have you been riding?" Zach asked, licking a smear of nacho cheese off his wrist.

"Not long," Sheila said. "This is only my second show."

"You're kidding," Andy said. "I wouldn't have guessed that at all."

"We won't keep you," I told the twins, but they planted their feet, still looking at Sheila.

"Give us a call if you ever want to get together and ride," Andy said. "We have the best arena in town."

When they walked away, Sheila waved to them, then pinched my arm. "Those boys are *cute.*"

"They're jerks," I told her. The last thing I needed was Sheila getting all moony over the Pope twins.

We turned around and my father was staring at us with his head cocked and his jaw flexing. "Who were you talking to?" he asked. I stepped away from Sheila to show that I hadn't been part of it.

"Those boys who won," Sheila said. "They're really friendly."

"Listen," my father said and his voice was low and careful. "You have a choice to make and I want you to make it right here and now."

Mrs. Altman looked at me with wide, worried eyes and I shook my head at her. I couldn't help.

"Do you want to have friends?" my father asked. "Or do you want to win?"

Sheila's face flushed and she looked up at my father with her lips parted. When she answered, her voice was thin and whispery. "Win?"

"What?" my father asked.

"Mr. Winston," Mrs. Altman interrupted. "I'm not sure I like—" but my father held one hand up in her direction and she fell silent.

"You have one job while you're here," my father told Sheila. "If you're not going to take it seriously, I'm not going to waste my time with you."

Sooner or later, my father gave this speech to every client. It was his way of keeping them focused, protecting them against people like Bud Pope who would try to lure them away from us. But as I watched my father look into Sheila's eyes, I felt a stir of uneasiness.

"I want to *win*, Joe," Sheila said again, and this time her voice was low and even, dangerous. My father smiled.

"Then you will," he told her. "I promise."

Mrs. Altman folded her fingers together and brought her hands up beneath her chin. "This seems a little extreme," she said quietly. "They're just children, after all. And those boys' father seemed so kind and helpful."

I thought of Valerie Hayes and wondered how well she had really known my sister, how many friendships Nona had kept secret from my father. But I looked at Sheila Altman, her wide, hopeful face and honest eyes, and realized that it didn't matter. As long as my sister had lived in Desert Valley, she was never going to run off with one of our competitors, never going to take her business elsewhere. Mrs. Altman looked around and saw that people were nice or that they weren't. She couldn't understand the way things worked, the way we needed her daughter, needed her money.

"Once I saw Bud Pope hit a horse," I said and all three of them looked at me. "With a riding crop."

"Oh, dear," Mrs. Altman said.

"Right across the face," I said. "Hard too. It made a big noise."

My father tilted his head at me. He despised Bud Pope, said he was a swindler, the kind of man who told his own kids to lose if they were competing against one of his clients. But I had never seen Bud hit a horse, and my father knew it.

"Well," Mrs. Altman said. "We'll just stay far away from *him*."

On the drive home, I sat with my back against the window and my legs stretched out across the seat of the truck. I could feel the grit on my scalp, the tight, hot glow of a sunburn stiffening my face and arms. We were nearly home when my father took one hand off the steering wheel, setting it on top of my foot. "Want me to take you out for a steak dinner?" he asked.

My stomach was swollen on the burgers, hot chocolate, and soda pop that Mrs. Altman had bought me throughout the day. I wasn't the littlest bit hungry. And even if I were, we couldn't afford a steak dinner. "Okay," I said.

Two days later, Sheila fell. It wasn't anything fantastic. In the middle of her lesson, she tried to nudge Cap into a canter. He balked, then hopped out with his back legs. Sheila tumbled off the side like she'd been shot through the heart.

My father sprinted across the ring. By the time I got there, he was already helping Sheila to her feet. Her hands were skinned and her chin was bearded with dirt. "You're-okay-you're-okay-you're-okay-you're-okay," my father kept saying, holding her upright with one hand and feeling down her limbs with the other.

Sheila's face was white, her lips trembling. "Is Cap okay?" she asked.

Across the arena, Cap snorted and tossed his head, pacing back and forth at an agitated trot. "He's fine," my father told her. "He's just worried about you."

My father looped Sheila's arm over my shoulder and guided my hand to her waist. "Alice will take you inside," he said, and I bent my knees to support her weight.

"Inside?" I asked. "Inside the house?" There was a bathroom in the barn and a refrigerator in the tack room. Sheila Altman had never been inside our house.

My father took a few steps toward Cap and the horse bolted in the opposite direction, dragging his reins through the dirt. "Let her sit down," my father said without taking his eyes off Cap. "Get her out of the sun."

I took slow, tiny steps out of the arena and through the barn, hoping that Sheila would suddenly straighten and declare herself fine. But she sagged against me as I walked, touching her fingertips to her mouth and stumbling over her feet. "I feel really strange," she said. "My lips keep shaking."

Inside, the house was dark and quiet. We hadn't opened the curtains in days and the air was thick with the greasy smell of the fast-food dinner we'd eaten the night before. I felt my way through the darkness and lowered Sheila onto the sofa. "My legs feel weird," she said.

"Do they hurt?" I asked, stumbling over a pair of my father's boots as I crossed the room to turn on a light.

"No," she said. "They just feel weird."

The mismatched lamps on either side of the sofa flicked on and Sheila blinked several times, then looked down at her hands. "You probably think I'm a crybaby," she said.

"You're not crying," I told her.

Sheila leaned back against the sofa and her eyes circled the room. I cringed at the pile of laundry on the foot of the stairs, the stained carpet, the cereal bowls from breakfast crusting on the table. "Wow," Sheila said. "Is that your sister?"

She was staring at the rows of pictures on the living room walls. "Yeah," I said. "That's Nona."

"Oh, my God," Sheila breathed. "She's, like, a *movie star.*"

"Thanks," I said.

Sheila stood and gimped toward the wall, rubbing her hip as she moved. "Look!" She pointed. "Here's one with Cap!" Sheila traced her finger over the caption printed at the bottom of the picture. "*Winona Winston on Yellow Cap,*" she read aloud. "*Six National Points.* What does that mean?"

"You compete for points," I told her, hoping she would sit back down in case she tripped on something and hit her head. But she watched me with her eyebrows raised, waiting for an explanation. "The more you win, the more points you get. When you ride in local shows, you earn local points. In national shows, you get national points. In world shows, you get world points. Get it?"

"Who wins the points?" Sheila asked. "The horse or the person?"

"It depends," I told her. "There are different classes for different things. But you compete for both."

Sheila looked back up at the picture. "And Cap has *national* points?"

"He has *world* points," I said. "My sister does too. They won them together."

Sheila stepped away from the wall and eased back onto the sofa, letting her eyes sweep across the pictures. Then she leaned forward into her hands and started to cry.

"Are you okay?" I asked.

Sheila shook her head and I edged toward the kitchen, thinking she might need water splashed onto her face.

"Alice, tell the truth," she whispered and I stopped. Sheila lifted her eyes over the tops of her fingers and I could see the tears spilling down her face into the cups of her hands. "Am I good enough for him?"

By the time Mrs. Altman came for Sheila, we had her mostly cleaned up. The shadow of a bruise was beginning to form along her jaw and the palms of her hands were a little raw, but she was walking and talking like a normal person again.

Mrs. Altman clutched Sheila against her chest, then stepped back to look at her. "We have to go to the emergency room," she said.

"You don't," my father told her. "I promise, you don't."

"Just to be sure," Mrs. Altman said, then narrowed her eyes at the barn. "That *horse!*"

"It wasn't Cap's fault," Sheila said and Mrs. Altman led her toward the car. "He probably got stung by a bee—that's what Alice said."

I tried to catch my father's eye, but he was hurrying in front of the Altmans to hold the car door open for Sheila. After she was inside, he put his hand on Mrs. Altman's shoulder. "She's all right," he said. "She's a lot tougher than she looks."

Mrs. Altman closed her eyes. "I know," she whispered. "It's just to be sure."

After they were gone, my father resaddled Cap and took him out to the arena, riding him at a full gallop. I went inside the house and opened the curtains. From the window, I watched Cap's coat darken with sweat. His head began to drop, a sign of exhaustion, but my father kicked him on. While I waited for him to finish, I folded the laundry and rinsed out the breakfast dishes, then lit a candle that was supposed to smell like apple pie. I walked the candle around the living room, trying to chase away the greasy burger and horse sweat smells, but the apple pie smell made me dizzy and I had to blow the candle out.

When I went back to the window, the sun was setting and I expected to see my father in front of the barn, waving me out to help feed the horses. But he was still in the arena. Cap's neck and legs were foamed with sweat and thick cords of saliva whipped from the corners of his mouth. I squeezed my eyes shut and flexed my whole body, trying to reach my father with my thoughts. *Stop, stop, stop,* I begged until my hands shook from clenching and my teeth ached in my jaw. When I opened my eyes, the last pink of daylight had drained into darkness. They were still running.

Upstairs in Nona's room, I turned on the light and closed the door. We had shoved a few things in there since she left—a couple boxes of Christmas tree decorations and some clothes of my mother's that she told us could not be kept in her own room and could not be thrown away—but beneath that, it was exactly the same as it had been when Nona lived there. A pile of dirty clothes lay beside the dresser and a paperback novel was open facedown on the bedside table, keeping her place.

Outside, I could sense Cap's gait in the distance, the weight of his body pounding against the ground. I walked across the room, and the floorboards seemed to tremble beneath my feet, the earth buckling under the force of Cap's punishment. I picked up Nona's pink telephone and stretched the cord into her closet.

I sat on the floor between my sister's fleece bedroom slippers and a pair of silver sandals I had never seen her wear. The hems of her skirts brushed the top of my head, and up through the floor, I felt the pounding move into my chest, pulsing through my arms and into the palms of my hands. My father wasn't going to stop. The earth would break. The house would fall. I would be buried under rubble, smashed to pieces. A tiny part of myself believed it was about to happen. A tiny part of myself wanted it.

I turned the phone over in my hands. In the past few weeks, I had stolen a hundred glances at the phone book, had traced the number in my head a thousand times. There was nothing inside my body but noise—it flattened my lungs and pumped through my limbs. My fingers moved over the telephone keys like they were underwater, my entire body drowning in the din of my own heartbeat. It rang five times before he answered.

"Mr. Delmar?" I asked.

There was a pause on the other end of the line, a silence as deep and unknowable as the sky. Everything inside myself went perfectly still. "Alice Winston," he said.

four

On television, the weatherman said that it was the hottest summer Desert Valley had seen in fifteen years. We hadn't had a single rainy day since early spring, and outside, the sun glared down like a raw wound, bleaching the wooden fences and wilting the trees. The town passed a ban on irrigation and by early July, the ground had turned the color of bone. It was all anyone could talk about: *When will it rain? Will there be rain? Where is the rain?*

Desert Valley's history was written in weather. Throughout my life, I had heard the stories: In the early seventies, there had been a freak coverage of damp, wet weather that bred mosquitoes the size of bumblebees. Five years before that, a season of wind had stripped the trees bare and left the land as clean and polished as a well-washed dinner plate. On the other side of town, houses and shopping malls sprouted up like exotic gardens, glistening with their newness and drawing in people who liked warm weather and mild winters. The boarders carried tubes of lotion in their handbags that they squirted onto their fingers and smoothed over their arms. Even Sheila Altman, who loathed their very presence, would line up to receive a dollop. "My mom calls me her little flower," she told me by way of explanation. "If I don't moisturize regularly, I just shrivel up."

The people who lived on our side of town had been born here, and their parents before them. There were no new restaurants, no clean

white houses. No one complained of dry skin. As the valley trans-
formed around us, the locals relied on the history of weather to dis-
criminate between those who could be trusted and those who could
not. Men older than my father gathered in the Co-op, where we
bought our feed, to compare the current climate to that of their
childhood. In the early forties, there had been a heat wave that
stretched across the better part of an entire year. "No fall," they
reminded one another. "No winter. Just God-blasting sunshine for
nine whole months."

There had been another devastating heat wave in '66. Livestock
died of thirst and starvation; men went bankrupt. To add insult to
injury, a series of fires had followed the drought, swallowing whole
farms and leaving families with nothing. "You remember that, don't
you, Joe?" they asked and my father turned to them, nodding.

"Seemed like we'd never come back from that time," he said and
they reached out and squeezed his arm, drawing him into their private circle.

In the greater sense, my family had always been misfits. My
grandparents had built the house we lived in, raised their family,
then watched as my father's older sisters left one by one. After my
father married my mother, the grandparents bought a motor home
and gave both house and barn to my parents, following their lost
daughters across the wide-open spread of the country.

My sister and I had grown up marred by the absence of the aunts
we didn't know and the grandparents who had given up everything
to follow them. Our grandfather had been something of a hero—
generous and well liked by his neighbors. The fact that he would
pick up and leave his home behind had always been an indication
that there was a certain sickness in our family, a reason to mistrust
us. As much as the locals doubted the intentions of those who moved,
new and fresh, into the valley, they doubted those who left it even
more.

The week after Jerry came for Nona, my father had taken me to a
posse picnic. I stood beside him, damp and sticky in my summer
dress, while plates of meat sweated fat under the sun. A week was
long enough for most of the men to hear that something had hap-

pened out at our barn, to notice Nona's absence. When pressed, my father had given a single, colorless explanation: "She's a teenager."

The other men had nodded. "Hormones," they agreed. "Selfishness." Teenagers were wild and unpredictable, they said. Stubborn. And though they sympathized, spoke of the universal problem, their faces betrayed their true thoughts as they stole glances at their own children: my father had done something wrong, made some dreadful mistake in the raising of my sister that had brought this misfortune onto his head.

After the circle around us broke, I heard them murmuring to one another, stealing looks in our direction, trying to sort it out. "Think about the mother," they whispered, and I dropped my head, pretending not to hear. It was something particular, something that existed in our family and our family alone. And I closed my eyes, searching inside myself for the answer. I was Nona's sister, bred and raised in the same exact space she had been. It sent a shiver of excitement through my limbs. We were different, she and I. If my sister was somehow damaged, somehow *wrong,* then I must be too.

But in the end, my father remembered the fires and the drought that preceded it. He had survived the mosquitoes. And ultimately, he had been responsible for the creation of my sister, who, for a time, seemed incapable of doing any wrong by our community. She won trophies and titles and money that made even the stodgiest old-timers tip their hats when she entered a room. But now she was gone. She had run away with her cowboy, and the weather had marked the land with its latest injustice. Even if she came back, she would not be able to speak of this new crisis. She would not be one of us.

"It's weird," Sheila told me. "I never would have thought so much about something like the weather until I knew your family. I mean, it doesn't make much difference how hot or cold it gets to regular people, but if you live off the land—"

"We don't *live off the land,*" I interrupted and Sheila made a face.

"I just mean that your horses do," she said. "Don't be so touchy."

In the afternoons, a hot, dry wind swept clouds of dirt across our pastures, chasing the horses into corners. There was going to be a hay shortage—no way around it. Already, people were beginning to look as far away as Denver to stock up on winter feed. During the day, I would catch my father behind the barn, counting hay bales and cursing under his breath.

Sheila was right, of course. Our horses depended on the weather, on the delicate balance of rain and sunshine. And our livelihood depended on our horses. As the worry began to form creases in my father's face, stooping his shoulders and souring his expression, I knew that the panic should have been contagious. But I watched the land turn to dust and felt nothing.

At night, my dreams were filled with water. It fell from the sky or rose up out of the ground, spilling through the house and washing over the furniture. In one dream, it came up through the bathtub drain. In another, a tiny sip of water swelled inside my mouth until I could not swallow fast enough. Night after night, it pulled me under, catching my wrists and tightening around my neck like a thousand icy fingers.

"Do you worry about when it will rain?" I asked Mr. Delmar. It was the fifth time in as many days that I had called, the fifth time in as many days that he had not asked me why or told me to stop.

"I'm pretty sick of this heat," he said, and through the phone I could hear the tinkling of ice cubes against his teeth as he took a slow drink of something, then swallowed. "But I wouldn't say that I *worry.*"

"The canals are really low," I told him. "Yesterday in the paper, there was a picture of a couple little kids wading across one."

"I saw that," he said and took another sip. "Are *you* worried about the drought?"

"Not at all."

Three weeks had passed since the night I first called him. We had talked about Polly, about how much I missed her, how I didn't know what to do with myself now that she was gone. He had understood this, or at least said that he did. And it was easy to keep talking. I told him about birthday parties that hadn't happened and stories she had never told me. Through our nightly conversations, Polly Cain was reborn as the closest friend I never had. She had held my hand while she learned to rollerskate, had braided my hair during slumber parties, and cried into my fingers when she failed a spelling test. And slowly, it became my history too.

It was wrong—I knew it was. But the thought of dialing his number, of waiting for his voice to come through the other end of the line, filled me with a thrill of guilt, a giddy sense of shame. Every time I hung up the phone, I promised myself that it would be the last, that I would not call again. But the sun would begin to set and I would find myself crouched in my sister's closet, holding her phone on my lap like a ticking bomb. I kept waiting for the night he didn't answer, the night the phone would ring and ring and I would know that it was over. But every time I called, there were fewer rings before he picked up. And then he began to answer by saying my name, knowing for certain that I was the one on the other end of the line.

The first night I called, he asked how the reading list was coming along, and I had to confess that I hadn't started it. There was no way to explain that we were short on money, that my father would never drive me to a bookstore so that I could get a head start on my English class. I hadn't even looked at the list since the day he handed it to me.

"I thought you might be calling to tell me that *The Hobbit* changed your life," he'd said.

"Will *The Hobbit* change my life?" I asked.

"I doubt it."

Sometimes we talked about nothing—old movies and new music, the way the desert looked at sunset or the sound the wind made in the evenings. Sometimes, we didn't mention Polly at all.

But she was there. Always. Like a breath on the line, she listened and waited. She was between us, responsible. She had led me to him, and I wanted to be grateful. I wanted to be sorry. But of all the new feelings that were beginning to stir inside me, remorse was not one of them. Who was Polly Cain anyway? One less girl with straight brown hair and no accomplishments to her name. One less girl who might have been anybody. I listened to Mr. Delmar talk, asked him questions and told him stories, and all the while the questions played through my head like a scratched record: *Is this the way* she *talked to you? Are these the words you said to her?*

"I'd love to get out of here for a while," he told me. "Just until the heat dies down."

"Me too," I said.

"Where would you go?" he asked, and I tried to think of someplace exotic, someplace that would show him how rich my imagination was, how deep my longing.

"I don't know," I said finally. "Where would you go?"

"It wouldn't matter," he said. "So long as it was by the ocean."

I had seen the ocean once, when I was seven. Nona had a show in Nevada, and afterward, my father drove us six hours out of our way to San Diego. We got to stand on the beach for two whole hours before the sun set and the water disappeared into dark noise. Nona and I had kept back, sitting on the sand. But my father took off his shoes and pulled the cuffs of his pant legs up over his knees, letting the waves roll over his white feet. "This is the Pacific," he kept saying. "The Pacific *Ocean.*"

Eventually, Nona tiptoed in. Afterward, she told me it was like being eaten alive, the way the water pushed her one direction while the ground pulled another. They both called to me, said that if I didn't go in, I would regret it afterward. I'd always be sorry to have come so close and not touched it.

I had seen oceans in movies, of course, had carried an idea of them around in my mind the way I carried ideas of panda bears and the Statue of Liberty. But up close, I was paralyzed. So much water all together looked nothing like water at all. It was steely and hungry and alive, something with lungs and teeth and a thousand secrets. I stayed on dry ground.

Now, I imagined a different sort of ocean: the ocean that Mr. Delmar and I would travel to together. He would come for me, help me pack my bags into the back of his car, and we would drive across the country, stopping at strange little restaurants, eating foods I'd never heard of. The ocean we arrived at would be flat like glass, the sand as white as snow, and we would sit side by side on brightly colored beach towels, sipping exotic drinks out of coconuts. He would read books aloud and I would write long letters to my sister and mother, telling them about all the places I had seen, all the beautiful things they were missing.

"We could go right now," I said, twisting the belt of Nona's bathrobe around my finger.

He laughed. "A few more days of this heat," he said, "and I just might take you up on that."

In the barn, it felt like things might be settling down. Sheila had placed sixth in a few of the shows. My father seemed pleased with the improvement and Mrs. Altman just about had a heart attack every time her daughter came out of the arena with a ribbon. Bud Pope kept tipping his hat in Sheila's direction and sending his sons over to flirt with her, but ever since my father's ultimatum, Sheila did her best to keep away from them. She always smiled politely when they spoke to her, but she dropped her head to avoid eye contact and made up excuses to slip away before a conversation could begin.

Sheila had yet to invite a single friend out to watch her ride, but the boarders wrote check after check. Once a week, my father drove to the lumberyard and filled the back of his pickup with sawdust for Toy Boy, then charged Patty Jo three times the amount he paid for it. "It's not like she's the type of woman who's gonna have any idea what sawdust costs," he reasoned. Late at night, we refilled the jugs of Sierra's store-bought water with water from the hose and neither Jaycee nor Sierra seemed to notice. With the extra money, my father built an awning over the pens he'd made outside for our show horses.

I had hit a sudden growth spurt and over the course of a few weeks, my clothes became too small for my body. I was getting ready to tell my father that my shoes were making me limp and my jeans were beginning to cut off the circulation at my waist, but then our air conditioner started making noises like a cat in heat. Then it stopped altogether.

My father spent a whole day on the roof, hammering and banging and swearing loudly enough that I could hear him from inside the barn. When he finally climbed down, he kicked the ladder with the toe of his boot. "I guess it's busted," he said and slumped down on the ground. I sat beside him and sucked in my stomach to keep my jeans from pinching. "Do you ever wonder when things will just be easy?" he asked.

"Yes."

We sat there for a moment, not speaking, and then he stood up and brushed the grass off the back of his jeans. "Well, it's not going to be today," he said and went inside the house.

We bought some fans from a discount store and set them up in the windows of our house. But when we turned them on, they only moved the hot air around, so that standing in front of them felt like standing in front of a hair dryer. My mother's room was upstairs, where it was hot enough to make a person nauseated during the afternoons. So my father and I took turns wrapping bags of ice in dishrags and carrying them up to her.

"I feel like my face is melting off," she told me.

"You could go downstairs," I said, and she fanned herself with one limp hand.

"Is it much better down there?" she asked.

"Not really."

My mother gave me a thin smile, then leaned her head back against the pillow and closed her eyes. "How's the new favorite doing?"

"Sheila?" I asked and my mother nodded without opening her eyes. "She's okay. She took sixth place in her Western class last week."

"Good for her." My mother set the bag of ice across her forehead, opening one eye. "Those clothes are too small for you, baby."

"Air conditioner first," I told her. "New clothes second."

Downstairs, my father was sitting at the table in his boxer shorts with the newspaper spread in front of him. "Mom's not looking so good," I said and he waved me to his side.

"Look here." He tapped the newspaper with his index finger.

"Is someone selling an air conditioner?"

My father grinned at me. "There's an auction this week."

"We can't buy any horses right now," I told him and his forehead creased.

"We can *look,*" he said. He was bouncing his leg under the table and I knew that it didn't matter what I said. In his mind, he was already at the auction, walking through lines of pens, looking for the best horse as if we had the money to pay for it.

"We still need a stud," he said, nodding in agreement with himself. "And we could take Sheila. It would be a good experience for her."

"I don't think she'll care," I told him while he scrolled through the information with his finger.

"This is a big auction," he said. "Sellers are coming from all over the place. It'll be good for the barn if we make an appearance." When I didn't answer, he tapped his finger on the table. "Plus, it's in Clover City. That's an hour away. And the truck has air-conditioning."

It was clear from the get-go that my father was prepared to make more than an appearance. The morning of the auction, he hitched the empty horse trailer to the back of the truck while we waited for Mrs. Altman to drop off Sheila. When he saw me watching, my father broadened across the shoulders. "What?"

I glanced at the roof, where our gutted air conditioner sagged like a dead tick. "Nothing," I said.

On the drive to Clover City, Sheila sat in the middle, talking with my father about what was next for her and Cap. I leaned my head against the window and stared out as the desert passed in streaks of sage and sand. Now that Sheila was beginning to place in the equitation classes, my father told her, it was time to start working on some of the specialty classes: trail, reining, and showmanship. "Do you think we're ready for those?" she asked, and my eyes darted sideways as my father patted her knee.

"We'll just start working," he said. "You're a fast learner."

At the auction, Sheila and I trailed behind while my father perused the pens, clicking his tongue to make the horses look alert, running his hands over their necks and muzzles, standing back to get the full effect of their forms.

A crowd of men had gathered at the end of the row, and Sheila and I stayed close to my father as he nudged his way to the front. The mare was a paint horse, pure white with patches of brown across her face and back. She paced in her pen, tossing the tangles of her snow-white mane and holding her head high as she snorted and stomped at the ground.

She turned to face us and the crowd around me inhaled in a single breath. The mare's right eye was the shade of melted chocolate, soft and deep and perfect. Her left was a pale, empty blue—the color of ice in winter. "Creepy," whispered Sheila.

Bud Pope stood among the horse's throng of admirers with his arms slung over the rail of her pen. When he saw us, he nodded sharply at my father, then winked at Sheila. "Morning, princess." She looked straight ahead, as though she hadn't heard him. When he turned away, she smiled into her shoulder.

Zach and Andy stood like bookends on either side of their father, bored and sweaty. "Alice-bo-*Balice*," Andy greeted me and Zach hooked his fingers into the corners of his mouth, pulling it flat and poking his tongue between his chapped lips like a lizard. I kept my eyes on the mare, pretending not to notice.

"What's the story?" my father asked the mare's handler.

"She's young," he said. "And a little crazy."

"Just the way you like your women, right, Joe?" Bud Pope said and the men around him laughed. A flush crept up my father's neck.

"She broken yet?" my father asked.

"Nope," the handler said. "Never even had a saddle on her back."

My father nodded and the handler motioned to the mare with his head. "She's got good blood, though. Her mama was a hell of a horse—ran in the Kentucky Derby once. And her daddy, well, just look at her. You can't beat that coloring."

It was true that her markings were something special—the white as pure and perfect as untouched snow, a canvas on which the soft brown patches of color seemed too precise and well placed to be anything less than intentional, a masterpiece in composition. But my father shrugged to show that he wasn't terribly impressed. "Not broken, though . . ." he said and glanced over his shoulder to let the other men see the full scope of his disinterest.

"Just means you won't have to fix some other jackass's mistakes," the handler said.

Sheila nudged me with her elbow. "Broken?"

I cupped my mouth with my hand. "It means, can she be ridden," I whispered back.

"And this horse can't?" Sheila's forehead wrinkled, pulling the blond lines of her eyebrows together.

It made sense that Sheila wouldn't know about training. Since she'd begun riding at the barn, my father hadn't worked with a single young horse. All of his time had been devoted to her.

"It means we would have to break her," I told Sheila, then glanced at my father. "I mean, if we bought her."

We walked back to the trailer so that my father could think before the bidding started. Sheila leaned against the truck, fanning her neck with her hand while my father sat in the front seat and opened his wallet. He thumbed through the stack of bills, his mouth moving silently as he counted.

"Wow," Sheila said as she watched. "You guys are *rich.*"

"Where did that come from?" I asked.

My father winked at me and wadded the bills back into his wallet. "Sawdust and fancy water."

My jeans were pinching at my sides, squeezing my stomach over the waist so that I felt like a tube of toothpaste. "It's boarder money?" I asked. "What about bills and clothes and hay for winter?"

My father glanced at Sheila, then gave me a look. We weren't supposed to talk about money in front of clients, unless we were collecting it from them. "What about the air conditioner?" I added.

My father cleared his throat and got out of the truck, pushing the door closed with his knee. "Sheila," he said. "Will you run around back and check that I put a halter in the trailer?" Sheila grinned and ran around behind the truck, clapping her hands.

"We're gonna buy a horse—we're gonna buy a horse," she sang to herself.

"Think about it," my father told me when Sheila was out of earshot. "We buy that mare today for a little bit of money, then train the hell out of her and sell her for three times what we paid." He rapped his knuckles lightly on my forehead. "It's what's called an *investment.*"

"Like those new saddles were an investment?"

A look crossed my father's face like thunder, but Sheila came around the back of the trailer, announcing that there was, indeed, a halter, and the words my father might have said froze inside his mouth. He touched the knuckle of his thumb beneath my chin, tilting my head so that my eyes were looking straight into his. "Watch yourself," he whispered, then turned, smiling, to Sheila.

The mare's name was Darling Peaches 'N Cream, which was a bad sign right off. Nothing ensured that a horse would be a killer more than giving it a cutesy name. At shows, it was always a Doll-Baby or a Honeybunch that ended up stomping some kid half to death in the middle of the arena. But if anyone else had noticed this trend, it didn't seem to make much difference when the bidding started.

It took four men to load her into our horse trailer and once she was inside, the trailer shook and rattled until I thought it might come apart in pieces. "I salute you, Joe," Bud Pope said, touching his fingers to the rim of his cowboy hat as he passed. "If nothing else, you're a man who likes a challenge." Then he winked at Sheila and headed toward his rig with the twins scuffing their feet behind him.

"Later, gator," Andy said to me. "Don't run off marrying any strangers now."

During the drive home, the truck rocked and the trailer fishtailed as the mare kicked and stomped. When we pulled into the driveway, Patty Jo and Jaycee came out of the barn to watch my father unload the mare. He opened the trailer door and Darling stood inside with her nostrils flared and her ears flattened against her head. She had kicked through the rail of the trailer gate and was holding one hind leg bent at an awkward angle beneath her.

Sheila stood on her tiptoes to see. "Oh, my God!" she said. "Her leg is bleeding!"

The muscles in my father's jaw flexed as he climbed into the trailer to get a better look. Darling bared her teeth and he held one hand up to her. "Bite me," he warned in an even voice, "and I'll knock your lights out."

My father kept his eyes on the mare's head as he ran his hand down her hind leg. She tried to jerk away, but he pushed her sideways, pinning her against the inside of the trailer so that she couldn't kick.

"Is it bad?" Sheila asked.

"She'll live," he said.

I stood behind the trailer and watched as my father slid the lead rope loose with one hand, then clicked his tongue to back the mare out. There was a skittering of hooves and then she threw her head with such force that it struck the roof of the trailer, bone on metal, and the whole thing vibrated with noise. Darling jerked sideways, shaking her head, and my father coiled the rope around his hand.

"I don't think she wants to go out backwards," Sheila called to him and I touched her arm to quiet her. "Joe's gonna get hurt," she whispered.

"Everyone gets hurt," I told her.

The mare tried to twist, but my father held her head tight by the halter, keeping her faced toward the back. With the coil of rope, he tapped lightly on her chest and she came out fast and reckless, her hooves scattering sprays of gravel as she yanked my father into the driveway.

Patty Jo and Jaycee stood at a safe distance, watching. "What a looker," Jaycee said, and my father wiped the sweat from his upper lip with his shoulder.

"I need to wrap that leg," he said and nodded toward the barn. "Alice, go get a bandage and the twitch."

In the tack room, I had to rummage through three bins before I found the twitch. I stood for a moment, holding it between my hands. The twitch was made from two pieces of metal hinged together at one end like a nutcracker. Only instead of cracking a nut between the metal pieces, it was supposed to be placed over the softest, most delicate skin of a horse's nose, then squeezed. It was the surest way to keep a horse still, and the nastiest. I couldn't remember the last time we'd had to use it. As I walked through the barn, a cold fear crept into the palms of my hands—someone was going to have to hold the twitch while my father wrapped the leg.

When I came back out, Patty Jo and Jaycee were giggling into their hands and Sheila was gazing up at my father with perfect awe.

My father pinched the twitch around Darling's nose and her ears flattened. She tried to pull back against the pressure, but my father tightened his grip and her head dropped. He motioned to me with his free hand. "Think you can handle it?"

It didn't matter if I thought I could or not. I was the only person present who couldn't sue my father if the mare crushed me into pieces. My fingers were shaking, but I reached up and took the ends of the twitch in both hands.

"Good and tight now," my father said and patted my shoulder. "You're okay."

As he moved around to Darling's back leg, I could feel the wet heat of her breath on my forehead. My father crouched down and I lifted my head, trying to force my lungs to exhale. He touched the leg and Darling threw her head, lifting me off my feet by the twitch. "Hold her!" my father barked and I gripped the handle with everything I had.

Her ears flicked back toward my father and her nostrils widened, snorting a spray of salty moisture into my face. "Ew," Sheila said, but I closed my eyes and squeezed harder.

I made my mind focus on anything but the possibility of the mare bolting and dragging me across the gravel driveway to my death. I tried to think about Nona in Idaho, eating bread from a flowerpot, or the perfect white beach where Mr. Delmar and I would order drinks with tiny umbrellas and watch the sunset. Horses could smell fear, and as I looked into the glass blue emptiness of Darling's eye, I tightened my face to show that she wasn't any meaner than I was. "I'm not afraid of you," I whispered.

My palms ached against the metal handle. My back tensed and the muscles in my legs burned as I struggled to keep upright. The mare rolled her eyes and I tightened my grip. I didn't feel my father step up behind me, and when he unhinged my hands from the twitch, I fell back against him, my legs as loose and weak as two elastic bands.

He unhooked the twitch from Darling's nose and used the palm of his hand to rub at the raw, red creases that cut across the flesh of her muzzle. When he brought his hand away, a smear of blood darkened his palm. He stared down at the blood on his hand and when he turned to me, his expression was blank. "You've got one hell of a grip, kid," he said finally.

Patty Jo and Jaycee were watching with their mouths open, the lines of their eyebrows frozen in perfect, lifted arcs. "Mr. Winston," Jaycee said, "what *is* that awful contraption?"

"We never use it," my father told her quickly, shoving the twitch into his back pocket to hide it from view. "The mare's too much horse for Alice. She couldn't keep her steady otherwise." Patty Jo and Jaycee smiled stiffly when I looked at them, then shifted their eyes sideways.

"Did I hurt her?" I whispered. The palms of my hands throbbed with bursts of fire and I could feel the dampness of my own blood trickling between my fingers.

"It's a long way from her heart," my father said, and I wiped my palms on my blue jeans, dipping my head so that I wouldn't have to see the horrified faces of Patty Jo, Jaycee, and Sheila.

My father walked Darling through the barn to the arena while the rest of us followed. I slowed my pace, hooking my hands behind my back. No one turned to look at me. No one spoke. I felt myself shrinking into a shadow as I walked the length of the barn alone. The burn in my hands spread up my inner arms, through my shoulders and neck, smoldering between my ears. If my sister had been there, she would have been able to calm the horse with the sound of her voice, the ease of her touch, the unnameable force that came from somewhere deep inside her. Without the twitch, I never would have been able to hold the mare. She had been in more pain than I was— it was the only reason I had any power at all.

"We'll keep her out here tonight," my father said and let Darling loose in the arena. She lifted her tail and trotted across the ring, shaking her head to loosen the ache from the twitch while I stood to the side.

"She's a real beauty," Patty Jo said quietly and stepped beside my father, resting her elbows on the fence.

"Her mama was a racehorse," my father said. "Just watch the way she moves."

In the arena, the mare's mane and tail glistened in streams of white ribbons as she broke into a canter and arched her neck, lifting a cloud of dust behind her. When she reached the far end of the arena, she turned to face us, stomping one slender leg against the ground. For a moment, just a moment, her eyes rested on mine, and I felt the weightless knowledge of her stare, the recognition. *I'm sorry,* I mouthed. But of course, she couldn't understand. Of course, it made no difference.

"What on earth will you do with an animal like that?" Jaycee asked, but my father didn't answer. His eyes were on the horse, on the future she might carry with her. I had seen this expression on his face before—it was the way he'd looked at every new horse, the way he'd looked at my sister. His eyes were filled with possibility, with fame and money. In that moment, the rest of the world did not exist.

"Watch the way she holds her head," he said, and Sheila climbed up on the fence beside him. He laughed out loud and I followed his finger with my eyes as he traced the curve of Darling's neck. "One in a million," he whispered. "God's perfect creation."

The fire was pumping up through my arms, spilling down the back of my neck, into my throat and chest. Everyone's eyes were on the mare. No one saw me turn for the house. No one saw me start to cry.

"Do you believe in God?" I asked. I had spent the whole of the evening locked inside Nona's closet, crying into the soft fleece of her bathrobe until the inside of my body felt scraped and hollow and my throat was raw.

"Hang on a second," Mr. Delmar said. "I might need another drink for this conversation."

I leaned back against the wall, touching my fingers to the sticky centers of my palms as I listened to him crack ice cubes from a tray, dropping them like bulbs of crystal into his drink. "Okay," he said after a minute. "What was the question?" On the other end of the line there was a flicking noise, followed by the slow hiss of burning paper—a cigarette.

"God," I said. "Do you believe in it?"

"*It?*"

"Him," I said. "Her. Father, Son, Holy Ghost. Whatever. Do you believe?"

"Do I believe in God." There was a moment of silence, a tinkling of ice cubes against his teeth as he took a sip from his drink. "No."

I held the phone between my ear and shoulder, flexing my fingers to feel the tear and burn in the linings of my palms. "Me neither."

He took a long breath of cigarette smoke, then exhaled, and I imagined him sitting outside, the smoke curling up into the black nothing of desert sky. "I believe in divinity," he told me. "I believe in grace."

"Like, not tripping over stuff?"

"Like, the goodness that works through people," he said, and I could tell by the soft edges of the words on his tongue that he was smiling. "The God inside humanity."

"So you don't believe in hell?"

"What's the point in believing?" he asked. "Everything we imagine hell to be, all the pain and atrocities, all the suffering and loneliness, it already exists. It's all around us all the time."

"And heaven?" I asked. "It's here too, real and all around us?"

"What do you think?"

I bit my lip, unable to answer. "What about animals?" I asked finally.

"What about them?"

I had waited for the tears to stop before I called him, waited until my whole body was empty and dry, hard as a fist. But now I felt the sadness rising again inside my chest. "It just seems like there should be someone, *something* out there that cares about them, cares that they existed, that they suffered or didn't." My voice rasped across my tongue, thickening my words and tightening behind my sinuses. "Something out there ought to be watching over them."

There was a moment of silence and I clenched my fingers into my palms, digging my nails into the raw, open centers of my hands until I gasped with pain. Fire shot through my wrists and inner arms, pulsing into my shoulders. But still, I squeezed harder. This is pain, I thought to myself. This is real.

"Alice," Mr. Delmar said softly. My name felt fresh and alive inside his mouth, something full of potential, something that was just beginning to exist. "I want you to hear something."

On the other end of the line, I could hear papers rustling, drawers opening and closing, the thump of his footsteps on carpet. "Close your eyes," he told me. I tilted my head back against the fabric of my sister's clothes and closed my eyes. "Now listen."

I could hear a door open, then shut on the other end of the line, the creak of his chair as he sat down, the stir of night around him as he began to read. "'Oh this is the animal that never was . . .'"

The inside of Nona's closet disappeared, the house, the world around it, leading me into someplace new, a place he had never taken Polly Cain, a place that belonged only to me. "'. . . It had not *been*. But for them, it appeared in all its purity. . . .'"

This day, and all the long, lonely days that had come before, they were not real. My nightmares of water, of struggle and fear, they were all just imaginary, created out of nothing.

"'. . . They nourished it, not with grain, but with the mere possibility of being. And finally this gave it so much power that from its forehead a horn grew. . . .'"

His voice, that was real. The plastic cup of the telephone trickling sweat into the curl of my ear, that was real. This moment, when the world was hidden behind the lids of my eyes, was real. I was here. He was speaking. It was real.

"'. . . One horn . . .'"

And in the darkness, I could see him, could taste his words in the lining of my mouth.

"'. . . It drew near to a virgin, white, gleaming—and was, inside the mirror and in her.'"

For a moment, the last word hung in the air, untouched, unwavering. And then there was another soft whisper of burning paper, the hiss of white ash falling like snow to the ground, the circle of his mouth drawing smoke into his lungs, holding it there, letting it go.

✦ ✦ ✦

When I came back downstairs, my father was standing in the living room in bare feet and boxer shorts. "I was looking for you," he said and a spasm of panic jerked through my spine.

"I'm right here."

"Go put on your swimming suit," he said.

"What for?"

"Because I told you to." He held his hand out, snapping his fingers beside my ear. "Then come out behind the barn."

When I found my swimsuit in the back of a drawer, the straps cut into my shoulders and I hunched over, trying to make myself shorter. Outside, it was dark, but the heat didn't feel any less intense. The gravel driveway burned the pads of my bare feet and I hurried through the barn, wondering what sort of awful, messy task required a bathing suit instead of regular clothes.

I came through the back of the barn and stood, squinting into the darkness. There was a splash of water and my father whistled at me. "Over here," he called.

I walked toward the sound of his voice, then stopped. Next to the arena was a round water bin, one of the largest that we owned. My father poked his head over the edge, his hair wet and slicked back to his skull. "Check it out," he said and rested his hands on the metal rim. "Our own private swimming pool!"

"That's what the Kills drink out of," I said, unsure what was happening.

"I cleaned it out first," my father told me. "Get in."

I had heard of people having strokes in severe heat and I tried to see my father's face in the darkness, to tell if it was sagging or lopsided, to be sure he wasn't suffering from some sort of brain damage. "Isn't there a ban on water?" I asked.

"There's a ban on irrigation," he said. "I'm not irrigating."

I stepped over the edge and knelt down on the metal floor until the water covered my shoulders. "Nice, right?" my father asked.

"It feels good," I said and he rolled onto his back, floating in the shallow water.

The sky was black as ink, the stars flickering by the thousands. "People from the East might act like their way of life is so much better than ours," my father said. "But I'll tell you what, they never see a sky like this."

I sat beside him in the water and tried to think if we knew any people from the East.

"It's one of the only things your mother ever liked about the desert," he said, his hands moving beneath the water, sending soft ripples lapping up against the metal edge.

I held my breath. My father never talked about my mother. Not ever. "What is?" I whispered.

"The sky," he said. "She grew up in the Midwest, you know?" In the darkness, I nodded, dipping my chin into the water. Nona had told me how our mother first came out to the barn, back when the house used to belong to my grandparents, and my grandfather gave riding lessons on the weekends. This was all I knew of my parents' history, that my mother had taken lessons from my grandfather, then married his son. When my parents got married, my grandparents retired, leaving the desert, the house, the barn, and all the horses for my parents to build their new life on.

My knee was almost touching my father's elbow beneath the water, but his eyes were on the sky and I made myself rigid, afraid that even the movement of air through my lungs might remind him where we were, might break whatever spell he seemed to be under and silence him completely. I felt suddenly light inside my skin, weightless, and my eyes closed, trying to locate myself. Maybe I was still upstairs in my sister's closet, still listening to the waves of Mr. Delmar's breath. This was all a dream. My body, my breath, my entire life, it was all just pretend.

In the distance, I could hear the hum of barn lights, the creaking choir of crickets in the pasture beyond us. "She was such an oddball when she moved here," my father said, his voice sleepy, his eyes still watching the sky above him. "This strange little flower. She was always talking about how the desert dried her skin and the air made her hair brittle." He laughed out loud and I took a slow, careful swallow of air, holding it inside my chest.

"Once," he said, "I told her to put mayonnaise on her hair, said that it was what we did for the horses to keep their tails shiny. And she did it! Smeared it all over her head. She washed and washed, but it wouldn't come out. For days, her hair looked all wet and greasy—this big, oily mess. She smelled like a salad rotting in the sun. I would sniff the air around her and say, 'What's that smell?' And she would hit me and scream, 'I *hate* you, Joe Winston!'"

My father's body was shaking with laughter, sending the water across the bin in even rolls that splashed up onto my neck. "God," he said to the stars. "What a funny kid."

I waited for him to go on, to say more about her, about who they had been when they used to belong together. But the only sound came from the ripples of water that his hands made as he moved them beneath the surface.

I lowered my shoulders into the water, dropping my arms until they sank beneath the dark surface of waves. The water lapped across the palms of my hands, curling my fingers with pain. This was real.

In the black sky, I followed the imperfect pattern of stars, trying to trace their endless trail with my eyes. Behind us, in the arena, I could hear the thumping of Darling's hooves as she broke into a trot and moved, invisible, through the darkness. I wanted to ask my father what we were going to do with her, how he would ever find the time to train her, where we would keep her when we had to use the arena. But then I thought of the look that had crossed his face when he watched her. She was still full of promise, still perfect in her mystery. For this one day, he could look at her like she might be the answer to all his prayers, the end of every worry. Once, he had looked at Sheila Altman that way, and before her, my sister. There must have been a time, back before I had knowledge or language or memory, when he had looked at me that way too.

Tomorrow, the sun would rise and deaden the land beneath its indifference. My father would remember the hay shortage, the empty white envelopes in their little drawer, the air conditioner. Tomorrow, the new mare would kick or bite or break a bone and prove that she was no different from any pretty new horse that had come before her. Tomorrow, in the honest truth of daylight, our own private swimming pool would be only what it was: a rusty metal bucket made for watering livestock.

Upstairs in my sister's closet, I had closed my eyes and seen a place I hadn't known existed. There was no anger, no loneliness, no jagged, icy fear gnawing at the wires of my body. For that one moment, the noise inside my head had turned still and silent. If hell was real and true and all around us, then heaven was too. And so I said nothing. I let my father's moment last. I let it go on until it ended.

five

WHEN THE AFTERNOON temperature swelled up over 103 degrees, my father finally surrendered to it, announcing that only a fool would work in such heat. My father hated laziness, but more than that, he hated fools. So we stopped riding in the afternoons. We had to wake up earlier in the mornings and work later into the evenings, making use of the parts of day that only threatened the intensity of the oncoming heat.

My father said that there was plenty to do during the hottest part of the day that didn't involve dehydration or death. We set up fans and folding chairs in the barn, using the afternoons to polish the show saddles. When we were finished, we organized the grooming equipment, the first aid kits, and then the tack room refrigerator. After that, there was nothing to do with the long, useless stretches of heat except sit and wait for them to pass.

By one in the afternoon, the barn and everything inside it felt sticky and unreal. We slouched in the folding chairs, playing rummy with the grimy deck of cards my father kept in the tack room and sipping sodas from the refrigerator. And while we were able to sit out the hottest part of the afternoon on workdays, weekends offered no such escape.

Horse shows stretched across the entire day, regardless of temperature, and Mrs. Altman and I sat on the bleachers with the sun beating down on our bare shoulders, drinking icy soft drinks from the concession stand and shielding our eyes with our hands. Mrs. Altman wore a wide-brimmed sunhat and thick, shaded glasses. In her purse, she carried tubes of sunblock that she insisted on rubbing onto my arms and face every few hours. "You'll be grateful some-day," she promised each time I resisted. "When you get to be my age and your skin is still as pretty and smooth as it is now, you'll thank your lucky stars that Sheila's silly mother made you wear sunscreen."

We waited for Sheila's class to enter the arena, and Mrs. Altman glanced at her wristwatch, then turned to squint out at the parking lot. "Mitchell might come out today," she explained.

"Sheila's dad?" I asked and she nodded. Mr. Altman had yet to attend a single horse show, but I had never thought much about it. Mrs. Altman took so many pictures each week that it seemed unlikely her husband missed much.

Sheila's class filed into the ring and Zach Pope blew me a dramatic kiss as he passed, then dropped his chin, laughing silently into his chest. "Those boys have a crush on you," Mrs. Altman said, smiling.

"They just like to make fun of me," I told her.

"That's how you can tell," she said.

"Sheila's the one they like," I told her politely. "They're always flirting with her."

"That's just because their father tells them to," Mrs. Altman said. "He's trying to win her into taking lessons from *him.*"

I turned to look at her and she lifted one eyebrow at me, tilting her mouth into a wry smile. "I'm catching on."

The riders lined up in the center of the ring, and Mrs. Altman leaned sideways to whisper through her fingers. "I think Sheila has a shot at fourth, don't you?"

"Fifth at least," I told her. It was a small class and several of the riders were much worse than Sheila.

When they called Sheila's name for fifth place, Mrs. Altman and I stood in the stands, cheering and clapping our hands above our heads. Sheila grinned and waved at us. Outside the arena, my father gave her a giant hug and they headed back toward the trailer.

Once they were out of eyesight, we sat back down and Mrs. Altman turned in her seat to scowl at the parking lot. When she saw me watching, her face cleared. "I guess he got tied up with work."

"What does he do?" I asked.

She leaned forward onto her knees, swirling the melting ice in her paper cup and peering into it with one eye. "He's a professor at the college," she said. "He teaches astronomy."

All this time, and I had never heard Sheila mention that her father was a college professor. "Wow," I said. "He must be really smart."

She smiled into her cup. "He is."

Mrs. Altman seemed lost in thought and in that instant, I wanted to tell her about Mr. Delmar, how he was the smartest person I had ever known, how he had read every book and seen every movie and had an answer for every question I asked him. But then I thought of what she'd said about the Pope twins making fun of me, about how *that* was the way you could tell if someone really liked you.

I tried to think back over all the phone conversations, and though I could remember Mr. Delmar laughing at some of the things I'd said, he'd never made fun. I wanted to ask her if Mr. Altman had made fun of *her* when they first met, if that was the way she knew that he would be the man she married. As I was about to speak, her face suddenly brightened and she turned to me.

"You know what we need right now?" I shook my head. "Ice cream sandwiches! Doesn't that sound like a little piece of heaven?"

My pants were cutting into my waist, squeezing my hips and pinching my thighs. If I ate another bite of food, I was sure that I would burst right out of them. But she seemed so excited, as if the very idea of an ice cream sandwich had chased all the dark thoughts right out of her head. "That sounds nice," I said and she clapped her hands.

While she was gone, I sat in the sun alone, watching the fourteen-to-eighteen class canter their horses around the arena. This was the class my sister would have been riding in if she were still here, the class she would have won with her hands tied behind her back. We hadn't gotten a single letter from her since the one that said she was in Idaho, and though my father said there was nothing to worry about, that she was just busy or preoccupied, I felt a greater stir of uneasiness with every day that passed. Nona had left without telling me anything about Jerry. Now she was gone, and I couldn't ask her if he was smart, if he teased her, if he showed up when he told her he would. I tried to picture them together in Idaho, eating steak dinners in restaurants, and for the first time, I suddenly wondered if everything was going as well as she said it was.

"Have you ever been in love?" I asked.

Mr. Delmar didn't answer and I wound the phone cord around my finger, wondering if I had asked something I shouldn't have, if I had, finally, gone too far.

"Yes," he said after a moment.

"How did you know?" I asked. "I mean, when you first fell in love, how did you know that's what it was?"

Through the phone, I could hear the sound of a car backfiring, the gentle swirl of breeze around him—he was outside.

"I just knew," he said finally.

"But what does it *feel* like?" I asked. "*How* did you know?"

"Okay, okay," he said. "Let me think a minute."

Upstairs in my sister's closet, the heat was almost more than I could bear, the air so thick it felt like I was breathing underwater. The sweat on my palms made the phone slippery and hard to hold so that I had to keep changing hands and wiping my palms dry on the hems of Nona's skirts.

"I lost a lot of weight," Mr. Delmar said. "I could stand in front of the mirror and count my ribs through my shirt."

"That's how you knew you were in *love*?" I asked.

"It's hard to explain," he said. "When you're first in love, it *fills* you. You don't need anything else—not food, not sleep, not money or friends or family even. I felt dizzy and light-headed, sick, and stupid almost."

"Stupid?"

"I nearly flunked out of college. I went to the classes, but I couldn't make myself pay attention. The whole world could have ended around me and I wouldn't have noticed."

I tried to picture Mr. Delmar in college, taking tests and writing papers, wasting away on love.

"You're not buying this," he said. "I can tell."

"I believe you," I told him. "It's just . . ." I wanted to ask who she was, the girl who made him starve himself and nearly flunk out of college, the girl who might have kept him from graduating and becoming an English teacher, the girl who might have made it so that I never met him. "It's just feeling sick and dizzy? Losing weight? Maybe you had a tapeworm."

He laughed and my face burned with embarrassment. "What?" I asked.

"You," he said. "You're a funny kid." My heart exploded inside my chest and I couldn't find the words to answer. The light was dimming around me, the air swelling inside my lungs. "For someone so smart, you're kind of a dope."

My father left the new mare alone for over a week—giving her leg time to heal. We moved her from the arena into the round pen where we had once kept Bart. My father said that once she was trained, we would be able to keep her the way we kept the rest of the show horses—in a small, square pen where she could walk little circles while she waited for someone important to buy her.

My father worked with her in the mornings, before the sun could fill the sky with its fury and chase every living thing into the shade. He lunged her for hours, standing in the center of the round pen and cracking a riding crop against his boot to make her run circles around him. Exhaustion was the key ingredient to breaking young horses, driving them into the ground until they were drenched with sweat and so bone-tired that they wouldn't even notice the additional weight of a saddle on their backs, the additional weight of a person.

But no amount of exercise could seem to numb her senses. Every time my father put a saddle on her back, Darling would rear and buck, twisting her body in midair, thrashing herself into the fence or throwing herself to the ground and rolling until the saddle broke under her weight and had to be thrown away.

So my father went to plan B: During the hottest part of the day, he would lead her into the empty arena and hold her tight as he cinched the saddle around her. Then he tied one rein to the side of the saddle so that her head wrenched sideways and her body curved into a C. At this angle, she couldn't buck, couldn't roll, couldn't take a step forward. She was frozen in the center of the ring, stationary, powerless. Once her head was secured, my father walked out of the arena and closed the gate, leaving her to stand and sweat beneath the sun. "A few days of this," he said, "and she'll be eating out of the palm of my hand."

Patty Jo was grooming Toy Boy in the barn, and she stopped to look out at the arena where Darling stood with her body twisted and her head low. Her legs were rigid and the sunlight caught in the dead blue of her left eye, making it glow like the center of a flame. Even from a distance, it was clear that she was not submitting to the heat. She was merely enduring it.

Patty Jo shuddered next to me and I waited for her to say something about the extremity of my father's methods, something about cruelty. But when he came through the barn, Patty stepped sideways, shaking her head in amazement. "I had no idea how difficult it was to train a young horse," she said.

"It isn't always so hard," my father told her. "Some of them take to it easy. But others . . ." He held up his hand and shrugged toward the arena. "Well, they're all different."

"I think it's amazing what you do," Patty said, and my father and I both looked at her. She was the only boarder who came out alone, and without her girlfriends or thermoses full of champagne, she was quieter, easier, more like anybody else. "People like myself just *ride* horses," she said. "You make it possible."

A flush of pink crept up my father's neck and he lowered his eyes to the barn floor, bouncing the toe of his boot against the wall. "It has to be done," he said after a minute. "If horses had any idea how large they were, how strong, they'd be impossible to control. They'd be killers."

When my father took my sister and me to the Kill Sales, he always explained how it was experience, someone else's brutality, that had turned the horses crazy and made them into the sort of monsters that people believed could not be fixed. And yet, again and again, he proved them wrong. He never trained the Kill horses by means of exhaustion or forced submission. In the end, it was the sound of his voice and the consistency of his touch that turned them peaceful and shaped them into horses that anyone could manage. I watched Darling sweat beneath the sun and wondered what my father understood that I did not, what he saw inside of her that told him sound and touch alone would never be enough for her.

"Well, I think it's amazing," Patty Jo said, and her voice dropped into a throaty whisper. "Really, you're so talented."

Patty smiled and my father bit his lip, his face glowing from her compliment. It was the sort of exchange that might have happened anytime, between anyone. But it didn't. It happened there and then, while I stood between them, watching.

"How old do you think Patty Jo is?" I asked Sheila. My father had gone to the lumberyard for more sawdust and we were playing cards in the barn, holding cans of cold soda against our necks and faces.

Sheila scowled at her hand of cards. "Older than she wants to be."

I laughed and Sheila looked up from her hand, pleased to have said something funny. "Was that mean?" she asked, then laughed into her shoulder. "It's just, all those women—the way they're always laughing? The way they talk to each other? It's like they think they're *our* age."

The boarders whispered and giggled like children, addressing each other as *girls*—"Girls, we need more drinky-drinks" and "I've had the most fabulous idea, girls!" Their skin was freckled with deep suntans and they had tiny lines around their eyes and mouths, but their bodies were small and trim, their clothes youthful, their voices light and bubbly. And while I didn't want to pay attention to them, didn't want to admit that I noticed them at all, they always seemed to be having more fun than anyone else. I couldn't stop watching.

"They *are* kind of strange," I admitted.

Sheila blew her bangs off her forehead. "My mom hates them," she said.

"Really?" I couldn't imagine Mrs. Altman hating anybody.

Sheila discarded, then looked up at me through the pale white feathers of her eyelashes. "She says you have to be careful around women like that."

"Careful how?" I asked.

"She says that women like that ask questions like they care about you, but really, they just want to swallow you up. They want to take everything that's yours." Sheila lowered her voice and raised her eyebrows. "She calls them *catfish*."

The boarders were always asking me questions while I cleaned stalls, and I never thought twice before I answered. They asked how old my mother was (thirty-six), where my family came from (here), how long my father had been working with horses (forever). Once in a while, they would ask my father about grooming equipment or tack. It never crossed my mind that they were asking questions because they cared about us. I just thought they were making conversation, being polite. Now I wondered if there was something more behind their curiosity, if they wanted to swallow us whole and take everything that was ours. They were all rich and pretty with big houses and perfect white smiles. What did we have that any of them could possibly want?

My father said I had to wear a dress to the posse banquet, which put us at odds for the entire day. *Banquet* was a loose term for the party that the sheriff's posse threw each summer. A potluck, people showed up in pickup trucks, carrying dishes of greasy food covered with cellophane and wearing cowboy boots so that they could dance in the arena without worrying about the horse droppings.

"I don't see why I even have to go," I told my father while we were feeding the horses that morning. In the past, Nona and I would eat hot dogs by ourselves, whispering and laughing as we came up with various ways to describe the dancing styles of drunken posse members. "Cowboys on crack," Nona would say. "I can't tell if Mr. Sheldon's trying to swing or having a seizure." Without my sister to keep me company, I would spend the evening alone.

"You have to go because *I* have to go," my father said.

"I'm not feeling well," I told him. "I think I might be getting a stomach bug."

"Then you better bring a bucket to puke into."

That was that—subject closed. I spent the rest of the day giving my father the silent treatment and he spent the rest of the day not noticing. When the sun finally set, I changed into the dress I had worn the year before, then stood in front of the mirror. It was too short now, and my knees looked large and naked beneath the flowered hem, my shoulders stooping to compensate for the tightness of the fabric across my chest.

Surely, my father would see me looking like a giant in a child's dress and he would understand. He would feel sorry for me, would know without being told that I couldn't possibly survive the evening. But when I came downstairs, he was busy rummaging through our cabinets, looking for something to take to the banquet. Pickings were slim, and he finally settled on an open bag of potato chips and a half-empty six-pack of beer. "Let's go," he told me.

Outside, Patty Jo was loading her saddle into the trunk of her car and she whistled at us across the driveway. "Well, aren't *you two* a sight?" My father's ears flushed beneath his freshly washed hair and I slouched against the truck without answering. "You must have a special evening planned."

"Nah," my father said, touching his fingers self-consciously to the front of his button-down shirt. "Just a posse thing. A party, I guess. It's nothing important."

Patty clasped her hands together and shimmied her hips in front of her car. "A party!" She sighed. "There's nothing I love better than a party."

Before my father even opened his mouth, I could sense the words that were going to come out of it. I turned to glare at him, to silence him with the force of my will, but he didn't so much as glance in my direction. "Would you like to come along?"

Patty grinned, then held her hands out to her sides, turning a slow circle in front of us. "I'm not really dressed for it."

She was wearing tight blue jeans that hugged the curves of her tiny hips and a black T-shirt with a V-neck low enough to expose a hint of freckled cleavage. "You look great," my father said. "Besides, it's nothing fancy."

The drive to the Posse Grounds was quiet and uncomfortable. Patty asked how things were going with Darling and my father told her things were going fine. She said how much she enjoyed riding at our barn and my father told her he was glad. I sat between them in the pickup truck, tugging at the hem of my dress to make it cover my knees and holding myself rigid so that I wouldn't lean into Patty when we turned corners.

When we arrived at the banquet, my father headed toward the food table with Patty Jo while I trailed behind. A small stage had been set up in the center of the arena and though the band was still getting organized, people had already begun to gather around, drinking beer from bottles and tipping their cowboy hats in greeting. The younger children chased one another around the perimeter, screaming and pelting one another with ice from the coolers while their parents shouted halfhearted threats to make them settle down.

Although my father had brought only three beers, there seemed to be no shortage. By the time the music started, he and Patty were each on their third. I hovered around the food table, nibbling nachos off a paper napkin and watching as Patty Jo's head tipped back with laughter every time my father spoke.

I was too far away to hear what they were saying to each other, but still, I strained my ears in their direction, squinting my eyes to read their lips. Women like that, I thought to myself, will ask you questions like they care. I thought of Mrs. Altman, warning her daughter to watch herself around Patty Jo and the other boarders. *Catfish.* I said the name inside my head, letting myself taste the ridge and slope of the word. *Women like that want to swallow you whole.*

"Alice Winston."

When I turned around, Janice Reardon stood behind me slurping on a Popsicle. She was wearing a flowered dress and a pair of dingy pink fairy wings on her back that knocked into the people around us as she stepped closer. Popsicle juice melted down her hand, and she turned her arm sideways, licking a smear from the inside of her wrist as she looked me up and down. "That dress is too small for you."

Janice's own dress gaped in open ovals down the buttoned front, revealing pale patches of flesh beneath.

"I knew you'd be here," she said.

"Wow," I told her, trying to sound distracted. "You must be psychic."

Janice twisted her mouth sideways and glanced off into the distance, deciding whether to let my nastiness pass unnoticed. "I guess you must know everyone here," she said finally.

In the center of the arena, the band was pounding their instruments and jumping around onstage. "Let me hear you *scream*!" the lead singer shouted into his microphone, and the crowd lifted their beers into the air, toasting in a single, wordless holler.

"I guess," I said.

"My stepdad brought us," she told me and pointed out into the arena where a pudgy man in a cowboy hat was dancing an awkward two-step with an equally pudgy woman. "My real dad lives in Iowa. I'm going to visit him next week. He's going to buy me a new stereo."

"That's nice," I said.

Janice's chin was wet with the melted syrup of her Popsicle, her lips tainted orange. "Colleen's back," she said, and though I didn't want to, I leaned in to hear her better. "She came home last week."

I thought again of the white building with no windows where Colleen had lived with other girls who had tried to kill themselves. I pictured them sitting in a circle of folding chairs, holding hands while they told their stories. "Have you seen her?" I asked.

"No," she said. "But Sharon has. She says Colleen's skinny now. And she talks about Jesus a lot."

So that was how they cured them. I readjusted the picture in my mind. They didn't just hold hands and talk. They starved. They prayed. They talked about how Jesus loved them. Jesus died for their sins. Jesus wanted them to live.

"Is that your mom?"

I followed Janice's gaze out to the arena where Patty Jo sat beside my father in a folding chair, laughing with her mouth open. "No."

"I didn't think so," Janice said. "She doesn't look anything like you."

In the arena, my father held two fresh bottles of beer between his knees, cracking them open and handing one to Patty. She took a delicate sip from the bottle, then leaned sideways to whisper something into his ear, resting her fingers in the crook of his arm. "My mother's at home," I said. "She has cancer."

Janice's face froze, her mouth opening into a sticky circle of shock. "Oh, Alice."

"Have fun in Iowa," I said and wadded my paper napkin into a ball, setting it beside the tray of nachos before I walked away.

An hour passed, then two, then three, and still my father sat out in the folding chairs with Patty Jo. The band sweated and the cowboys kicked up dust around them, swinging their wives in wobbly circles and pausing only to slurp beer from the endless supply of bottles. I sat on the fence alone, waiting for my father to stand and dig his keys out of his pants pocket, a gesture that the time was up, our duty had been served, and we could go home. But unlike at posse functions of the past, my father seemed entirely unaware of the time.

My father never really cared that much about his posse membership. He went to the meetings and directed traffic at the rodeos. He showed up when they called him and carried a dead girl out of the canal when no one else would do it. All this came from a sense of obligation, rather than a real love for the work. My grandfather had been a member of the sheriff's posse before he and my grandmother bought their motor home and took off across the country after my aunts. Before him, my great-grandfather had been a member as well. There weren't any real advantages to belonging to such a group. It was just something you did if you lived on our side of the valley and were a man.

In the past, my father had dragged my sister and me along to picnics and banquets, then spent his obligatory two hours talking about horse feed and vet bills with the men who had known him since he was a child. He was always civil, nodding in the right places and shrugging agreement at their various philosophies on horse training and barn maintenance. But at home, his lip curled as he told us who mixed sawdust into his grain to make it last longer, which man drugged his show horses when they were lame so that they would still be able to compete. My father made it clear that Nona and I were to be polite and friendly at posse functions, that we were to use our manners and not behave in a way that might look bad for our barn. But he also made it clear that the other posse members were different from us. They were crooks and cheaters. They were not our friends.

But now my father sat in the arena, laughing and talking, holding one finger to his ear as he leaned forward to hear Patty Jo better. The sky darkened above me, and I thought of Mr. Delmar, alone in a house I had never seen, waiting for the phone to ring. Somewhere, far away, my sister was climbing into bed with a man I didn't know. I imagined her, wearing the T-shirt and boxer shorts she always slept in, curling the form of herself around Jerry in their bed, unaware that tonight was the night of the posse banquet, that I was sitting by myself, passing the time alone.

In the arena, the posse members drank and danced and shouted in unison when the band called out to them. Patty Jo dipped and shimmied her shoulders in her folding chair, bobbing herself up and down until my father set his beer in the dirt beside him and held one hand out to her. She grinned and slipped her fingers into his. The cold bar of the fence ached against my thighs as I watched them stand, then join the throng of laughter and sweat and breathless motion that closed against the stage. I had never known that my father could dance.

His face was pink and gleaming with sweat as he twirled her one way and then the other. Patty laughed, pausing from time to time to wrap her arms around her middle and pant at the ground. But she always righted, always reached her hand back into his. Their fingers closed around each other's and their feet moved in unison, shuffling through dust and horse dung. Then the crowd shifted around them and they were gone.

"Alice-bo-*balice*."

The Pope twins appeared on either side of me, leaning their arms onto the top rail of the fence so that their elbows brushed against my hips. "Hey," I said, shifting my weight and drawing myself together to avoid their touch.

"We saw you," Andy said from my right. "Talking to that fat girl."

"Yeah," Zach added from my left. "The one with the wings."

"She's just a girl from school," I told them. "We're not friends or anything."

The twins climbed onto the fence, sandwiching me between them. I could smell the oniony scent of their sweat against my body, could feel the damp grit of their skin against mine, and I reached down to tug the hem of my dress over my naked knees. They each held a half-empty beer bottle in their hands and Zach tapped the lip of his against my thigh.

"Where'd you get those?" I asked.

"Swiped them," Andy grinned. "Jealous?"

I lifted my chin, refusing to answer.

"Want a sip?" Zach asked and held his bottle in front of me, tilting it from side to side.

"Bet she won't," Andy snorted. "Alice is a *good girl.*"

Out in the arena, my father was twirling Patty Jo in circles, his face glowing, his hair slick with sweat. Janice Reardon's family had left more than an hour ago. She was probably at home right now, in her little bedroom, packing for her trip to Iowa. Colleen Murphy was warm and safe in her parents' house, praying to Jesus for the strength to make it through another day. Nona was in Idaho or Kansas or somewhere else I'd never been, sleeping with her body curved around the shape of her cowboy-husband. Across the valley, Mr. Delmar was smoking cigarettes and sipping from his icy glass, wondering why I hadn't called yet.

I reached sideways, yanking the bottle from Zach's hand, then tilted my head back to chug its contents. My throat filled with cold foam, my forehead lightening as I swallowed the last drop. I handed the empty bottle back to Zach and he stared at it for a moment before opening his mouth to speak. "Well, *okay,*" he said and Andy tipped his chin backward, baying at the sky like a wild dog.

"Here," he said and handed me his own bottle. "We've each had two, so you better drink fast to catch up with us." My stomach felt like a deflated balloon, sunken and sloshing with liquid, but again I lifted my chin toward the black sky and opened my throat, finishing Andy's beer without pausing for breath.

"Damn," Andy whispered when I'd finished. "You might be Nona's sister after all." He nudged me with his shoulder so that I tipped into Zach, who teetered on the fence rail then reached sideways, digging his fingers into my thigh to keep from falling. My skin pinched beneath his grip. It should have hurt. But I stared down at his hand on my leg, his pink knuckles and grungy nails, and felt nothing.

Out in the arena, the band members bobbed their heads in unison, their voices raspy after so many hours of singing and yelling to the crowd. Around them, the posse members blurred together in the cloud of dust, spinning and dipping and lifting their beer bottles into the air, my father and Patty Jo lost somewhere among them.

Andy belched once, loud and wet, before announcing we needed more beer and volunteering to go and steal three fresh bottles. He jumped down, and the fence shook beneath us. Zach gripped his fingers tighter into my leg to keep his balance. "Be back in the time it takes a Winston girl to fall in love," Andy said.

Zach and I sat in silence for a moment. Slowly, his fingers loosened on my leg, but he didn't take his hand away. "Isn't it hard to steal beer?" I asked finally.

Zach shrugged beside me. "It's not like anyone's paying attention," he said.

In the arena, Bud Pope was dancing with Valerie Hayes, swinging her in circles so that her red hair rose around her like a flame. She looped her arms around his neck and his hands slid down her waist until they were cupping the back pockets of her blue jeans. "Do you like your father?" I asked.

The fabric of my dress felt damp and warm beneath Zach's hand, and I couldn't tell if it was from my sweat or his. "I don't know if you've noticed," he said, "but my dad's kind of a dick."

I turned to look at him and his face was so close to mine that I could feel the heat of his breath on my skin, could smell the stolen beer, stale and sour on his tongue. And then he dipped his head closer, and the world went still.

In movies, kisses were soft and smooth, mouths joining, eyes closing, heads tipping to expose the slender white slope of a woman's neck. But as Zach pressed his face into mine, our noses flattened against each other and I could feel the sandpaper of his chapped lips opening and closing against my own. The tip of his tongue found the tip of mine, two dry, rubbery muscles wrestling inside a waxy cage of teeth. There were no trumpets, no shivering sighs, no flutters of frantic heartbeats inside my chest. When he pulled his head back, he blinked several times, then lifted his hand from my leg and touched his fingers to his lips as if he was unsure who they belonged to.

"What'd I miss?" Andy said, handing two fresh bottles up to us. Zach straightened, reaching for his bottle with the same hand that had rested on my thigh. His eyes were glassy, staring straight ahead at the dancing crowd as he took a long, gulping swallow of beer. "Nothing," he said.

The band was packing their instruments into the back of a van when my father and Patty Jo finally wobbled toward the truck. Their elbows were linked, their laughter rising up into the black sky, and my heart pounded in my throat as I followed behind them. I had just finished my fourth beer and I was sure that they would smell the liquor on my breath, see my legs trembling as I tried to climb into the truck. But inside, my father only fumbled with his keys, dropping them twice before fitting them into the ignition. He never even looked at me.

We drove home along back country roads with the windows open and the radio blaring. My father leaned back in his seat as he steered the truck, holding his arms rigid in front of him and squeezing one eye shut while he and Patty sang along to the radio, their voices pounding off-key on either side of me.

The truck lurched back and forth and my body felt loose and liquid around me. "This has been the best night of my life!" Patty shouted over the music, then reached her arm out the window, letting the air push between her fingers. The truck wove on the road and I tipped sideways into her. I wanted to right myself, but my head was heavy, my eyelids dipping closed even as I willed them to open.

Patty shifted beside me, wrapping one arm around my shoulders

and squeezing me against herself as she and my father sang along
with Neil Diamond:

> *Hurtin' runs off my shoulders*
> *How can I hurt when holdin' you . . .*

Her body was damp and warm against mine, smelling of beer and
sweat and spicy perfume. Inside my head, my thoughts swam
together, raw and wet and unnamable. But somewhere inside that
sticky mix, I felt Patty Jo's body, real and whole and alive. It didn't
matter who she was, who she had been earlier tonight, who she would
be tomorrow. This whole night had been a blur of make-believe, a
world stirred together in pretending. And so I let her hold me. I kept
my eyes closed, letting myself pretend that she was someone, anyone,
who loved me.

six

"HOW MANY DAYS has he kept her out there?"

The television was off and my mother sat in the window with one leg pulled to her chest. Her nightgown caught up around her knee and I stared down at the rail of her exposed shin, the slender white slip of her anklebone. In the arena, Darling stood alone with her head cinched to her shoulder, her coat gray and oily with sweat.

"This is the sixth time," I said, holding out a fresh bag of ice.

My mother looked at the ice, then turned back to the window without reaching to take it. "Do you think it will work?"

The waist of my jeans was pinching into my skin and the ice bag burned in my hand, pulsing a dull ache through my wrist and forearm. "I'm not sure," I told her. "She's kind of nutso."

My mother's shoulders straightened, lengthening her neck and tilting her jaw so that I could see the cords of her throat moving beneath her skin. "How much did he pay?" she asked.

Three thousand, seven hundred and fifty—that was what she went for in the end. Seven men had bid, including Bud Pope. But my father's jaw was steel, his eyes tight and focused. The rest of the bidders eventually lost interest. When it was over, my father paid $1,347 in cash, then split the rest between two credit cards. "I don't know," I said.

"You don't *know*?" my mother asked.

"I don't remember."

Her eyes narrowed and we stared at each other for a moment. Her gaze sliced straight through me, cold and empty. "What a good girl you are," she whispered.

A flush burned in my cheeks and I wasn't sure if it was from the heat of her bedroom or the dull, smoldering series of secrets that seemed to be spreading through me. My father and I had not spoken once of the posse banquet, had not even mentioned the fact that we'd attended. Patty Jo had returned the next day to groom Toy Boy without ever mentioning the dance, the beer, the drive home. And so that night had turned into something else that no one talked about, something else that probably never happened.

My mother's whole body shivered and she shook her head as if she were waking up from a dream. "I'm sorry," she said and reached to take the ice from me. "The heat." She touched the ice to the back of her neck. "It's running my wires together."

"It's making everyone a little crazy," I said.

"I've noticed." She nodded out toward the arena, and I wasn't sure if she was talking about the mare or about my father.

"Dad'll get her trained," I promised.

"I can hardly wait," she said.

The day my father mounted Darling for the first time, Sheila and I climbed onto the arena fence to watch. The Catfish lined up beside us, passing a bag of frozen grapes and sipping from their paper cups. "Do you think she's ready for this?" Sheila whispered and I shrugged. My father hoisted his foot into the stirrup, tightening the reins in his hand. It didn't matter if she was ready or not.

The mare's ears flattened and her neck arched. She stood perfectly still in the center of the arena, nostrils huffing, back bowed. "Is this normal?" Bitsy asked. Darling's ribs were heaving with breath, her tail tucked beneath her. My father waited, but she didn't move. Slowly, he adjusted his seat on top of her, then brought his heels into her sides. As soon as they touched, all hell broke loose.

The mare seemed to spring from every angle, leaping straight off the ground, then twisting as she came back down, slicing the air with her hooves. She reared, then bucked, then turned her body in midair, pounding herself into the ground and whipping my father's head. He held tight with his legs, loosening his upper body so that he moved like a piece of elastic on her back. The Catfish gasped, inhaling in a single breath while Sheila covered her face with her hands. "She'll kill him," Patty Jo whispered.

Through the clouds of dust, I could see my father's head tipping forward, his hands working the reins, pulling her one way as she twisted the other. She flung herself sideways into the fence, scraping his legs along the wooden rails. But he stayed on.

When there was nothing left for her to try, she ran. She crossed the arena at awkward angles, sliding to stops and spinning in the opposite direction when she reached the edge. But slowly, she joined herself with the rail until she was galloping the arena in full, even ovals. The sweat foamed in the creases of her chest and stomach, soaking down her legs, and her mouth lathered with saliva around the bit. "Look at that," Patty Jo whispered when it was clear that my father was not going to be killed, when it was clear that he was, in fact, riding her. "Jesus Christ."

He brought her into the center of the arena and pulled back on the reins, slowing the mare to a halt. She stood before us, her coat soaked with sweat, her body heaving with breath. My father sat for a moment, then swung his weight sideways, dismounting in one smooth step.

And the crowd went wild.

The Catfish stood in a line, doing a cheerlike dance complete with kicks and hand motions, whooping and whistling through their teeth while Sheila jumped up and down beside them. "Yeah, Joe!" she called. "That was awesome!"

"Truly amazing," Patty said, and my father grinned.

He led the mare out of the arena and Sheila climbed onto the gate, swinging it open for him. The Catfish gathered around, each breathlessly recounting the moment she thought it was over, the moment she thought he was done for. My father stood with his face gleaming. "All in a day's work," he said.

"Work *schmerk*!" Bitsy gasped. "You're a bona fide fucking *god*!" The Catfish refilled their cups from their thermoses, adding an extra one for my father.

"A bona fide fucking *god*!" they toasted, then drank. My father tilted his head back, draining his cup in a single swallow.

They refilled again, then again, toasting to bravery, then speed, then the pure stupidity that would make a human being climb onto the back of a horse that had never been ridden. I kept waiting for my father's face to clear, for him to call a stop to such a ridiculous show and tell everyone to get back to work. But he stood among them, laughing and toasting and drinking. Sheila skipped circles around him and he scooped her up by her armpits, spinning her around until she squealed.

"Alice," Bitsy said when she saw that I was still sitting on the fence. "Aren't you just *amazed* by your old dad?"

My father looked at me, and for the first time, a hint of the familiar flickered across his face, a brief shadow of reality. "Aw," he said. "She's seen this sort of thing a thousand times before. She's just thinking it's not anything special." He turned back into the circle of Catfish and they grinned up at him, refilling his paper cup for another toast.

Beside him, the mare stood with her ribs heaving. The corners of her mouth were foamed with pink—blood and saliva, the same blood that had caused everyone so much horror, so much revulsion, when I had drawn it with the twitch.

My father was wrong. I was not thinking that this was nothing special. I was thinking that if any of them lived out at the barn, instead of visiting when they felt like it, they would know that riding a horse once didn't mean that it was broken. Just because the mare stood beside him now, torn and bloodied into exhaustion, it didn't mean that she was any different than she was a few hours ago. Nothing had happened. Nothing had changed. Just because my father had managed to stay on her back, it didn't mean that anyone else in the world would ever be able to do the same.

"Holy shit," my father said when everyone was gone. He flopped down on the sofa, his big toe sticking up through a hole in his sock.

His face was still flushed, his hair damp at the roots. He closed his eyes, drumming his fingers against his chest like he was listening to music. "She was smooth," he told me. "I mean, *really,* it was unbelievable. She turns like she's on rails. Even when she was jumping and thrashing around, it was like riding water. Like sitting on top of whipped cream. She's a champion, Alice. I'm not kidding you."

I leaned against the edge of the dining room table, watching him grin up at the water-stained ceiling. I thought of Darling, alone outside in the pen where we used to keep Bart, her back stained with a saddle of sweat, the tender lining of her mouth raw and swollen.

"Sitting on top of her," he said. "It was like this *rush,* this burst of fire, this *storm.* I felt like, oh shit, I don't know."

"A bona fide fucking god?" I asked and his eyes snapped open.

"Hey," he told me. "Watch your language."

I bit my lip, ready to apologize, but my father was still smiling, his fingers twitching with excitement, his knees, scraped and bloody from the fence, bouncing inside his ripped blue jeans.

The phone rang and my father sat up, then bounded across the living room to answer. "That'll probably be the local media," he joked.

"Why?" I asked. "Do we owe them money?"

"Good evening," my father chirped into the phone. "Winston Stables. Joe Winston here, horse trainer extraordinaire."

I slid down onto the sofa, resting my chin on my hands and fighting the urge to roll my eyes. My father listened for a moment, then turned his back to me, pressing his finger into his ear. "What?" he whispered. In the stifling heat of our living room, a chill crept across my skin.

My father nodded silently into the phone, his breath slowing, his shoulders stooping into a curve. The call ended and my father stood, staring at the receiver.

"What?" I asked.

The color had drained from his face and he shook his head without answering. My stomach turned inside itself, flipping and churning up into my throat. "Did something happen?" I whispered. "Is it Nona?" My father slid the receiver back into its place, then crossed the room to the sofa, sinking himself into it.

"Daddy," I whispered, using her name for him. Her word. "Daddy, tell me."

When he lifted his face to look at me, his skin was chalky, his expression blank. "That was the grandparents," he said finally. "They're coming."

Jack and Ruby were my father's parents. Though the house and barn had once belonged to them, they hardly ever came to visit. Before he retired, Jack had worked as a chiropractor out of a little office in front of the house that we now used for storage. I couldn't remember the last time I'd seen them.

"When?" I asked.

"Now." My father glanced at his watch, then stood and crossed to the table. "Tonight. We've gotta hustle." He swept the nest of loose newspapers into a pile with his arm, then bent over the table, using his thumbnail to scrape a Cheerio that had cemented itself in dried milk.

"Where will we put them?" I asked. My father slept in the guest bedroom and I was suddenly afraid that the grandparents would be put in Nona's room, cutting me off from both closet and telephone.

My father glared at me. "Less talk. More hustle."

I vacuumed while my father repositioned lamps and rugs over stains in the carpet. When we finished, I held open a garbage bag as my father stuffed the old newspapers inside. This all seemed like a lot of fuss for nothing. Jack and Ruby lived in a motor home, after all. It wasn't like the concept of clutter would be so unfamiliar to them.

My father turned around and scanned the room, wiping his forehead with the back of his arm. "Good, good," he said. "So now we just have the kitchen, and . . ." His eyes traveled across the hall to the stairs, then up. "Shit," he whispered.

"What?"

My father's shoulders sank as his eyes rested on the top of the stairs. "I have to tell your mother."

It didn't seem fair that I should have to clean the kitchen while my father went upstairs to talk to my mother. What would be the point of telling her anyway? It wasn't like she would rush downstairs and pick up a broom. He would just explain how the grandparents were coming, and then she would sit upstairs and think odd thoughts until they got here. "Why not let it be a surprise?" I said.

While my father was upstairs talking to my mother, I swept the kitchen floor and wiped all the counters with a spray that smelled like lemons and rubbing alcohol. Then I rearranged the inside of the cabinets, putting plates with plates, glasses with glasses. I gathered the giant plastic cups we'd accumulated from fast food restaurants and hid them in the back of the pantry behind cans of vegetables we never ate and an ice-cream maker I didn't remember us ever having used.

When he finally came back down, my father's feet were heavy on the stairs, his head dipped forward. He sat on the bottom step and leaned his head into his hands, massaging the base of his skull with his thumbs.

"So," I said. "Have you thought about where we'll put them?"

Ruby Winston was the fattest person I'd ever seen in real life. I stared up at her through the tiny rectangle of the motor home door and wondered how she would ever get herself out. She stepped down, the cracked pink soles of her feet lobbing out over the wooden heels of her sandals, using her hands to redistribute her middle as she squeezed herself out the door. "Great Lord," she huffed when she hugged me. "You've gotten huge."

Ruby rocked me back and forth against herself, pressing me into the marshmallow mass of her middle. Then she flung me sideways and reached for my father. "Oh, Jody," she gasped. "Oh, Jody, oh, God!"

My father's back stiffened and I watched him close behind the rolls of Ruby's fat. When he stepped back, she put her hands on either side of his face, squeezing his cheeks and pouching his lips between the flab of her palms. "Hi, Ma," he mumbled.

Jack was tall and trim, with silver hair and arms that shone smooth and bronze beneath the white of his ironed shirtsleeves. He patted my shoulder, then pulled me into a sideways hug. "Heya, kid."

The third member of their party was a small, piggish dog with a pointed face and fur like a dingy powder puff. The dog grunted when Ruby lifted him to introduce us. "Pom-Pom's the baby," she said. "And don't think he doesn't know it." She held him out to us by his armpits, his hind legs splayed, his toenails clenching air.

My father and I stood side by side, hot and grubby from cleaning. In all our preparation, neither one of us had thought to shower or change out of our work clothes. My father's hair was stiff with sweat, his T-shirt stained yellow at the neck and armpits. I could smell the barn in my own clothes, the sweet scent of sawdust and hay. My hair was tangled, my fingernails caked with dirt. Ruby looked back and forth between us, and her smile faded slightly. "We're missing someone," she said.

I turned to my father. Surely he would have told them about Nona. "Marian's inside," he said.

Ruby tucked Pom-Pom under her arm and swung the back door open, letting out another burst of excitement that sent her whole self rippling. "Marian-girl, it's been a *lifetime*!" I leaned sideways, peering around Ruby's middle and there, at the foot of the stairs, dressed and upright, was my mother.

She looked small and sparrowish beside the banister, her dress sagging from the rails of her shoulders, her shoes large and loose on the slips of her feet. My grandmother reached to hug her and I cringed, thinking my mother might dissolve into dust between Ruby's massive arms.

My father stepped forward, looping one arm around my mother's waist to keep her upright, and she gripped the back of his T-shirt with her fingers while he led her across the living room floor, then lowered her onto the sofa. "Marian's just getting over a bug," my father explained. "She's still a little weak."

Jack and Ruby exchanged a look and I stepped between them. "How long are you staying?" I asked.

Ruby's eyes stayed on my mother. "Just a bit," she said. "You know your Papa Jack. He has to have some time in the West every so often to keep his brain from blowing." Jack leaned in the doorway, gazing out at the barn with his arms crossed over his chest. It didn't look like his brain was anywhere near to blowing.

My father leaned forward and touched my mother lightly on the shoulder. "Are you all right?" he asked.

Her eyes lifted, dark and sunken on her white cheekbones. "I'm tired," she said.

Ruby shifted Pom-Pom to her opposite arm and fanned herself with one pink hand. "Jesus God, Jody, it's like an oven in here." Her whole body jiggled as she waved her hand in front of her face, her red cheeks shivering in waves as a trickle of sweat crept down from her hairline.

"The air conditioner busted," my father said.

Jack's eyes lifted to the ceiling. "Oh, yeah?" he asked. "What's wrong with it?"

"It's busted," my father repeated.

"I'll climb up there tomorrow and take a look," Jack said, and my father's lips flattened into a thread.

Ruby cooked dinner in our kitchen while my father and grandfather exchanged stilted conversation, talking about the drive, the weather, the heat wave. I set the table and my mother sat on the sofa, staring at the dark screen of our television as if there were something on it. I watched my mother out of the corner of my eye, wondering what my father might have said to her upstairs, what sort of arrangement had been made. I tried to think back to the last time Jack and Ruby had visited, to remember if my mother had dressed and come downstairs, if she had played this part before—the normal, happy woman recovering from a bug. But all that I could recall from the grandparents' last visit was Ruby's continual insistence that my sister was the spitting image of herself at that age and Nona's brief devotion to vomiting after meals.

When Ruby carried the food from the kitchen, my father looped his arm around my mother's waist, helping her rise and guiding her to the table. Ruby squinted at her over a dish of mashed potatoes. "You were sick the last time we visited, Marian," she said, and my mother blinked at her.

"Was I?" she asked. "How odd. I'm usually as healthy as a horse."

During dinner, Pom-Pom skittered around the table while we ate, whining and standing on his hind legs to beg for food. My father watched with one side of his mouth curled back in disgust. "Better not let that dog around the horses," he said. "We'll be scraping his brains off the floor."

"Don't think so," Jack told him. "Dog's brainless."

Ruby's mouth puckered like a prune and she took a piece of bread from her plate, sopping it in gravy before letting Pom-Pom lick it from her fingers. Across the table, my mother turned her head sideways, gagging silently into her shoulder. "So Alice," Ruby said. "How old are you now?"

"Twelve," I told her.

"Do you have a boyfriend?"

I dropped my eyes, shaking my head no.

"Your cousin Kissy's twelve too," Ruby said. "She's got *three* boyfriends."

My father gave Pom-Pom a little kick under the table and the dog grunted. "She sounds like a tramp," he said.

Across the table, my mother was staring at me, her hands folded on her lap, her plate of food untouched before her. "You're how old?" she asked.

"Twelve," I repeated.

"That can't be." Her face contracted and her lip began to tremble. She looked small in her chair, her dress hanging from the clothes hanger of her shoulders, her arms as thin as two cooked noodles. Her eyes circled the room, searching the corners, the ceiling, the walls behind us as if she'd suddenly awoken from a dream to find herself in a place she'd never been before.

Jack and Ruby stared at her without speaking and my father's eyes darted back and forth between them. "Marian," he said finally. His voice was barely a whisper, but her eyes turned to his and something passed between them, a silent exchange, an understanding. The confusion parted like clouds behind my mother's eyes. She turned her face to the grandparents and the corners of her mouth tilted into a watery smile.

"Time moves so quickly," she whispered. "I lose track."

"You don't have to tell me," Ruby said and pointed at my father with her fork. "Seems like only yesterday that this one was in diapers.

Lord Almighty, Jody was the most beautiful baby. He had these soft yellow curls and great big eyelashes. People would stop me all the time and say, 'Oh, what a perfect little girl!' " Ruby laughed with her mouth open, slapping her hand on the table. My father drummed his fingers against his thigh and turned to look at the clock.

"I didn't see old Bart out there," Jack said after a minute, cutting his meat into smooth, even strips across his plate. "You move him into the barn?"

"Bart's dead," my mother said, and across the table, my father met my eye in a moment of panic. We'd told her that Bart was in Nebraska, fat and happy on a farm. "He got sick and had to be put down."

Jack sat back in his chair, taking a moment to register the news. "Shit," he said. "When?"

"Last year," my mother told him.

Jack sighed up at the ceiling, then nodded and returned to his food. "What have you done about a replacement?"

My father was chewing his food slowly, rolling it around inside his mouth and watching my mother sideways. "I've got my eyes open."

"You've gotta have a stud, boy," Jack told him. "Barn's no good without one."

Everyone else was still eating when my mother stood up, her eyes on the staircase. "I think I'm going to turn in."

"You should," my father told her, standing. "You've had a long day." He kept one hand on her elbow as he walked my mother to the stairs, then leaned down and gave her a strange-looking kiss on the side of her head. Once she was upstairs, everyone stayed quiet for a moment. My mother's plate of food sat untouched on the table, her utensils clean, her napkin still folded beneath them. My father began clearing dishes and I jumped up to help.

"Must have been one hell of a bug," Jack said.

After dinner, I sat on the porch steps between Jack's knees, letting him work the muscles of my back with his thumbs while Pom-Pom sniffed around our yard, lifting his leg to mark every little rock and tuft of grass. Jack held a lit cigar between his teeth and the smoke curled around us while he adjusted my posture and rocked my head back and forth between his hands.

In the days when the house still belonged to my grandparents, Jack had made his money by adjusting the backs of ranchers. Horses were hard on the human spine, that's what he said, and men would shell out their cash to let him crack their bones and dig his thumbs into the muscles of their necks and shoulders. Even with all the years that had passed, old men would still approach my father at horse shows or in the Co-op, tilting their heads from side to side and rubbing at the small of their backs. "What I wouldn't give for a little of Jack Winston's treatment," they would say, and my father would nod apologetically. Whatever Jack's secrets were when it came to the human body, he'd kept them to himself.

"You feel that?" Jack asked me. "The way your back is all lined up?" I nodded. "That's the way it feels when you're sitting right."

Ruby lit a cigarette and squeezed herself onto the porch swing beside my father, the chains groaning under her weight. "I walked through the barn after supper," Jack told my father. "You've got a bunch of strangers in there."

"Boarders," my father said.

"Really?" Jack asked in a mild voice. "You're doing that now?"

On the swing, my father slipped a cigarette from Ruby's pack and held it to his mouth without lighting it. "Just for a while."

Jack's fingers pressed deeper into the muscles of my neck and the smoke from his cigar filled my nostrils and stung my eyes, spinning my head into a dizzy trance.

"Well," Ruby said after a moment of silence. "I didn't want to ask in front of Marian—it's plain as plain that her basket's slipping—but now it's just us. Let's hear about Nona."

"Not much to hear," my father mumbled, the unlit cigarette bobbing up and down between his lips. "She took off. Got married."

"Do you know the boy?"

"Nope."

Ruby stubbed her cigarette out on the arm of the porch swing, then lit another. "Must be more to the story than that, Jody. I need details."

"Why don't I help you with your things," my father said. "We've got the guest room made up for you."

"Later," Ruby said, and I turned between Jack's knees, watching my father, waiting for him to speak.

These were the details: Jerry's truck was turquoise with a white stripe across both sides. Nona's hair had been wet when she came outside to greet him, her feet bare, toenails chipped with candy-pink polish that glittered in the sunlight when she wrapped her legs around his waist and pressed her lips to his. Jerry was nineteen, with a loose walk and square, meaty hands that hung from his arms like anvils. As he helped my sister load her boxes into the back of his truck, Jerry's skinny legs bowed and his knees poked through the holes in his jeans. "Jesus Christ," my father had whispered. "If he'd been a horse, we would have had to geld him."

My father had tried to talk sense to Nona. When she stood on her tiptoes to kiss him good-bye, he put one hand behind her neck, holding her by the thick of her wet hair. "Don't be a jackass," he told her. "Use your head."

But Nona's face was smooth and serious, her cornflower eyes unblinking as she looked into his. "Kiss me good-bye, Daddy." When my father didn't move, she reached behind her head and loosened his fingers from her hair. She held his hand in hers for a moment, then brought it up to her mouth, brushing her lips against the back of his wrist before she let go.

Ruby puffed on her cigarette, exhaling in loud, pointed breaths: she was waiting. When my father cleared his throat in my direction, Jack took the hint. "Why don't you show me the new foals?" he asked, nudging me to my feet.

Without being given the choice to stay, I followed the glowing cherry of Jack's cigar into the darkness, slowing my pace and straining my ears to make out my father's voice on the porch. We rounded the corner of the house, and just before they disappeared from my view, Ruby reached out and lit my father's cigarette. "All right," she told him. "Start talking."

In the moonlight, the foals looked new and clean on the dark smear of pasture. Jack leaned against the fence, puffing at the last stub of his cigar and staring out at the lines of their silhouettes. "Did you see them born?" he asked.

"All but one," I told him and winced as the memory flooded through me—my stupidity and weak, worthless efforts, my tears. The birth of Ginger's foal had been witnessed by Sheila Altman alone. Now, in the dark, the foals were nameless slips of shadow, interchangeable. But tomorrow, in the daylight, Jack would see what my father and I had seen the night we brought Cap back from the canal: Ginger's colt was autumn red with a blaze of white down his nose and a single white sock on his left hind leg—the one that looked like Bart.

Jack dropped his cigar, snuffing it out in the dirt with the toe of his shoe. "Just between you and me," he said, "how are things holding up out here?"

I tried to think what the right answer was. "We had the barn painted," I said. "The trailer too."

"I saw that," he said. "Everything's nice and shiny, all right."

"So things are holding up well."

Jack shook his head, smiling into the darkness. "You know your father," he said.

My father. Just a few hours earlier, he had stood surrounded by the Catfish, grinning from ear to ear and toasting out of paper cups. And now he sat, sheepish, beside his mother, regurgitating the details of the day my sister got into the car of a stranger and didn't come back. There was nothing he could say that I didn't already know, nothing he had seen that I hadn't seen myself. It didn't make sense that he would want me to leave before he talked to Ruby.

But then I thought of Polly Cain, how my father had found her, seen her, carried the dead, empty weight of her through the water. And he had said nothing. All the time we spent together, the endless stretches of hot, wretched days, the long, silent evenings, and still there were things he didn't tell me, things I didn't know. Tonight, the grandparents would sleep in the guest bedroom and my father would climb the stairs to my mother's room, would lie beside her in her bed, sharing the same air, the same space, the same low rhythms of sleep as though they did so every night, as though they were anybody's parents.

"Yes," I told Jack. "I know my father." In a world of so many lies, what was one more?

When my father and I came outside to feed the horses the next morning, Jack was already on the roof. He sat, straddling one of the eaves of the house, his legs loose, his shoulders easy. The air conditioner was wide open beside him and he whistled to himself as he turned a piece of metal over in his hands. When he saw us, Jack grinned and waved. "How about that?" he called and pointed out to Ginger's colt in the pasture. "The old man left a legacy!" The air conditioner was running by noon.

After that, Jack turned to the water pump that had rusted in our side pasture and then the gate that wouldn't shut properly. My mother did not come downstairs for breakfast or lunch, and Ruby spent the morning in the kitchen baking cookies and casseroles and cleaning out the brown mucky water that had settled in the vegetable drawer of our refrigerator. At noon, she carried out a pitcher of cold fruit punch and a tray of ham sandwiches that she set up on the card table in the barn. Patty Jo and Bitsy were grooming their horses and Ruby waved them over. "I made enough for everyone," she said.

We stood around the table, eating off paper napkins while Sheila sat on the ground to pet Pom-Pom. Ruby called to Jack in the pasture, swearing that he would have a stroke if he didn't get out of the sun. But even the heat could not faze him. He continued to work, wiping his forehead with the blue handkerchief he kept in his back pocket and unbuttoning the top of his shirt to reveal a silver tuft of chest hair glistening with sweat in the sunlight. "Look at him," Ruby said from the barn door. "We're back less than a day and already he thinks he's John Wayne."

"Well," Patty Jo said as she nibbled a crust of sandwich. "I see where Joe gets his looks."

My father blushed at his feet and Ruby smiled politely, squinting slightly at Patty through the folds of her eyelids. After the Catfish returned to their horses, Ruby cocked her head at my father and lowered her voice. "Be careful there, Jody."

In the early evening, Jack came in from the pasture to help us feed the horses. Sheila and I had to drag a single bale of hay between us, but my father and Jack each lifted their own, throwing hay to one horse over the head of another and hoisting buckets of grain into pens as if they weighed nothing at all.

"Wow," Sheila whispered when Jack paused to light a cigar. "He's like the Marlboro Man."

"I see you still keep that going on," Jack said to my father, nodding toward the back pasture where we kept the Kill horses.

"Old Ace'll be thirty this year," my father said. Jack's eyes shifted sideways, locking for a moment on my father's.

"Ace was the first horse I ever rode out here," Sheila said brightly. She climbed onto the fence, blowing a kiss to Ace, who continued to eat without regarding her.

"What are you and Yellow working on now?" Jack asked.

"We're learning reining," Sheila told him. "And we're gonna start showmanship soon." She blushed, then smiled into her shoulder. "I mean, *I'm* learning. Cap already knows how to do all that."

"He's a hell of a horse," Jack said seriously. "You work hard, now."

"I am," Sheila told him. "Every day, I am." A shadow of self-doubt passed across her face, but I could tell that she appreciated Jack's honesty, his recognition of Cap's superiority.

For dinner, Ruby made lasagna. My mother came downstairs and stood, blank-faced and bleary-eyed, blinking at us. "The air," she said and held her hand up toward the vent. "I slept and slept. It was like I hadn't slept in a hundred years."

"Jack fixed the air conditioner," I told her. "It ran all day."

Jack winked at my mother and she crossed the room to stand before him, touching her palms to the sides of his face, her hands as pale and thin as two sheets of tissue paper against his skin. "Oh, Jack," she whispered and leaned her head against his chest. "I think I might just love you."

After dinner, Ruby washed dishes and I dried while my mother sat at the kitchen table, gazing out the window. Ruby hummed, rolling her wide shoulders in a little dance and pausing occasionally to feed Pom-Pom a scrap of food left over on a plate. I watched my mother sideways as I dried, her legs crossed underneath herself, her eyes half closed. The air conditioner kicked on, moving through her hair like a breeze. She had taken only a few small nibbles of her dinner and now she sipped at a glass of milk that Ruby had poured for her. "Small women need their calcium," Ruby said. "Keeps their bones from turning to dust." My mother's hand dangled loosely at her side and she stared out the window at nothing, tapping her fingers soundlessly against the fabric of her skirt, keeping inaudible time to the tune that Ruby hummed.

"I think we should ask them to stay," I told my father. He was smoking a cigarette on the porch, staring out at the front pasture.

"What?" he asked.

"The grandparents," I said. "We should ask them to stay for a while. We've got the room."

But my father didn't answer. He stood with his back to me and I crossed the porch to see what he was looking at. The sun had set and there was only the slightest purple left in the sky. In the front pasture, Jack stood alone, smoking a cigar. The broodmares grazed around him and the foals watched him with their ears up and their legs tensed to bolt. Jack's arms were loose and easy at his sides, his cigar glowing between his teeth. In the darkness, the foals' silhouettes tangled together as they stepped closer, then skittered back. The last pink of daylight was draining from the sky when one of the foals stepped forward, stretching its neck and reaching with its lips. Jack held out his arm and there was only a moment of hesitation before they touched, nose to fingers, and the sky went black.

"Do you ever sleep?" I asked.

It was two o'clock in the morning, the world silent, the desert sleeping, but still, he answered his phone when it rang. "I take naps," Mr. Delmar told me. "I sleep better when other people are awake."

On the other side of the wall, my parents were sharing a bed for the second night in a row. After my father said good night, I had waited with my ear to the wall and my breath quiet in my chest, thinking he might just sit until the house fell silent, then creep downstairs to sleep on the sofa. But the minutes passed and through the wall I could make out the low, watery sound of my father's snoring. If they had spoken to each other at all before falling asleep, I didn't hear the words.

"I have bad dreams," I told Mr. Delmar.

"About what?" he asked.

I wanted to tell him about the water that filled my bedroom while I slept, spilling through the windows, splashing up under the door. But it was too close, I knew, to her, too much like saying her name out loud. "I don't remember."

"You shouldn't be afraid of dreams," he said. "There's nothing in them that can really hurt you."

"I know that," I told him, disappointed by such a predictable response. It seemed too much like a grown-up comforting a child, my father telling me when I was six years old and terrified during a storm that thunder was no more than two pieces of air bumping together, using his hands to demonstrate, missing the point entirely.

"I'm not blowing you off," Mr. Delmar said. "I just mean that dreams are sort of an opportunity. You can confront danger without actually being in jeopardy."

"Oh," I said. Opportunity was a good thing, a chance, a promise— the gift of drowning every night and never being dead.

"Real life is a hell of a lot scarier than dreams," he added. "People are much more dangerous than anything your mind can make up while you're sleeping."

"Like bank robbers and serial killers?" I asked.

"Sure," he told me. "They're pretty bad."

I thought about the Catfish, about Ruby and Mrs. Altman sensing the same invisible danger within them, warning their children to take care. "Like people you can't trust?"

"Yes," he answered and his voice was quieter. "They're the most dangerous."

"How can you tell who they are?" I asked.

"That's easy," he said, inhaling slowly from his cigarette. "They're the people who are the hardest to stay away from."

On Saturday, Ruby packed a cooler full of sandwiches and sodas to bring to the horse show. Jack stayed down by the trailer, helping my father groom and saddle Cap, while Mrs. Altman and I followed Ruby to the bleachers. Ruby had dressed Pom-Pom in a pink cape and matching pink visor and she carried him under her arm while she climbed the bleachers, pausing every few steps to catch her breath. "Oh!" she wheezed. "I have missed the show days!" People glanced up at us as we passed, scooting sideways in their seats to keep out of Ruby's path.

I followed behind, stooping my shoulders and bending at the knees. My pants were too short and my shirt rose up around my waist. I had to curl my toes inside my shoes, hunching forward to keep the pale stripe of my stomach from showing. "Stand up straight," Jack kept telling me at home. "You don't want to be a grizzled old hunchback when you're older, do you?"

Ruby led us to the top row of the bleachers, then stopped. "I'd sit right up here," she said, pointing out her old seat. Mrs. Altman smiled, but her eyes darted across the crowd, uncomfortable with the attention Ruby drew. "And if Jody didn't come in first, I'd scream out, 'Spit on the judge, Jody! Spit on the judge!' That made them think twice."

"Good heavens," Mrs. Altman said.

Down beside the ring, Bud Pope walked up to my grandfather and Jack threw his arms in the air, laughing out loud and pumping Bud's hand. All morning long, members of the sheriff's posse had been approaching Jack, whooping out when they saw him, grinning from ear to ear, punching him lightly in the shoulder. My father stood to the side with his eyes on the arena, though Sheila was not riding in the class that was inside.

"Your husband still has a lot of ties here," Mrs. Altman said to Ruby while she watched.

"He hated to leave," Ruby told her.

"Why did you?" Mrs. Altman asked.

"We were getting too old for this kind of life," she said. "Jody was married, needed to start his own family. And my girls were all gone. A mother has to be close to her daughters."

"I understand," Mrs. Altman said.

Down by the ring, Sheila stood beside my father, resting her head on his arm as she watched the class inside. She had spent the whole morning clinging to him. For the first time, my father had entered her into a reining class and from the bleachers, I could see her lips stuttering across the same question over and over: *Are you sure I'm ready?*

"Well," Mrs. Altman said. "Your son certainly does a good job."

Ruby's face softened as she smiled down at my father. "I'm glad to hear it."

"He's wonderful with Sheila," Mrs. Altman went on. "She just adores him."

"Jody's a good boy," Ruby agreed. "Gentle, you know? Of course, he's spent his whole life with girls. Three older sisters, two daughters. There aren't many men who could do nearly as well with so many women."

"He's good with the horses too," Mrs. Altman said.

Ruby laughed. "Same thing."

Nothing seemed to impress clients more than watching my father train a horse. Sheila Altman's own progression as a rider had been slow, imperceptible to her mother. But Darling was another story. Every day, my father would saddle her and lead her into the arena. It always started out with the same rodeo, Darling flinging herself in every direction while my father hung on for dear life. But the Catfish and the Altmans could not have been more impressed. Less than a month ago, he couldn't even keep a saddle on her back and now there he was, an actual person, sitting on her back, staying on, taking her through turns and stops and lead changes. Even Ruby would waddle out to the arena to watch my father work with Darling. She stood close to the Catfish, listening in on their gossip and calling out warnings and encouragement to my father, who, for the most part, ignored her. "Watch her head, Jody!" Ruby would shout. "That's right, that's right, pull her left!"

Only Jack seemed immune to the excitement. He stood back beside me, leaning against the barn and puffing his cigar while the women formed their cheering section around the arena. "Just between you and me," he said, nodding out to the arena, "your pop's got it all wrong."

I watched the Catfish erupt in applause as my father pushed Darling through a series of violent bucks. "It's not about staying on," Jack continued. "It's about taking the fight out of them."

"This is how Dad always does it," I told Jack. "They settle down eventually."

"Your dad's a hell of a rider," Jack told me. "And that horse isn't stupid. In her gut, she knows she can't get him off. But she's not learning anything out there. She's just biding her time."

I felt like I ought to disagree with him, to defend my father's methods. But I watched the circle of women swooning at the fence, my father's ears blushing with the attention, and at my center, I knew that Jack was right. It wasn't betrayal, it was just the truth.

"She's got good lines," Jack said as he watched Darling move. "How much did he pay?"

"Just between you and me?" I asked. Jack nodded. "Three thousand."

"She'll be worth more than that," he said. "Considerably more."

"That's what Dad said."

Jack was quiet for a moment. "He knows the real thing when he sees it," he said. "I'll give him that."

Jack wasn't the only one. That morning, my father had loaded Darling into the horse trailer beside Yellow Cap. It would be good for her, he said, to spend the day at the show, to be around the other horses, the crowds of people, the loudspeakers. She spent the morning tied to the trailer, stomping and snorting, flattening her ears at every child who passed too close. By noon, the men who had crowded around Jack when they first saw him had gathered around our horse trailer to get a look at Darling. They whistled through their teeth and shook their heads at the ground. "A real looker," they agreed. "Full of hellfire."

"You ought to breed her," Jack said after the crowd had dispersed. My father was saddling Yellow Cap for Sheila's reining class and he looked over his shoulder at Darling, thinking.

"She's coming along," he said. "Besides, she's too young. We'd never get a good foal out of her at this age."

Jack shook his head, dismissing my father's concern. "We're not interested in the foal," he said. "And she isn't coming along half as fast as she ought to be. She won't be any good for a year anyway. Let's drive her over to Pope's place and have her taken care of."

My father scowled at Yellow Cap's girth strap and Jack snapped his fingers at him. "Think about it, Jody," he said. "You breed her now and next year, she'll be pregnant during the hottest part of the summer. Trust me, you'll be able to stick a kid on her back after that."

Late in the afternoon, Ruby, Mrs. Altman, and I resumed our places on the bleachers to watch Sheila's reining class. "She's scared to death," Mrs. Altman told us. "I don't think she slept at all last night."

"Nothing to worry about," Ruby said, patting Mrs. Altman's knee. "Jody wouldn't put her in there if he didn't know she was ready."

I sat beside them, silent. Reining was the last class of the day and unlike the others, it was solitary, a single rider at a time entering the arena. In the other classes, riders kept their horses slow inside the ring, focusing on precision and smooth, gentle strides. But in reining, speed was the key ingredient. The faster the horse performed the pattern, the more dramatic the effect, the whirling circles and spins, the long, sliding stop at the end. Sheila sat outside the arena, waiting her turn, petrified.

My father had told her beforehand that she could take the pattern as slowly as she wanted. "Don't try to impress anyone," he said. "Just try to get through the routine without making mistakes." Earlier that day, they had posted the pattern outside the announcer's booth and I had stood with Sheila, helping her memorize. Now, as the gate opened and Sheila moved Yellow Cap inside, her face was white, her eyes unblinking. The judge and his assistant sat in folding chairs along one side of the arena and when they tipped their hats at her, indicating that she could begin, Sheila only stared out at the wide, empty arena, without moving. Straight line to the far side of the ring, I thought. Two and a half spins to the right.

It didn't matter what my father had or had not told her about speed. Yellow Cap remembered reining, knew what he was supposed to do, and when Sheila finally touched her heels to his sides, Cap sprung across the arena, kicking up a cloud of dirt and sending Sheila bobbing sideways on her saddle. A spin was supposed to be tight and centered, the horse planting a single hind foot and rotating upon it like a top. But Sheila yanked her reins and shifted her weight sideways, off-kilter from the speed while Cap stumbled in a circle, confused. At the point when Sheila was supposed to begin galloping circles around the ring, she panicked. From the stands, I could see the fear freezing inside her mind, making her stupid. She tilted sideways on her saddle, her cowboy hat dipping down over her eyes, blocking her view.

Mrs. Altman covered her face with her hands as Cap raced recklessly around the ring, his circle widening toward the edge where both judge and assistant suddenly realized he was not going to stop and leapt from their folding chairs, tossing their clipboards over their shoulders and sprinting across the arena to get out of Sheila's path. Sheila and Cap came to a bumpy halt half a ring away from where the pattern was supposed to end. Once they had finished, Sheila held one hand to her chest, catching her breath, then lifted the rim of her cowboy hat, peering across the arena at the empty folding chairs tipped onto their sides, the judge and his assistant catching their breath on the opposite end of the ring.

"Think of it this way, honey," Ruby said and patted Mrs. Altman's thigh. "There's no place to go but up."

seven

My cousins were pageant girls. Ruby had volumes of scrapbooks devoted to each girl's history of crowns and banners, and she brought them into the house, spreading them across the kitchen table to show my mother and me. "They're your family," she said to us. "And you wouldn't even recognize them if you passed by them on the street. It breaks my heart."

Usually, I would not be permitted to sit inside the house in the middle of the day. But Sheila Altman was taking a small vacation from her lessons since the fiasco during her reining class. And while the temperature remained in the hundreds, the boarders made fewer and fewer appearances in the barn. Jack and my father continued working, but no one seemed to notice when I slipped inside the house.

Ruby flipped through the pages and there they were: the cousins I hardly knew, wearing sequins and feathers, smiling perfect posed smiles behind their masks of makeup. Ruby was right; if I passed these girls on the street, it would never occur to me that they were family. In truth, if I ever passed these girls on the street, I would probably cross to the other side.

"The younger you can start them, the better," Ruby told us as she turned the pages. She was eating potato chips from the bag and paused to wipe the grease from her fingers onto her pants before pointing to a picture. "Look here," she said. "Kissy was only six weeks old in this one. And she came in first."

The infant in the picture was sleeping, small and wrinkled like a little old man inside the frosted ruffles of her dress. On top of her head, a tiny crown sat within a nest of perfect blond ringlets. "She had a lot of hair for a baby," I said.

"That's fake," Ruby told me. "A bitty baby wig. You just stick it right on top of their bald little heads and, presto—hair."

"Isn't that cheating?" I asked and Ruby shook her head.

"Everybody does it."

Outside the window, Jack and my father were fencing off a piece of the back pasture. The foals needed to be weaned, Jack had said. We'd need a place to put them.

"Just look at that," Ruby breathed as she squinted to see them. "Aren't those the two most handsome men on God's great earth?"

It was late in the day and still the sun beat down on the parched land. Jack looked easy and comfortable in the heat as he supported a fence rail with his thigh. My father looked like my father. "I guess," I said and Ruby laughed.

"You're young," she told me. "You'll figure it out, won't she, Marian?"

My mother didn't answer. She sat in her chair with her legs tucked up beneath her, staring out the window. Ruby paid particular attention to my mother now, watching how much she ate, and poking food into her any time she had the opportunity. "I've got to fatten you up while I'm here," she kept saying. And though my mother still slept late and retired early, she seemed open to Ruby's efforts. "Drink your milk," Ruby would say, and my mother would flicker out of her trance, sipping from her glass like an obedient child.

As she turned though the pages, Ruby was quick to point out the falsities within each photo—hair extensions, eyelashes, false teeth used to conceal gaps from lost baby teeth. "You can see how much work it is," she told me. "It's one of the reasons we hardly ever get out here to visit you. Your aunts need me in the beauty trenches."

It was hard to tell how old my cousins were in the photographs. Sometimes I could catch a glimpse of skinny legs poking out beneath a hem of lace or a dimpled child hand holding a microphone. But their faces belonged to women, serious and sultry, their eyes full of secrets I couldn't yet imagine.

My mother slid a potato chip from the bag and held it delicately between the tips of her thumb and forefinger, considering the possibility of putting it inside her mouth. Pom-Pom danced at her feet and she bent forward, offering the chip to him and giggling as his tongue tickled the tips of her fingers.

Ruby watched with her fingers laced over her massive belly. "You're good with dogs, Marian," she said.

"I love dogs," my mother said.

"You should get one," Ruby told her.

"I had one once," my mother said. "His name was Cody."

"When you were a girl?" Ruby asked.

My mother shook her head, feeding a second potato chip to Pom-Pom. "When I was a little girl, all I wanted in the world was a dog," she answered. "But we lived in a small house—there wasn't even a yard—and so I was never allowed to have one."

This was the first time I had ever heard my mother speak of anything before her life at our house. I straightened in my seat, glancing across the table at Ruby to see if she sensed the rarity of my mother's conversation. But Ruby only smiled and nodded, glancing down at her scrapbook, running her fingers across the pictures of her other, more familiar granddaughters as my mother spoke.

"After I married Joe," my mother went on, "someone dumped Cody out on the desert and he found his way here—to us. He was so beat up. His head was caved in on one side and he limped like a little old man. But oh! He was the sweetest dog. When I was pregnant with Nona, he used to rest his head on my lap so that his ear was right beside my belly. I would say, 'Can you hear the baby, Cody?' And his tail would go *thump, thump, thump* against my leg." My mother turned to me, her eyes misty with the memory. "Do you remember that, Alice?"

My mother's smile was wet and fragile as she blinked at me. I couldn't remember the last time she had looked at me, the last time she had asked me a question. And so I didn't tell her that I hadn't known the dog, that I would never be able to remember something that had happened before my sister was born. I didn't tell her that until that very moment, I had never even known that Cody existed.

"He sounds precious," Ruby said finally.

"He was," my mother said and her face cleared, her smile fading. "He was precious. And then a horse kicked him in the head and he died."

My mother turned back to the window, letting the memory, the story, and the moment of happiness slip away into shadow. "I'm tired," she said, standing. "I think I'll lie down now."

Ruby and I watched her climb the stairs on her small, awkward frame. After she had disappeared past the top, Ruby reached across the table for my mother's glass, finishing the milk in a single swallow. Ruby looked up at me over the empty glass, then reached into her pocket for a cigarette. "Your mother is a different sort of person, Alice."

"I know that," I said. Ruby lit her cigarette and I kept my eyes down, afraid, as I always was when someone began to speak of my mother, that any reminder of myself, of who I was, might suddenly shut her up.

"Marian was just a girl when she first came out here," Ruby told me. "A little bitty thing. But Jody wasn't much more than a kid himself. Jack gave her lessons and Jody just fell head over foot for her. Of course, anybody could see why. When Marian was happy, the sun shined from her skin. You couldn't look away."

"But you didn't like her?" I asked.

Ruby shrugged. "Marian had her ways, even back then." She raised her eyebrows at me and I nodded to show that I understood what she wasn't saying. "She was never meant for this kind of life. It was plain as plain and I said so to Jody a million times."

"But he was in love," I said.

"But he was in love." Ruby sighed. "And nothing makes a person more selfish and pigheaded than being in love."

"Do you hate him for it?" I asked.

Ruby laughed and her cigarette bounced in her fingers, peppering the tabletop with white ash. "It's all water through the chute now," she said, wiping the ash from the table with the palm of her hand. "He did what he did and now here you are, and what would the world be like if you weren't in it?"

I didn't answer. The world would probably be the same.

Love. This was the word that changed everything. What people wanted, what they thought their lives would be, it crashed to pieces when they fell in love. This had been the case with my father, with my sister. It had been the case with Polly Cain.

The story of Polly had changed in my mind, what had become of her, how she ended. I had been willing to believe that she was simply clumsy, that her number was up, that she was just another person who was here one day and gone the next. But now, I couldn't think of Polly's last moments without thinking of Mr. Delmar. Love was enough to make a person stop paying attention, to make a person off balance and careless. And the wanting, the dark, empty space it left inside the body, the need that pounded against the rib cage and sobbed through the nighttime, it might be enough to make a person forget about putting one foot in front of the other. It might be enough to make a person step across the place where ground changed into water.

As we spoke more and more, as I waited away the daylight until I could slip into Nona's closet and dial his number, the other parts of my life began to dim. The person I had been before I knew him was drifting into a past life that felt more like dream than reality. I found myself counting away the minutes, finding ways to pass time until we could speak again. The heat, the desert, the barn filled with people I barely knew, they were all just make-believe, a story someone had told to me while I was half asleep. At night, the rest of the world disappeared into darkness, and my own secret world awoke.

It didn't matter how late I called, he always answered. "I read something today," he had told me the last time I called. "And I thought of you.

"'. . . We have lingered in the chambers of the sea by sea-girls wreathed with seaweed red and brown till human voices wake us, and we drown.'"

He did this more and more now, read from novels, magazines,

books of poems. I never asked the titles or authors and he never volunteered. Instead, I closed my eyes and let the words float through my mind in cloudy waves—my own private ocean. I tethered myself to the sound of his voice, his breath, the soft stirs of night rustling through the air around him. In this way, we passed the time together. The rest of the world vanished behind the perfect pitch of darkness and we, alone, remained behind. Surely, this was love. What else could it have been?

My father and grandfather had abandoned the fence for the day when I went outside to call them for dinner. Jack was standing in the front pasture with the foals gathered around him. I climbed over the fence and the foals skittered away as I started toward them.

Jack held up a hand in greeting and I slowed my pace, worried that I might be interfering with whatever strange practice he engaged in to keep them close. But he waved me over with one hand while he held the other out to the foals. He whispered to them, calling them back, and though they watched me sideways, they moved toward Jack, poking at him with their small noses. He reached into his pocket and held out his hand while the foals crowded around him, stretching their noses to his fingers. If I had been even a few feet farther away, I would not have seen the single white sugar cube cupped in the palm of his hand as he reached out to Ginger's colt.

All those afternoons that my father had watched Jack from the porch, swearing under his breath and wondering what the secret was, and now I knew. He was bribing them. "You're terrible," I said, and Jack shot me a wicked grin. "You know what bad habits that teaches them," I added. "It makes them biters. Dad would have a fit if he knew."

Jack held his hands to his sides as he started toward me, shrugging helplessly. "I'm the grandpa," he said. "I'm supposed to spoil them." He pulled another cube from his pocket, holding it between his thumb and forefinger, then touched his free hand beneath my chin, tipping my head back and setting the sugar on my tongue. "You'll keep my secret, won't you?" he asked.

The cube dissolved on my tongue, coating my mouth in warm, sweet syrup. I swallowed, then rolled my eyes at him, surrendering.

"Good," he told me and slung his arm across my shoulders. "Now stand up straight."

After the fence in the back pasture was finished, Jack began building a second round pen. "We don't *need* another round pen," my father said when Jack came home with a truck full of lumber.

"Can't hurt," Jack said, then looked at me. "Alice, tell him."

"We could use it for lunging," I told my father. "We could use it for equitation exercises." The wood was already bought, the space plotted out in Jack's head—directly across from the existing round pen. My father gave in. What would be the use in arguing? And so the new project was born. My father and grandfather spent the days sawing and hammering, measuring space and pounding poles into the ground.

Sheila Altman had finally come back and we mucked stalls while the sounds of hammering echoed through the barn. "I'm thinking of giving it up," she said, and I stopped, the pole of my rake sweaty in my palms. The air around us vibrated with the noise of building, and for a moment, I thought about pretending I couldn't make her out over the din. But Sheila stared across at me through the white feathers of her eyelashes. I had heard every word and she knew it.

"Why?" I whispered.

Sheila continued shoveling, sifting through the sawdust of Toy Boy's pen with her rake, lifting the droppings into the wheelbarrow. "You know why," she said. "Everyone does."

How long had I waited for Sheila Altman to see the light, to give in to reality and surrender? But now I imagined her gone, the afternoons empty without her lessons. Jack and Ruby were here now, building and cooking and making my mother drink her milk. But they were not going to stay. Sheila Altman was our only client. She was not allowed to give it up. "Because of the last show?" I asked her. "Because of one little class?"

Sheila raised her eyes, her gaze leveling mine. "I almost killed the judge."

"Nah," I told her, continuing with my work as though this conversation were no different from any other, discussing the superior look of Cap, the annoying laugh of the Catfish, the unbearable stretches of afternoon heat. "He had a huge head start. He was practically on the other side of the *state* before you ran over his folding chair."

Sheila stared at me, not fooled. "I suck," she said. "You know it. Your dad knows it. That judge and his assistant, the *whole wide world,* they all know it. I'm wasting everyone's time."

"You're nuts," I said, and Sheila stared at me with the wide, cutting eyes of a person who was not interested in flattery, not interested in falsity.

"Name one person," she told me, "just *one* who was ever any good at this without being born into it."

My mind flattened, blank and empty. She was only asking for a name. All I had to do was make one up. "Don't lie," she said, her voice dead with calm. She knew me. All those hours she had spent at the barn, raking and sweeping and shoveling beside me, but not until that moment did I realize that she understood so much.

I saw it then—the future. Jack was right about Darling, she wasn't coming along nearly as quickly as my father thought she was. The Catfish owned the barn now, cackling through the hallway with their wealthy, disinterested laughter. Sheila Altman was our path to freedom, our way out. Maybe I didn't think she could do it. Maybe I hated her for all the pretty possibility I didn't believe she was capable of living up to. But in that moment, none of it mattered. She was our hope. And that was something I wasn't willing to let go of. "My mother," I said.

Sheila blinked at me, uncertain. "Your mother *what?*"

"She wasn't born into it," I told her.

Sheila leaned on the pole of her rake, waiting.

"She came here for lessons, older than you—fifteen, I think. She didn't know anything. But she learned. And then she won." Sheila sucked her breath in through her teeth, her eyes misting over as she listened. "She worked," I said, filling in the details no one had ever bothered to tell me. "She worked until there was nothing left of her, until she wanted to fall to the ground she was so tired. But she didn't.

She kept going, kept working. And in the end, she won. She won and won and won and won. She was a star. She even had her picture in the paper once."

A single tear slipped down Sheila's dusty cheek, trickling a muddy stream to reveal the perfect apricot cream of her skin beneath. "And he fell in love with her," she whispered.

"And he *married* her."

Bud Pope's place was huge. We wandered through the corridors of the barn, passing the indoor arena, the air-conditioned stalls, the automatic watering system. Jack held Darling's lead rope and walked ahead, chatting with Bud while my father and I followed.

The drive out to Pope Equestrian Center had passed in near silence. Jack drove and I sat in between him and my father, my body swaying into theirs every time we hit a bump or turned a corner. "This seems like a waste of money," my father had mumbled while he slumped in his seat, his eyes turned out the window.

"No more so than paying three grand for a horse nobody but you can ride," Jack said evenly, and my father's body stiffened beside mine.

"I don't see how that's anybody's business but my own," he said.

"The posse boys talk," Jack said, winking sideways at me to show that he wouldn't betray my trust, and I sank back against the seat. Half the posse members had been at the auction that day. Bud Pope had been there. Any one of them might have told Jack how much Darling went for in the end.

"They'd do better to look after their own affairs," my father grumbled.

"Probably so," Jack agreed. "But they're interested in yours all the same."

My father leaned forward, staring past me at Jack. "You wanna share what you've been hearing?" he asked.

Jack shrugged. "Everyone knows you're hurting for money, Jody."

My head felt dizzy with heat, the backs of my legs sticking to the vinyl seat. People were talking about us, whispering behind our backs about the money we didn't have. All summer long, I'd been slouching in my tight clothes, waiting for my father to notice that I needed new ones. How many other people had seen what he had not? "It's a small town and people talk," Jack went on. "And it didn't help you any when Nona took off."

My father's eyes shot daggers across the front seat of the truck, warning Jack, who watched the road without noticing. "It's not good for business," Jack said, "when a man can't even control his own kids."

All the air seemed to suck itself from the cab of the truck, flattening my lungs into threads, forcing my mouth open. *I'm here,* I wanted to whisper. *Right here between you.* But my lips could not form the words, my breath unable to support the sound. Neither of them so much as glanced at me.

"Trust me, Jody," Jack told my father, and his voice was steady, reassuring, completely unaware of the invisible line he had just crossed over. "We're gonna get this mare taken care of. We'll wean the foals and get the colts gelded, have them registered—you should have done that ages ago. You're gonna feel like a new man when the barn's running the way it ought to."

"Barn's running fine the way it is," my father said, but his voice was thin, barely more than a whisper. Jack didn't answer, letting the subject, finally, drop.

It didn't matter what my father had said in the truck. Our barn looked dwarfed and shabby compared with Bud Pope's, and there was no point pretending otherwise. But we walked through the property and my father's face registered nothing. A part of myself wanted to look around, to inspect the long lines of clean fences, the even rows of feed bins, the warm-up rings and perfectly ordered shelves of equipment, but I stayed back beside my father, mirroring my face after his.

Jack had been wrong in the truck and I wanted to tell my father so. I wanted to set my hand in the crook of his arm and rest my head against his shoulder, to say that Jack had not been there, had not seen the load my father carried without breathing a word of complaint. But I had. I wanted to stand on my tiptoes and whisper into his ear:

Sugar cubes. Jack's a cheater. I wanted to say that we were doing just fine. We were getting by.

Bud led us out of the barn to a paddock where a bay stud was haltered and tied to the fence. The stallion's head lifted when he caught Darling's scent, his whole body arching and tightening into ripples as he stomped one foot on the ground. Darling nickered and skittered sideways.

The twins were standing beside the fence. "Alice-bo-balice," Zach called when he saw me. I hung back, staying beside my father.

"Banana-phanna-pho-*phallus*," Andy continued. He wrapped his arms around himself and squeezed his eyes shut as he kissed the air. My blood filled with fire and my hands went numb at my sides as the twins snorted with laughter.

I looked up at my father, beginning to shake my head. I wanted him to know that we were in this together, that I would not lend my support to such a waste of money, that I would protect him. My father's face was tight, his skin red, his expression steaming. He looked at the twins, then down at me. I opened my mouth, starting to ask what was wrong, what had happened. But before I could speak, my father reached down, snatching me by the side of the neck, his fingers digging into the tendon of my shoulder until I yelped with pain. I tried to twist away, but he tightened his grip, sending spasms of white-hot pain searing down my back, through my arm, numbing my brain with fire.

Again, I tried to pull away, but my head wrenched sideways and he brought his other hand up to the side of my face, tilting it up so that I was staring into his eyes, my body dangling uselessly from his hands. I tried to focus my vision through the pain, to see what was happening, what I had done. But the anger burned like a flame behind my father's eyes, flooding through his body, tearing into my flesh. "You keep away from those boys," he growled. "I don't want you anywhere near them."

My father let me go and I stumbled backward, my neck and shoulder clenching with pain, my mouth opening and closing, soundless. I looked up into my father's face, still red with fury. Inside my chest, the tears were beginning to form, the sobs rising. But they froze inside my throat, stopping at the back of my tongue, filling my mouth with a dull, empty ache. All the warmth, the sweet, gentle love that had swelled in my rib cage only moments before, now singed and crackled, burned and dead inside of me. I felt nothing. I could not have cried if my life depended on it.

"Don't worry," I said, my lip curling over my teeth as I looked into his eyes. Then I turned on my heel, wobbling toward the others, leaving him to stand alone.

Bud had tied Darling inside the paddock and was now crouched behind her, wrapping a leather cord in a figure eight between her hind feet. Jack and the twins stood to the side, watching with their backs to me. No one had seen a thing.

I stood between the Pope twins, daring my father to come after me, knowing he would not. In the paddock, Darling balked and tried to move sideways, but Bud tightened the cord and she stumbled, then stood frozen. "What's he doing?" I asked and Zach grinned at me.

"Hobbling her," he answered. "Tying her legs together."

The sun was glaring down, but I felt cold and dizzy, sick to my stomach. I circled my arms around myself, trying to stifle the chill that was creeping across my skin, the chatter hinged in my jaw. A deep ache pulsed through my neck and shoulder, but I kept my eyes straight ahead.

"Why?" I asked.

"You know," Andy said. "So she won't kick him in his money organ." Zach leaned forward, shaking with laughter, and I pretended not to notice. Breeding was strange and awkward to watch, large and clumsy, mechanical. But I had seen it a hundred times before. I had seen everything. Nothing that happened could surprise me. Nothing the Pope twins said would ever be enough to make me blush.

"Training's not going so well, eh, Joe?" Bud called over his shoulder as he loosened the stud's lead rope.

When my father didn't answer, Jack stepped between them. "Just trying to take some of the fire out of her," he explained, and Bud nodded.

"Well, this'll do it, all right." He unhooked the lead rope from the stud's halter, turning him loose inside the paddock.

The stud huffed and snorted, trotting up behind Darling and shivering with his whole body as he stomped at the ground. Her ears turned back and her nostrils flared, her limbs stiffening beneath her. She tried to move sideways, but the hobble held her and her eyes stayed straight ahead as the stud lifted himself, hooves digging into flanks, on top of her.

The stud groaned, flexing and rocking on his hind feet, his front hooves streaking dirt across the perfect white of her haunches. Darling's ribs heaved and her nostrils trembled in small, whimpering breaths. Her back legs shifted between the hobble. Behind me, I could sense my father watching from a distance. I stared into Darling's eyes and did not feel sorry for her, did not feel anything. My mind was blank, a tunnel of icy wind. Something flickered in the mare's eyes, an instant, nothing more, and the words sliced into the tissue of my body, stabbing like lightning through the air between us: *Kill him.*

I heard the sounds before I saw the movement, a crack of wood, a snap of leather, the raw, wet split of flesh. Her body seemed to extend from inside out, her head whipping back to break the fence rail at the same moment that her hooves cut backward, shredding the hobble that tied them together. The stud made a noise like a blown tire, then fell back on his hind legs, wheezing and wobbling, dropping to his knees in the dirt.

Jack and Bud began yelling, rushing toward the stud, then the mare, then each other in a storm of chaos. The twins stood on either side of me with their mouths open, their hands dead at their sides. Darling, free of halter, hobble, and stud, trotted easily across the paddock, then stopped and turned, regarding the whole useless crowd of us with the cold crystal blue of her unblinking eye.

At home, Jack led Darling back to the round pen, his face red. He had written a check to Bud Pope, covering the stud fee, the broken fence, the broken hobble, and the several weeks Bud expected his stud would have to lie low before being able to rouse his muscle again after such a furious kick. During the drive back, my father's eyes kept shifting sideways to me, but I watched the road ahead of us through the windshield, never acknowledging him. None of us spoke once during the entire drive.

Inside the house, the air conditioner was turned up full blast, a false winter in our living room. "Well?" Ruby asked when my father and I walked through the back door. My mother was nestled on the sofa, an afghan wrapped around her shoulders, a glass of milk on the end table beside her.

"She kicked him," I said and my mother rose up onto her knees. "She didn't."

"Broke the hobble," my father told them. "Snapped it between her legs like it was a piece of licorice. I've never seen anything like it."

My mother covered her mouth with her hand. "Oh." She giggled. "I bet Jack's angry."

Ruby began pumping my father for details about Bud Pope's place, and I could feel him watching me as he answered, his eyes following me as I crept around the perimeter of the room and slipped out the back door. Outside, the sun was small and white in the afternoon sky. I sat on the porch steps and touched my fingers to my neck, wincing as they brushed across the knot of pain.

Inside the barn, there was work to be done, stalls to clean, horses to exercise. I stared across the driveway, thinking of everything that had to happen before this day could be finished, all the hours still waiting to be filled. The sun beat down on my bare legs, but I couldn't feel the heat. I leaned my head against the porch railing, my body numb and heavy. The sob that had started to rise in my chest at Bud Pope's place had become caught inside me, and though I could feel it, sticking in my throat like a piece of soggy bread, I couldn't feel the sadness. I couldn't feel anything.

The screen door opened and shut behind me, feet scraping across the floor of the porch. My father stood for a moment, then sat beside me on the steps without speaking. I could feel him thinking, trying to gauge my silence. "That was something else, huh?" he said after a minute. I nodded without looking at him. "We're lucky she didn't split him straight open," my father went on. "We're lucky she didn't kill him."

My father cleared his throat, trying to sort the words out inside his head, trying to find the ones that would fix the piece of broken space between us. My body was lead against the porch rail, unable to move, unable to turn. I only heard the slight rustle of his shirtsleeve as his hand moved closer, lifting my hair off my shoulder, revealing the hot, tender prints his fingers had left upon my skin.

He inhaled, breath across gravel, and my lungs shivered inside my chest. The cold, clogging marble in the back of my throat melted into warm liquid, seeping down into my stomach, up through my sinuses, spilling over the rims of my eyes.

"The day he came for her," my father said, his voice quiet as he let my hair drop. "The day she left." I turned to him, waiting. The tears spilled over my lips, down my neck, and into the collar of my T-shirt, but I didn't move to wipe them away. "There was nothing I could have done to stop her."

"I know," I told him.

He nodded down at his hands, his face twisted. "The thing is," he said, and I had to strain to hear his words, "I didn't see it coming."

"She doesn't even write to us anymore," I whispered. "She doesn't even call." My nose was running, my lips wet and salty with tears.

"I don't understand it," he said. His head dipped forward, his eyes squinting. "She was always so open, you know? So clear."

I saw her then, my sister. She laughed with her whole body, mouth open, head thrown back. She sank to her knees when she cried, kicked things when she was angry. As a child, she liked to be carried, liked to sit on my father's lap. When she was older, she rested her head on his arm when she stood beside him, looping her thumb into the pocket of his pants, jawing the muscle of his shoulder with the point of her chin. She had been his darling, his baby, his pet. And then one day she'd left with barely a word of good-bye. How would he have ever seen it coming?

"And me?" I asked.

"You," he said and smiled down at his feet. "God only knows what's happening inside your head."

The sun was shining into my face, drying my tears, stiffening my skin. "Even when you were a baby," my father told me, "we never knew what to make of you. We'd try to hold you and you'd arch your back, squirming away." He turned his face to mine, and his eyes softened with seriousness, a moment of pure perfect truth. "You're like me."

We looked at each other through the blinding glare of sunlight. This was the closest my father would ever come to saying that he had been wrong, the closest thing I would ever get to an apology. And I tried to smile at him, my lips waxy with dried tears. I tried to show that it was enough.

"I guess I ought to go check on the mare," my father said, standing. He paused for a moment, laughing at the ground. "That crazy bitch."

After he was gone, I sat on the steps alone. Darling would not carry a foal this year, would not stand, swollen and pregnant, under the brutal sun of the following summer. I thought about my father, his moment of misplaced rage, the bruises that would stain my skin for days. He had said we were alike. And I wondered, now that it was all over, if he had watched Darling as closely as I had. I wondered if he had seen the same look in her face when the stud climbed on top of her, if he understood what had happened with the clear, centered certainty that I did: she never would have kicked if they hadn't tied her legs.

eight

THE DAY WE WEANED the foals, Sheila Altman climbed out of her mother's minivan waving a pink envelope at me. It was going to be the best slumber party ever, she told me. They were going to rent R-rated movies and order pizza and eat ice cream until they threw up. Sheila Altman did not turn thirteen every day, after all.

The invitation had my name in glitter across the front with stickers of pastel horses around the edges. I stared down without moving to open it. "You have to come," she said. "You're practically my best friend."

"She'll be there," my father said and I shot him a look. "Wouldn't miss it for the world, right?" Before I could answer, he took the envelope from my hands and opened it, scrolling through the information. "Six o'clock on Friday," he said.

"With a sleeping bag and pillow," Sheila added.

"Alice will be there," my father told her.

Sheila clapped her hands and ran into the barn, bouncing on the balls of her feet.

"Maybe I shouldn't go," I said to my father.

"It's a party," he told me. "You've been working hard. You deserve a little break."

"I don't really want to go," I tried again.

"It'll be great," he told me. So there was that to look forward to.

After we separated the foals from their mothers, we all stood around, watching their grief. They screamed and rammed their chests into the fence, running circles in the little pen, colliding with one another in clouds of dust. Their heads lifted, crying out in thin, anguished whinnies, slicing the air with their pain. Sheila watched and her eyes filled with tears. She reached through the rails of the fence, holding her hand out to comfort them, but they were blind with agony and fear. There was nothing she could do to make it easier.

"Why can't they just stay with their mothers?" Sheila asked.

"They gotta be trained," Jack told her. "Can't work with a horse that's still attached to his mother. They gotta grow up."

Sheila shuddered as she watched them and my father stepped behind her, patting her shoulder. "It seems bad now," he told her. "But they recover fast. A few months from now, we could put them back out in the pasture with the broodmares, and they wouldn't even recognize each other."

"Is that true?" Sheila whispered, turning to me. Her eyes were rimmed with red, her chin puckered.

We had never tried it before, but I nodded my head at her. "Absolutely," I said.

The tears spilled down Sheila's cheeks and she dipped her chin to her chest. "That's the saddest thing I've ever heard."

Over the next few days, the broodmares' udders swelled under the weight of their unnursed milk, cracking and bleeding as they stood in the farthest corner of the front pasture—the closest they could get to the sounds of their frantic, screaming foals. They paced and stomped and called out with their necks extended and their mouths open.

"What is that noise?" Mr. Delmar asked when I called.

Even from inside the closet, the sounds scraped through the air, mothers and offspring separated by a matter of yards, but still, lost to each other. "Just the television," I told him. "My mother's watching a show in the other room."

"Jesus," he said. "It sounds like someone's torturing rabbits."

Finally, the weight of the milk became too much to bear and, one by one, the broodmares surrendered to the pain, lying down on the dried grass, giving themselves over to agony and grief.

"Maybe we could milk them," Sheila suggested. "Just a little." On the other side of the fence, the mares rolled their eyes, groaning up at the empty sky as their wasted milk leaked tiny streams onto the brown grass.

Jack shook his head. "You'd be delaying the inevitable," he said. "We milk them now, they'd make more milk. It's kindest just to let them suffer." Jack lifted his chin and wrinkled his brow at the sky. "Weaning's always ugliest in drought years."

The mares moaned on the grass, their eyes glassy and open. The foals were silent now, their throats scraped empty of sound after two solid days of screaming. The wind had shifted, hiding their scents from their mothers. There was nothing left to do but wait for the pain to stop.

"Is it over?" my mother asked when I went inside the house. She and Ruby were sitting at the kitchen table, a deck of playing cards spread out before them. Pom-Pom was perched on my mother's lap and she dangled an Oreo cookie over his head.

"They're quiet, at least," I told her.

"Good," she said and shuddered in her chair. "That noise gives me nightmares."

Ruby discarded, then stood. "You hungry?" she asked. I shook my head and she started into the kitchen.

"I might like something," my mother called after her. "A sand-wich," she said, dropping the Oreo into Pom-Pom's open mouth. "Peanut butter and banana. No crust."

Ruby disappeared into the kitchen and my mother scooted Pom-Pom off her lap, then stood and crossed to the window. "I'm learning to play poker," she told me. "I've won six cookies so far."

"Good for you," I told her.

She swayed in front of the window, moving her hips to music that only she could hear. "Maybe I'll run away to Las Vegas," she said, her voice giddy, her shoulders shimmying. "I could wear feathers in my hair and blow onto dice for men in tuxedos. I could be Lady Luck!"

It was early evening and across the driveway, Mrs. Altman was climbing out of her minivan, standing to fumble inside her purse.

My mother's body stopped swaying, her knees locking in the window to watch. Mrs. Altman dropped her keys and bent to pick them up. When she stood, her head tilted sideways, sensing that she was being watched. My mother's eyes met Mrs. Altman's and both women froze like cats, staring at each other through the window. They stood for a moment, and then Mrs. Altman raised one hand in an awkward wave. My mother lifted her hand in return. Mrs. Altman smiled, squinting into the house, then fluffed her hair self-consciously with her hands and turned to walk into the barn.

"That's the little girl's mother," my mother whispered, dropping to the side of the window and folding a curtain around her chest as she bent sideways to peer out at Mrs. Altman's retreating form.

"Sheila's mother," I told her. "That's right."

"She's pretty," she said, then turned to look at me. "Do you think so?"

"Sure," I told her. "And she's really nice."

"She looks just like the little girl," my mother said.

"*Sheila,*" I said again, and my mother nodded, repeating the name without sound. "Her birthday's this week. Dad says I have to go."

My mother turned and her eyes fell like razors on my skin. "Of course you'll go," she said. She leaned forward, crooking her finger to draw me closer. "You'll go," she whispered, "and then you'll tell me what it's like."

"What *what's* like?"

My mother pecked her head forward, pushing my hair off my shoulder to speak into my ear. "Inside their house."

"I need a gift," I told my father.

He thought for a second, then handed me a box from a shelf in the tack room. "Here," he said. "I was gonna sell them to her mother anyway." I opened the box. Inside was a set of spurs.

"I can't take spurs to a *slumber party,*" I told him.

"Why not?" he asked. "What are you supposed to take?"

I held one hand up. "A *birthday* present," I said. "Earrings or hair barrettes or a pair of white ice skates."

My father's forehead creased. "Sheila doesn't *need* earrings or hair barrettes or a pair of ice skates," he said. "But she does need new spurs. And lucky us—we've got some. Now just wrap them up in pretty paper and they'll work fine."

I stared at him with my mouth open. It seemed like this whole slumber party thing could not possibly get any worse. And then, behind us, a woman laughed. I turned to look, and Patty Jo was standing in the doorway.

"Oh, dear." She smiled. "If ever there was someone who didn't understand the importance of a slumber party, I believe it is you, Joe." My father blushed and Patty Jo winked at me like we were in cahoots.

"If you'd like," Patty told my father, "I could take Alice and help her pick out something more suitable for the occasion."

My father smiled, his ears as pink as candy, and I felt myself shrinking between them, the box of spurs growing large between my hands. "It's okay," I told them. "These will work fine."

But my father took a step toward Patty Jo and lifted the box from my hands. "That's really nice of you," he said. He reached into his wallet and slid out a twenty-dollar bill. As he started to hand it to her, Patty Jo put her hand over his, pushing the money away.

"Please," she said. "After all the work you do for us, let me just do this."

I stood in between them, waiting. It was less than a second that they touched, less than a moment. But the air was still around us, the light dim, and I felt a sick, swimmy urge to be anywhere else, to close my eyes and see nothing, to not have known that it happened.

There was no denying that Patty Jo had taste. The necklace she chose had a silver chain that glistened against the black velvet lining of its box with a delicate silver horseshoe at the end, filled with tiny pink crystals. I never would have picked the necklace in a million years, but as soon as Patty Jo pointed, I knew that it was the perfect gift for Sheila, the thing she would have chosen for herself had she been there with us. I stood to the side while Patty paid the clerk extra to wrap the box in pink and white paper and wondered how she could possibly have such a sense of Sheila's likes when I, who probably spent more time with Sheila than anybody, would have been entirely lost on my own.

I held the present on my lap while my father drove across town to the party, tracing the delicate white bow with the tip of my finger. The houses in Sheila's neighborhood were large and white with rolling front lawns and rows of blooming flowers along the clean lines of their sidewalks. We turned onto Sheila's street and everything was lush and green. "I thought there was a drought," I said.

"Not at this end of town, I guess," my father told me. When he pulled the pickup into the driveway, my father stopped, leaning forward over the steering wheel to look up through the windshield at the house. "Jesus," he whispered.

We sat for a moment in silence, staring up at the bay windows, the white pillars on the front porch, the French doors. "Well," my father said finally. "I guess I'll see you tomorrow."

"Aren't you going to walk up with me?" I asked.

My father rapped his fingers against the steering wheel. "The grandparents are waiting," he told me. "Besides, it's you who's invited. They don't need to see me."

"It might be the wrong house," I said, and my father pointed at the mailbox where a bouquet of pink and white balloons was fastened with silver ribbons.

I looked down at my grubby green sleeping bag and my faded pillowcase. That morning, in an act of desperation, I had torn Nona's closet apart looking for something that might fit me. But where my own clothes were too small, Nona's were too large, and I made do with a combination of both, half my body loose and swimming in her sagging shirt, the other half constricted and squeezing out over the waist of my pants. "It might be nice for you to just say happy birthday," I said weakly.

My father leaned across me to open my door. "You can say it for both of us."

By the time I reached the front porch, my father was gone. I rang the doorbell and Sheila squealed when she answered, throwing her arms around my neck. "Alice, my God! I'm so glad you're here!"

"Happy birthday," I told her and held out the present. From somewhere in the background, I could hear the sound of girls laughing and screaming, strangers spinning into a party frenzy.

"You can put the present in the kitchen," Sheila said and pointed. She was flushed and breathless, holding one hand to her chest in a dramatic effort to catch her breath. "Crystal just choked Dr Pepper through her nose," she gasped. "I have to get a towel."

Sheila disappeared and I stood for a moment in the front hallway. The house spread around me in all directions, the pale peach walls stretching up into high, vaulted ceilings, the carpet plush and white beneath my feet. I started in the direction Sheila had pointed, but rooms opened into other rooms and I felt a stir of panic rise inside my throat. This was not going to end well. I was going to get lost or spill or break something. Everything inside the Altmans' house was shiny and clean, not a speck of clutter anywhere. The walls were lined with pictures of Sheila. She was on skis, wearing bathing suits on beaches, sitting beside Christmas trees, hanging upside down by her knees from a jungle gym. Mrs. Altman's whole purpose, it seemed, was to follow Sheila around with a camera, recording every single second of her clean, pretty life.

I thought about calling Sheila's name, about screaming into the winding hallways that I was lost, that I needed help. But then I rounded a corner and found myself in the kitchen. The refrigerator towered above me, silver and humming. Copper-bottomed pots and pans hung above an island in the center, and the table was piled with brightly wrapped presents. Mr. and Mrs. Altman stood beside the back door, speaking in low voices. "You didn't say anything before," Mrs. Altman told her husband.

Sheila's father held his hands up helplessly. "Night lab," he said. "I really thought I told you."

I stood for a moment, unsure whether I should leave or make my presence known. But my mouth was dry, the gift sweaty in my hands. I shrank back against the marble counter and waited for them to see me.

"It's Sheila's birthday," Mrs. Altman whispered, and from across the massive kitchen, I thought I could see her lip quivering. Mr. Altman's forehead creased, but before he could respond, his eyes lifted, catching me in the background.

"Hey there, Annie," he said and waved at me.

Mrs. Altman's eyes cut sideways into him, narrowing dangerously, and I started to back out of the kitchen. But Sheila came running up behind me, skidding on the tile floor in her pink socks. "Present goes there," she told me and pointed to the table.

I crossed the room with my head lowered, placing Patty Jo's gift on top of the others. Mrs. Altman was staring at her husband with her lips pressed thin, her eyes blinking quickly.

"Hey now," Mr. Altman said to Sheila. "It won't spoil the party if this old fogy isn't around for a while, will it?"

"Bye, Dad," she said breathlessly, then looped her arm through mine, tugging me out of the kitchen. "Come see my room."

All of Sheila's friends looked like Sheila. They sat clustered in her bedroom, fresh and smiling with straight white teeth and cheeks flushed pink with excitement. They laughed with their mouths open and screamed into their fingers, crawling across Sheila's bed and pawing through her dresser drawers as though her things were merely an extension of their own. Sheila bounded across the room to join them and I slouched against her dresser, winding my arms around myself and trying to look like I was having fun.

It wasn't hard to stay in their periphery. They talked about people I didn't know and places I'd never been. When the food came, I ate it. When they put on videos, I watched. I smiled when they smiled and laughed when they laughed. The party went on around me and it looked like I was participating in it.

For all their thrills and chills, Sheila and her friends were sound asleep by midnight. I lay beside them in the darkness, listening until every breath was slow and long. Then I lifted onto my elbows, careful not to make a sound, and peered at the clock on the VCR: 1:30. Mr. Delmar would still be awake.

I tiptoed through the nest of sleeping bags, worried that the sound of my heartbeat might wake them all. But I had spent the last hour and a half lying in the darkness, planning out what I would say if I was caught. If anyone stirred, I would say I had to go to the bathroom. I would say I was feeling sick—too much pizza. I would say that I had been so moved by Jennifer Beals's performance in *Flashdance* that I couldn't even begin to fall asleep.

I retraced my steps through the house, searching for the telephone. Two rights and a left would be the living room. One right, two lefts, the bathroom. I touched my fingers against the wall as I wound through hallways in the darkness, counting my steps, peering into shadowy doorways. When I came around the corner, the kitchen was dark except for three dim lights above the sink. Mrs. Altman stood beneath them in her bathrobe, smoking a cigarette and sipping a glass of red wine as she looked out the window onto the street.

I stood for a moment, afraid suddenly that this whole thing, the party and videos, the trip to the mall with Patty Jo, was all just a dream. Mrs. Altman didn't smoke, didn't drink, didn't wear a shabby bathrobe and stand alone in darkened rooms. Any moment now a pipe would break, a cloud would open, and the whole world would fill with water, making this night no different from any other.

But then Mrs. Altman's eyes lifted in the reflection of the window, her head tilting sideways as she saw me. "Alice?" Her voice was thick and sleepy, her face stripped clean of makeup, naked as a raw potato between the frame of her yellow hair. "Is everything all right?"

I wasn't sure. This was Mrs. Altman's house, wasn't it? And that was Mrs. Altman. But she was in a bathrobe. Her hair was messy. She was smoking a cigarette. Nothing was right.

"I was coming back from the bathroom," I said. "I got turned around."

The smoke from her cigarette swam around her head, framing her face like a blue halo in the darkness. I started to back out of the room, but Mrs. Altman crossed to the kitchen counter and patted it for me to join her. "Want a dish of ice cream?" she asked.

I glanced over my shoulder, half hoping that Sheila would suddenly appear behind me, giddy and breathless, to drag me back to her bedroom so that one of her friends could paint my toenails. But the house was silent and sleeping around us. No one was coming for me. "Thank you," I said and climbed onto a stool.

Mrs. Altman crossed to the freezer, spooning a ball of peppermint ice cream into a bowl. After she handed it to me, she leaned against the counter, inhaling from her cigarette and watching me eat. "Are you having an all-right time at the party?" she asked.

I nodded. Behind Mrs. Altman there was a humming noise and then a sudden blossoming of water outside the window as the sprinkler system came to life. "You have a really pretty house," I told her, and she smiled into her wineglass.

"We designed this house ourselves," she said. "I mean, *I* did. *I* designed it." She glanced around the kitchen at the high vaulted ceilings and clean white walls. "See the cupboards?" she told me. "They're exactly the right height for me to reach every shelf. I don't even have to stand on my tiptoes."

I licked my spoon and Mrs. Altman held out her hands, offering up the whole house. "It was how Mitchell convinced me to move to this town," she said. "The cost of living is so low, we could build our own house and have anything we wanted. Not like California."

"Did you live by the ocean?" I asked.

"We lived in Berkeley," she told me. "That's where Sheila was born."

I had no idea where Berkeley was, but I nodded as if that had answered my question.

Outside, a flash of headlights passed on the street and Mrs. Altman looked over her shoulder at the window. The car disappeared past the house and she turned back to me and took another sip of wine.

"I sometimes wonder what would have happened if we'd stayed there," she said. "What it would have been like to just live like everyone else."

I could see the tint of wine on her teeth as she spoke, a rim of purple along the inside of her lips. "I sometimes wonder what that would be like too," I told her.

Mrs. Altman's eyes lifted and her face cleared as she looked at me. Something between us felt suddenly open, stripped naked of pretending. "Alice?" she whispered. I looked into her eyes and knew before the words were spoken what the question was going to be. "What's wrong with your mother?"

The kitchen was breathing around us—the dishwasher steaming, the refrigerator humming through its huge, steely lungs. Everything inside this house was alive, functional, clean and pretty, and working the way it ought to. Everything was in its place. "She's sad," I said.

I waited for Mrs. Altman to tell me that that wasn't what she meant, that there must be something more—a reason. But she dropped her chin to her chest and nodded into her glass. "I'm sorry," she said.

"She starts crying and she can't stop," I told her. "Sometimes she cries until she can't move, until she can't stand, and my father has to carry her."

Mrs. Altman stubbed her cigarette out in the kitchen sink. "Has it always been that way?"

"Since I was born." I thought of what my father had said on the porch the day he touched my hair to see the bruises on my neck, the day we had not bred Darling to Bud Pope's stud: I was a baby who did not like to be held. My mother had handed me to my sister. She had gone upstairs. And until Jack and Ruby pulled into the driveway in their motor home, she had not come back down.

Mrs. Altman pressed her lips together, considering this. "It's like that for some women," she said after a moment. "Sometimes women get sad when they have their babies."

"Why?" I asked.

"Having a baby," she told me, "it opens something inside of you. It's almost like the world splits in two, you're so open. All different sorts of things can rush inside of you, can fill you up. Some women fill with sadness."

"Did you?" I asked, and she smiled.

"It's hard to explain," she said. "Loving something so much—you're not prepared. It's so big, so ancient and animal. It's terrifying." She made one hand into a fist and held it to her chest, showing me—*terrifying*. "It can make you feel crazy."

I thought of my mother, her fear of noise and light and people, her dreams of dead kittens.

"When I was in labor with Sheila," Mrs. Altman told me, "it was like I was someone else. There was so much pain." She took a last swallow of wine and set her empty glass on the counter. "At one point, I was looking around the delivery room for something to kill myself with."

I set my spoon in my dish. "And afterwards?" I asked. "Did you fill with sadness?"

Mrs. Altman's eyes drifted away from me, returning to that moment. "Afterwards," she said, "I filled with electricity. I couldn't stay in bed. I kept jumping out to use the phone." She held one hand to her wine-stained mouth, laughing. "It was the middle of the night, but I was calling everyone I knew, telling them, 'I had a baby! I had a baby!' The nurses kept saying, 'Mrs. Altman, you need to stay in bed.' But I couldn't hold still." She was smiling and I watched her face, waiting for her to remember that I was there. But she was somewhere else, lost and happy in the memory of a place I'd never been.

Another set of headlights crossed the window and Mrs. Altman turned to look, then pulled another cigarette from her bathrobe pocket and lit it with a tiny silver lighter.

"I didn't know you smoked," I told her as she started to inhale. Her eyes moved from the window to my face.

"Guilty secret," she said. "You won't say anything, will you?"

I shook my head. "I don't do this very often," she told me. "But still, it would worry Sheila if she knew."

Another car passed on the street and Mrs. Altman's eyes moved like lights to the window. There would be no phone call tonight. And wherever he was, maybe he was thinking about me, wondering where I was and why I hadn't called. Bad things happened, after all. People slipped and fell, went crazy with sadness, walked out the back doors of their perfect, custom-built houses and left wives and families to watch from windows, waiting for them to return. That was the problem with getting used to people—you had to miss them when they were gone.

It was nearly two in the morning when I finally slid off my stool and went back to bed, leaving Mrs. Altman in the dim light of the kitchen, smoking her lonely cigarette and rinsing my ice-cream dish under the sink.

✦ ✦ ✦

Five days after we took their foals, the milk had dried in the brood-mares' udders and they hung, sagging and crusted, from their mis-shapen bellies. The mares were on their feet now, nibbling at the sun-scorched grass and lifting their heads each time the wind shifted, searching the air for hints of their stolen offspring. On the other side of the barn, the foals huddled together in their section of the pasture, whimpering into one another's manes and refusing their hay.

"What if they never eat?" Sheila asked. She stood at the fence, whispering words of comfort to them, holding her hand between the rails to coax them toward her. The foals stayed in the far corner, exhausted from terror, frozen with grief.

"Give them time," my father told her. "When they're through with their suffering, they'll eat."

Sheila watched them through the fence, powerless to ease their pain. "You're sure?" she whispered and my father nodded.

"It's just nature."

Jack and my father had finished building the second round pen and without another project waiting, Jack turned his attention to the foals. He began filling out registration papers, pacing through the barn as he thought of names, asking suggestions from anyone who would pause to help. Sheila was particularly delighted by this task. At home each night, she wrote lists of potential names for the foals, then brought them into the barn to try them out on Jack. Her sug-gestions were absurd, but Jack listened earnestly, nodding and think-ing and taking the time to explain why each one wouldn't work.

"Skippy," she read from her list.

"Bland," Jack told her and she crossed it off.

"Angel Dream."

"Fussy."

"Secretariat."

"Taken."

"Do you think it's a good idea to let Jack name the foals?" I asked my father while we forked sawdust out of the back of his truck.

"Why not?" he said. "It keeps him busy."

"Frank Sinatra," Sheila's voice wafted from the barn. "He's my dad's favorite singer."

"What if he picks a dumb one?" I asked.

My father shrugged. "He's paying the registration fees," he told me. "He can name them Hughie, Louie, and Screwie for all I care."

Jack told my father that it was as good a time as any to geld the colts. They were still traumatized from being weaned off their mothers. They probably wouldn't even notice. My father hesitated. Gelding meant a veterinarian and a veterinarian meant money. It could wait a month or two, my father said. But Jack waved this suggestion away. He scheduled the veterinarian to come on a Saturday, when the rest of us would be at a horse show. He would stay behind to supervise.

"You sure?" my father asked.

"Ugly business, castration," Jack said. "Best the women aren't around."

My mother would sleep late and stay inside the house. Jack alone would be present to write a check when the procedure was finished. "What the hell?" my father told him. "Have at it."

At the show, Sheila and I sat inside the truck during lunch, eating the ham sandwiches Ruby had made and wrapped in wax paper. Sheila bent forward, working on her list of names with her tongue poking out the corner of her mouth. "Thunder Flash," she read.

"Lame," I said, and she made a face, then rubbed the name out with her eraser.

"I wonder how it's going back at the house," she said. "I feel really bad for the colts."

"Jack's there," I told her. "He'll look after them."

"I love your grandparents, don't you?" she asked. "Look how much they've done for the barn."

"They're kind of like Mary Poppins," I said.

"Yeah," Sheila told me and blew her bangs off her forehead. "If Mary Poppins drove an RV and smoked a lot of cigarettes." Sheila's lip curled slightly, showing her disdain of smoking. An image of Mrs. Altman in her bathrobe flashed through my mind, and I looked down, pretending to focus on my sandwich in case my face might reveal anything to Sheila.

"So your dad's a professor at the college?" I asked.

Sheila wiped the sweat from her forehead with her hand, leaving a smudge of dirt in its place. "Uh-huh," she said. "He studies stars."

"I guess he works at night a lot," I said, and she gave me an odd look.

"Well, yeah," she told me. "All the time. That's when the stars are *out*."

"It must be nice to have a dad who knows so much," I said.

"I guess." Sheila folded her list into quarters, then slid out of the truck. I scooted sideways in my seat, following her. "We've gotten to take some cool trips because of it," she told me. "But it can be a pain." She crossed to Cap, breaking the crust of her sandwich into pieces and letting him lip them off the palm of her hand. "One time we had company, and my dad made my mom and me act out an eclipse with Tupperware lids. It was so embarrassing. I wanted to die."

"How come he never comes out to watch you ride?" I asked.

"I don't know." Sheila shrugged, bored with the conversation. "He's not that into the things my mom and I like. But it doesn't really matter. He wants us to do things that make us happy. As long as we are, he doesn't worry."

"Oh," I said. I thought of Mrs. Altman with her eyes on the window, her cigarette burning between her fingers, her little glass of wine clutched to her chest. "And you are?" I asked.

Sheila turned to me over her shoulder. "Use words," she said. "And I am *what?*" I thought about saying something smart and nasty. A part of me wanted to hurt her feelings, to make her feel bad. But a bigger part wanted to know the answer.

"Happy," I said. "You and your mom, you're happy?"

Sheila rolled her eyes at me. *"Duh."*

I waited for a moment, but she was bending over her show saddle, getting ready for her afternoon classes. She wasn't going to explain further. I guessed that meant yes.

By the time we got home that evening, the vet's truck was gone. The sun was low in the sky, the air still shimmering with heat. Ruby went inside to get dinner started and check on my mother. I wanted to follow her inside, to take a cold shower and sit beneath the vent in the living room with my hair wet and clean on my neck. My mother would have heard us pull in and would be coming down the stairs, groggy from the cool air, the day of sleep. In the kitchen, Ruby would cook and my mother would sit at the table, curled like a white spider in her chair, her eyes sleepy, her head propped on her hands. I wanted to sit beside her, taking in the smell of dinner, the soft noises Ruby made while she cooked. But the horses needed to be fed and so I turned, scuffing my feet through the gravel, and followed my father into the barn.

Out back, Jack was standing next to the foals' pen. The colts stood among their half sisters, still and stupid with pain. Before we even reached the fence, my father stopped. "What happened to the other one?"

I stood on my tiptoes, counting. One of the colts was missing and I looked up at my father. Something had gone wrong. One of the colts had been ill and we hadn't known it, had been too weak for castrating, had died, bleeding and moaning, among his stronger brothers.

But when Jack turned to us, he was smiling. He pointed over our shoulders and my father and I looked. While we were gone, Jack had moved Darling from Bart's old round pen and put her into the new one. In her place stood Ginger's colt. "Alice, Jody," Jack said. "Meet your new stud."

My father's body went slack beside mine. "What?"

Jack leaned back, looping his thumbs into his pockets and grinning at us. "I've called all over the place looking for a replacement for old Bart," he told us. "Nothing came close. But this little guy—" He held his hand out. "It came to me in a dream the other night—the next generation! It's brilliant!"

My father nodded, absorbing the information. We followed Jack to the round pen. Inside, Ginger's colt looked naked and miserable without the company of his brothers and sisters. He stood with his head low, and his ears drooping. "He's sort of young to be a stud," I said.

Jack rapped his knuckles lightly on the top of my head. "He'll get older, won't he?"

My father stood with his knuckles white on the fence rail, his mouth opening and closing, trying to find the words.

"You're not happy," Jack said.

"It would have been nice to know," my father told him. "To have some input."

"Bart was a hell of a horse, Jody," Jack said. "You wouldn't have found better in ten years. I had to call in about seven favors to get him back then. And your mother just about popped her pillow when she found out how much he cost."

"How much?" I asked.

"Too much," my father said, and Jack looked at him in shock.

"Bart's bloodlines traced back to Eclipse," he said. "Open your eyes, Jody. This little guy's a legacy. You raise him up right, you could charge a thousand bucks a pop—*at least.*"

"Bart was a waste of money when you bought him, Dad," my father said. "People out here don't pay that sort of money for breeding. They wouldn't pay it for Bart and they won't pay it for his look-alike. We're not in the racehorse business."

"Well, maybe that's your problem," Jack said. "Look at Pope's place." My father's eyes narrowed. "He puts his energy into the barn, into building the reputation, and everything else comes naturally. You focus too much on the little things, Jody, and you don't see the big picture. It's always been your problem."

"Bud Pope has family money," my father said. "That's the only thing in his whole life that comes to him naturally—*money.* Everything else, he steals. Just like the rest of us."

Jack held up his hands. "Let's not get defensive," he said. "I'm just trying to help. I sent in the papers, paid the fee to register him as a stud. I'm doing you a favor."

At this, my father's head snapped up. Jack had sent in the papers. It was final, then. Ginger's colt was our new stud.

"What did you name him?" I asked.

Jack smiled and clapped me on the back. "Well," he said. "At least someone around here has brains enough to ask the right questions." Jack leaned forward onto the fence rails. "Miss Alice Winston," he said. "Let me introduce you to Royal Red Richard."

This was legacy, then. Bart's full name had been Royal Red Bart. But Ginger's colt was still small and slender, with thin legs and large, knobby knees. The name fit him like an oversize sweater. "What are we supposed to call him?" I asked. Referring to one of the horses as Richard just felt wrong.

"He's a stud," my father said, his voice gruff with the acceptance of this fact. "You won't ever need to call him."

Bart had been huge, his chest massive and gleaming, his face tight with muscle. Every part of him seemed to arch and flex when he moved, the ground trembling when he stomped, the air shivering around him as he lifted his head to call out to a mare. The colt stood trembling on the far side of the round pen, whimpering slightly through his tiny, pointed noise. He didn't look anything like a stud.

"Still, though," I said. "We ought to have something."

"You need a name?" my father asked me. "Just call him Dick." My father turned and started back to the barn.

"You'll need a name when you ride him," Jack said.

"We don't ride our studs," I told Jack, and he looked at me, shocked.

"Well, that's a real waste," he said. "Nothing worse than a useless animal." My father turned, looking at him. "Bart never looked better than when he was inside the ring."

Jack was remembering wrong, I was sure of it. My whole life, the only person in the barn who would have possibly been able to handle Bart had been my sister. And she had never been allowed. It was my father's rule that we couldn't go near the stud. Sometimes, when my father wasn't home, my sister and I would dare each other to see who could get closest to him before he turned and snorted, making us scream and run away. But she had never ridden him. I would have known if she had.

"No one ever rode Bart," I told Jack.

"That isn't true," he said, and my father's head snapped up. "Marian rode Bart."

"No way," I said, looking at my father. He seemed confused, as if trying to remember. He paused beside the fence and I could see the memory working through him, finding itself inside his mind. He nodded slowly. It was true. "Did she show him?"

Jack shook his head. "You gotta be eighteen to ride a stud in a show," he said. "She was too young. But she rode him out here. It was goddamned amazing. Do you remember that, Jody?" he asked. I turned, expecting my father to be angry, but he was smiling at the ground, remembering.

"It was beautiful," he said.

I felt suddenly misplaced between them, as if this might all be a joke, a prank to see how much I would believe. My mother could barely maneuver herself down the stairway, could barely support the weight of her head upon the white thread of her neck, could barely muster the energy to sustain a single conversation from beginning to end. And now I was supposed to believe that she had been the type of girl who would have mounted a stud—a *young* stud—and ridden his wild, springing body around the arena. I was supposed to believe that not only had she managed to stay on, but that she had done it well, had been *goddamned amazing,* had been *beautiful.* And I was supposed to believe that she did all this by choice. "Why?" I asked. "Why did she ride him?"

Jack shrugged. "Because I made her."

My father's face cleared at this, his eyes narrowing as the happy memory, the *beautiful,* evaporated from his thoughts. This was the place where he and Jack separated, where they were not going to agree on the past. "You *made* her?" I repeated.

"Your mom might seem like a frail little thing to you," Jack told me. "But she was a brilliant rider. Brilliant. The thing about Marian is that she can do anything, so long as someone tells her she has to."

My father's jaw was flexing, his lips white as chalk. "You don't even know her," he said, and Jack laughed.

"You might have married her, boy," he said, "but I taught her how to ride."

My father's face was reddening, his hands heavy at his sides. I stood back, thinking he might be about to blow. But if Jack noticed, he didn't let on. "I bet dinner's nearly ready," he told us, clapping his hands. "Probably ought to get ourselves cleaned up."

After he was gone, my father turned to me and I waited, hoping he would explain about Bart, about my mother, about anything that

Jack had just told us. "You remember the rule about studs?" my father asked finally, looking sideways at the ground.

"Not to go near," I said, and he nodded. My father followed Jack into the barn and I stood alone for a moment. Inside the round pen, Ginger's colt let out a mournful whimper and across the way, Darling crossed inside her own round pen, stretching her neck to nicker back at him. A few days ago, I had stood in the pasture with Jack while Ginger's colt and the others crowded near. There had been no reason to stay separate, no reason to be afraid. But now he had a name, a purpose, a position—his whole life decided for him. He was a stud. He would stay in this pen alone. And I would be afraid of him.

I turned and followed my father and grandfather through the barn, leaving the new stud in his new pen, alone, crying for his mother.

"Do you know anything about horses?" I asked Mr. Delmar and he laughed out loud.

"No," he said. "Do you?"

"Not really," I told him. "But there's one thing. This horse named Eclipse was, like, the most famous racehorse ever. Two hundred years ago or something. And there are still horses alive that are related to him."

"That doesn't seem impossible," he said. "Two hundred years isn't such a long time."

"It might be longer," I said. "But people have kept track, all this time. They write it down and can trace it all the way back through the fathers."

"That's a peculiar piece of information to have," he said. "But it's interesting. Strange name for a horse though—Eclipse."

"People say he was born during an eclipse," I said.

"Is that true?"

"I'm not sure," I told him. "I think I read it somewhere."

"Well," he said. "It's a good story anyway."

"Have you ever seen an eclipse?" I asked.

"Solar or lunar?"

"I don't know," I told him. "What's the difference?"

"Solar eclipses are pretty rare. The moon passes in front of the sun, and the sun disappears."

"Does it get dark?"

"Just for a minute," he said.

I thought of Sheila Altman and her mother, acting out an eclipse with Tupperware lids for a house full of company. "I'd like to see that," I said.

"Life is long," he told me. "I'm sure you will someday."

The grandparents left us with as much ceremony as when they had arrived. They said they were going, and then they went. It was evening—Jack liked to drive at night—and the barn was empty, the clients all safe in their nice homes. My mother, father, and I stood out on the porch to hug them good-bye. Ruby cried and Jack cleared his throat. Pom-Pom begged at my mother's feet.

When Ruby turned to my mother, she put her hands on either side of her face and looked into her eyes for a long moment. "You're okay," Ruby whispered and my mother closed her eyes, nodding silently. I watched without speaking, my chest tight, my throat aching.

When they were gone, my father started down the steps, then stopped, turning to my mother. He looked at her for a moment, then reached for her hand, holding it lightly in his. Her eyes were red and gleaming, but no tears slipped down her face. They stood, touching at the fingers. "Thank you," my father said and she nodded. He let her hand drop and headed down the porch steps, across the driveway and into the barn.

My mother took a deep breath, looking around the outside air. How long had it been since she had come through the back door, since she stood outside the house? For a moment she stood, seeing the land, breathing the air, and then she turned to go inside. Tonight, my father would return to the guest room, leaving the bed my parents had shared before I was born, the bed where they had made me. We would go back to eating our dinner in silence, carrying small meals upstairs that my mother would stare at without touching. Everything would be the way it had been before. "You could stay," I told her. "You could stay down here for just a while."

It was mostly pretending—I knew that. Still, it was better than telling the truth, better than letting things be the way they were. I was sure that if she looked at me, just looked at me, she would see that life was better this way, that everyone was happier. I was sure that she would understand. "You have to stay," I whispered.

But when my mother's eyes rested on mine, there was nothing inside them but sadness. "I can't," she said and leaned forward, touching her lips to the top of my head. "I'm so sorry, baby. I just can't."

nine

THREE WEEKS BEFORE school started, my father broke his leg. There was nothing spectacular or heroic about the story—he was fixing a beam in the rafters of the barn and he slipped. The doctors said that the break was one in a thousand; if he had landed any other way, it might not have broken at all. They put my father in a cast that went from toe to hip and gave him a pair of crutches. Whether the break was just that bad or whether my father never gave it a chance to heal properly, the leg would never be the same. From that point forward, my father would be able to feel the weather in his knee. From that point forward, he would never walk without a limp.

I have one memory of that morning. It's small, a few seconds maybe: My father is walking through the barn, twirling a hammer in his fingers. One of the barn cats crosses in front of him and he pauses for a moment, bending to scratch the cat at the base of her tail. She rubs against his shins, squinting her eyes up into his face through the syrupy sunlight of midmorning. My father clicks his tongue at her, rubbing her belly as she flops onto the floor. And then he stands and continues through the barn to get the ladder. After so many years, I'm not sure if the memory is real or something my mind created. But I remember it as real, and so there it is: the last time I ever saw my father walk without pain.

He was fast on crutches, gliding in long, quick strides so that I had to jog to keep up with him. Still, his frustration boiled beneath the surface, and he would often toss the crutches aside and hobble on his cast in order to have the use of his hands. Sheila and I would find the crutches propped against haystacks or splayed across the tack room floor. With my father nowhere in sight, we took turns running with his crutches through the barn and vaulting ourselves up on them so that our feet lifted off the ground.

"Your father's amazing," Patty Jo told me. In the afternoons she stood at the back of the barn, watching while my father dragged hay bales with one hand or wobbled on his broken leg to push a wheelbarrow full of sawdust. "He just won't go down."

Even with the pain, the cast, and the brutal, unwavering heat, my father could not sit still. During Sheila's lessons, he hopped on one foot across the arena as he called instructions out to her. Sheila and Cap had survived the two most recent horse shows, completing their reining classes without threatening the lives of the judges. Considering this a success, my father decided to move on to showmanship.

Showmanship, Sheila declared before her first lesson, was going to be a piece of cake. How hard could a class be where you didn't even have to *ride* the horse? I smiled and nodded, climbing onto the arena fence to get a good seat. It was Sunday, and Mrs. Altman stood beside Sheila as she haltered Cap for her lesson, smearing sunblock onto her daughter's shoulders. It was all about presenting the horse, Sheila explained to her mother. Cap was the most beautiful horse in the ring, hands down. All she had to do was groom up, lead him in, and, presto—Sheila Altman would be rolling in blue ribbons.

Half an hour into the lesson, Mrs. Altman dropped her head, letting her yellow hair fall across her lips to whisper to me, "This doesn't seem like it should be so hard."

Out in the ring, Sheila stood red-faced beside Cap, her hands shaking from concentration, her tongue poking sideways out the corner of her mouth. I put my hand over my mouth to whisper back. "It's a lot harder than it looks," I told her. "You have to get the horse to stand exactly right—to set up." In the ring, my father hopped around Cap on one foot, lifting each of his hooves and setting them down in the right position. "You see that?" I asked Mrs. Altman when my father finished. "The way Cap's feet are all lined up now? They have to be like that every time. And she has to be able to do it without touching him."

"That's impossible," Mrs. Altman whispered.

On the ground, Sheila had even less control than she did in the saddle. When she tried to make Cap trot beside her, he sank his feet into the ground, staring blankly into her face as she threw the weight of her whole body against the lead rope. When she tried to make him turn, he stepped on her feet. When she tried to make him set up, he widened his stance, shifting his weight and rolling his eyes as he dropped his sheath and sent a flood of urine splashing onto her boots and jeans. *"Fuck!"* Sheila screamed, and I stumbled backward off the fence, pretending to choke so that they wouldn't see me laughing.

"Sheila," Mrs. Altman gasped. "Apologize to Mr. Winston." But Sheila was crying too hard to hear.

"I'm so sorry," Mrs. Altman said to my father. "I don't know where she learned language like that."

My father started toward Sheila, but his cast wrenched at an awkward angle and he caught himself on the fence, wincing up at the sky. "It's okay," he said when the pain had passed. "She probably heard it out here."

Mrs. Altman stood beside the arena, wringing her hands helplessly at Sheila's sudden outburst and the ruined state of her expensive clothing. I watched my father's forehead crease as he tried to find words to comfort her, some anecdote of another client who had faced similar difficulties, then gone on to mop the floor with the competition. But there was no such anecdote. Sheila was the first of our clients to be urinated upon during a lesson.

"Well," my father said and reached for his crutches. "I guess that's probably enough for today."

For the next two days, my father hobbled through the barn with his face screwed in thought. There were only a few shows left before the season was finished and he didn't want it to end on a sour note for Sheila. "I don't think making her compete in showmanship at this point would be good for her self-esteem," he told me over dinner.

"Especially if she's covered in horse piss," I added, and my father glared at me from across the table.

"But if I don't put her in, she'll be discouraged." My father sawed at his meat with his knife, thinking.

The answer came to him in the night, and the next morning my father haltered Ace and brought him in from the back pasture. "You're not serious," I told him. "You can't put *Ace* in the ring!"

"Sure I can," he said. "It's just a local show, after all. And look at the way he stands! Sheila won't even have to do anything." At the hitching post, Ace stood with his feet aligned perfectly. But his hooves were long and scraggly, his mane and tail matted, his eyes crusted with dirt. "It will help Sheila's confidence," he told me. "At this point, I think it's more important for her to feel like she's doing well than to look good."

Sheila listened, her head cocked in confusion, when my father explained his plan to her. "It'll only be for a couple of shows," he promised. "Just until you get the feel for it."

Sheila stared at Ace with her nose crinkled. The horse's eyes were half closed, his lower lip sagging to expose a row of streaky brown teeth. "He isn't very *showy*-looking," she said finally.

"Aw, don't worry about that," my father told her, patting Ace's rump so that a cloud of dust lifted from his coat. "Alice and I'll get him all clipped and cleaned. Trust me, by the time he walks into the ring, you won't even recognize him."

And so Ace came out of retirement. Each morning, before the sun could gain too much force, Sheila would put Yellow Cap's show halter on Ace and lead him into the ring for her lesson. In the arena, Ace stood perfectly still and obedient while Sheila practiced moving around him, learning the positions. Again and again, his feet lined up evenly without Sheila having to so much as tap the lead rope beneath his chin. "See?" my father told her. "You're a natural."

Beside her, Ace's eyes dipped closed and a tiny grunting snore creaked through his lips. "I think he's asleep," Sheila said.

My father hopped forward, looking. "Oh," he said, unconcerned. "If he does that in the ring, just wait till the judge isn't looking, then give him a little poke."

Ace wasn't the only horse in our barn who had suddenly found his position altered. My father's cast made it impossible for him to ride, and, worried that Darling might backslide without a daily workout, a new plan was formulated. Bud Pope's stud had not been able to make any sort of impression on the mare, my father said. So maybe it was time to let the women have a go at it.

Out in the front pasture, the broodmares lifted their sunken heads when my father opened the gate and led Darling inside. They were all slower than she was, all heavy on their feet, misshapen by old age and the constant burden of pregnancy. But even from a distance, Darling sensed the true nature of her situation: she was not welcome here. She skittered sideways, whinnying and pacing in front of the gate.

Under normal circumstances, the broodmares were less than animated, clopping slowly across the pasture, nibbling at dried grass and swishing their tails halfheartedly at flies. But the minute Darling was released into their presence, their entire dynamic reinvented itself before our eyes. They attacked singly, two at a time, or all together, flattening their ears and baring their teeth, chasing Darling into corners where she could only cower helplessly as they turned their backs to kick.

My father stood at the fence, watching as Ginger and Sally unleashed a series of kicks into Darling's chest and shoulders. "Damn," he chuckled. "They're pretty swift for a bunch of old bats."

"Why are they being so mean?" Sheila asked, and I shook my head. Less than two weeks before, they had been flattened to the ground with pain, whimpering in grief, deadened by loss. And now they chased Darling across the arena with their tails up and their ears perked, as quick and alert as a group of yearlings.

"Horses get used to their groups," my father explained. "They don't much care for outsiders. Besides, they've had a rough month. Now they have someone to take it out on." Sheila shuddered beside me and my father balanced on his crutches to pat her shoulder. "Don't worry," he said. "They won't do any real harm to her. But they'll give her a decent workout. And they might teach her a little something about respecting her elders."

Each morning, my father would halter Darling and support himself on one crutch as he led her from the round pen. Across the way, Ginger's colt pawed and whinnied, panicking himself into a sweat at the absence of his only companion. He spent the days alone in his pen, pacing on the pencils of his legs, crying out in raspy, inconsolable misery while, on the other side of the barn, his mother chased Darling into corners.

Leaving Darling in the pasture overnight would defeat the purpose, my father explained. The broodmares would get used to her, begin to accept her presence. But removing her in the evenings kept her unfamiliar, separate, and she returned each morning as a stranger. At night, my father led her back, dirty and limping, and Ginger's colt would perk his ears at the sight of her, his small nostrils trembling. Beside the back pasture, his brothers and sisters curled together in their pen, forgetting him a little more with each passing day. But night after night, Darling came back. He would stretch his neck toward her, grasping with his pointed nose through the wide space between them, a space so wide that they would never touch. And they passed the night together, crying out from their twin pens, sharing their suffering, their isolation, through the long hours of darkness until the sun rose, soaking the sky with color, and my father returned to take her away from him.

In the front pasture, Darling didn't attempt to graze. She had given up trying to outrun the broodmares and now she merely lowered her head to them, allowing them to bite and pummel her. My father watched and called this progress. If a man had beaten the horse like that, it would have been abuse. Horses battering other horses, my father said, was just nature.

Sheila and I nodded to show that we agreed, saying that it was better this way. We looked at Ace, the sunken side of his face, his stooped hindquarters, and told ourselves that there were worse fates than a pasture full of bitter broodmares—there were guns and knives and men with hammers. There were rendering plants. And though we said all these things out loud, still we found ourselves creeping away from my father to stand at the pasture gate where we would wince at every kick, every bite, every chase that ended with Darling cowering in a corner, diminished and defenseless against the broodmares' number, their rage, their sudden position of power.

Sheila chewed on the end of her braid as she watched. "Are you excited about school starting?" she asked.

In less than a week, I would be in seventh grade. Mr. Delmar would be there. I would get to see him every day. "I guess," I said.

"Do you have a lot of friends there?"

"Tons," I told her.

Across the pasture, Darling grunted as Ginger's hooves cut into her shoulder. "You're lucky," Sheila said after a moment. "I don't have so many."

I turned to look at her, but her eyes didn't move from the pasture. "What about all those girls at your birthday party?" I asked.

"They're not always so nice to me," she said. "Sometimes they're kind of mean."

Sheila Altman had perfect skin and perfect hair. She lived in a big perfect house with her rich perfect parents. The fact that even the smallest fraction of her whole perfect life might be somehow difficult, somehow unpleasant, was just too much to believe. "What do they do to you?" I asked.

She took a deep breath. "Sometimes they leave me out. If I don't do what they want, they go to the movies and don't invite me. They don't let me sit with them in class. They make me eat lunch by myself." I could hear the muscles straining in her throat, the tears she would not shed. "Last year, they got mad at me and passed notes to everyone, telling them not to talk to me."

I didn't have a single friend at school and ate lunch every day at a table by myself. The only real friend I had ever had was dead, and on top of that, the friendship was a lie. But no one at school ever went out of her way to be mean to me. No one had ever passed a nasty note with my name inside. "Oh," I said, because I didn't know what else to say.

"It turned out okay, though," Sheila told me. "After the note thing happened, that's when I started taking lessons out here. My mom thought it would be good for me to do something that didn't have anything to do with my friends, to have something that was just *mine*."

I nodded. Sheila Altman was going to win or not win. My father could devote his entire life to her, could work with her until they were both old and gray. The rich friends he dreamed of were never going to come here, never going to sign up for lessons or exchange their parents' money for the show saddles that had spent the summer gathering dust in the tack room. Sheila Altman had never been the girl who was going to save us.

"School starts next week," Sheila said miserably. "And I just wish this summer could go on forever."

The sun still beat down upon the land without any promise of rain or relent. But even so, the sun was beginning to rise later and set earlier. School would start and the show season would end, taking the last of summer with it. No amount of wishing on Sheila Altman's part was going to make it different.

Sheila turned to me, her expression stripped and dangerous. "I think it's sinful what Joe's doing to that mare," she said, and the frost of her blue eyes cut straight through mine. It was the first time she had ever spoken out against my father, the first time she had shown anything but blind adoration for him or anything he did.

"He has to break her," I told Sheila. "He *has* to." She stared blankly as I spoke, her opinion unwavering. "You know how much worse it could be," I reminded her. "Whips and chains and hammers. This is just *nature*."

In the pasture, Darling stumbled to her knees, then heaved herself up on her trembling legs. A fresh ribbon of blood streaked across the white of her hip, but Sheila watched without flinching. "Pain is pain," she told me. "I don't care who causes it."

That night, I watched my father sort through his white envelopes at the table. His cast was propped on the chair beside him and he drummed his fingers on the table, cursing under his breath as he scribbled numbers onto scraps of paper. Darling was not broken and Sheila was not winning. The show season was nearly over and with his broken leg, my father would not be able to train the young horses. A cold wave of fear churned inside my stomach. But when my father saw me watching, his face cleared and he swept the empty envelopes into a pile with his arm.

"Got a call yesterday from a guy," he said. "Daughter wants to start riding lessons. They're coming out tomorrow to have a look."

"She's going to start lessons here?" I asked. Another Sheila Altman, she would begin bright and hopeful, shining with the money of her parents, with all the hopes and promises my father gave her. And then, she would fall. She would lose. She would turn one day to look at my father and she would say the word: *sinful.* How long after that before she saw the rest? One day, she would look around and see all the fabrications and inconsistencies, she would see us for what we were: thieves and liars. One day, not so terribly far in the future, she would decide that life must be better someplace else and, saving herself, she would leave.

My father stuffed the empty envelopes back into their drawer, then slammed it shut, all his problems disappearing. "It'll be great," he said. "They sound really excited."

But the next day when their silver car pulled into our driveway, nothing about the family seemed the least bit excited. The father walked around the front of the car to open the door for his wife, who dipped her head forward, surveying the barn over the rim of her smoky sunglasses. The parents stood beside their car for a moment, looking around at the dead grass in our yard, the broodmares whaling on Darling in the pasture, the bald knobs of my ankles poking out beneath the cuffs of my pants, and they exchanged a doubtful glance. The daughter was young, seven or eight, and she climbed out of the backseat and wrinkled her nose at her parents. "This place smells like horse poop."

They followed me through the barn with their arms crossed over their chests, keeping close together as though they were frightened that they might catch something. Inside the ring, Sheila was working with Ace on showmanship, and my father glided toward the edge of the arena on his crutches, leaning over the fence to shake the parents' hands.

"Joe Winston." He grinned and the couple introduced themselves.

"Little Katie here's awfully excited to start riding," the father said. The daughter was standing beside him with her arms looped behind her back. She looked over at the foals, still thin and gangly, but no longer the adorable babies that might have sent little Katie rushing to coo at them only a month earlier. She glanced over her shoulder at the round pen where Ginger's colt stood, stained with sweat and dirt, whimpering mournfully.

"Why is that little horse all by himself?" she asked, and my father's smile tightened.

"Well," he said after a minute. "We're really glad that you wanted to come by."

A year ago, this would have been the point when my sister led Yellow Cap into the ring, riding him in slow, even circles, taking him over jumps, tossing her honey-colored hair so that it shimmered in the sunlight. The parents would have stood back to watch while their daughter climbed onto the fence, gaping. What little girl wouldn't want to be like Nona?

But now, Sheila Altman stood in the arena, tapping at Ace's front foot with the toe of her boot to make him set up properly. The parents' faces stiffened as they took in his flea-bitten coat and stooped hindquarters, the concave curve of his disfigured head.

"My daughter has been around horses her whole life," my father said finally, gesturing to me with the rubber tip of his crutch. "And she gets real good grades."

So it had come to this. My good grades were now the only thing we had to offer, the only halfhearted promise my father could make. The parents looked down at me and I nodded to show that it was true. "Straight A's," I added, trying to help. They smiled politely.

"What do you think, Kates?" the father said to his daughter.

Little Katie turned a slow circle, taking in the barn, the pasture of Old Men, the grungy cast on my father's leg, and the arena where Sheila Altman stood sweating in her T-shirt. "I liked the other place better."

That was that. They climbed back into their silver car. And before it could even begin, it had ended.

"I never got around to the reading list," I confessed.

That night, I'd cleaned out my backpack and found it there: a scrap of yellow paper scrawled with his handwriting, all the books I hadn't read, the good intentions lost inside the stretch of phone calls and horse shows and endless days of sweltering heat. "I meant to read them," I said. "Really, I did."

"Don't worry about it," Mr. Delmar said, the exhale of his cigarette hissing through his teeth. "The list is bullshit." Inside Nona's closet, my body hummed with electricity. *Bullshit.* In a few short days, school would start. And what would happen then? Who would we be to each other? I had heard him swear, had heard him smoke and drink and talk about God. I would be different from my classmates, from all the girls who had spent their summers swimming and tanning and taking family vacations, from all the little people who sat in their little desks. I would be special.

"I've liked the poetry," I said. It was a partial truth. I didn't really listen to the poems he read, didn't try too hard to understand them. What I liked was the sound of his voice as he spoke the words, the spaces between them—not here, not there, but somewhere separate and secret and private, a place that only belonged to him, a place he let me visit.

"I'll tell you one thing," he said. "You won't find those poems on any middle school reading lists." I thought of all the English classes I had taken, the vocabulary quizzes and spelling tests, the books they made us read a chapter a night—blind girls and boys who lived in trees.

"I don't really get the books we read in school," I admitted. "They seem pretty dumb."

"Those books are a total waste of time," he told me. His voice was thick and I wondered suddenly if I had awakened him, if he had dragged himself from bed to answer my call, to hear the sound of my voice. To talk to me.

"Why do they make us read them?"

"Somebody made them read those books when they were young," he said. "So now they make you read them. America," he snorted, "is a country completely void of imagination."

"You've just been living in the desert too long," I told him. Weeks earlier, I had asked where he was from and he told me Michigan.

Since then, I'd imagined it as a state full of green, flowering trees and sweet-smelling grass. I had looked it up on a map: Michigan, nestled at the top of the country, reaching its fingers toward Canada—a state filled with water.

"It's the same everywhere," he said.

"I don't believe you," I said.

"What happened to culture?" he asked. "To greatness?" Through the phone, there was a clatter, the sound of glass breaking on the floor beneath him. But he didn't pause or explain, didn't seem even to notice. "Where's John Wayne?" he asked. "Where's Elvis?"

I wasn't sure what we were talking about anymore, what any of this had to do with imagination or reading lists. "They're dead," I told him.

"Amen," he said.

John Wayne, Elvis, all the men who had written all the poems I didn't quite listen to—they had died before I was even born. Maybe greatness had died too, maybe the whole country was just a big, empty graveyard of forgetting. And maybe, if the wide-open nothing had always been your home, you couldn't feel bad about it. Maybe you couldn't even imagine that there had ever been anything more.

"The world is ruined," he told me. "And no one even cares."

The whole conversation felt suddenly dangerous and forbidden. When he read to me, my body became quiet in its center, my mind smooth and sleepy. But now pinpricks of uneasiness were rising on the back of my neck, a cold, clammy soup churning inside my stomach. I had been born too late, missed too much. The world was ruined. And it was the only one I had ever known. "I care," I whispered.

On the other end of the line, he was silent. "Then maybe there's hope," he said finally.

I nodded without speaking. Caring was not enough, not nearly. Things went on as they always had. In the front pasture, the broodmares beat the show mare, shrinking her, changing her. It was not out of cruelty or anger or greed. They beat her because they could, because they were animals, because it was their nature. We allowed it, encouraged it, used it to our advantage. And then, Sheila Altman had watched with the pure, unclouded vision of her perfect blue eyes and given it a name: *sinful.*

"There ought to be more," I told him.

"More than what?" he asked.

"Caring," I said. "Grace. There ought to be so much more than that."

"Jesus," he said. "You listen to everything I say. I'll have to be more careful."

"If grace is the only thing out there to hope for, if no one's even paying attention, then what's the point?" I asked him. "Why does anyone bother with anything?"

"If you figure out the answer to that," he told me, "I want to be the first person you tell."

"You'll be the only person."

The next day, my father came home with a school bus. He parked it in front of the barn, then hopped down the steps on one leg, reaching behind him for his crutches. "What's that?" I asked, and he looked at me like I was simple.

"A school bus."

"What's it doing here?"

"New gig," my father told me. "Just for a while."

My heart hiccupped in my chest. The bus was as big as a billboard, a giant, hideous heap in front of our barn. There was no way to hide it, no way to lie it away. He would drive it around town, sit behind the wheel in school parking lots. No one would assume he was doing it for fun. Everyone who knew us would understand: we needed money.

He started into the barn and I jogged to keep up. "Can you drive a bus with a broken leg?" I asked.

"Sure," he said.

"I mean, are you supposed to?"

"Oh," he said. "I knew the guy—he owed me a favor."

"What guy?" I asked.

My father turned, cocking his head at me. "A posse guy," he told me. "You got any more questions, or can I get back to work?"

I shook my head. There was nothing more to ask, nothing more to say. It was already done. If one posse member knew that my father had taken a job driving a school bus, the rest would know by the end of the week. They would tell their wives. They would tell their children. My stomach shrank into a stone as I pictured the wicked grins of the Pope twins. I could hear their nasally laughter inside my head, could feel the nasty jokes already forming inside their wormy little minds. *The wheels on the bus go round and round . . .*

"I won't ride in it!" I called after my father and he shrugged without turning.

"Okay."

Back inside the barn, I forked halfheartedly at the dirty straw in Heathcliff's stall. I pictured my father driving a bus full of my classmates, swerving around cars that moved too slowly and cursing out the window at people who cut him off. School had always been bearable because no one really paid attention to me. No one knew who I was. But now I imagined my father letting the school bus get low on gas, as he did with our pickup, then gunning the ignition to find a gas station before it ran out completely, driving up on curbs and running stoplights until the bus flipped over, killing everyone inside. I would be Alice Winston, the girl whose father murdered the middle school. Alice Winston, the girl whose father drove a bus.

When I heard Patty Jo's car grumble into the driveway, I ducked behind the door of Heathcliff's stall, not wanting to have to explain the bus. Her boot heels clipped across the barn floor and she paused just on the other side of the door. "Are we hosting a field trip today?" she asked.

I held my breath, unsure if she was directing the question at me or the barn in general. Before I could think how to answer, my father's voice did it for me. "New gig," he said, and I crouched lower onto the ground, afraid they might suddenly see me and I would have to explain why I was hiding.

"How awful." Patty laughed. "Why on earth would you do something like that?"

There was a moment of silence before my father answered. Through a crack in the stall door, I could see their feet, my father's cast tinged gray with dirt, the shine of Patty Jo's pointed cowboy boots, the stitched hem of her perfectly creased blue jeans. "Show season's ending," he said finally. "Leg's busted. Got bills to pay." It had not been there when he spoke to me. But now, in front of Patty Jo, there it was, deep and raw in the low whisper of his voice: shame.

My father shifted his weight on the rubber tips of his crutches and Patty inched backward on her heels. "God," she said. "I'm such a bitch."

"No," my father said quickly. "It's a joke. Pay's for shit. But it's just something to get us through a month or two. It's temporary."

"We don't pay you enough," Patty said. "The girls and I—you work so hard, do so much. We should pay more."

My breath froze in my chest. This was the answer, the solution, the way out. But instead of encouraging the suggestion, my father sighed with resignation. "This is the business," he said, "feast or famine. Well, famine or worse famine, anyway."

Patty rocked forward on her toes. "Do you ever think about walking away?" she whispered.

"Selling the place?" my father asked. She didn't answer and he moved sideways on his crutches, sinking down into the folding chair and dropping his hands between his knees so that I could see the tips of his fingers curling into his palms. "This is all I've ever done," he said. "It's the only thing I'm good at."

"You're lucky then," she said, and my father laughed.

"You're the first person to call me that."

"I'm serious," she said, and he stopped laughing. "To know that there's something you're good at, it's a real gift. I've never had that."

"You're a decent rider," my father said, stretching his legs forward so that they were only inches away from the toes of Patty's boots.

"There was this place my family used to go in the summers," Patty Jo said. "They had horses and that's all I did, all day every day. Jumping was my favorite."

"No kidding," my father said. "I wouldn't have taken you for a jumper."

"I've always been small," Patty Jo explained. "The boys I dated as a girl, they wanted to sit me on their laps, carry me around. My parents always worried about me, always kept me closed away like a little doll. But that feeling when you're jumping—it's like flying, like freedom. My whole life, all I ever wanted was a horse. I begged my parents. And then I begged my husband. He thinks I'm crazy." She laughed. "Maybe I am. I'm sure I sound that way."

On the other side of Heathcliff's stall, I waited for my father to make his excuses and rise, to move away from her. Being small was not the same thing as being poor, and I waited for him to lose his patience and say so. Patty Jo owned a champion horse that she groomed without showing. My father drove a school bus. They might as well have lived on different planets.

"That's how it was for my wife," my father said, and my hands went dead at my sides. If there was one subject that was off-limits with clients, with strangers, with anyone who did not share our last name and most of those who did, it was my mother. "People were always wanting to pet her and carry her around. But on a horse, she was large, powerful. She couldn't stay away."

"Why did she stop riding?" Patty asked.

A long silence followed, something secret and hidden, a world that no one had ever shared with me. And though I could only see their feet, I could feel the connection passing between them. If I had been able to see their faces, I was sure I would have seen it too, would have understood the thoughts they shared, the words they left unspoken.

"You can't blame yourself," Patty said quietly. "No one can be entirely responsible for another person's disappointment."

Her words seemed to pull all the air from the barn until the space around me filled with warm, dead nothing, and my breath turned stale in my lungs. Through the crack of the stall door, I watched Patty Jo's foot slide forward, the glossy triangular toe of her boot stopping just before it met the grubby heel of my father's cast.

And nothing happened. I watched and waited as they stood on the other side of the door, not speaking, not touching, until the moment was finished and they went their separate ways.

The next morning, my father woke up early and hauled the jumps out of the front office, where Jack had once seen his patients. By the time I came outside, he was already in the arena, hopping on one foot as he dragged the jumps across the ring in pieces. We had not had the jumps out since Nona left. Sheila was still eons away from being able to negotiate Cap over fences. There was simply no point.

But when Patty came out that day, she looked into the arena and her mouth crept up into a secret smile. "What an odd coincidence," she said, and my father shrugged.

"Thought that horse of yours might be getting a little bored with ground work," he told her.

My father didn't usually let other people ride in the arena while he was giving lessons, but Patty Jo worked with Toy Boy, taking him over the jumps while Sheila practiced showmanship with Ace, and my father didn't object. Slowly, he began making suggestions to her, turning away from Sheila to give Patty little tips, to point out flaws in the way she held her hands or prompted Toy Boy forward.

Soon, he'd abandon Sheila altogether. "That horse is a fucking *jumper*!" my father whooped as he watched, and Patty Jo beamed.

It was true. Toy Boy was sleek and muscled, arching himself over the jumps as if they were nothing at all. And though Patty rode well, with clean lines and a good seat, the horse's skills were clearly beyond her own. "You have to trust him," my father told her, resting his hand on her knee so that her face turned pink. "Close your eyes. Turn your face sideways as you take each jump." He slid his hand up the length of her thigh. "Just *feel* him beneath you. *Believe* that he will get you over it."

I sat on the fence and watched as Patty and Sheila waited their turns for my father's attention, nodding reverently at everything he said, revolving around him like planets.

"Is Patty Jo taking lessons now?" I asked my father at dinner.

"I'm helping her out," he said.

"But she's not paying."

"I'm just giving her a few pointers is all."

I looked up at the ceiling and pretended to think.

"What?" my father asked.

"Oh," I said. "I was just wondering how that must make Sheila feel. Here she is, *paying* for every little thing, and Patty Jo gets pointers for free. I hope she doesn't say anything to her mom."

The truth was that Sheila didn't even seem to notice Patty Jo in the ring, much less care that she was there. Sheila's focus was entirely on Ace, her forehead creased, her cheeks burning with concentration. The last thing Sheila would ever think about was money—who was paying for what and how much.

My father gave me a look across the table, and my cheese sandwich turned to cement inside my mouth. "Business is like a game, Alice," he said, and his head dipped forward, his spine curving in a moment of exhaustion. "Everyone has their own set of rules."

Advanced English was a small class—there were only thirteen of us. On the first day, Colleen Murphy took a seat beside Janice Reardon, who leaned forward and shielded her mouth with her hands as though she was about to whisper. But when she asked, "Are you doing all right?" her voice was loud enough that I could hear from all the way across the room.

I squinted from my desk, trying to find the marks on Colleen's neck and wrists. But I couldn't see anything wrong. Her attempt at suicide hadn't even left scar tissue.

I looked around the classroom while I waited for the bell to ring. The picture on Mr. Delmar's desk—the woman by the waterfall—was gone. When he walked into the room, I lowered my eyes, letting my hair fall in front of my face. That morning, I had dressed in a combination of my own clothes and Nona's. I sat in my desk feeling crooked and unbalanced, parts of myself bursting at the seams while others hung like twigs in sacks.

When he called roll, Mr. Delmar read my name off the roster like I was anyone else, and I answered without lifting my eyes. I wasn't sure what was supposed to happen now. We had a secret. We knew something that no one else did. Pretending otherwise made my heart flutter in my throat and my blood turn to ice. Perhaps now that school had started, things would have to be different. Certainly he would not be able to stay up so late into the night, his voice lazy, his laughter easy on his tongue. There would be a schedule. There would be rules.

But that night when I called, he answered as if nothing had changed.

As long as we were at school, we stayed apart, avoiding each other's gaze. And yet, through the drapery of my hair, I could sometimes catch him watching me in the classroom. In the cafeteria, I could feel his eyes find me in the crowd. I knew his whistle—could hear him coming around a corner or passing in the hall outside my classrooms.

At home, I labored over every English assignment. When he handed back the homework, I waited until I was outside before I scanned the paper for comments. Every red checkmark felt like a knife slash across my throat. I imagined him grading, seeing the error, and thinking of me as a stupid girl, a poor speller, a person who mixed her modifiers. And then I would want to kill myself.

But on the phone, we never mentioned school, never brought up the fact that we had seen each other just hours before, that he had spilled coffee on his shirt or that I had stumbled over the pronunciation of *hyperbole* when it was my turn to read aloud. In this way, we inched forward. I kept calling. He kept answering. And though inside my head, I couldn't think that we were doing anything wrong, someplace deep inside my core felt dark and clenched with fear. In some way I could not name, we weren't playing by the rules. Eventually, there would have to be a price.

Walking home after school, the canal was empty beside me, dried like bone from the drought. I was struck at the blankness of the canals without water, the sand and grass and shallow slopes. With every shift of wind, the weeds rustled around me, inhaling the desert air like lungs, whispering along the banks of the canals. There were no white shadows, no lonely ghosts. But still, I felt her watching me, judging me, knowing that I had crossed, uninvited, into a place that had once been hers alone. "Go away," I whispered during my walk. "There's nothing here that belongs to you."

"Do you think she's pretty?" my mother asked.

"Who?" I had been sent upstairs to check if my mother was hungry, to see if she needed anything. But now I stood and watched while she sat in the window. Ever since Jack and Ruby had left, my mother had stayed upstairs. My father had returned to the guest room and my mother had slipped back into her world of silence, her world where nothing happened and nothing changed. But even this world was not safe. My mother had a window. And it didn't seem that she could keep away from it.

"The rich woman," my mother said without turning away from the window. "The one he's teaching to jump."

The sun streamed through the window, filling my mother's hair so that it glowed like melted chocolate. Patty Jo was pretty, I thought, with a bright, animated face and clothes that smelled like the women's magazines Nona sometimes stole from the dentist's office. My mother was younger, with smooth, pale skin and a delicate jaw-line. But her frailty and isolation wavered just below the surface, dulling her, fading her slowly away. Patty Jo burned like a flame in comparison to my mother, her life force leaping from within, her laughter like music. *Pretty* had nothing to do with it.

"She's okay," I said. "She pays a lot to keep her horse here."

"He spends more and more time with her."

Out in the arena, Patty Jo turned her face sideways as my father had instructed and Toy Boy sailed easily over the jump. My father cheered and Patty Jo held up one hand, waving like a beauty queen as she and Toy Boy cantered a victory lap around the ring.

"It's just a game," I whispered, and my mother turned from the window, her eyes searching mine for an explanation I couldn't give her. Once upon a time, my father said, my mother had wanted to be powerful. She'd ridden and competed and won. And then one day, she'd stopped.

Suddenly, I wanted to remember her, the way she looked at this instant—the sun gleaming in her hair, the soft, lineless curve of her neck. I tried to burn her image into my mind, so that years later, I would be able to recall it. So that I could see her there before me as I did now, the fragile, transient state of her beauty, and remind myself of who she was, of who she might have been had she lived in any world except for this one.

✦ ✦ ✦

We pulled into the Posse Grounds on the day of the second-to-last show with a full horse trailer. In addition to Yellow Cap and Darling, whom my father still brought along every week to attract a crowd, that morning he'd loaded Ace and Toy Boy into the trailer as well.

My father said that Toy Boy was a champion, and that Patty Jo was depriving the horse of his basic rights by keeping him out of the show ring. Patty could win her division with her eyes closed, my father had told her. And though I hadn't expected her to agree, Patty Jo said that the competition might be fun. She'd ridden in a few shows as a girl. She said they were full of *camp.*

The rest of the Catfish came to the show to support Patty Jo. They followed Mrs. Altman and me to the bleachers, carrying along their little thermoses and stacks of paper cups. When they offered one to Mrs. Altman, her spine stiffened and she said, "No, thank you."

Up in the bleachers, the Catfish laughed and drank and leaned their heads into one another's shoulders to point out anything that might be campy. *"Bolero ties,"* Jaycee chuckled to Bitsy as she pointed to a couple of men sitting near us. "That's fucking *hilarious.*"

Mrs. Altman's cheeks flushed pink at the language and she angled her body away from them, directing her attention to the side of the arena where Sheila stood with Ace, preparing for her first showmanship class.

Over the past few days, my father and I had groomed Ace until I thought his skin might fall away under the pressure of our brushing. We conditioned his mane and tail, clipped his whiskers, and patted baby powder into the spots on his flanks so that they would look white instead of dingy gray. Even with all our work, Ace was still what he was: an old horse who had once been beaten half to death with a hammer.

That morning, Sheila had braided his mane and tied the ends with pink ribbons, then haltered him in the show halter the Altmans had bought for Yellow Cap. It was dark, polished leather with silver studs that caught like jewels in the sunlight. But it sagged from Ace's misshapen skull, the studs ridiculous and misplaced against the flea-bitten gray of his coat.

Inside the ring, Ace clopped along obediently beside Sheila, setting up without being asked and holding his position while she moved around him for the judge. "Damn," Bitsy breathed beside me. "That's one *ugly* horse."

Ace might have been the ugliest horse in the ring, the ugliest horse in the world, but he set up as well as any seasoned show horse, following along beside Sheila without a hitch as she led him through the walking pattern. In the end she took second, placing between Zach and Andy Pope, whose mouths dropped into mirrored caves of shock when they realized they'd been split apart by Sheila.

Mrs. Altman and I stood in the stands, cheering and clapping, bobbing our heads beside each other in a spontaneous dance of happiness. This was the first time Sheila had placed above fifth. Of course, she started crying.

Outside the ring, she cried onto my father's shirt when he hugged her. She cried into her mother's hands, into her own shirtsleeves, into the braids she'd tied in Ace's mane. She cried on my shoulder and on the red ribbon she'd been awarded as she exited the arena. "This is the happiest moment of my entire life," she sobbed. The rest of us stepped sideways as Mrs. Altman snapped a series of pictures with her tiny camera, saving the moment for her absent husband, making it last forever.

During the lunch break, I stood beside my father while he saddled Toy Boy for Patty Jo's jumping class. Patty had been too nervous to saddle the horse herself and had instead climbed the bleachers to join the Catfish for a last-minute drink. "Darling seems pretty calm today," my father said.

"I guess so," I told him. She stood tied to the trailer, head bowed under the heat. We had not bothered to wash or groom her and her coat was grungy and stained with blood and sweat and hoof prints.

"I was thinking you might like to ride her in the reining class," he told me.

I stared at him. I didn't show. Not ever. Nona showed. I cheered.

This was the way it had always been, the way it was always supposed to be. "Well, I wouldn't," I told him.

"It'll be a piece of cake," my father continued. "I promise, if it was a big deal, I wouldn't ask you to do it."

My heart sank, small and shrunken inside my chest, a useless pea pod of a thing. "We just need to get her used to the ring, and I can't do it. You'll be in there by yourself. Just trot her through the pattern. You don't have to do well—you don't even have to canter her if you don't want to. It's just so she can get a sense of the ring."

I took a step back and my father began leading Toy Boy toward the arena where Patty was waiting, wringing her hands with nerves. Mrs. Altman came up beside me, her face still gleaming from Sheila's win.

"Is everything all right?" she asked, and I nodded without answering. I was afraid that if I said even a single word, my heart would freeze into stone and there would be nothing left of me at all.

Patty Jo rode well inside the ring. From the stands, I could see her dropping her vision to take the jumps, closing her eyes or glancing sideways, letting Toy Boy do the work as my father had instructed her during Sheila's lessons.

He had been right, my father. Toy Boy was built for jumping, sleek and sculpted, easy with the task. Like Sheila, Patty Jo also took second place. But this time, it was the Catfish who stood in the stands, screaming and cheering, kicking their feet in a choreographed dance. "That's our *girl*," Bitsy hollered beside me. "That's our little winner!"

I moved through the rest of the day like a dead person, the minutes ticking toward the end. In the late afternoon, Mrs. Altman helped me change in the back of the trailer, putting my hair into a French braid, then pinning it up at the base of my neck. She smoothed the stray wisps of my hair behind my ears and I steadied myself on the side of the trailer as a fresh wave of nausea rose in my throat. "Are you all right?" she asked and I nodded without answering. "It's the heat," she told me.

I started out of the trailer and Mrs. Altman took my hand. "Alice," she said. "You don't have to do this if you don't want to."

I looked up at her, her wide mother-eyes and heart-shaped face, and wondered what it might be like if that were true. What it might be like to live in a world where there were trips and vacations, where acting out an eclipse with Tupperware lids was the worst sort of trauma and your parents bought you a horse when people were mean to you at school. It was hard to believe that Mrs. Altman lived only on the other end of town. Her world was so far away from mine.

"I could speak with your father if you wanted," she offered, and I shook her hand away. The mare would kill me in the ring before I let my father hear from Mrs. Altman that I was too scared to ride her.

"I'm fine," I told her. "It's not a big deal."

When I turned around the corner of the horse trailer, my father and Patty Jo were unsaddling Toy Boy, their fingers overlapping on the girth strap. I stood, waiting for them to see me, for my father to drop his hand, to pull away, but his eyes stayed locked on Patty's. I started to say that I was ready and that we might as well get it over with. But before I could speak, Patty lifted my father's hand to her mouth, pinching the tip of his index finger between her teeth.

The fear that had been humming through my veins suddenly turned cold and silent. Patty Jo saw me and froze, my father's wrist light in her fingers, the pad of his finger on her tongue. My father followed her gaze and the three of us stood, unmoving, unblinking.

"Alice," he said, and drew his hand away from Patty's, pushing his fingers up through his hair.

"I was just showing your father my ribbon," Patty said and flashed a mouthful of perfect white teeth.

"Second place," my father said with forced brightness. "Not too shabby for a first-timer, right?"

As the reining class began, Patty and Mrs. Altman joined the Catfish in the bleachers. I stood beside my father, empty and unbalanced on my feet. The moment was over and I wondered now if I had imagined it. My father didn't look at me, didn't try to explain, didn't apologize. He helped me mount Darling, then stood in front, holding the reins, keeping her steady. One by one, the other riders entered the ring and went through the motions of the pattern. "See?" my father kept saying. "It's nothing."

And I watched. The other riders loped through the pattern, their horses slow and sleek with show training. But I could feel Darling beneath me, her ribs warm against my legs. I tried to make my mind focus on the pattern—the spins and circles, the sliding stop at the end.

My father spoke to me in a low voice as the other riders went, but I couldn't concentrate on his words. "Everyone else is doing simple lead changes," he told me. "So don't feel like you have to do anything fancy." *Small circle to the right, lead change.* "You don't even have to take her above a trot if you don't want to." *Small circle to the left, lead change.* Sheila came out and the gate was open into the length of the empty arena. "Okay," my father said. "Just take her through it. All you have to do is stay on."

I turned my head to the bleachers and Mrs. Altman made a double thumbs-up at me. Patty sat beside her, blank and smiling—*I was just showing your father my ribbon.* My father let go of the reins and I felt the tension in Darling's steps, the spring of her knees, the lightness of her feet on the ground as we walked under the covered arena. The gate closed behind me and I was on my own.

As soon as the open space of the arena stretched before us, I could feel the mare's body tighten beneath me. And then I knew it: the broodmares, the kicks and bites and days of beatings—none of it had worked. She was not smaller, not meeker. She had endured them, just as she had endured the days she spent tied up in the sun. She was nobody's pet. There would be no trotting. Her mother was a racehorse and she was going to run. Everything came back to bloodlines.

The mare would run and I would not be able to stay on. She would throw me, stomp me, kill me. There would be pain. I waited a moment, waited for the fear, the dread. But it didn't come. If this was it, my moment to die, then it was. The world was ruined. So be it.

I don't remember touching my heels to her sides, don't remember loosening the reins. I only thought the word inside my head: *Go.* And her body sprang beneath me.

The speed knocked me out of myself. For a moment, I was afraid she had leapt out from underneath me, leaving me to watch from the far side of the arena. I felt myself slipping back over the saddle, losing myself in the blur around me. The speed stole my breath, my vision, any control I'd ever thought I had. It was gone. All of it. It was over. I was over. So be it.

But then I saw it—the point between her ears where the world was still in focus, the place where we were seeing the same thing. Everything else turned into pounding: hooves, heart, fear, speed. The dust rose from the ground beneath, and my legs fused to Darling's sides. In that moment, we were a single body—destined to crash, destined for death. I felt the tuck in my own spine as she spun, the dig of the single point of her hoof as we lifted and rotated around it, the sky and earth and bleachers bleeding into smears around us. In my head, I counted—*one, two, and a half*—and we lifted, springing toward the other side of the arena. In the center, we turned and my stomach rolled into my chest as she shifted beneath me, changing her lead in midair, coming down on her opposite foot in one single, breathless motion. As we came around the arena I felt the speed swell inside myself and I let her go, let it all go. There was nothing left except the point between her ears, the core of her body clenched beneath mine. Through the blur of dust and heat, I saw the end of the fence approach before us and I thought we might crash straight through, might rise over the top and lift into air, into flight, into whatever came in the moments when life ended and the next thing began.

The word appeared behind my eyes: *Stop.* And we sank. Her hind feet glided through the dust like sled blades through snow. The dust rose in clouds around us. And it was over.

The world came back from the inside out. Heartbeat, breath, dust, judge, audience. There was a moment of silence and then an explosion of sound, cheering, the Catfish standing in the bleachers, doing their little dance, while Mrs. Altman bounced beside them, clapping her hands above her head.

My tongue was dry and coated with dust, my lips stuck over my teeth so that I had to work my jaw to free them. I turned Darling toward the gate where the Pope twins hung from the fence with their mouths gaping open. Beside them, my father hopped up and down on his good leg, waving one crutch above his head and slapping the metal rail of the fence with his free hand. "That's my kid," he whooped. "That's my *baby*!"

And after that, it was a whole different game.

ten

THE NEXT DAY, the rain started. The winds began in the morning, the sky darkening over the blue mountains to the east, sinking under the weight of itself in long, dark fingers that reached toward the ground. By noon, the horizon had vanished behind the mass of gray clouds and the air shivered with a sweet, damp chill. We were all inside the barn when the rain began to strike the roof like handfuls of pebbles, deafening the world beneath.

At first, we rushed outside to stand underneath, shocked and silenced by the downpour. The Catfish toasted with their little paper cups and Sheila and I linked arms, skipping around the driveway while the water flattened our hair to our skulls and soaked through our clothing. My father hobbled out on one crutch, then stood, looking up at the sky and wiping the water from his face with his hands. "Don't stop," Sheila sang as she danced circles around me, stretching her palms up toward the clouds. "Don't *stop*."

And it didn't. The earth swallowed and swallowed until it could hold no more, until the land turned to liquid and the roads ran like rivers. Basements flooded. The water crept into the barn, soaking through bags of grain and pooling on the concrete floor. Sheila and I jumped through the puddles, splashing brown water onto each other's legs while my father used brooms and shovels to try and push it back outside. Out in the pastures and pens, the horses sank to their ankles in mud, dipping their hindquarters and lowering their heads beneath the pelting water.

The school flooded, first the gymnasium and then the library, so that we had to keep rerouting ourselves around the oncoming water. When the electricity went out, advanced English lit candles and sat in a circle on the floor, while Mr. Delmar read a short story aloud about a planet where it rained all the time and the sun shone only once every seven years. At the end, Janice Reardon broke out weeping. "I'm just so *sensitive!*" she gasped through her hiccups and Colleen patted her head like she was a dog.

"On that note," Mr. Delmar said, "why don't we call it a day. I don't think they can keep you here without electricity. Be free."

The class gathered books and papers around me while I stood in the shadowy darkness and waited. The candlelight made everything feel misshapen and make-believe, crawling shadows across the floor and flickering ghostly patterns along the walls and chalkboards. When everyone else had gone, Mr. Delmar looked up into the darkness and saw me. "Well, hello," he said.

It was the first time we'd looked right at each other—the very first, since the day I'd met him, the day I'd walked into his classroom and asked for a reading list. I wanted to tell him about the water, spilling from my dreams into the world. I wanted to tell him about my father and Patty Jo, what I might have seen, what I couldn't explain or even remember exactly. I wanted to tell him about the blue ribbon nestled inside my backpack. Throughout the day I had opened the zipper to peek in at it, glowing like an ember, and stroke my fingers over its cool, silky surface. I wanted to tell him about the slips of images that shivered through my mind each time I looked at the ribbon: the speed, the sound, the tight, thrumming center where I had joined with an animal and disappeared. I wanted to tell him about that moment of connection, that moment of forgetting, of letting everything else go. I wanted to tell him that I had survived it, to pull the blue ribbon from my backpack and say the words: *I won.* And more than anything, I wanted to tell him that the feelings I'd had when I saw my father's hand in Patty Jo's, the spasms of cold, sick fear that had shot through the back of my throat, into my teeth and tongue, into the backs of my eyes and the beds of my fingernails, had been nothing, forgettable, so entirely insignificant, compared with the feeling of people clapping and cheering, the sound of strangers whistling, the whole upheaval of the world as they called my name.

But the candles flickered ghosts across the walls, the wet wind crying like a lost child outside the window, streaking the glass with its tears. "I'll be home by five," he said. I nodded in the darkness, then backed out of the room.

After that, they canceled school altogether. At home, the arena had turned into a lake. Sheila's mother didn't drive her out—what would be the point? But when I got home, Patty Jo's car was parked in front of the barn and I hesitated in the driveway, uncertain for a moment what was expected of me, if I was supposed to go into the house or into the barn. Since the show, my father had been careful with me, grinning and proud, never mentioning that anything had happened before the reining class. The whole day blurred together in my mind—Ace and Sheila, my father and Patty Jo, me and Darling tearing across the arena, the speed and silence, the eruption of cheers at the end.

Since then, my father had not asked for my help with feeding or cleaning, had not told me to hurry up in the morning or called me back outside after dark. "Take some time for yourself," he'd said when we got home from the show. "Go have a hot bath and I'll make dinner." So that's what I did. He told me not to worry about feeding the horses and so I didn't feed them. And I didn't worry.

But now, I would walk into the barn. I would walk in because it was my barn, because I lived there and Patty Jo did not, because if nothing that had happened so far had killed me, nothing ever would.

Inside the barn, they sat on folding chairs. Patty Jo's hair was wet and my father had a garbage bag tied around his cast. "There's the little star," Patty said when she saw me. I stood in the doorway without smiling, without saying hello.

"We've been waiting for you," my father said.

"Here I am," I told them.

Patty Jo was all smiles, all happiness, and she stood, brushing her wet hair out of her face. "You have a real gift, Alice," she gushed. I leaned in the door frame, bored, unwilling to be infected. "But gifts can need help sometimes," she went on, pretending not to notice. "Gardens need tending. I've been talking with your father and I would really love to help you out. I'd be honored to sponsor you." She blinked at me, waiting for my response.

"I don't know what you're talking about," I said.

My father stood up, heaving the weight of his cast onto the wet barn floor. "Your clothes are too small for you," he said. "Patty wants to buy you new ones."

I looked back and forth between them, wondering what this had to do with gifts or gardens, how new clothes could possibly contribute to training or future blue ribbons. "When?" I asked.

Patty blinked at me. "Whenever you want."

I set my backpack on an empty folding chair. "Now," I told her. "I want them right now."

The inside of Patty Jo's car smelled like perfume and leather, and I sat in the backseat, tracing my fingers over the power locks and windows, buttons that warmed seats and adjusted headrests. My father rode up front, and though he didn't speak, I could feel him thinking, looking around at the inside of the car. He reached up, fingering a string of seashells that dangled from the rearview mirror. "Those are from Hawaii," Patty told him, and my father pulled his hand back, dropping it into his lap as though the shells were priceless and delicate, a piece of art on a wall with a sign beneath that said *No Touching.*

"You've been to Hawaii?" I asked, and Patty met my eye in the rearview mirror.

"Only twice."

We walked into the mall, shaking the rain from our hair. The wet tips of my father's crutches made squeaking noises on the tile floor and I stood beside him, unsure what would happen next. "Well," he said after a minute. "Go to it."

I was careful at first, checking price tags and only choosing things that I needed. But Patty Jo flipped through the racks, pulling out clothes and piling them into the salesgirl's arms. My father stood to the side, awkward and displaced. For a moment, I felt frightened.

This was all wrong, all different. It was too much. But when he saw me, his face cleared and he nodded. "You've been working hard," he told me. "You deserve a few good things." And so I loaded my arms, taking anything that caught my eye, anything that might fit me.

In the dressing room, I made piles around myself, then peeled off my clothes and stood in my underwear. In the mirror, I turned sideways, sucking my stomach into my spine so that my ribs jutted like bony fingers beneath my skin. My hair hung down my back in wet tangles and I raked my fingers through it, trying to make it smooth.

I had spent my life in jeans and T-shirts, cutoff shorts and cowboy boots, clothes that I could get dirty, could stain or tear or wear through at the knees without feeling guilty, without feeling anything at all. The clothes in the dressing room had buttons and collars, lace cuffs or small bright flowers sewn along the hems of the jeans. These were clothes that girls at Sheila Altman's school wore, clothes for girls who didn't ever spill or trip or muck stalls after school. I slid into them, shivering at their lightness, the soft, smooth shimmer of the fabrics.

I looked in the mirror and there I was—all the right size, wearing pretty clothes that fit me perfectly. I changed into a different outfit and looked at myself again, holding my arms out to my sides, turning to see my body from different angles. I squatted, then stood on my tiptoes, lifting my arms above my head—*This is what I look like when I'm reaching.* I cocked one hip and put my hand at my waist, the way that Nona always stood. Then I sat on the little stool in the corner of the fitting room—*This is what I look like when I'm sitting down.*

I turned and looked and turned and looked—*This is what I look like from the right side, from the left side, from behind. This is what I look like standing on one foot.* And then I imagined Mr. Delmar looking at me. I pictured myself walking into advanced English in my new clothes, making my way across the room, sitting down at my desk. A chilly flutter of excitement spread up through my spine, my whole body shivering to life right in front of my eyes.

When I came out of the dressing room, my father and Patty Jo were standing outside, waiting. "How did everything work?" Patty asked.

My arms were weighted with clothes and I dumped them into Patty's. "I want all of these," I told her. "And I want shoes and earrings and I want to wear some of it home."

My father scanned the pile and then my face. I could tell he was weighing it out in his mind, wondering if it was too much, if I was taking advantage. But I knew what his conclusion would be before he had reached it, and I stood beside Patty Jo, waiting for him to catch up. "Anything else?" he asked with a raised eyebrow that a week earlier I might have taken as a warning.

"Yes," I said. "I want to get my hair cut."

At the salon, my father sat off to the side, shifting in his seat to adjust the awkward angle of his cast and leafing through women's magazines without looking at them. Patty had driven us all the way to the other end of town, where she got her own hair styled. "My girl's the *best*," she promised.

She stood behind me in the mirror, discussing what was to be done. "We don't want it too short," she said, and her girl nodded.

Patty Jo ran her fingers through my hair, indicating what the length should be. "Get rid of the dead ends," she instructed. "And some of the weight."

I sat in my chair, watching myself in the mirror while they moved around me, figuring it out. *This is what I look like with wet hair. This is what I look like when I wink, when I swallow, when I lift one eyebrow.*

"Maybe some layers?" Patty's girl asked. "Give it more movement?"

"And tapered around the face."

"*Yes.*"

The blades of the scissors flashed silver against my dark hair, cutting away the dead ends, the weight. "Your mom sure knows a lot about hair," the girl said, and in the mirror, I saw my father's head lift.

Patty's face tensed. "Oh," she said, laughing nervously. "I'm just a friend of the family."

I stared at myself in the mirror as Patty's girl snipped away at my hair, lifting it between her fingers, letting it fall. She didn't ask for any more explanation, why a friend of the family would pay for my haircut, why she would give instructions or drive me through the rain in her sweet-smelling car. And I didn't ask either. I had stood beside Patty while she paid for my new clothes and shoes, the heap of tiny sparkling jewelry she'd helped me pick out by holding it up to my ears and throat to see which worked best against my skin. Altogether, my new wardrobe cost more than my father and I spent on food for an entire month, more than I had ever seen in any of my father's white envelopes. But Patty opened her wallet and selected a single gold card from a spread of others without even glancing to see which one it was.

She was doing this because she was impressed with the way I'd ridden in the show or she was doing it because she was guilty over having been caught with my father's hand in her mouth. She was rewarding me or paying me off. And maybe it should have felt wrong. Maybe I should have said no thank you, told her that I didn't need her money, her good taste, her hair girl. But when I thought about it, really sat myself down and *thought* about the whole situation from top to bottom, what I came to was this: I had won that reining class, won it fair and square. I had worked and sweated and cleaned stalls, had eaten greasy food off of paper napkins and lived in a house without an air conditioner during the hottest part of the summer. I'd worn clothes that didn't fit me and been nice to people I didn't like. I had earned these good things, every single one of them. So keep them coming.

After we left the salon, Patty Jo took us out to dinner. We sat, the three of us, inside a cozy booth and she ordered a bottle of wine for herself and my father while I sipped a cherry Coke made with real cherries. Outside, the rain beat down against the window, the roads swelling with brown water. But inside, candles flickered on the white tablecloths and the waiters wore black bow ties. Our steaks came sizzling on our plates, so tender and juicy that I barely had to chew the meat before I swallowed.

When the check came, my father squinted down at it. "Holy shit," he whispered. "I don't think I've ever paid more than twenty dollars for a meal in my entire life."

Patty Jo leaned forward, laughing. "Poor Joe," she said, splitting the last trickle of wine between her glass and his. "Doing all the work and missing all the fun." She reached to take the check from him and her hand hovered above his for a moment before settling on the paper and slipping it from his fingers. My father looked down at his hand, the place where she had nearly touched him, and blushed in the candlelight. Across the table, I turned my head from side to side, feeling the swish of my hair on the back of my neck, clean and light and silky, and pretended not to notice.

At home, I spread my new clothes out across my bed and took my time modeling each outfit in front of the mirror, lifting my hair off my face, then smoothing it along my jaw, twirling as fast as I could to make it fan out around my shoulders. In the bathroom I dug beneath the sink and found a case of Nona's abandoned makeup, then sat cross-legged on the counter, experimenting with the tiny tubes and pale, starry powders.

Within a day, I had memorized every reflective surface in our house, the mirrors in the bathroom and my bedroom, the windows, outside looking in during daylight, inside looking out in the darkness. The china cabinet had glass panels in the front that were less than ideal, reflecting my body only in outlines, but still, it was something.

The day that school finally started up again, I took my time to prepare in the morning, choosing carefully from my closet of new clothes. The rain had lessened, but the ground was still soggy with mud, and I curled my toes inside my old shoes, carrying my new ones in a bag. At school, I changed in the girls' room, then hid my old, muddy shoes in the bottom of my locker.

"Ooo-la-*la*," Zach Pope said when he passed in a group of eighth-grade boys. I kept my eyes straight ahead and didn't answer. In advanced English, I crossed the room and took my seat like it was any other day. I kept my head down, pretending to put the finishing touches on my homework assignment. But when Mr. Delmar called my name in roll, I looked up, right straight into his eyes, and answered. Anyone else in the room might not have noticed, but he paused. Our eyes locked and the corners of his mouth tilted upward, a tiny, secret smile. And then he winked. It was an instant, maybe less, before he lowered his eyes back to the attendance sheet and called out the next name on his list.

During science class, Janice Reardon abandoned her Bunsen burner to come and stand in front of mine. "I was looking for you," she said.

"And now you've found me," I told her. "Good work."

Janice's hair was pulled into a messy ponytail and tied with pink and blue pompons, her fingernails colored in with streaky red marker. "You look different," she said.

I lowered my head over my burner, trying to look like I was concentrating on the experiment. "Well, I'm not," I mumbled.

Janice crossed her arms over her chest, squinting at me through the scratched lenses of her safety goggles. "I know."

A chill fluttered through my spine, and I turned my head to feel my hair move across the back of my neck, light and shiny. Janice Reardon was a joke, everyone thought so. Her opinion meant nothing.

I tapped my open science book with my pen. "I have to finish this," I said.

Janice looked sideways at the clock, gauging if I had enough time, then climbed onto the empty stool beside me. "I was talking to my friends," she told me, then paused, raising her eyebrows pointedly. "You know, Abigail, Sharon, and Colleen? I was telling them how your sister ran off and your mother has cancer and your father has to drive a school bus just to make ends meet, and they said it would be okay if you ate lunch at our table."

Janice leaned back on her stool, waiting for my gratitude. I imagined crossing the cafeteria to Polly's table, sitting in her chair, talking to her friends. But I couldn't think what the point would be. None of them had spent as much time thinking about Polly as I had. None of them knew about Mr. Delmar. They might have been the girls who sat beside her while she ate her lunch, but none of them knew her the way I did.

Besides, Janice Reardon wore strings of paper clips as necklaces and purple shoes with Velcro straps. I didn't need her charity.

"Thanks, but no thanks," I said.

I could feel her mind working circles inside her head, making excuses for me. My sister had run away. My mother had cancer. "I feel sorry for you, Alice Winston," she said finally. "Really, I do."

After school, I waited in the girls' bathroom until everyone had left, then changed back into my old shoes. On the walk home, the canal rushed beside me, swollen and gorged, sloshing water up over the lip while the sky growled above. "I could give you a ride," my father had offered that morning as he climbed into the bus, but I refused. Now I crept along the weeds, keeping my eyes on the canal.

On television each night, they tried to estimate how much damage the valley had suffered. The repair needed after the rain stopped would likely take years to complete. Up in the mountains, chunks of land had fallen away, causing mudslides that flowed down the cliffs like rivers of concrete, uplifting trees and rocks, swallowing everything in their path. Around the rim of the valley, cars were crushed, homes destroyed. Whole sections of road had washed completely away. The worst, they told us, was over. In a few days, the sun would shine again. Homes would be rebuilt, roads repaired.

But alongside the canal, there were no such promises. The water rushed, fierce and hungry. I pictured it rising, spreading across the entire valley until the town disappeared beneath, a sunken ship lost forever on the ocean floor. Maybe when it happened, I would float to the surface. Maybe the blue ribbon, worn and grubby in my backpack, and the memory of myself inside the ring—the lightness of my body, the pure, perfect silence—would be enough to lift me. And from up above, I would peer down into the watery ruin of the town, trying to remind myself what it had been like to live there, to recognize the place that had been my home before the rain came and everything old was lost.

"Have you ever been really good at anything?"

"Not really," Mr. Delmar told me.

"Aren't you pretty good at tennis?" I asked.

"Nah," he said. "I took a class in college is all."

"But you coach the team at school," I said. I was careful—this was the closest we'd come to mentioning Polly Cain since school started. The conversation suddenly felt weighted and fragile. I didn't want to cross the line that would break anything.

"It's one of the rules," he said. "All the teachers have to do something extracurricular: newspaper, French Club, yearbook—"

"The yearbook's really crappy," I interrupted.

"And a hell of a lot of work, I bet," Mr. Delmar said. "Tennis only meets for a couple of months, and we don't really have a court. That's why I took it."

This didn't match the idea I had of him—the idea I had of any adult, that he might make decisions based on what required the least amount of work. I thought suddenly of Patty Jo, paying for the expensive dinner at the restaurant, and of my father, turning pink at the mere idea of her touch. *Poor Joe, doing all the work and missing all the fun.* "But you like teaching, right?"

"It isn't what I want to do forever."

A slippery fear crept inside me at the idea that he might find something else he liked better, that he might go away. "I think you're a really good teacher," I said.

"I like teaching English lit," he told me. "At least, I think it's important."

Outside of seeing him, English didn't make much difference in my life. The things I learned in math could sometimes come in handy. But it never seemed to matter much to anyone what books I'd read or that I knew the difference between similes and metaphors. "It's more important than shop," I said. "Right now we're making birdcages. Nobody even has a bird."

"That *is* a waste of time," he said.

"There are a lot of people who do the same thing their whole lives," I told him.

"I know," he said. "I feel really sorry for them."

I tried to imagine anything I could do for my entire life, anything I was good enough at that someone might pay me to do it. I'd been repeatedly complimented on both my penmanship and my ability to whistle through my fingers like a boy, but these skills seemed unlikely to pay off in the long run.

"My father has done the same thing his entire life," I said.

"What does he do?" Mr. Delmar asked.

Inside Nona's closet, her clothes hung on their little plastic hangers like forgotten ghosts. They were out of date now, out of fashion. They were cheap. "He's a professor," I said. "He studies the stars."

"Well, if you're smart enough to do something like that," he said, "you don't really need to look around for something better."

Above me, a tea-colored stain tinted the ceiling where our roof had leaked, and I pictured the house in the life where my father was a professor, the high ceilings and apricot carpeting, the green lawns and rosebushes lining the driveway. "It's all he's ever done," I told Mr. Delmar. "The only thing he's good at."

"You're lucky," he said. "You've got good bloodlines."

When the clouds finally parted, the sun shone down and the moisture rose like steam, hazing the horizon and curling in smoky fingers through the chilly morning air. Quenched and confused, the land began to awaken, the ground turning green and purple, the air soft and damp. The breeze smelled like flowers, trees budding in sprouts of pink and white. And by the middle of October, it was spring.

"That's the desert," people kept saying, holding their hands up to the sky.

"Yeah," my father grunted. "When it's not kicking your teeth in, it's a hell of a place to live."

At home, the horses were frisky in their pens, perking their ears and nickering into the wind. Even the foals, who had been nothing but morose since their weaning, nipped playfully at one another in their pen. The arena was still too sloppy for riding, and the afternoons passed in long, lazy stretches. There was nothing to do but wait for the ground to dry. Still, Patty Jo came every day.

And she brought me things: hair barrettes and pens that wrote in purple ink, a leather backpack as smooth and soft as warm butter. We never made much of these exchanges. "I thought this might be nice on you," she would say, or, "I saw this in a window and it looked like you." And I would take the gift, shrugging my thanks and tossing it inside the house until I had the time and privacy to really look at it, to run my fingers over seams and turn price tags over in my hands, to spin slow circles in front of the mirror.

The second time Patty invited us to dinner, my father had to think about it. His bus route had run late and the horses needed to be fed. He looked small and tired on his crutches, his spine curved, his hair damp at the roots. Two of the girls on his route suffered frequently from car sickness.

Patty Jo blushed at his hesitation, holding her hands up in apology. "Why not?" my father said before she could speak. "I deserve a little cheering up."

The third time she asked us to dinner, my father didn't even pause. "It'll beat anything we've got in the refrigerator."

She continued to ask and he continued to accept. A new routine began. After his bus route, my father would shower and change into clean clothes, coming outside with his hair damp and his face smooth from shaving. At the restaurants, I sat between them or across from them, eating crème brûlée and thinking about whatever new gift awaited me at home.

Our dinners were an education. Patty took us to a different restaurant each night: sushi, Thai, French-Polynesian. My father and I modeled our manners after hers, placing our napkins across our laps, keeping our elbows off the table. At first, my father had held his wineglass cupped in his hand. Now he held the stem between his fingers, swishing the glass before he drank. Even with all his effort, the affect fit him wrong. His hands were calloused, his fingernails stained with permanent grime. And though he swished and swallowed, his eyes darted continually to Patty Jo's, checking himself in her expression. Under normal circumstances, my father was not a person who ate salad, not a person who would touch snail or eel or anything pink. But if Patty Jo recommended it, he put it into his mouth, rolled it around on his tongue, and swallowed.

During our dinners, Patty told us how our food compared with meals she had eaten in other cities: steaks she'd had in New York, foie gras in Paris, *nigiri* in Tokyo. My father stopped eating when she spoke, leaning back in his seat to watch her remember all the places he had never been, all the places he would never go. Patty's son went to college in California and she told us of her visits there, the different stores and restaurants, all the things that didn't exist in Desert Valley.

"We've been to California," my father said, proud to have something in common with Patty Jo.

"Isn't it wonderful there?" she asked, and my father nodded. "Where did you stay?"

"Oh," he said. "We didn't stay there. We were just driving through."

Patty's head tilted as she considered this and she motioned to the waiter for another bottle of wine.

"Sheila's from California," I said. "They moved here so that her dad could get more for his money."

Patty laughed. "Oh, sweetheart," she said. "That isn't *his* money."

"It isn't?"

"Good Lord, no. Altman's just a little college professor. He doesn't make *real* money." Patty cocked her chin at me, lifting one eyebrow as if this were obvious. "All that glitters there belongs to the missus." She dropped her voice. *"She comes from good people."*

I couldn't believe this. Mr. Altman had been to college himself, he knew about stars and planets and solar eclipses. I stared at Patty, wondering what *real* money was and who out there was making it. "What's your son in college for?" I asked.

"He's going to be a doctor," Patty told me, rolling her eyes as if this were something her son was doing expressly to annoy her. "Don't get me wrong," she added. "It's a noble profession, blah, blah, blah. But doctors are aliens. They speak another language. When Alex comes home now, he and his father sit around talk-talk-talking. I don't understand a word they say."

My father straightened in his seat and I thought he was reacting to the mention of Patty Jo's husband. These were the two things that never came up in conversation during our dinners: the doctor who paid for them, and my mother. But my father gestured to me across the table. "Alice could be a doctor," he said. "She's a brain and a half."

Patty's eyes rested on mine and she smiled. "Alice Winston," she said. "What *will* you be?"

In Patty's voice, the question sounded dreamy, full of possibility, and I wanted to have a good answer. Something romantic and spectacular. At school, they had given us questionnaires to help determine our careers. We spent an afternoon filling in bubbles to indicate how much we liked children, the outdoors, and working in stores. But in the end, it was fruitless. A glitch in the software caused the computer to spit out identical answers on each form, predicting that every student in the entire school would grow up to be a marine biologist.

"I don't really know," I said at last, and Patty reached across the table, touching the knuckle of her index finger to the knuckle of mine.

"That's the best way to be," she told me. "You can take your time with life. The whole world is open to you."

I was eating the food she'd ordered and wearing the clothes she'd paid for. Believing her felt easy.

And so we went on, our pretend family. Every day, the arena dried a little more. Soon, Sheila Altman would return, ready for her afternoon lessons. The Catfish would swarm the barn, making up for lost time. The final horse show of the season had been delayed indefinitely, but it would be rescheduled. My father would enter me in the reining class. I would have to do it again.

But for now, we ate and drank and talked about everything except who we were and why we were out together. If Patty Jo noticed the raised eyebrows from women at nearby tables or the double looks she got from waiters when she reached for the bill, she never let on. And as I became used to linen napkins and waiters holding my chair for me, it began to seem as though things had always been this way, as if this were the way they would always be.

So of course, it couldn't last. Of course, the moment I stopped missing her was the moment she came back.

eleven

IT MIGHT HAVE BEEN anybody's old pickup truck parked beside my father's school bus. "Whose is that?" Patty asked as she pulled into our driveway, and my father shook his head, fumbling to get his crutches out the car door. When he didn't answer, she turned in her seat. "Alice?"

The truck shone beneath the floodlights, turquoise with a white stripe. "I'm not sure," I mumbled and followed my father out of the car.

We walked through the back door and they were waiting for us, sitting on our furniture, drinking sodas from our refrigerator. My sister was smaller than I remembered. When she wrapped her arms around my shoulders to hug me, I could feel the ridges of her collarbone pressing into my throat, the ladder of ribs jutting beneath her tank top. "You got so tall," she breathed.

Behind her, Jerry sat at the dining room table with his hands wrapped around his soda can. "You remember Jerry," Nona told us, and he lifted his eyes, his head tipping in a brief nod.

Nona took a step toward my father, then stopped, stooping her shoulders as she shoved her hands into her pockets. I waited for my father to say something, to ask her where she'd been, why she hadn't written, and why, after so much time, she would ever think she was welcome here. But he balanced on his crutches without speaking.

"We need a place to stay," Nona said, and my father held her gaze only an instant before blinking his consent.

"Aren't you going to ask about his leg?" I asked, and Nona turned to me.

"He fell," she said. "Mom told me."

"You've talked to Mom?" Everything was moving too quickly. Everything was wrong.

"You guys were gone," Nona said.

"We were with a client," my father said, and I wanted to kick his crutches out from under him. Where *we* had been couldn't have been less important.

"I know," Nona said. "Mom told me."

Jerry shifted in his seat and I stared, trying to see if he was somehow hurt. My father had always said that Jerry would break his spine in the rodeos, that he'd be crippled for life and Nona would come home destitute. But Jerry sipped at his soda without lifting his eyes. Nothing about him looked broken or crippled.

"We could bring in our stuff," Nona said finally, and Jerry rose to his feet at the suggestion.

"Alice can help," my father said without looking at me. Alone with my sister, he would get to the bottom of things, would say what needed to be said. So I followed Jerry outside.

We had never been introduced, never spoken to each other, and I waited for him to tilt his head in my direction, to say that he'd heard a lot about me or offer some sort of explanation for why they were back. *Your sister's been missing her family and I couldn't keep her away any longer. She wanted to finish high school. She wanted to show again.* But he climbed into the truck without saying a word.

They didn't have much, a ratty duffel bag and a few cardboard boxes. I leaned against the school bus, watching Jerry toss the boxes onto the ground without offering to help. When his back was turned, I lifted onto my toes, peering inside the window. The cab was littered with hamburger wrappers and empty cigarette packs. A dingy blanket was wadded on the floor, and on the dashboard, a road map had been crumpled beneath a pair of my sister's socks.

When the truck bed was empty, Jerry moved into the cab, rustling through the garbage on the floor and shaking the cigarette packs until he found one that made noise. His heel caught on the blanket, smearing a crescent of mud across the faded pink. When he reached down to free his foot from the tangle, the blanket tugged sideways, revealing a black pole. For a second, I thought it might be a cane, and I cupped my hands around my face to get a better look through the window.

Perhaps Jerry had been injured after all, a part of himself crushed to smithereens, and he was merely concealing the pain that seared through his body with every step he took. But as I squinted into the truck, I could see where the pole bent like an elbow into smooth, curved wood. It was not a cane, and I sank back onto my heels as the image worked itself through my mind.

Through the window, Jerry's eyes locked with mine. In the movies, there were two sorts of men who had guns: heroes and criminals. Inside the truck, Jerry reached down, yanking the blanket back across the floor, then climbed out, locking the door behind him. He turned to face me and I could feel the fear rising inside my chest like ice water. Jerry was not a hero.

I waited for him to tell me that I hadn't seen what I thought I had, that it was none of my business, that if I said a word to anyone, he would tear my heart out through my throat. But Jerry bent down, piling every last bag and box into his arms, then turned for the house.

Inside, Nona and my father stood on opposite sides of the room, not looking at each other, not speaking, while Jerry piled the boxes next to the stairs. My heart spun inside my chest, my thoughts blurring together like smears of paint. Jerry and Nona were not visiting. They were moving in. They would eat at our table and take showers in our bathroom. And suddenly, all the unanswered questions, all the explanations left unsaid, drained from my mind as I realized that they would be staying in Nona's bedroom.

"I need a telephone," I said, and all three of them turned to look at me.

"What?" my father asked, blinking at me through the dim light of the living room.

"I need a phone," I repeated. "In my bedroom."

"I could run a line from Nona's room, I guess," my father said. "But I'd have to get some stuff at the store."

"I need it tonight," I told him. If my father asked for explanations, I would say that advanced English was difficult—I had to call people in my class for help with the homework three, four times a night. The conversations were long. Drawn out. I couldn't use the phone in the living room—I had to concentrate.

But my father seemed relieved by the request, fishing his keys from his pocket as he turned toward the door. "Don't forget to buy a phone," I called after him. "Any color but pink."

Jerry went outside to smoke and Nona looped the threads of her arms across her chest as she watched me. "You have a secret," she said.

My sister smiled, but her cheeks were sunken, the skin beneath her eyes gray and sagging. "I have lots," I told her.

Nona rolled her eyes. "I haven't been gone *that* long."

I didn't know how to answer. The world had changed since my sister left. Horses had been bought and sold. Bones had broken. Nona had missed the drought and she had missed the flood, and now we stood, separated by a canyon of time. There was no way to tell her how long she had been gone. There was no way to begin.

"Why are you back?" I asked, and her eyes narrowed slightly.

"Because I am," she said. "Is that a problem?"

"No," I told her. "I just think you should have a better reason."

My sister slept for days after that, emerging from her bedroom at irregular times to fix herself a plate of food or sit half asleep on the porch swing, smoking cigarettes and gazing across the pasture at nothing. My father gave Jerry a tour of the barn, pointing where we kept the feed and tack and grooming supplies. Jerry slouched along behind, not speaking except to mumble the occasional "Yes, sir."

"We're show people," my father said. "I don't want to see any of that rodeo shit out here."

"Yes, sir."

Jerry was as skinny as a girl, with ropy arms and bowed legs that made him look underfed and insectlike beside my father's broad shoulders.

"Our clients are classy people," my father added. "So keep it clean."

"Yes, sir."

"I guess that's about it," my father said at last, giving Jerry a sideways look that indicated he neither liked nor trusted him. "If you've got questions, Nona can help you out. She knows the way things work."

But Nona did not set foot in the barn. In the afternoons, she would sometimes rouse herself from sleep, then wander, eyes bleary, hair tangled, into my mother's room, where she would prop her bare feet on the bedside table and smoke out the window. And though she rarely laid eyes on Jerry during the day, at night, he climbed the stairs to her. I would lie awake in my bed and listen to the sounds of their breath, those loose, aching gasps that swelled like waves on the other side of the wall, and wonder what could have possibly happened out there to make them come back here.

"How long are they staying?" I asked my father.

"I don't know," he said. "Awhile. I figured you'd be happy to have her around."

My thoughts spun together inside my head. My sister had gone away and left a piece of the world empty. But her sudden presence felt as wrong as her absence, something jammed in where it didn't belong, a school bus in front of a barn.

"Why are they here?" I asked, and my father took a deep breath.

"They need a place to stay," he said. "What should I have told them? No? Go live in a ditch?"

Jerry had a truck. It wasn't like they'd have to sleep on the ground. "They're having sex in our house," I said. "Did you know that?"

My father jumped like I had thrown cold water on him. "Jesus Christ, Alice, I don't want to be thinking about things like that."

"Neither do I," I told him. "So I think you ought to tell them to stay someplace else. Jerry could be a serial killer, for all we know. Nona might be brainwashed like Patty Hearst. I mean, why haven't we heard from them in so long?" My father held out one hand, silencing me before my next question could form.

"They're here," he said. "That's the only answer I've got."

With no one else offering explanation, I began to imagine my own answers. I played them through my head like movies, all the scenarios that could have resulted in Jerry and Nona climbing into their beat-up truck and driving across the wide-open spaces of the country to end at our back door.

During the afternoon, I inched Nona's bedroom door open, watching her chest heave as she slept. Her stomach sloped beneath the hem of her T-shirt, her navel sunken in the white bowl of her hipbones. It was a frantic, hungry sleep—her mouth open, tongue tasting the stale air of her bedroom as it moved over her lips. In her waking state, my sister was groggy and listless, slow to respond and easy to forget herself. She wandered downstairs in her bra and underwear, then stood, staring blankly into the open refrigerator. But her sleep was filled with worry, her body tossing, her lips trembling. This was not the sleep of a girl returning from a yearlong honeymoon. This was not the sister who had drawn smiley faces into the margins of her letters.

And so I imagined drugs. I imagined that Nona and Jerry had fallen in with a bad rodeo crowd and spent their nights in dark rooms, shooting heroin and wasting away like Sid Vicious and Nancy Spungen. I imagined that another cowboy had fallen head over heels in love with my sister, and Jerry, drunk and dangerous, had snapped the man's neck in a jealous rage. I imagined that together they had robbed a bank and driven across the country like Bonnie and Clyde, lost in an orgy of crime and whiskey, the shotgun propped between them like an extra limb.

"We're dying to get a look at your mysterious sister," Bitsy told me in the barn. The Catfish had finally returned, but with the arena still too wet for riding, they stood around drinking from their paper cups and rooting for distractions.

"All she does is sleep," I said.

"*Well,*" Bitsy breathed, and cast an admiring look to the back of the barn where Jerry was shoveling sawdust into Toy Boy's stall. "He must have worn her out."

When it came to basic maintenance, Jerry was a machine. By the time I got home from school each afternoon, he had already exercised our show horses and cleaned all the stalls. He was small, with a wiry frame, but he could lift bales of hay like they were nothing at all, carrying one in each hand and tossing them with the same ease I might use to throw a pillow from one side of my bed to the other.

"He's obviously got a lot of energy," Jaycee added, and the rest of them giggled into their paper cups.

Patty Jo stood apart from the conversation, sifting absently through her grooming equipment and watching the road from the front of the barn. With Jerry taking care of the horses, my father took extra bus jobs, shuttling sports teams to games and picking up field trips at the post office. Sometimes he didn't get home until evening.

"I suppose they ran out of money," Bitsy said lightly, and I straightened, waiting to hear her reasoning. Perhaps Jerry was only a mediocre cowboy whose winnings couldn't keep them in hotel rooms and steak dinners. Perhaps a foul and violent temper had gotten him banned from the circuit.

But before Bitsy could explain, Patty Jo turned, her eyes leveling the crowd of us. "I suppose it's none of our business."

A hush fell over the Catfish, and their eyes darted back and forth, a thousand silent exchanges. "Well," Bitsy said with forced brightness, "fiddle-dee-dee," and the conversation shifted seamlessly onto something else.

"Maybe your sister's sick," Sheila told me the next day. It was the first time she'd been out to the barn since the rain had started, and like the horses, she seemed restless and cranky at having been cooped up for so long. She paced circles around Cap, scowling at the tangles in his mane. "I hope you guys have been taking care of him while I was gone," she said.

"What could Nona be sick with?" I asked. Illness had never occurred to me.

Sheila stood on her tiptoes, her tongue poking sideways out her mouth as she tried to loosen the tangle with her fingers. "Mononucleosis makes people sleep a lot," she told me. "You get it from kissing people."

"How do you know?" I asked.

"They told us at school."

It figured. Sheila went to a better school than I did. At my school, they had only told us about getting pregnant. "Well, it can't be that," I told her. "Jerry's healthy enough, and he's the only person she could have caught it from."

Sheila paused to clean her currycomb, her eyebrows knitting together in thought. "Do you know that for sure?"

Sheila had yet to lay eyes on Nona, but I could sense her impulse to disapprove, to be the better owner of Cap. Still, a new image flashed through my head, Nona kissing cowboys right and left, catching a disease, coming home to sleep herself to death.

"She knows, right?" Sheila asked, her eyes darting to the house. "About me and Cap?"

I had figured that the barn would be the first place Nona went after she climbed out of Jerry's truck, that she would run to Yellow Cap's stall before even going inside the house. But eight days had passed and she had yet to step foot in the barn. She had yet to ask about him.

"Well, it doesn't matter," Sheila said when I didn't answer. "She left *him,* after all. She has no reason to expect that he'd still belong to her."

"Have you ever heard of mononucleosis?"

"The kissing disease?" Mr. Delmar asked.

My thoughts swam back to the posse banquet, the taste of Zach Pope's tongue, like dust and beer, the grit of his chapped lips pressed to mine. Apparently, this was how disease spread, strangers kissing strangers until everyone retreated into bedrooms, closing doors and curtains, and fell asleep, leaving the world, at last, to itself. But the posse banquet had taken place more than a month ago, and I hadn't noticed any increased need for sleep. Besides, Zach Pope was neither particularly bright nor especially good-looking. I was probably the only person who had ever kissed him.

"Can you die from it?" I asked.

"You just sleep a lot," Mr. Delmar told me. "Why?"

I tried to think how I could tell him about my sister, about her going away, then coming back drowsy and shrunken, weighting our life with the brooding presence of the man she'd left us for. Mr. Delmar would be able to explain things. He would come up with ideas I hadn't, ideas I might never come up with on my own. But I didn't know how to explain, how to even begin to weave Nona's story through the new life I had made for myself, the life I had made for him.

"*You* don't have it, do you?" he asked.

"No," I told him, but a flush crept up my neck at the suggestion. As far as Mr. Delmar knew, I might be a girl whom boys lined up to kiss. In that other life, where my father studied stars and my mother ran business meetings, I would have grown up wearing expensive clothes and paying professionals to cut and style my hair. Polly Cain and I would have slept over at each other's house, staying up all night to talk about boys we thought were nice or cute or had thick eyelashes, kissing our hands for practice, preparing for a life that neither of us would have.

"It's a dangerous world," he said. "You have to be careful."

"Are you careful?" I asked.

He paused, hissing a match to light a cigarette. "All things considered, I would say that I am very careless."

Mr. Delmar read books and coached tennis. When I asked a question, he always had an answer. This was not carelessness. Careless people married strangers. They forgot the ages of their children. They kept a gun, or something that looked like a gun, concealed on the floor of their truck by a dirty blanket. They walked beside water on a windless day and slipped, fell, died alone. "I don't believe you," I said.

He sighed, and I could feel something shifting between us, a sadness spreading through the cord of my new telephone. "You don't know me that well," he said finally, and my stomach filled with lead.

"I know you're smart," I told him. "And nice and funny. I know you're a good person."

I could hear him breathing on the other end of the line, the air moving through his lips, across his tongue, into his throat and lungs, then turning to silence as he held it there, thinking. "You're a lovely girl," he said at last. I closed my eyes, letting the words form behind my eyelids in soft, pink letters: *lovely girl.* "And I know you're lonely."

Inside my mind, the words shivered, changing shape and color, the pink draining into soggy gray. *Lovely* was not so far away from *lonely.* A single letter was all that kept them from being exactly the same.

"I see you at school," he told me quietly. "You sit by yourself, walk to class alone."

Other girls sat in clusters, leaning over desks to pass notes or braid beads and ribbons into each other's hair. They laughed with their mouths open at each other's jokes, screamed with delight at each other's successes, cried on each other's shoulder at any shared misfortune. Of course, Mr. Delmar would notice this. Of course he would notice that I had no such group of girls to wind myself into.

"Things have been hard for you since last spring," he said, and in the spaces between his words, I could feel the weight of what was left unsaid: things had been hard for me since I had lost my best friend, since Polly Cain had died and left me all alone. "But you're too special to stay so separate. You need friends."

The old Alice Winston had never needed friends. School had always been a job, punching in, doing time, punching out. As a child, my life revolved around the barn, my father, and my sister. Nona had gone away and left a hole, but the empty space had deepened in the time she'd been gone, changing shape. Now she was back, my whole family once again under the same roof. Even as my sister was beginning to rejoin the world of the living, spending less time asleep and more time wandering aimlessly through the house, I knew that we could never return to the life we'd had before she left. And even if we could, it was no longer the life I wanted.

Mr. Delmar saw my life the way it should be, full of potential and possibility. In his eyes, I was smart. I was lovely. I was special. If he thought I needed friends, then I would find some.

The next day Kelly and Rachel invited me to eat lunch at their table. I crossed the cafeteria behind them, swinging my hair from side to side and ignoring the weight of Janice Reardon's gaze following me from the other side of the room.

It was surprisingly easy to get along with the cheerleaders. All I had to do was look bored by everything they said, and they loved me. "Tryouts are long over," Rachel told me. "But maybe we could fudge the rules for you. Can you do a cartwheel?"

I chewed my soggy hamburger and imagined myself dressed in a little red and white skirt, wearing one of the football players' jerseys at school on game days like the other cheerleaders did, standing in clusters with them, winding my hair around my finger and wrinkling my nose at the rest of my classmates like they were a slow-spreading disease. I imagined Mr. Delmar in the stands during the football games, watching me on the field with the other cheerleaders.

> *Hi, my name's Alice and you've got no choice,*
> *I'm gonna run you over in my new Rolls-Royce!*

I was pretty sure I couldn't do a cartwheel, but I shrugged, committing to neither cartwheel nor interest in joining the squad.

"It doesn't matter," Kelly said quickly. "You have really shiny hair."

In the mornings, I spent more than an hour in the bathroom, blow-drying my hair and styling the ends with a curling iron Patty Jo had bought me from her salon—*the good kind,* she'd told me. "Hey, Duchess!" Jerry would call as he banged the door from outside. "Move it along, will you? I gotta piss."

But I took my time, applying lip gloss and turning to see my hair from every angle. Although our dinners had ended, Patty Jo continued to bring me gifts, sneaking little boxes of earrings into my hands while the other Catfish were preoccupied, motioning me into the tack room to present me with a new blouse, a silver bracelet, a pair of pink socks with lacy cuffs.

"Where do you shop?" Rachel asked while we were changing clothes for gym class.

The truth was that I had no idea where most of Patty's gifts came from, only that the clothes felt smooth on my skin and smelled like a rich woman. "My mom travels for work," I told her. "She buys most of my things in California."

"You're such a lucky bitch!" Rachel gasped. I could feel the muscles of my face tightening beneath my skin—no one had ever called me a bitch before. But Rachel's eyes were gleaming with approval and I smiled, accepting the compliment of her jealousy.

"It's weird that we never really noticed you before," Amy said, and the rest of the cheerleaders nodded. "I mean, you're so *obviously* supposed to be hanging out with us."

Up close, the cheerleaders didn't seem much different from everyone else. They had better hair and wore more makeup than most of the seventh-grade girls, but sitting at their table or standing next to them in line, it wasn't hard to find the imperfections that might be unnoticeable from farther away. Amy had wide-set eyes and a nose that was too long for her face—a fact she tried to conceal by wearing extra rouge and lipstick to draw the attention away. Beneath her cake of foundation, Rachel had small constellations of pimples on her chin and forehead, and Kelly had a thick stomach that pudged over the waist of her jeans when she forgot to suck it in. As far as I could tell, the only real difference between the cheerleaders and the girls they didn't speak to was where they sat during lunch.

"Well," Rachel said, looping her arm through mine as we started out the locker room. "Maybe we never noticed you before, but better late than never, right?"

I did not particularly enjoy their company, didn't find them especially fun or interesting, but I nodded. All those years I had been unnoticeable, hiding behind my hair, slumping my shoulders, scuffing through the hallways alone. There was no way to get that time back, and so there was no point in thinking about it. What was important was today, tomorrow, the day that came after. What was important was knowing that all I had to do to be better than other people was act like I was.

Friday night, my father got word that the final horse show of the season had been rescheduled for the following weekend, and on Saturday morning, he gathered us all in the barn to discuss what needed to be done in preparation. My father was nearly giddy, laughing with his chin tipped back as he spoke with Mrs. Altman, teasing Bitsy and Jaycee about the dance they had performed in the stands every time one of us had placed or won. "I hope you've been practicing your little routine," he told them. "I've got a feeling about this last show."

I leaned against the tack room door, watching as my father glided through the barn on his crutches, joking and smiling. Of course he had a good feeling about the final show. Nona was back.

The Catfish were mulling around, sifting through tack and grooming equipment. Patty Jo stood among them, nodding and laughing. But her eyes moved to my father, watching as he spoke to Mrs. Altman about the price of the following week's lessons.

When my sister walked into the barn, everyone fell silent. Her hair was tied in a greasy bun, her feet bare. She stood for a moment, blinking into Cap's stall, where Sheila was leaning against his shoulder, stroking the tips of his mane with her fingers. Nona stared at one of the signs Jaycee had taped to the barn wall about Heathcliff's sensitive sinuses, then lit a cigarette. "You told me to come out here," she said to my father, exhaling a ribbon of smoke sideways through her lips.

If my father noticed the stares, the strange silence that had settled over the barn the moment my sister entered it, he didn't let on. "Great." He grinned. "Everyone's here." He introduced Nona and Sheila went suddenly shy, staring at her feet and stealing quick, nervous glances at my sister.

My father turned to Sheila and Mrs. Altman, explaining his new plan. Nona would give Sheila a few lessons before the last show. She knew Cap better than anyone, he said. She could help with showmanship. Mrs. Altman watched Nona smoke her cigarette and her smile tensed. "Well," she said after a minute. "That would be fine."

"What do you say?" my father asked Nona.

Her eyes had settled on Cap's monogrammed blanket, the halter stitched with his name in gold. Inside his stall, Sheila stood with her eyes lowered, her blond hair parted down the center and held in place with glittery barrettes. "Whatever," Nona said, and turned back for the house.

The crowd dispersed and I followed my sister up the porch stairs, leaning against the railing as she settled on the swing, lighting a new cigarette from the old one before tossing the butt onto the lawn. "What's with them putting his fucking name on everything?" she asked.

I glanced toward the barn, nervous that Mrs. Altman might be close enough to overhear us—she wouldn't want Sheila taking lessons from a person who used the word *fucking*.

"Dad will buy you a new horse," I said, and Nona's eyes lifted, leveling with mine. I wanted her to cry, to yell, to throw a temper tantrum in pure Nona fashion, to be the person I remembered. But she only stared at me, her expression blank, her eyes cold.

"I don't care," she said. "I'm through with all of it."

"Not with showing," I said.

"With *all of it*," she repeated.

"Then why are you here?" I asked.

Nona dipped her head forward, her eyes closing as though even the effort required to hold her head up was too much for her. "Things got hard out there, Alice," she said finally. "They got really hard."

"Things were hard here too," I told her, and she shook her head.

"It isn't the same."

I started to object. Nona didn't know what it had been like to watch Cap's registration papers change into the Altmans' name. She didn't know the way the posse members had looked at us, the way they'd kept their children away from me after she'd left, like I was infected with some disease that might spread, making an entire community of children who ran away before they were grown, who left their families with work and debt and a hollow, hungry hole. She didn't know about Polly Cain, who had died, kicking and struggling in the murky brown canal water, feet away from where I walked home every single day of my life, and our father, who had lifted her body and carried her onto dry ground three days too late to save her.

But before I could open my mouth, before I could even begin to form the words, she held her hand up. "You can't understand," she told me. "It's different out there. Believe me."

And so the conversation ended. I didn't have a chance to tell her about Patty Jo and the Catfish moving into the barn, making it their own, tangling their lives into ours so that now, when I looked around, nothing here would ever be enough to make me happy, nothing would ever be good enough. It wasn't that I didn't believe her. I believed her entirely. Things out there, they had to be different. They just had to be.

The arena was still patchy with mud when my father saddled Darling and took me out to ride. I told my father that I would not practice reining while Patty or Sheila were in the ring, and so he woke me early in the morning, before anyone had arrived out at the barn.

I had spent the weeks since the last show reliving the reining class in my head, allowing my muscles to flex with the memory of speed and connection, the ecstasy of triumph. But now, Darling's legs were black with mud from her pen, her mane gray with rainwater. The ride was flawed and sloppy, her head wildly high, her legs slipping, splashing mud up onto my jeans and boots as I tried to maneuver her around the ring.

The reins slipped in my fingers, and my feet slid out of the stirrups. Out of the corner of my eye, I saw Jerry leaning against the fence, watching, and my mind singed into black, empty panic. Darling's spins unraveled and her halts bounced me over the front of the saddle.

"That's okay, that's okay," my father kept saying until he finally threw his crutches into the mud and screamed, "God *damn* it, Alice, get her going!"

I would not cry. Not in front of my father, not in front of Jerry. I locked my jaw, trying to remember what I had done differently at the show, trying to re-create the space that had filled my head. I closed my eyes and let my memory travel back to that day, my father's hand against Patty Jo's lips, the look on his face, the wide, empty arena stretching open and dusty between the points of Darling's ears. But now the memory was jarred and broken, scattered with gifts and clothes and dinners in warm restaurants with waiters who called me *miss, sweetheart, bella.* I opened my eyes and the ground was wet, the sky streaked with white cotton clouds, the audience of cheering strangers replaced by Jerry, who watched with his eyes calm and his jaw set.

I could not control the horse, couldn't keep my body still on top of her lurching body. Whatever I had found that day in the ring, whatever secret part of myself that had stayed so long hidden, now retreated back into my bones and intestines, shielding itself from me, making me as useless and forgettable as I had been before.

When I finally climbed off the horse, my father took the reins without meeting my eye. I handed Darling over, waiting for him to say that it wasn't worth worrying, that I hadn't practiced before the last show and look how well that turned out. But he gimped out of the arena on one foot, leading Darling back into the barn without saying a word. I followed behind, lowering my head so that I wouldn't have to see Jerry's expression when I passed.

He followed a few paces behind, and I could hear his feet sinking through the mud. But I didn't turn to acknowledge him, didn't slow my pace to allow him to catch up. I passed through the barn, and when I reached the house, my sister was on the front porch, smoking a cigarette in her pajamas. "How'd it go?" she asked.

Jerry came up behind me, resting his elbows on the porch rail. "It was okay," I said.

Nona lifted her bare foot to Jerry's hand, balancing on one leg. He smiled slightly, pinching her toes with his fingers before she pulled away and sank herself onto the creaking porch swing. "Big day planned?" he asked.

Nona stretched her hands above her head, the shadows of her nipples pressing beneath the taut white of her tank top. I looked away, embarrassed. "I'm supposed to work with the rich girl today." She yawned. "Try to help her not suck so much when she's showing my horse."

Jerry leaned forward over the porch rail, tilting his chin at her cigarette. Nona walked the swing forward with her heels, stretching her arm to hold the cigarette in front of Jerry's mouth. He inhaled in three quick puffs, and my sister lifted her feet, letting the swing rock her away from him.

"He's not your horse," Jerry said. "Your pop sold him to Sheila."

Nona's eyes traveled to the barn. "He's mine," she said. "He was mine before I ever laid eyes on him. He'll be mine forever."

"There isn't a horse that can't be replaced," I said, and Nona's mouth twisted sideways.

"Thanks, *Dad.*"

Jerry climbed up the porch steps and sat beside my sister on the swing. She repositioned herself against him, looping her leg across his thigh. "Besides," I added, "Sheila's crazy in love with him. She won't sell him back."

Jerry put his hand over Nona's knee, rubbing it in slow circles as she held the cigarette between his lips to let him inhale. "It doesn't matter whose name is on the registration papers," Nona said. "She can't even ride him."

"How do you know?" I asked.

"Mom told me."

Jerry's hand moved up Nona's leg, massaging the inside of her thigh with his thumb. She closed her eyes and leaned her head back against the swing. I stared right at them, waiting for them to notice me, to realize that they were not in their bedroom, to stop. But Jerry looked only at Nona, working his thumb up her inner leg, watching as her mouth opened and closed in tiny, silent swallows of air.

"I don't know why you're asking Mom anyway," I said, and I could feel the meanness spreading through me like a thousand icy pinpricks. "She doesn't even come downstairs."

Nona shrugged without opening her eyes. "She came downstairs for the grandparents, didn't she?" she asked. "Pretended to be the good wife for them, pretended to be the good mother?"

My face was burning, my fingers clenching into my palms. Yes, our mother had come downstairs. She had sat at the table while we ate, nodded blankly while we spoke. But there had been no pretending. There had been no good wife. No good mother.

I wanted to ask why Nona suddenly cared so much what our mother said, anyway. Before she ran off with Jerry, my sister had not spent any more time with my mother than I had. She had carried up plates of food. She had closed curtains. She had done the bare minimum of obligatory duties just like the rest of us.

But before I could point this out, Jerry's forehead wrinkled in thought. "These are your mother's folks?" he asked, and Nona shook her head.

"My father's."

"Our mother doesn't have parents," I added sharply.

Nona opened her eyes, lifting her head to look at me. "Of course she has *parents,* Alice. What do you think? She grew on a tree?"

Jerry snorted and I glared at him. "Who are they then?" I asked.

"Her mother was a teacher," she said.

"And her father?"

"He left when she was little. Just took off in the middle of the night without saying one word. It's one of the reasons she's the way she is."

"And what way is that?" I asked.

Nona tilted her head at me. "Screwed up."

"She isn't *screwed up,*" I told her, and I could hear my voice rising, scraping through my throat like a reckless wind. "She's just sad."

"Fine," Nona said. "It's one of the reasons she's *sad.*"

I closed my eyes, trying to center myself, trying to stop the shaking in my fingers that had begun out in the arena. "No, it isn't."

Nona sat up, putting both feet on the ground so that Jerry's hand fell away from her leg. "Jesus, Alice, do you have to argue with every single thing I say?"

I shrugged and Nona blew her bangs off her forehead.

"All I'm saying is that she doesn't leave her bedroom," I told her. "She doesn't have any idea what's been going on out here."

The corners of Nona's mouth lifted into a crooked smile. "She knows you have a crush," she said, and my blood turned to ice inside my veins. "She knows that you spend all night every night on the phone with him, talking about love and poetry."

"Mom's insane," I whispered.

Nona's lower lip jutted into a mock pout and she reached her hand out, patting me on the head like I was a small child. "*No,*" she said, her voice syrupy. "She's just *sad.*"

I yanked away from her touch. "What do you know about anything?" I hissed. "You haven't even been here."

She shook her head at me as she stood. "What do you know about being sad?" she asked. "You're just a kid."

"I know you don't need a reason," I told her, but the door slammed. She was already inside.

Nona's cigarette burned between Jerry's lips, and he reached up to remove it, biting the inside of his cheek to keep from smiling. I felt raw and naked in front of him, as though Nona's words had stripped away the lining that separated me from the rest of the world. When I was a child, Nona had been my protector, putting herself between me and anything that might bring me harm. She had covered my eyes when a horse had to be put down, let me sleep in her bed during thunderstorms, drew my father's attention to herself on the rare occasions that he'd been angry enough at me that something might have come of it. But something had been lost in the time since she'd left. Something had been taken.

"What?" I snapped.

Jerry brushed the back of his hand across his lips, wiping the smile away like a smudge of dirt. "You've got a crush, huh?" he asked.

I wanted to rush at him and claw at his face with my fingernails, to make him scream and cry and beg for mercy, to crawl back into his ratty truck and never come back. "For your information," I told him, "I have a *boyfriend*. And he's *much* older than I am."

"Is that a fact?"

"It is," I said. "And if I asked him to, he would come here and rearrange your crooked teeth."

Jerry smiled. "What does Daddy think of your older man?"

"Maybe you haven't noticed," I told him, "but my father doesn't much care what I do."

"I've noticed," he said.

My whole self was boiling over, steaming. I glared at him to let him know that I didn't care what he thought, that just because my sister married him in some crappy little Kansas courthouse, just because she had sex with him in her bedroom, it didn't mean a thing to me. He was not my brother, not my family. Nothing he noticed meant a thing.

✦ ✦ ✦

"If you leave something behind," I said, keeping my voice low so that my mother wouldn't be able to hear me through the wall, "and then come back for it, does the thing still belong to you?"

"It depends," Mr. Delmar said. "Be more specific."

I thought of the last graded essay he'd handed back in class and cringed. *To Kill a Mockingbird was a very good book in which a lot of interesting things happened,* I'd written. The red ink of his handwriting gashed the margin: "More specific here." Stupid Alice Winston and her stupid, nonspecific details.

"Let's say I had a backpack," I began and then thought better of it. "Let's say I had a green backpack with purple polka dots and on the last day of school, I left it. When I came back in the fall, would it still be mine?"

"If no one else had taken it," he said.

"What if someone had?" I asked.

"Did someone steal your backpack?"

"No," I told him. "Answer the question."

"It depends," he said. "Did you just forget to take it home? Or did you leave it behind because you didn't want it anymore?"

"Does it matter?" I asked.

"I think so," he said. "If you leave something behind because you don't want it, it's gone. But if you lose something, well, it belongs to you forever. Whether you ever see it again or not."

So that was the difference.

"My sister and her husband are staying with us," I told Mr. Delmar.

"I didn't know you had a sister," he said.

"She's been gone," I told him. "She left when she got married. It's been a year since we've seen her."

There was a pause on the other end of the line, the pop of a refrigerator door opening, the crackle of an ice tray as he twisted it in his hands, then dropped the cubes into an empty glass. "Why has she stayed away so long?" he asked.

This was the question, the one without an answer. My sister had been busy, had been preoccupied, had been stranded in the woods without a phone or a post office. She'd been shooting heroin, robbing banks, killing strangers in cities all across the United States. She'd been having sex. "Her husband goes to medical school in California," I said. "It's a lot of work and they can't ever get away."

"Wow," he said, taking a slow sip from his glass, the ice cubes clinking against his teeth. "Medical school."

"He's taking a break from it now," I said. "They needed some time off."

"I can understand that."

"I don't like him," I said.

"Why not?"

I thought. "He's always watching everything I do," I said finally. "But he hardly even speaks to me."

"Maybe he's just shy," Mr. Delmar suggested.

I pictured Jerry sitting beside Nona on the porch swing, his hand moving up her leg, the square, meaty center of his palm nearly covering her thigh. Right in front of me he did this. Making her dip her head back, making her close her eyes. "Maybe," I said.

"People who have jobs like that," he told me, "people who have to work so hard, I think that the focus can sometimes make them seem a little strange, a little disinterested in the rest of us."

Jerry worked hard, there was no doubt about that. He was wiry and restless, waking early and staying up late. Once in a while, I would catch him resting, his eyes on the road in front of our house, watching it as if he expected it to do something. But these brief pauses were rare. Mostly, he shoveled sawdust and lifted hay bales, sweating and panting and ignoring everyone around him.

"I figure, even if people are assholes, you can learn something from them," Mr. Delmar said. "No one's a complete waste of time."

"Is that true?" I asked.

"I don't know." He laughed. "But it can't hurt to think so. It can't hurt to give people the benefit of the doubt."

I thought about this. I was all doubt—there was no benefit inside of me. "Maybe you should give the guy a chance," Mr. Delmar said, reading my thoughts. "Ask him some questions. Maybe you'll find out he's not so bad. Maybe you'll learn something."

I wanted to disagree, to say that Jerry had bowed legs and a smirking expression, that he ate with his fingers and belched when he drank, that he couldn't possibly know anything about anything. But for Mr. Delmar, I would try. I would change into old jeans and a T-shirt and pick up a pitchfork for the first time in weeks. I would clean stalls beside my sister's husband. I would ask him questions about himself. I would try to learn something.

And, of course, Mr. Delmar was not wrong: Jerry, it turned out, knew everything there was to know about Elvis.

The first half hour we spent mucking stalls together was strained with awkward silence. I asked about his family and he said he had none. I asked about the rodeos and he said that they were just that: rodeos. I asked where he came from, and he said nowhere in particular. But then I asked what books he'd read. After that, I couldn't have paid him to shut up.

From Jerry I learned that Elvis made thirty-three movies and released over 150 albums and singles. Jerry had been to Graceland twelve times, had seen where the King slept and sat and ate his breakfast. "There are a lot of people out there who would say they could tell you about Elvis," Jerry explained, "who say they know all the secrets. But those are the people who get caught up in hype, the ones who focus on scandal or money or drugs." He shook his head as he lifted a forkful of soggy straw into the wheelbarrow. "Elvis was so much more than that."

"He was a pretty big star," I said finally, adding the single piece of information that I knew of Elvis Presley.

"He was more than a star," Jerry told me.

Jerry didn't just know about Elvis's career, he knew about his life. He had read ten different books on Elvis. *"Ten,"* he told me and set down his pitchfork to hold up all of his fingers.

Elvis had been born poor. Even though he was a star, he was lonely. No one ever really understood him. He took good care of his mother. He had a twin brother who died.

"Did you take Nona to Graceland?" I asked.

"Twice," he told me. "We thought about getting married there, but your sister said it would be tacky. I guess I see her point—so many tourists wandering around."

My whole life, I had never heard my sister so much as mention

Elvis Presley. The idea that she might have been married in his back-yard was harder to imagine than the courthouse in Kansas.

"What's it like?" I asked, and Jerry stopped for a moment, lean-ing against the stall door to light a cigarette.

"Unbelievable," he told me. "But sad. You wander around and it's like, *he lived here.* You walk where he walked, see what he saw. And it really hits you: he's gone. This whole big life, just . . . *gone.*"

Jerry watched the ground as he spoke, holding his cigarette between his thumb and forefinger. Toy Boy nickered and Jerry reached out without looking, patting his neck.

"I knew a girl who died," I said and Jerry raised his eyes.

"Yeah?"

"Her name was Polly," I said. "Last year, she drowned in the canal."

"She was your age?" he asked and I nodded. "Were you friends?"

"We'd been in school together since kindergarten. We walked the same road home every day." Jerry puffed at his cigarette as he lis-tened. Standing there in my old grubby clothes with my hair pulled back into a bland ponytail, I felt like a kid again. Not the old Alice, dumb and weak and good at nothing. But like any child, anywhere. "No," I told him. "We weren't friends."

Toy Boy stood with his eyes half closed, little groans of pleasure creaking through his lips as Jerry scratched his chest. "Almost makes it worse, doesn't it?" Jerry asked, and when he looked at me, I felt the jolt of connection between us, plug to socket.

"Why did you come here?" I whispered.

Jerry dropped his cigarette onto the ground, stubbing it into the straw with the toe of his boot. "The world's a fucked-up place, baby sis," he said. "Why does anyone do anything?"

In the afternoons, after he had finished his bus route, my father worked with Patty Jo on jumping while my sister worked with Sheila. Even with his broken leg, my father was animated when he gave lessons, gliding alongside or hopping up and down in the cen-ter of the arena.

Nona had a more casual approach. She sat on the fence, smoking cigarettes and looking bored while Sheila and Cap practiced show-manship in front of her. She never took over, never demonstrated or so much as laid a finger on Cap. But Sheila didn't seem to notice. She watched with her eyes wide with respect, making mental notes of every little thing that Nona said. She began wearing her blond hair in a messy bun, began standing with one hip cocked when she wasn't working, mirroring Nona.

"See the way his ears are pointed back," Nona told Sheila. "He's not paying attention to you." And Sheila nodded reverently, clicking her tongue to bring Cap's attention back to herself.

After each lesson, Sheila stood with me in the barn, repeating everything my sister had told her. "Cap's high-strung," she said. "He needs to feel challenged to perform well. I've been focusing on how to make him do what I want, when really, I need to be thinking of us as a team, need to be thinking about what he needs from *me*. Isn't that the smartest thing you've ever heard?"

"Sure," I said.

The final show was only a few days away, and I had yet to ride Darling the way I had that day in the ring. Every time I tried, my father yelled and Jerry stood watching while Darling stumbled, out of control, beneath me. I tried to make it small inside my head, tried to remind myself that it didn't matter, that regardless of what happened at the final show, I would still have my leather backpack and my expensive clothes, still have my shiny hair and the whole cheer-leading squad to eat lunch with. But inside the arena, I would look sideways, seeing Jerry's face, the picture he had of me—I hogged the bathroom. I couldn't ride a horse.

"Your sister is absolutely amazing," Sheila went on. "It's like she watches and she just *understands*. She sees it all so clearly. I do what she says and it works."

Out in the arena, Patty Jo brought Toy Boy to a halt in the center and my father stood beside her, brushing his fingers over her knee as he spoke up to her. Her head lowered while she listened, her hand moving down her leg toward his.

"I can't imagine what it must be like to have a sister like Nona," Sheila gushed, her face pink as she fastened the buckles of Cap's blanket under his stomach, then led him into his stall. "She's about the coolest person I've ever met."

In the arena, Patty's fingers met my father's, then crept across the whole of his hand, palm pressing palm.

"You can have her," I said, and Sheila stopped, cocking her hip at me.

"Huh?" she asked.

"She's yours," I told her. "My father too. My whole life—you can have it."

"Alice," Sheila said, and her voice was suddenly thin and nervous. "Don't act crazy."

"For real," I told her. "I'm not using it anymore."

At the last horse show of the year, everyone stared at my sister, pointing and nodding and whispering to one another. *Well, look at that,* they mouthed silently. *I'll be damned.*

Nona stood beside Jerry, pretending not to notice. Before showmanship, she gave a few last-minute pointers to Sheila, then walked around the fence to stand directly behind her, whispering instructions when the judge had moved far enough way that he couldn't hear. Mrs. Altman sat with the Catfish up in the stands and when Sheila took first place, she nearly fell off the side from cheering so hard. Sheila came out of the ring and burst into tears, wrapping her arms around my sister's neck. "You're a wizard!" Sheila gushed. "A goddess! A miracle worker!"

Nona stiffened, but she patted Sheila's back. "Okay," she said.

During the jumping class, Patty Jo took first place and repeated a similar display with my father when she came out of the ring, kissing him on both cheeks. "You've changed my life," she whispered. "I swear to God, I don't think I can remember ever being as completely happy as I am right now."

No one paid a speck of attention to me until I came out of the horse trailer dressed for reining. Nona raised her eyes to me. "Those are my clothes," she said.

That morning, I had paced beside the trailer while my father loaded Yellow Cap, Toy Boy, and Darling into the back. "I don't want you to worry about a thing," he told me. "It's the adrenaline that does it for you. I'm sure of it. You'll get in front of the crowd and it will be just like it was last time."

But it wasn't adrenaline. It couldn't be. Because that was all there was when I rode Darling at home—adrenaline pumping through my body like a river of fire. And it made no difference. At home, I had been able to convince myself that it didn't matter, that I still had school and Mr. Delmar and the cheerleaders lining up to be friends with me. But now that I was at the show, now that I looked at Darling and the stands full of strangers and posse members and clients and parents of Bud Pope's students, my knees softened and my legs trembled beneath me.

I tried to think how I could get out of it. I could pretend to be sick, could cut my hand with a hoof pick, could fall backward off the top of the bleachers—which would probably only break my leg and not kill me.

Nona was quiet, eyeing me in her old clothes as she talked Sheila through her equitation routine. But before reining, she came up to me, shoving her hands into her pockets and keeping her eyes on the ground. "I could do your hair for you," she offered.

I sat between her legs while she combed my hair, pulling it back and pinning it up, smoothing her fingers through the tangles. "There," she said when she was finished. "You look good."

"It's too loose," I told her.

"It's supposed to be," she said. "When you stop at the end, just throw your head a little—they won't even notice. Your hair will fall down and it'll look like you stopped so hard that it knocked your braid out. Trust me, they love shit like that."

It wouldn't matter about my hair. Nona hadn't seen me on Darling, hadn't seen the mess we were inside the ring. But Jerry had, and he followed as I led Darling toward the arena. My father was leaning against the fence with Patty Jo, not paying attention, and Jerry put his hand on my shoulder. His eyes were serious, his face screwed in thought, and for a moment, I figured he was going to tell me some new fact about Elvis, something he'd left out in our earlier discussions. I glared at him, ready to be annoyed.

"It isn't about control," he whispered. "It isn't about concentration."

He slid his hand down my arm, resting his fingers lightly on my hip. "You want to be tight *here,*" he said, then smoothed his hands down his own hips, making a frame around the space between his crotch and navel. "Put all the fear right here. Just stuff it down until it's like a knot, a cold, hard fist clenched right in your gut."

Jerry's jaw was hard, his eyebrows knitting as he balled his fist into his stomach. Then he reached out, touching the pads of his fingers to the center of my forehead. "And here," he said, "be empty." His skin felt cool and dry against mine and I closed my eyes, trying to let my thoughts drain away. "Look right between her ears, nowhere else. Don't think. Don't feel. Make your mind as blank as the sky in summertime. Okay?"

There it was: the exact description of how I had done it the first time. He had explained precisely the way it felt to ride in the last show, the way it felt to win. "Okay," I said, and he held his hand out, helping me mount the horse.

"She'll do the work," he told me. "All you have to do is stay on top of her."

And he was right. The gate opened and I sat on top of Darling, stuffing every spasm of fear into the pit of my stomach until it churned and hardened and my mind filled with cold, empty space. For the second time, we swept across the arena, gliding through our spins, lifting clouds of dust around us as we shifted through our lead changes. At the end, Darling tucked beneath me, sliding into a perfect stop. I tossed my head ever so slightly and my hair spilled down my back, the crowd inhaling in a single, stunned breath. At the rail, my sister cheered and screamed beside my father. Patty Jo blew kisses at me and the Catfish danced in the stands.

We came out of the arena and my father took Darling's reins as I slid onto the ground. "What'd I tell you?" he asked Nona as he shook me by the shoulders. "What'd I *tell* you?"

Nona threw her arms around my neck, spinning me in a circle and jumping up and down. "Jesus fucking Christ!" she gasped. "Maybe it runs in the family after all!"

The Altmans and the Catfish gathered around us, clapping me on the back and kissing my cheeks while the earth settled back around me. "I don't know how she does it," my father told them. "I swear to God, I don't."

Through all the cheering and gasping and congratulatory hugs, I could still feel the tightness pressed inside myself, the vast, open nothing ringing between my ears. Everyone else could gape with wonder, could question how I'd done it, what sort of miraculous gift must have been bestowed upon me at birth. And though I stood among them, letting them pet me and kiss me and tell me how no one else could have done better, I could not tap into their perfect, ringing joy, could not shrug off their questions and compliments, could not begin to offer an explanation. Because there, standing behind them all, was Jerry, not looking at me, not saying anything.

After the show, Patty Jo took the whole crowd of us out to dinner. At the restaurant, they pulled four tables together to seat us all. I sat between my father and Patty Jo, their arms brushing against mine, their heads dipping forward to smile at each other in small, secret exchanges. While the rest of our party was distracted with menus and drink orders, my father reached behind me, pulling at a loose thread on the collar of Patty's shirt. His forearm rested against the back of my neck, sliding against my hair. Beside me, Patty blushed down at her menu, her eyelids dipping closed as my father's fingertips grazed the delicate line of her jaw. It was a moment, maybe less, before the waitress turned her attention to Patty Jo and my father's hand fell away from her face, resting on my shoulder, giving it a little squeeze as if that had been his intent all along.

When I looked up, Jerry was watching from the other side of the table. I squared my shoulders beneath my father's arm, trying to make the embrace look natural, as if my father hugged me all the time, as if there was nothing at all awkward or peculiar about him putting his arm around me.

But Jerry's lips crept up into a half smile. *Smooth riding,* he mouthed. A few days earlier, I would have hissed between my teeth at him, but now, I felt a warm glow spread up my neck at his approval.

Thanks, I mouthed back, and my father turned his attention back to his menu, letting his arm drop from my shoulder.

During dinner, Sheila hooked her blue ribbon on the front of her shirt so that it hung down like a necktie, and Mrs. Altman ordered champagne for the table. They brought glasses for everyone, including Sheila and me. We toasted to the summer, to the show season, to the flood. We toasted to Patty Jo, Sheila, and me, to my father, and to our stable—the finest barn in town.

At home, we put the horses away and my father glided inside the house on his crutches, humming beneath his breath. But Jerry and Nona dragged their feet and I waited outside with them. My head felt light and spinny from the speed, the win, the champagne, and I tottered on the heels of my boots as I followed them through the barn. Nona held my blue ribbon up to the side of my face in the barn light. "It brings out your eyes," she told me, then wobbled forward, catching herself on my shoulders. "Sorry." She giggled. "I'm a little drunk."

Jerry came up behind me and, in a single motion, lifted me by my waist, hoisting me up onto his shoulders as easily as he lifted the bales of hay. Nona leaned forward, laughing into her knees while Jerry spun in circles, galloping through the barn and pawing in Nona's direction like a wild horse. I gripped his hair, laughing and screaming as he chased my sister out into the darkness.

Outside in the round pen, Ginger's colt was trotting back and forth with his ears perked and his tail raised, greeting Darling, who nickered at him from across the way. Nona rested against the fence, catching her breath. Jerry lifted me off his shoulders, setting me down beside my sister, and the three of us settled beside the fence, watching the colt pace beneath the moonlight.

"He's a good-looking horse," Jerry said, and Nona smiled.

"He's the spitting image of our last stud," she told him.

"What's his name?" Jerry asked, and I covered my face with my hands, still dizzy from the chase.

"*Richard,*" I told him, and my sister burst out laughing.

"That's god-awful!" she said.

"Royal *Red* Richard," I added, and Nona leaned into my shoulder, giggling into my hair while Jerry shook his head.

"That's the shittiest horse name I've ever heard," he told us. "And I've heard some shitty horse names."

"I can't believe Dad went for the new model," Nona said. "He couldn't stand Bart."

"What do you call him?" Jerry asked, and I shrugged.

"He's a stud," I said. "We don't call him anything."

"This little guy'll be a hell of a horse when he's older," Jerry told us. "Look at his head." I stood between them, resting against Nona's arm. "Needs a better name, though."

Ginger's colt trotted the length of his pen under the moonlight, the early hints of muscles rippling, the weight of his hooves thumping against the dusty ground. "He *is* pretty," I said, seeing for the first time what Jack must have seen straight off—the power, the strength, the perfect arch of his neck.

"He's a rock star," Nona agreed, and Jerry leaned forward, grinning at her.

"The King," he said.

There was nothing official about the moment, nothing put on paper, nothing signed or sealed. But in the end, it didn't matter. Jerry spoke the words and they stuck. Unintentional as it might have been, Jerry had given him a name. For the rest of King's life, he would belong to Jerry.

That night in my dreams, the rain was soft against the window, the sky silver and shimmering above it, a lake suspended in air. I wandered the dark hallways of the dream-soaked house, the carpet damp on my bare feet, past my mother's room and the guest room where my father slept, separated from his wife by watery walls that trickled with streams of glistening raindrops.

Inside my dream, I reached Nona's room and the door was open, the light on. Her bed rocked like a raft on the ocean, tilting and floating along the floor of her bedroom, touching against the walls then floating back to the other side. Nona sat cross-legged on her bed, licking at the pink icing of a cupcake while Jerry slept beside her, his naked arm thrown across her bare thigh. Without waiting for invitation, I climbed onto the bed and Nona scooted to the edge, making room for me in the middle. The sheets were soft and warm against my skin and Jerry rearranged himself without waking, stretching his arm across me to touch the perfect white knob of my sister's anklebone. I leaned my head against her shoulder and her hair smelled like frosting, her skin smooth and light against mine. The bed floated across the room, padding against the walls, and I let my body soften into the mattress, sinking my head into the sweet-smelling mound of their pillows. "I'm so tired," I whispered to Nona, and she licked the pink icing from her fingers before touching my hair.

"You should go to sleep," she said. She slid her body down against mine and lifted the covers up over our heads, shutting out the light. In the darkness of my dream, she and Jerry reached for each other around me, their legs touching between mine, their fingers lacing through my hair, their arms winding around my shoulders until we were all three tangled in a human knot, until I could not tell where I stopped and they began.

twelve

WITH THE SHOW season finished, Nona's approach to Sheila's lessons changed. Most days, she would saddle one of the Old Men for herself and she and Sheila would ride down the driveway, onto the road, and out of view, plodding along at a lazy walk. Nona said that riding a Kill horse down the road didn't really count as riding—she was still retired. She said it was good experience for Sheila, though she didn't say it with the slightest amount of conviction. And my father shrugged approval, using the time to work alone with Patty Jo in the arena.

Each afternoon, Nona and Sheila walked the country roads on their horses. Sometimes they were gone for an hour. Sometimes they were gone for three. Once, they came back with an armload of wild asparagus they had picked alongside the canal. Another time, they came back with milk shakes.

"Jesus," Nona said, resting her elbows on the hitching post while Sheila led Cap into the barn after one of their afternoon rides. "Her *life.*"

"What about it?" I asked.

"She's been to Egypt," Nona said. "Did you know that? I mean, fucking *Egypt*!"

"Her dad's a professor," I told her. "They go around looking at stars."

"Must be nice," Nona said.

I didn't know how to answer. Nona had spent the last year traveling around, going to places I had never been, seeing things I had never seen. "I guess," I said.

"Life is so easy for people like that," Nona went on. "And they don't even know it."

I thought of telling her about Sheila's friends at school, the ones who made her eat alone and passed notes to everyone in her class, telling them not to speak to her. But I watched Nona's face constrict with thought and I knew it wouldn't be enough to change her mind. "You've been a lot of places," I told her.

"I'm never gonna go to Egypt, Alice," she said.

"You don't know that," I told her. "Life is long."

"I *know*," she said. "Okay? I know."

I looked ahead at my own life and there it was: eighth grade, high school, and then a long, foggy tunnel that could lead to anything, a road to anywhere. My life was still unformed, a wide-open mystery. How could anyone *know* anything?

"How much do you charge that little girl's mother just to walk around with her?" Jerry asked, and Nona gave him a dark look.

"Enough to pay for your supper," she said.

Jerry's jaw flexed and his eyes narrowed, but Sheila came bounding around the corner of the barn and their faces cleared as they turned away from each other.

The whole world seemed to behave better when Sheila walked into view. It was like everyone understood that she was new, untouched. No one wanted to be the first to get her dirty.

"What are we talking about?" Sheila asked and cocked her hip sideways, standing beside my sister like a shadow.

"The complications of the world," Jerry said, and Nona cuffed him on the back of the head.

Jerry and Nona were like this with each other—coarse and quick to snap. I watched them throughout the days, sniping and growling at each other, shooting daggers of ice from their eyes.

"Your sister and her hubby are about the cutest thing I've ever seen," Bitsy told me, and the rest of the Catfish gathered around.

"I don't think they get along that well," I said and they laughed.

"Oh," Patty Jo said, "that's young love for you."

"What is?" I asked.

"Spats and fights and feuds—it's all the sexual energy," Jaycee explained.

"That's right," Bitsy told me. "It's practically erupting from the tops of their heads."

At night, after the horses were fed and the clients had gone home, my father would go inside and Nona would change the radio station in the barn from classical to oldies. She and Jerry would sit on the folding chairs, smoking cigarettes and drinking the beer that they stocked inside the tack room refrigerator. During the day, they were strange with each other. But at night, in the barn, with the music staticky on the speakers and the horses nickering night noises through the barn, my sister and Jerry seemed easy in each other's company. Their limbs loosened and their voices lightened with laughter.

After I finished my homework, I would wander out to the barn and sit beside them, sneaking sips from their beer bottles and listening to the sounds of the crickets. During the day, Jerry rarely spoke to anyone. At night, my sister and I talked while he listened. "So who asked about me?" Nona asked, and I slid my hand across the table, stealing a sip of her beer.

"I don't know," I said. "A few people, I guess."

"Be specific," she told me. She was smiling, her cheeks glowing pink. "Names and details." Jerry shifted in his folding chair, wetting his lower lip with his tongue as he watched her.

"Valerie Hayes asked about you," I said. "She said it was a scandal when you left."

Nona grinned and clapped her hands. "A scandal," she repeated and winked at Jerry. "Well, that's something."

The corners of Jerry's mouth turned up slightly and I wanted to have more to say. "A *total fucking scandal* is what she said exactly," I told them, and Nona tossed her hair back, laughing up at the ceiling. I reached again for her beer and neither of them moved to stop me.

"That's hilarious," Nona said. "Who else?"

I couldn't think of anyone else we both knew, anyone else who she would ever believe had talked to me. "Ruby asked," I said finally, "when she and Jack were here."

Nona's lower lip pouched into a fake pout. "What?" she said. "No boys asked about me?"

Jerry leveled her with his eyes, slouching in his chair and stretching the heels of his cowboy boots out in front of him so that they thudded on the concrete floor. Nona giggled. I wasn't sure what was happening, but suddenly the conversation had evaporated into the dusty night air and neither of them was looking at me.

Jerry lifted his hand and turned his palm up, crooking his finger at my sister. She stood and the corners of his mouth lifted into a smile as she crossed the floor to stand in front of him. For a moment, they only looked at each other, then Nona stepped forward, straddling Jerry's lap. He put his hands around her waist, lowering her onto his lap. His fingers slid down her waist until the squares of his palms rested on her back pockets, pulling her into him. She dipped her head to kiss him and her yellow hair fell forward, closing like a curtain, leaving me behind.

"Did you know that Elvis Presley had a twin?" I asked.

"Jesse Garon," Mr. Delmar said. "He was stillborn."

This seemed an unlikely detail for both Jerry and Mr. Delmar to be aware of. They had nothing in common, their lives spreading in opposite directions. "Why do you know that?" I asked.

"Common cultural knowledge," he said. "Why do you?"

I thought of trying to explain about Jerry, about my sister, about them being back and living in our house and probably having sex at this very minute. But he thought that my father was a professor and my sister's husband was in medical school. I didn't know how to explain about Jerry and his knowledge of Elvis without giving it all away. "The same reason," I told him.

"I wouldn't have taken you for a big Elvis fan," he said.

"Well," I said carefully, "he was such a big star."

"The biggest," he said. "The first great American sex symbol."

I thought of Elvis with his greased black hair and wagging hips, his white socks and shiny guitar. Everything, it seemed, came down to sex.

"Have you had sex a lot of times?" I asked, and on the other end of the line, Mr. Delmar choked on his drink.

"I'm not sure," he said after he'd composed himself. "What constitutes *a lot?*"

"I don't know," I told him. "How many times have you done it?"

"How many *times?*"

"Well, with how many people?"

"A gentleman doesn't discuss those things, Alice."

"Are you a gentleman?" I asked.

"I'm a man with a gentle nature," he said. "Is that close enough?"

"Okay then," I told him. "How old were you the first time?"

"You're making me blush, Alice."

"*How* old?"

"I was a late bloomer."

"Fifteen?" I asked.

"Jesus Christ," he sputtered. "I'm from Michigan!"

"Eighteen?"

"Around there."

"Nineteen?"

"I was twenty," he said. "Satisfied?"

They had told us all about sex at school, about getting pregnant and getting AIDS. *Don't have sex.* During sex ed, our home ec teacher had explained where our fallopian tubes were and that we had been born with all the eggs we would ever have. "I'm not going to have sex until I'm married," Janice Reardon had declared afterward while people averted their eyes so that they wouldn't have to listen. "I want to get into a good college."

"What does that have to do with anything?" I asked, speaking before I could remember my own rule about not engaging Janice Reardon in conversation.

"After girls have sex, their math scores drop," Janice told me knowingly.

"That's insane," I said.

"They've done research, Alice Winston," she told me. "It's well documented."

I had repeated this entire conversation to the cheerleaders at lunch, and they leaned forward, laughing into their corn dogs. Kelly and Rachel both had boyfriends in the eighth grade, and though they had not gone all the way with them, they knew about things like hickeys and petting. Once she had controlled her laughter, Rachel gave our entire table a demonstration on how to give a proper blow job, using her corn dog as a prop. The key, she told us, was to open your throat and cover your teeth with your lips—you didn't want to bite him. I watched with the rest of the cheerleaders as they clapped and whistled. But I wasn't entirely sure that this proved anything. A blow job was not actual sex and even if it was, the cheerleaders were mostly in the lower math classes, still learning fractions and long division. A severe head injury would probably not affect their math scores.

"How old was she?" I asked Mr. Delmar. "The girl?"

"The same age."

"And was it her first time too?"

"She said it was," he told me.

"Do you think she was telling the truth?" I asked.

"I did then," he said.

"But you don't now?"

"I don't know what I believe anymore," he told me.

"Why would she lie about something like that?" I asked, and he took a breath as he lit a cigarette.

"I don't know," he said. "Why does anyone lie about anything?"

When I was in second grade, I told my teacher that my mother had been killed in a boating accident. It wasn't a very good lie. We didn't own a boat and even if we had, this was the desert—there weren't a lot of opportunities for tragedies of the nautical variety. Still, my teacher was young and new to the experience of working with children. She was moved by my hardships. For the week or so before she found out the truth, my teacher went out of her way to make up for the fact that my mother was dead. She gave me extra gold stars on spelling tests and braided my hair during recess. She let me sit on her lap during story time. Of all the students in her class, I was the only one whose mother had been killed in a boating accident—I was her favorite.

But Desert Valley was a small town and it didn't take long before my teacher learned that my mother was not dead. She called our house and talked to my father, who told her that I had an active imagination, that I had recently watched a biography of Natalie Wood on television and had probably just gotten confused.

This explanation was not nearly good enough. At school, my teacher told me that truth was sacred, that a person was only as good as her word. I ought to know, she told me, how bad other people had it. There were children in the world who couldn't afford school or clothes or food, children whose parents were sick or dying or held their hands to hot stoves when they got mad at them. In China, my teacher told me, baby girls were drowned in buckets when they were born, just for being girls instead of boys. With so many terrible things happening in the world, why would I ever pretend that my mother, who was healthy and alive and sitting right that moment at home, was dead? It was bad luck, bad karma to make up such a story. I was tempting the universe. What goes around, my teacher said, comes around.

So I told her that I was sorry, that I had not known about babies drowning in buckets, had never heard of parents holding their children's hands to hot stoves. I never meant to tempt the universe. But it didn't matter what I said. From that point forward, my teacher never braided my hair or let me sit in her lap again. When I scored a perfect ten on spelling tests, I got a single gold star, just like everyone else. At the time, she had seemed like the most beautiful woman in the world, with red hair and green eyes and skin speckled with pumpkin-colored freckles. I would have given anything just to make her look at me, to make her spend an extra second speaking to me, to make her smile when her eyes met mine. But these were the things I could never have explained. And in the end, it didn't matter at all. Now, when I think of her, I don't even remember her name.

"It was the funniest thing in the world," Nona said, laughing into her beer as she told Jerry the story. "Dad answered the phone and was like, *A boat?*"

Jerry shook his head at me from his folding chair. "That's pretty fucked up," he said, and I blushed. "Why'd you say that?"

I bit my lip, trying to think of the answer. *My mother* is *dead. My mother has always been dead.* But this was not anything I was allowed to say, not anything that anyone would ever want to hear. Before I could think of something better, Nona waved the question away with her cigarette.

"Alice was always saying loony things," she told Jerry. "Even when she was itty-bitty, we never knew what was going to come out of her mouth."

Jerry cocked his head at me, trying to understand this. I looked away, busying myself with peeling the label off Nona's beer bottle.

"It's because she's so smart," Nona explained, her voice slurred with alcohol. "The world could never keep up with her brain."

I started to smile at the compliment, but when I raised my eyes, Jerry was still staring at me. "Maybe it's because she was just a kid," he said. "Maybe she was trying to figure out why her mother never went outside."

Nona's back straightened at Jerry's suggestion, her neck lengthening, her chin lifting. Sitting across from her, I could feel my own body stiffening. We were allowed to talk about our mother, how she said strange things and stayed away from the world like she was allergic to it. But no one else could. The silence between Jerry and Nona felt suddenly strained and heavy, and I understood that even though they were husband and wife, Jerry was not a member of this club. He was not allowed to talk about our mother.

"It wasn't always that way," Nona said finally, her voice controlled and careful, weighing the words inside her head before she spoke them. "She used to be normal. Well, closer to normal anyway."

I watched her face, trying to gauge if this was the truth or if she was merely spinning things so that Jerry wouldn't think his wife had craziness in her blood. But Nona's eyes were misty with remembering, her thoughts so far away that I couldn't begin to decipher them.

"My mom and dad used to go out together," she continued. "When all the work was done, they'd get into the truck and just drive around the valley listening to the radio, looking at the stars, finding plots of land they wanted to buy when they got rich. They would come home all smiles and laughter, talking about the house they would build themselves, the barn that would be theirs and theirs alone. He would hold her hand and she would rest her head on his shoulder, letting him dance her around the living room while he pointed out all the things they would leave behind—the old furniture and the stained carpet, the house that Jack built."

Nona paused, taking a sip of her beer, and her eyes welled, her smile trembling. "Do you remember how they used to dance together?" she asked, and when she looked at me, her face shifted as she realized that I did not, could not remember. Everything good between my parents had existed in the time before I was born. She looked away, sorry to have bragged her happy memory in front of me.

But I didn't want her pity. "It doesn't matter now," I said. "They aren't in love anymore."

Nona's beer tipped sideways in her hand. I watched the lip, waiting for it to spill. "Why would you say that?" she asked.

I stared at my sister. "He barely even looks at her," I said. "They barely even talk."

Nona shook her head. "You don't understand," she said, and I stood up.

"You've been gone," I told her, and my voice felt tight and strangled inside my throat, the voice of a stranger.

"There are some things that don't change," Nona told me. "Not in one year. Not in ten."

"So what happened then?" Jerry asked, and Nona blinked at him.

"Things got hard," she whispered. "Things fell apart."

"That doesn't happen overnight," Jerry told her, and Nona shook her head. He didn't understand.

"We had this cat once," Nona said, taking another slow sip from her beer. "This scraggly old barn cat—Ham."

"I don't remember that," I said. Our barn cats had always just been that—barn cats. We didn't give them names.

"You hadn't been born yet," Nona said and gave me a sideways look, annoyed with the interruption. "I was, like, five. *Anyway.* It got sick. All skinny and greasy with dead, glassy eyes and sores all over."

"It was dying," Jerry said, and Nona nodded.

"We didn't have any money. I mean, *none.* And so Dad just picked the cat up by the scruff of the neck with one hand and a two-by-four with the other and walked around behind the barn. We heard one loud crack, and that was it. No more Ham."

"Were you messed up?" Jerry asked.

"Not me," Nona said. "Not so bad. But Mom." Her eyes lifted then, resting on mine, and a chill passed between us, a common understanding. Our mother.

"What did she do?" Jerry asked. Nona's eyes winced a moment with mine, then flickered back to Jerry.

"She just flipped," she said. "She screamed and cried and threw herself at him, clawing at his face and chest, sobbing how much she hated him." Her eyes moved back to mine. "She came apart."

"And then she fell," I said.

"And wouldn't get up."

"Was that the first time?" I asked.

Nona's shoulders sagged, her expression flat and empty. "I think so," she said. "If it happened before, I don't remember."

Jerry stood up, crossing the barn for Nona's pack of cigarettes. "I'm not sure I'm following," he said.

Nona tossed her hair behind her, shaking the memory away. "It doesn't matter," she said and stood, striking a match to light Jerry's cigarette. "It's just old stupid stuff that doesn't matter to anyone."

The day my father got his cast removed, he came home and rolled up his pant leg to show us. His leg was as thin as a noodle, the muscle gone, the skin sagging around the bone of his shin and knee. He had been hoping that once the cast was gone and the crutches returned, it would be as if the break had never happened at all. But without cast or crutches, my father seemed less mobile than he had before. Walking the length of the barn, he would have to pause, holding himself upright against the wall and bending to massage his knee and hip with his fingers. He couldn't crouch to pick hooves or repair a thrown horseshoe. He couldn't maintain his balance to carry hay bales or push a wheelbarrow. He couldn't mount a horse.

"I never thought I'd be a guy who had to walk with a cane," he said to Patty Jo when she suggested that it might help.

"Not forever," she told him, squeezing his shoulder for emphasis. "Just for now. Just until the muscle comes back."

And as she had once taken me shopping for new clothes, she now took my father to buy a cane—something simple and inconspicuous. Something elegant. They went off together in Patty's car and didn't come home until late. The cane Patty picked out had a beech-wood shaft and a stitched leather handle.

"What do you think?" my father asked when I caught him staring at his reflection in the glass doors of our china cabinet. I thought the cane looked completely out of place with his faded blue jeans and stained T-shirt. "Patty thinks it makes me look dignified," he added.

"It looks expensive," I said.

"It was."

"Can you get it dirty?" I asked, and my father turned sideways to see his profile.

"I probably shouldn't."

"What good is it then?" I asked him. "If you can't use it in the barn."

My father shrugged. "Not that much to do out there anyway," he told me. "Jerry's got things under control."

As my father did less and less out in the barn, Jerry did more and more, cleaning stalls and exercising the show horses. He never grumbled or complained about the extra work. Spare time made him restless and when all the work was finished, he would pace through the barn, searching for something else to do. He reorganized the tack room and swept the barn floor, moving the grain bins to clean behind them.

"Sit still," Nona snapped at him. "You're making me fucking crazy."

But Jerry could not sit still. And the day he took a halter out to

King's round pen, I followed behind him, climbing up on the fence to watch. King skittered away from Jerry when he opened the gate. Jerry stood perfectly still inside the round pen with his arms lowered and the halter hanging from his fingertips. In the opposite pen, Darling stood with her ears perked forward, watching.

The minutes passed and King took a few uncertain steps toward Jerry, his nostrils widening as he sniffed the air around him. His hooves clopped through the dust until he stood an arm's length away, but still Jerry made no movement. King stretched his neck, his nose poking close to Jerry's shoulder, rustling the collar of his shirt with his breath. Jerry lifted his hand slowly, palm up, holding it so that King could get his scent. The horse jumped sideways, then crept close again. I sat on the fence, holding my breath silent in my chest as the dance continued, forward, back, until they touched.

Jerry ran his hand lightly over King's neck and chest. Every time the horse moved away, Jerry's body went still, waiting until he approached again. At last, he lifted the halter, touching it to the side of King's face, letting him sniff the fabric. Then he backed slowly out of the round pen, closing the gate behind him.

"What are you doing?" I asked.

"Somebody's gotta start working with him before he gets too big," Jerry told me. "He'll be wasted otherwise."

"Dad won't like it," I said, and Jerry gazed at me only a moment before turning back to the barn.

"Then I guess we're lucky he isn't around much."

Sheila Altman had auditioned for a community production of *The Sound of Music* and was cast as Louisa—the bratty one, she told me. She said that rehearsals were going to be intense. Until the play was over she would not be able to spend as much time out at the barn. I expected my father to object to this, to tell her how important it was to keep practicing, keep preparing for next year. But he seemed pleased by her news, telling her that she ought to take some time for herself now that the season was done and that of course we would all come see the play.

With all the free time, my father spent longer hours working with Patty on her jumping, or driving around with her in the afternoons, looking at tack and equipment. They never returned with any new tack or equipment, but if anyone besides me noticed this, no one mentioned it.

Without Sheila's lessons to occupy her time, Nona wandered through the barn, chatting with the Catfish or watching Jerry muck stalls without offering to help. Every afternoon, Jerry worked with King in the round pen. After a few days, he could halter him, then lead him. Soon, he had attached a lunge line and stood in the center of the pen, clicking his tongue and tapping the end of the lunge line against his thigh to make King trot circles around him.

"The only part of that horse that matters is his dick," Nona told Jerry. "You're wasting your time."

"Then let me waste it in peace," he answered.

Nona narrowed her eyes at him, ready for a fight. But Jerry turned his attention back to King. My sister waited a moment, then stalked away, leaning against the fence of Darling's pen to light a cigarette and glower at Jerry from a distance.

"It can't hurt to halter train him," I told my sister. "I mean, we'll have to put a halter on him when we breed him."

Nona shook her head at the ground and I climbed up on the fence beside her. "I don't see why *Jerry* has to do it," she snorted. "It's none of his business. Why does he even care?"

During the day, my sister and her husband gave better and better impressions of people who could not stand the sight of each other. But at night, when they drank together in the barn, they would soften around the edges, letting their bodies brush against each other, touching their knees together, lacing their fingers. They would dance and they would kiss. And then they would climb the stairs to Nona's bedroom and close the door behind them, disappearing into the dark noise that filtered through the walls of my bedroom, the shivering groans and frantic gasps of their bodies joining together. They didn't really hate each other—this is what the Catfish had told me. It was just sexual energy. It was young love.

"Maybe he's bored," I told my sister. "Maybe he misses the rodeo."

Nona's head snapped sideways, leveling me with her eyes. "Maybe you should mind your own business."

It had never been this way before, Nona so angry with everything, with everyone. There had always been arguments. Before she left, my sister and father would yell and stomp and give each other the silent treatment for days. But there had always been an element of play about it, a gentleness. Mostly, I thought they were both the kind of people who just enjoyed a good fight now and then. But now it was different. Something inside Nona seemed to recoil at everything around her, including Jerry. Including me.

Darling stuck her head over the fence and I scratched behind her ear, watching as her eyes closed and her nostrils trembled in pleasure. Inside the barn, there was an eruption of shrieking laughter from the Catfish, and Nona dropped her chin to her chest, massaging her temples with her thumbs. "Those bitches are driving me crazy," she said. "I can't believe that Dad would just *prostitute* our barn out to strangers."

"We had bills to pay," I told her.

"No," she said and nodded at Darling. "He had toys to buy."

I started to say that our father hadn't known he was going to break his leg when he bought Darling, that there had still been a small chance that Sheila might kick it into gear and become the kind of superstar who would save us from poverty. But Nona's eyes were clouded and I only said, "Whatever the reason, we needed the money."

"It's just, all these *people,*" Nona said. "I hate these kinds of people."

"What kinds?" I asked, and Nona lit another cigarette.

"Dumb rich people," she said.

"These are the people we've always had out here," I told her.

"Yeah," she said. "Well, it bugs me now. All these women—they have *everything.* And everything is the biggest damned drama. *Boo-hoo-hoo,* they can't go to Greece this year, or *wah, wah, wah,* someone's husband cheats on his wife."

"Who?" I asked. "Whose husband does that?"

Nona glanced over at me as if she had forgotten I was there. "Mr. Altman." She smirked. "Sheila's dad."

I climbed off the fence and stood in front of her. "How do you know that?"

"Patty Jo told me. She's seen him with some other woman. It's why he never comes out here."

"Does Mrs. Altman know?" I asked.

"Who cares?" she said. "It's not like her life would end. She'd still have her money and her house and her perfect pretty face."

"Maybe she's in love with him," I said.

Nona took a slow drag off her cigarette, then dropped the butt onto the ground. "Maybe she is," she said. "But people like that have so many other things. Love doesn't mean as much to them."

I took a step back, trying to process this information. "Look," Nona said, hopping off the fence. "Patty Jo's an attention hog. She probably just made it up anyway. Forget I said anything."

In the opposite round pen, King trotted easy circles around Jerry, and Nona paused, her jaw jutting sideways as she watched. "All those years Dad spent hating Bart," she said. "And then what does he do? Runs right out and replaces him with Junior."

"It was Jack," I told her, and she snorted.

"Figures."

"He did other stuff too," I said. "He fixed the air conditioner and the water pump. He paid the registration fees for all the new foals."

Nona shifted her weight, cocking one hip as she looked me up and down. "Jack's the one who beat Ace half to death," she said, and my body jerked from the inside out, the air around me sucked to the rims of the earth.

"You're lying," I said.

"You aren't a baby anymore," Nona told me, her voice prickling with ice. "You're old enough to know the truth. It happened when Dad was a kid. Jack was trying to put shoes on Ace. Ace kicked and Jack just snapped, beat the hell out of him while he was tied to the hitching post. Nearly killed him."

I wanted to hold my hands against my ears. But it was too late. The words filled my head like smoke, the picture forming behind my eyes: Jack, his square, freckled hands. A hammer, smooth and heavy. Ace, young and still perfect, cowering beneath the blows, hooves scraping concrete, blood and hair, the deep, wet noises of flesh giving itself over. Bones breaking. And my father, a child, watching it happen.

A sickness rose inside me, cool and slippery in the back of my throat. I didn't have to believe it. This information, I didn't have to accept it. Stories got twisted over time. Memories changed shape. My sister had not witnessed anything she'd said. It didn't have to be truth if I didn't want it to be. But even so, it was there. The event flashed through my mind and I saw it happen. Real or not, it would stay in my mind, a scar on something that had moments before been flawless. It would be there forever.

I looked into my sister's eyes, so calm, so empty, and I hated her.

"You don't know anything," I hissed. "You come back here and pretend you understand. But you haven't seen anything. Jack and Ruby came, and everything was better while they were here. Things that had been broken forever started working again. We all ate dinner together. No one could even get close to the foals, then Jack went out there and, *boom,* they fell in love with him."

"That all might be true," Nona said. "Jack might have acted like a saint among men while he was visiting. But he has a temper like nobody's business and he nearly killed Ace." She pointed at Darling. "So now Dad spends his life fixing up hot chicks and loser guys. What do you think Fred would say about that?"

"Fred?" I asked.

"You know," she told me. "That shrink guy who thought that everything stood for something else."

My sister had never been good in school, couldn't remember names or dates or formulas. She didn't study or practice or care. She didn't read books. I felt as if I were being lifted by the top of my head, straightening, lengthening, until I was staring down at her from far above. Until she was nothing but a speck. Nona might have been the better rider. But I would always be the smart one. *"Freud,"* I told her.

"Oh, I'm so sorry, Alice," Nona snapped. "I'm not a scholar. If you remember, I dropped out of school to get married."

"Yeah," I said. "How's that working out?"

Nona's face constricted, her mouth pulling sideways, her eyes welling with tears. And suddenly, my sister looked old. The skin around her eyes was thin and tired, the lines of her cheekbones more pronounced.

"You weren't here," I whispered finally. "Jack and Ruby are good people."

Nona's shoulders stooped. "No," she told me. "They're *regular* people. Just like you and me and everyone else."

Inside the barn, the Catfish were grooming their horses and Patty Jo stood among them, combing through Toy Boy's mane while she waited for my father to finish his bus route.

"Hi," I said.

"Well, hi," Patty said and put her hand to the side of my face. "You're all flushed, Alice. What's wrong?"

Everything was wrong, the whole wide world and everyone in it. Nothing anywhere was right. The palm of Patty's hand felt cool and smooth against my face, and as I looked up into her eyes, I could feel the tears beginning to burn behind my own. My hands were trembling, my feet numb inside the expensive shoes she had bought for me.

Patty Jo had told my sister about Mr. Altman, so probably, she had told the other Catfish as well. Probably, she had told my father. If my sister knew about Jack beating Ace with a hammer, my mother knew too. I thought of her sitting in her dark bedroom and wondered how much she saw from her little window, how much she heard through the paper-thin walls. All these years, I had thought we were protecting her, shielding her from the ugly world outside. But now I looked up into Patty Jo's perfectly drawn face, her curled eyelashes and straight white teeth, and wondered how I could have ever believed that I was protecting anyone from anything. The world was what it was. There were no secrets. There were only things that went unsaid.

"I know what will make you happy," Patty whispered and crooked her finger at me, leading me into the tack room. Inside, she turned on the light and bumped the door closed with her hip. "I brought you a little something."

She held out a plastic shopping bag. I peeked inside and saw the green suede jacket she had worn the day she first brought Toy Boy out to the barn. "Do you know what this is?" she asked, and I nodded.

"It's yours," I said.

"I was wearing this the first time I met you," she told me and pulled the jacket out of the bag, shaking it to loosen the wrinkles.

"Do you want to give it away?" I asked.

"I want you to have it," she said.

I stood with my arms stiff at my sides as Patty slid the jacket onto me and adjusted the collar. "You look beautiful," she breathed. "The color makes your eyes stand out like lights."

I took the jacket because it was easier than turning it down, because it matched my eyes, because it made me look beautiful. I took it because it smelled like Patty—money and possibility—like all the places I had never been and all the things I had never seen. I took it because the world was what it was, and turning down a suede jacket that fit perfectly wouldn't make things any different.

thirteen

SHEILA ALTMAN SAID that *The Sound of Music* was going to be the best production Desert Valley had ever seen. On the few days a week that she came out to the barn to work with Cap, she practiced her songs in front of me, dancing around the barn with her arms up over her head and kicking her heels out as she sang about goat herders and edelweiss. She put her pale hair in braids and looped them over the top of her head. "What do you think?" she asked me. "Do I look like a little Austrian girl?"

"You look like yourself," I told her. "In braids."

Sheila scowled and combed her hair loose with her fingers. "The costumes will help," she said. "My mom's sewing mine, so I know it'll be good."

Of course, Mrs. Altman would know how to sew. She had probably made every Halloween costume and school pageant outfit that Sheila ever wore. Of course, Sheila's costume would be good. And if anyone ever doubted, there would be plenty of pictures to prove it.

"Is your dad helping too?" I asked.

"Nah," she said. "He could have helped with sets, I guess. But he's pretty busy with work."

I studied her face, trying to gauge if there was any suspicion inside of her, any doubt. Nona had told me that Mr. Altman had a girlfriend, and it seemed that if this was something a person who had never met him could know, his own daughter would have an inkling. But Sheila twirled around Cap on her toes, her face flushed, her eyes sparkling as she sang, *"Me, a name I call myself, Far, a long, long way to run . . ."*

"He must work a lot," I said.

Sheila stopped in midtwirl, her mouth twisting to the side in annoyance. "You made me lose my place," she grumbled.

"Sorry."

"My dad *does* work a lot," she said. "That's why I have a nice house and nice clothes and a beautiful horse like Cap. Dad makes a lot of money."

I searched her eyes. If Patty Jo knew where the Altmans' money came from, certainly their own daughter knew. But Sheila only blinked at me, waiting for the conversation to end so that she could resume her singing. Sheila lived in the same house with her mother and father, saw their interactions, heard their conversations. And she didn't know them at all.

"I just thought it might be hard, having him be so busy with work," I said finally, and Sheila cocked her head to one side.

"Well, it isn't."

I nodded and Sheila lifted back onto her toes. "Now," she said, clearing her throat. *"Let's start at the very beginning, a very good place to start . . ."*

Sheila had once told me that I was her best friend. Best friends, I thought, would tell each other everything. This was the way I imagined my friendship with Polly Cain—the two of us whispering in the hallways and passing notes to each other during class, sharing everything about ourselves until every story, every fear and hope, had blended together and we were mere extensions of each other, two bodies sharing a single memory, a single life. And in that life that never was, I certainly would have told my best friend that people were talking about her father, that people were saying he had a girlfriend, that he cheated on his wife.

But as I watched Sheila Altman dance through the barn, I knew that we were not the kind of friends that Polly and I might have been. I owed her no secondhand information. Besides, just because Patty Jo had said something to my sister, that didn't make it true. In the world that existed on the other side of the valley, where the lawns were green and the sidewalks were lined with flowers, what Mr. Altman did or didn't do in his spare time couldn't have mattered less. What mattered was that Sheila had everything. And Mrs. Altman had Sheila.

"I can't even believe how spoiled that Sheila is," Nona said later that night. My father and Patty Jo had gone shopping for stirrups hours earlier and had yet to come back. The sky was dark, the barn quiet, and Nona and Jerry were drinking beer in the barn, bobbing their heads to the tinny music that wafted from the speakers above.

"Aw," Jerry told her, taking a slow drag from his cigarette. "She seems like a nice enough kid."

Nona glared at him. "What do you know? You haven't spent even a minute talking to her."

"I have no reason to talk to her," Jerry answered. "I'm not the one getting paid to teach her to ride." His voice had an edge to it and his eyes hooked onto my sister's. He didn't have to say that Nona only rode around with Sheila, that she wasn't teaching her anything. His eyes said it for him.

"Well, if you *did* talk to her," Nona began, ignoring the look he gave her across the card table, "you'd know that she's spent her whole life getting every little thing that she wants. Tell him, Alice."

I looked back and forth between them, feeling the heat of their anger, the unspoken words swelling in the air like smoke. Jerry took a slow sip from his beer and lit another cigarette. "You don't know anything about that little girl," he told Nona. "You're just jealous because Yellow Cap belongs to her now."

I could see Nona's heartbeat fluttering beneath her T-shirt, the cords tightening in her neck. "Her mommy and daddy might have paid for him," she whispered. "But he's mine."

I waited for Jerry to cave in to her, to apologize, to make things right between them. But he held her gaze, unwavering. "He's not."

Nona stubbed her cigarette out on the barn floor, then stood. "If you don't believe me," she whispered, "I'll show you."

My sister crossed the barn to Cap's stall and clicked her tongue at him. His gold head appeared in the doorway and Nona swung the stall door open. "Come on out," she told him.

"Don't!" I said, but she didn't pause.

Cap took several steps forward until he was standing completely free in the barn. I jumped up, blocking the doorway so that he couldn't bolt. Jerry stood and widened himself beside me, stretching out his arms. "What the hell are you doing?" he asked.

Nona stood beside Cap's head and lifted her arms as though she were holding an invisible lead rope. When she began to walk, Cap moved alongside her, matching his pace to hers.

"Whoa," Nona said quietly and Cap stopped. My sister made small noises with her tongue, whispering words we couldn't hear. Cap's ears twitched and his weight shifted as he adjusted his feet, setting up perfectly in showmanship form. Nona stepped back to present him to us, and Jerry and I dropped our arms to our sides.

"Ta *da*!" she said, clapping her hands at her own accomplishment.

"Very impressive," Jerry said in a low voice. "Now put the pony away."

Again, Nona lifted her hands as if holding a lead rope, and again, Yellow Cap followed. She stepped into him and he turned on his heel, then walked beside her through the barn and back into his stall. Once he was inside, Nona closed the door and held her hands out to us. She hadn't touched him once.

"Now," she said evenly. "Tell me again what isn't mine."

Jerry sank back into his chair, cracking open a fresh beer. "If that horse was so important to you, maybe you shouldn't have left him behind to be sold off to strangers."

Nona's face constricted, her cheeks and neck darkening in splotches of red. "Alice, tell him," she whispered. "Tell him that Cap belongs to me."

Sheila Altman could practice for the rest of her life, and she would never be able to do what my sister had just done. Yellow Cap would never follow her blindly, never walk on water for her. But my eyes traveled sideways to Cap's stall where his embroidered halter hung from its hook. If the Altmans ever moved to a different town, they would take Cap with them. My sister would never see him again. It wouldn't matter what he would or wouldn't do for her.

My sister waited a moment for me to speak, and when I didn't, she burst into tears, her shoulders heaving, her mouth wrenching open. Jerry and I glanced at each other, startled by the sudden burst of emotion.

"You can both go to hell," Nona hiccupped, and turned for the house. "Right straight to hell."

Jerry and I sat for a moment in silence, unsure what had just happened. "It's your fault," I said finally, holding one hand up in an oath. "She was never like this before. My hand to God, she wasn't."

Jerry leaned back in his chair. "It's getting late," he said without taking his eyes off the wall in front of him. "Probably past your bedtime."

I glared at him, but it was a waste of expression. He never even glanced sideways at me. "Fine," I said and turned to go. "I guess you'll just be going to hell alone tonight."

"Sweet dreams," he said, and I stomped into the house.

Nona and Jerry didn't speak to each other for days after that. They ate their meals at different times, standing over the kitchen sink or sitting alone at the table. In the evening, Jerry drank alone in the barn while Nona went through her closet, trying on her clothes in front of the mirror and staring blankly at her reflection.

Late at night, I would hear Jerry's footsteps on the stairs, making his way to my sister's bed. On the other side of the wall, I lay awake in my bed and listened to the rustle of his clothes as he undressed, the thud of each boot hitting the floor. But there were no more squeaking bedsprings, no open-mouthed gasps or shuddering breaths. And night after night, I waited for one of them to give in to the other, to apologize or make amends. But night after night, there was nothing but silence.

"The temperature out here's a bit chilly lately," Patty Jo told me. The seasons were shifting, the air crisp and cool, the green beginning to fade from the landscape. But Patty tilted her head toward the house and I knew she wasn't talking about weather. My sister was smoking a cigarette on the porch and when Jerry walked up the steps, she angled her body in the opposite direction. He went inside without a word, slamming the screen door behind him.

"They had a fight," I said.

"That would have been my first guess."

My father had an afternoon job transporting a high school wrestling team to a match, and Patty Jo wandered through the barn while she waited for him to return, running her fingers along the walls and pausing to pet the horses when they stuck their heads over their stall doors. Sheila sat cross-legged on the floor, polishing her show saddle and humming under her breath without ever noticing the exchange between Nona and Jerry.

"They won't even talk to each other," I told Patty Jo.

She sighed. "That's how it starts."

"How what starts?"

Patty leaned against the barn wall, looking down at the pointed toes of her black boots. "Do you know what I would do, Alice," she asked, "if I could do it all over again? Do you know what I would want?"

Her voice was quiet and I felt a stillness in the air around us, a weight in the words she was about to say. I glanced down at Sheila, but her mouth moved soundlessly over the words of her song—*So long, farewell, Auf wiedersehn, good-bye*—her mind lost in another world.

"What?" I asked.

"Just a little apartment somewhere, with my own little things, where I could sit and read and do whatever I wanted. I would just be *me*—by myself."

"What about your husband?" I asked, and Patty Jo lifted her eyes. "What about him?"

The conversation felt suddenly dangerous and wrong. I stared into Patty Jo's eyes, waiting for her to remember who I was. "Don't you like being married?"

She held my gaze, her eyes calm, her voice serious. "Marriage," she said quietly, "is the most expensive ticket to nowhere."

"You don't really think that."

Her eyebrows lifted into perfect arches. "Look how far it got your sister," she said. "Look how far it got your father."

A cold fear crept up the back of my throat and I felt all at once naked in front of her, as though she were staring through every secret I'd ever had, every lie I had ever told.

On the floor, Sheila blew her bangs off her forehead. "*Everybody gets married,*" she said.

Patty Jo's eyes stayed locked on mine, fierce and unyielding. "Marriage isn't the answer, Alice. Do you understand me? It's not the way out."

My tongue was dead inside my mouth, my lips frozen. But I nodded. Yes. I understood.

"Some people *love* being married," Sheila said in a knowing voice. "Look at my parents. They've been married fifteen years and they're still totally happy."

A storm crossed behind Patty Jo's eyes and I saw a moment of meanness flicker in her face, a spasm of disgust. But she set the palm of her hand on Sheila's head and closed her eyes, her voice softening as she said, "Then they're really lucky, sweetheart. And I'm happy for them."

"Do you want to get married?" I asked.

"Don't you think you should at least give high school a *try* first?" Mr. Delmar said.

There it was: that little line we sometimes crossed. I didn't know what it meant, but my stomach stirred and I blushed into the phone receiver. "You know what I mean."

"I do," he said, "know what you mean."

"So do you want to?"

"I don't know," he said. "Maybe someday." There was a hiss and a breath—his cigarette. "I was engaged once. It didn't work out."

"To the woman in the picture?" I asked. "The one that isn't on your desk anymore?"

"What good observation skills you have," he said. "Yes. To her."

"Why didn't you marry her?"

He paused to inhale. "She was finishing school in Michigan and I was teaching here. We were just apart too much."

"Did you love her?" I asked, though I already knew the answer, already knew that she was the one who had made him starved and stupid, the one who said she had never been with anyone besides him.

"Yes," he said.

"What happened?"

"She met someone else."

"While you were still in love with her?"

"Yes."

"And when it was over?" I asked. "Did it kill you?"

"It killed me," he said. "And I was dead."

"And then what happened?"

"The phone rang."

At school, Janice Reardon had wanted nothing to do with me since the day I declined the invitation to sit with her at lunch. So when she came up to my desk after advanced English, I figured she was just trying to get a look at the grade I'd received on the latest essay. I held my paper to my chest to cover the red B+ at the top, and Janice rolled her eyes. "I'm not trying to copy you, if that's what you're worried about."

"I'm not," I mumbled and stuffed the paper into my notebook.

"B-plus, huh?" Janice asked, leaning forward to see. "I got an A."

"Whoopee for you," I said. "What do you want?"

Janice was wearing the pink fairy wings that she'd had on the night of the posse banquet, and she heaved her backpack onto one shoulder, making the wings tilt sideways behind her. "I'm having a séance," she said. "Everyone's coming."

"Will Karen Carpenter be there?" I asked, and Janice narrowed her eyes.

"Abigail, Sharon, and Colleen will be," she told me. "And I think you know who else."

Polly.

"There are questions that need answers," Janice said, raising her eyebrows for emphasis. "About that day."

The day she drowned.

"About what happened."

Did she fall or did she jump?

Across the room, Mr. Delmar was erasing the chalkboard, and I could feel his attention turning toward us. A sudden fire swept through my brain. Polly Cain was *our* world, his and mine. If Janice Reardon said the name out loud in front of him, if anyone did, the spell would be broken. The world would come apart. She was *my* best friend. *I* was the only one who could give her back to him.

"Okay," I said.

"Okay what?" Janice asked.

"Okay, I'll come."

It was an ordeal, of course. Janice Reardon acted like she was planning the storming of Normandy with all her lists and dates and preparations. Apparently, certain times were better for contacting the dead than others—I guess they were more likely to take the call.

"You're in charge of bringing fresh flowers," Janice told me a few days later. Her face was red and I could tell that the pressure of the position she had assigned herself was about to give her a conniption.

"Why?" I asked.

"You can't do a séance without them."

"That's ridiculous," I said.

"I'm entirely serious, Alice Winston," she told me. "If you want to do this right, we have to have fresh flowers." Janice leaned forward to whisper in my ear, peeking sideways in case anyone might care enough to listen in. "The *spirits* are *attracted* to them."

I didn't see how Janice expected me to find fresh flowers in the fall desert, but when I mentioned this, she said that I was bright and imaginative and that she was sure I was up to the challenge.

"I need to go to a flower shop," I told Patty Jo. "Will you take me?"

She did a little roll with her shoulders and clapped her hands. "What's the occasion?"

"I'm going to contact the dead tonight."

Patty's face went slack, so I revised: "It's my best friend's birthday tomorrow and I want to give her flowers at school. Will you take me?"

Patty was thrilled. She told me that the relationships a girl had with her friends were the most important in life, and if I took good care of those relationships, I would never be sorry. She said that buying flowers was a *lovely* gesture and wouldn't my best friend be the luckiest girl in the whole school when she got the bouquet. At the florist's, Patty walked through the aisles, pointing out anything that included a stuffed animal or a balloon. "What do you think?" she asked and I shrugged. Flowers were flowers, I figured. Dead people probably weren't that particular.

When I saw the bouquet of white roses wrapped in silver paper, I reached for Patty's arm. With all the things I didn't know about Polly, I did know that her mother had carried a white rose at the funeral. "Those," I said.

"Oh, honey," Patty said. "Those are lovely. They *are*. But they're not very, well, *fun*. Wouldn't something like this be better?" She pointed to a bunch of red and purple flowers inside a mug with a teddy bear on it. A heart-shaped thought bubble above the bear's head read, *For a beary special someone*. "And when the flowers die," Patty told me, "your friend will have a nice little mug to keep forever."

I turned back to the white roses. "Those," I said again.

And though Patty seemed uncertain, she reached for her wallet. "She's *your* friend." She smiled. "I'm sure you know her best."

At home, Patty Jo hurried out to the arena to practice jumping in front of my father while I rushed upstairs to hide the roses inside my closet. When I came back down, Nona was drinking with the Catfish in the barn. Sheila stood to the side with her head down and her arms crossed over her chest. "Patty said she took you to buy flowers," she said, her voice flat and sullen.

"So?" I asked.

"For your best friend's birthday."

Out in the arena, Toy Boy sailed over a jump and the Catfish cheered in the barn, whistling through their teeth. Patty Jo stood in her stirrups, waving at them while my father balanced on his cane to clap. But Sheila kept her eyes on mine, searching my face. *Best* meant favorite—a friend that I liked better than her.

I shrugged to show her that it wasn't a big deal, then turned to join the Catfish. Sheila stood beside me, swallowing her sadness and pretending to watch Patty jump so that she wouldn't have to look at me. And so we saw it, all of us, right as it happened.

Out in the ring, Toy Boy stumbled. It was small, a hiccup in his gait, but it startled Patty Jo and she opened her eyes, turning her head toward the jump ahead of her. She hesitated, unsure whether to pull him back or urge him on, and her intentions divided, her hands jerking the reins back as her legs kicked him forward. Patty's body lifted forward to take the jump and Toy Boy's sank backward into a halt. From the doorway of the barn, it seemed to happen underwater. Patty tipped forward and Toy Boy rose back, the top of his head moving toward the front of her face. They met and there was a crack, bone on bone, and noise that sounded like a dish breaking on concrete. Beside me, Sheila screamed.

The rest I remember in slices: Jerry appearing like a ghost beside me, then sprinting into the house, the jerking, off-balance gait of my father's run as he crossed the arena toward Patty, the blood soaking down the front of her shirt when he pulled her from the horse. She wrapped her arms around his neck, smearing blood onto his face and neck. It poured down her chin and onto the floor, her feet streaking through it as my father half carried, half dragged her into the barn.

Patty's hand moved toward her mouth and Jerry appeared again beside me, catching her arm at the wrist before it reached her lips. "Ice," he said, and handed her a bag of frozen peas, wrapped in my sister's T-shirt.

"Oh, Jesus," Patty gurgled. Her eyes rolled wildly, and her feet slipped beneath her so that Jerry and my father had to keep catching her, keep holding her upright. "Oh, Jesus, Jesus."

The sweet, sticky smell of blood filled the barn and looking at her, it was hard to tell where exactly it was coming from. It pumped, dark and thick, seeping from her nostrils and the corners of her eyes, spilling from her lips and down her chin. Beneath it, her face looked wrong, her nose crooked, sideways, bent at an angle in the middle. When she opened her mouth, we saw it: the shattered fragments of broken teeth, the gaping bloody holes. The Catfish gasped and wept beside one another, shielding their eyes with their fingers. "What?" Patty choked. The Catfish turned away, crying into their hands, unable to look at her.

"What!" she screamed and turned my father's face to hers, smearing his neck with streaks of blood. Her nose was too high on her face, her eyes swollen into slits.

Jerry turned to Jaycee over his shoulder. "The hospital," he said, and she stared at him with her mouth open. "The car." He took her arm and shook her slightly. "You need to drive her." Jaycee's body jerked and she ran for her keys.

"It's okay," my father said, and Patty wrapped her arms around the back of his head, spiking his hair with blood.

"Oh, Jesus, Jesus."

Beside me, Sheila leaned forward and threw up into her hands.

"It's okay," my father said again, shifting his weight to support Patty's.

"Am I ugly?" Patty sobbed. "Oh, Jesus, am I going to be ugly?" The Catfish touched her shoulders, averting their eyes from her face as they shushed and petted her.

Jaycee pulled her car in front of the barn and my father lowered Patty into the front seat. Bitsy climbed into the backseat and closed the door on her seat belt, slamming it again and again without looking to see why it wouldn't close. Jerry leaned across, handing her the bag of frozen peas and lifting the buckle of the seat belt back inside. The door closed and they were gone.

My father turned and limped to the hose, spraying the blood and vomit from the barn floor while the horses paced and cried in their stalls. The remaining Catfish wandered aimlessly behind him, gathering purses, picking up the things the others had left behind. The cement floor of the barn was wet and colorless, the evidence running in rivers out the barn door and pooling in the dust, soaking into the ground, tinting it red. One by one, the Catfish touched their fingers to their faces, feeling their lips and teeth, the bridge of a nose, and the air would seem sweet and sickly as the moment replayed itself, passing from one mind into another.

They climbed into their cars, heading for the hospital, murmuring that they would call, that they would keep us updated. Nona took a step toward them. "Tell Patty . . ." she said, then trailed off. She looked at the rest of us to help her fill in the blank. I opened my mouth to speak, but my tongue reached for my teeth with its tip, feeling the evenness, the delicate bone that ran along the roof of my mouth. My father was spraying the hose, his jaw tight, the bloody handprints beginning to dry and flake from the skin of his face and neck as he rinsed Sheila's hands under the hose water. And so Nona left the rest of her sentiment empty. We had no message.

By the time Mrs. Altman came for Sheila, the air had tightened with chill, the smell of wood smoke sifting through the air. As soon as Mrs. Altman got out of her car, Sheila began to cry. It was the first sound she had made. Jerry stepped forward, explaining to Mrs. Altman what had happened to Patty Jo. He kept it brief and simple, giving stark, colorless details. But even so, Mrs. Altman's eyes welled, her hands moving to her mouth, palms pressing into her lips.

"My God," she whispered.

After the Altmans left, I sat on the porch steps and Nona sat beside me. The sun was beginning to set, and through the lengthening shadows of the barn, we watched my father and Jerry unsaddle Toy Boy in silence, then return to the arena to kick dirt over the clumps of blood, the glints of broken teeth. My memory jumped like a stone across a lake, filling my mind with noise—the sound of glass breaking, blood spilling, a woman screaming, *Will I be ugly?* My stomach forked and I imagined my own face coming apart in pieces, splintering like wood, damaged and broken forever.

Nona brushed her lips with her fingertips, then shook her head and stood. "Wanna get out of here?" she asked.

"Okay," I said.

We didn't tell anyone we were leaving. Nona grabbed her purse and the keys to Jerry's pickup. For a while, we just drove. Nona smoked out the window and I leaned against the passenger door, watching the open land pass in the purple twilight. The events of the afternoon swirled together inside my head, the chilly sweet air of the flower shop, the pools of blood on the barn floor, the sounds of Patty Jo's face breaking apart.

"It's awful that it had to happen," Nona said finally. "But at least it happened to her."

"Because you don't like her?" I asked.

"Because she has money."

I thought about this. Patty Jo's husband was a doctor. As far as medical care went, she would get the best of the best. "If something like that happened to you or me," Nona said, "you know what we'd be?"

"Ugly," I said.

"Fucked," she said.

And so I told myself it was lucky, lucky that it had happened to Patty and not to me. She would be cared for, repaired and rebuilt. Nothing had been done that couldn't be undone.

"Do you think Patty Jo will come back to the barn?" I asked.

Nona tossed her cigarette out the window, steering with one hand to light another. "Only if she had her brains knocked out along with her teeth."

"You came back," I said.

"I didn't have a choice."

The truck bounced over the dirt road, and at my feet, Jerry's gun thudded beneath the wadded blanket. I stretched my leg forward, tracing the barrel with the toe of my shoe. The sky was deepening, and the last slip of sunlight disappeared behind the mountains. Back at the barn, Jerry would have noticed that his wife and truck were missing. He would be feeding the horses or eating his dinner over the kitchen sink, and maybe he would be worried. Maybe he would think that this time, he was the one she was leaving behind.

"What happened?" I asked.

"A kid got killed," she said. I closed my eyes, feeling the bounce of the road beneath the truck, the length of the gun sliding along my foot. "He was a bronc rider, like Jerry, on the same circuit. We saw him every day. And then he was dead."

I pressed the arch of my foot over the gun, rocking my shoe across the barrel. "Someone killed him," I whispered.

"He was thrown," Nona told me. "He hit the ground and his neck cracked. He was dead before anyone even got to him."

I opened my eyes. This story had nothing to do with Jerry, nothing to do with Nona or money or secrets. "So?" I asked.

"So we saw him *every day,"* she repeated. "And then one day he was just *gone.* Do you know what that *feels* like?"

"Yes," I told her.

Nona's cigarette trembled between her fingers. "It could have been Jerry," she whispered.

"But it wasn't," I said.

"But it could have been."

"So he just gave it up?" I asked. "He got scared and walked away?" This did not fit the picture of Jerry that I had inside my head.

Nona's eyes were reddening around the rims, her lips wet. "What if I lost him?" she whispered. "What if one day, he was gone and I was all alone?" She glanced sideways and our eyes met. "I couldn't live without him," she told me. "I would die without him."

"You made him quit," I said.

"What if I lost him?" she repeated.

And I thought of the silence, the space. "You're losing him now," I told her, and her eyes spilled over.

"I know."

When we pulled back into the driveway, Nona turned the truck off and turned sideways to face me. "The very first time I saw him," she said, "he walked right up to me, and do you know what he said?"

I shook my head.

"He told me I was the reincarnation of Priscilla Presley." Nona dipped her head to dab her eyes with her shirtsleeve, and when she looked up, her face seemed softer, her eyes lost in the memory of their first meeting. In all the time since she'd been back, this was the first time I'd seen my sister look truly happy. And so I didn't tell her that a person had to die before she could be reincarnated. I didn't tell her that Priscilla Presley was still alive.

Jerry was waiting for my sister in the driveway, and as soon as she laid eyes on him, the smile vanished from her face, the happy memory draining away behind her eyes. Jerry grabbed her by the arm, shaking her. "Where the hell have you been?" he asked.

Nona yanked away, glaring at him from underneath the sheen of her hair. "A friend's," she said.

"Who?" Jerry demanded.

"*God,*" she said. "Nobody. Just some girl I used to know."

"You're lying to me," he told her.

Nona stomped into the barn and Jerry followed. I hung back, watching them fight and wondering why my sister didn't just tell the truth: we'd been nowhere, seen no one. There was no reason to lie. Jerry reached for her arm again, gentle this time, but she slapped his hand away. Knowing that I could not follow them, I turned and left them, fighting about all those things that didn't matter.

I was nearly inside the house before I saw my father on the porch. Through the inky darkness, I could barely make out his silhouette. His cane was propped beside him, and he sat, staring into the barn, a beer in one hand, a lit cigarette in the other. For a moment, I thought he was watching Nona and Jerry, but even through the shadows, I could sense that he had no interest in them.

"Have they called from the hospital?" I asked finally, and his chair creaked beneath him as he shook his head no.

Out in the barn, Nona and Jerry circled each other beneath the lights, their voices rising in words I couldn't make out, their bodies tight and aimed like guns. I sat down beside my father's chair, pulling my knees to my chest and trying to think what I should say, what I would want to hear if I were him.

"You could go there," I told him. "To the hospital. You could go and see her."

In the darkness, my father cleared his throat. "I don't think so."

"She's going to be okay," I said, and my father set his hand on top of my head. "Her husband's a doctor."

"I know," he said. "She's in good hands."

Out in the barn, Jerry's head dropped forward in defeat. He extended one arm to my sister, and she thought for a moment, then stepped forward, looping her fingers through his. As quickly as it had begun, the fight was over. My father sat with his palm resting on my hair, and we watched without speaking as their bodies swayed together under the barn lights, dancing to music that we were too far away to hear.

+ + +

I waited until my father had gone to sleep before I pulled the roses out of my closet and slipped back the silver paper to look at them. They had wilted slightly on top of my shoes, their petals tinged with shallow brown around the edges. But it was dark. No one would notice. I crept down the stairs, outside, and winced as my shoes crunched on the gravel.

The moon was hidden behind the clouds, and I walked down the dark road with the rose stems cool in my fingers, the paper rustling in the breeze. When I reached the canal, I could hear the water beside me, sipping through the grates and slapping against the grassy edge. The canals were low and quiet now, sinking daily. The ground had dried, and the grass was beginning to wilt with the cool weather that came at night. Soon, it would be winter and the canals would be empty for the second time in a year.

There had been some argument between Janice and Sharon over where the séance should be held. Sharon thought that we should meet closer to the school, where Polly's backpack had been found. But Janice had wanted to meet closer to my house, where the body had finally been discovered. Abigail and Colleen had stayed silent, not wanting to choose sides. So I was the tiebreaker. They had come to me at lunch the day before, stopping Rachel in the middle of a story about how she hid her hickeys from her mother with a combination of turtlenecks and scarves. "The question," Janice explained tensely, "is how long a person would stay alive in the water. It's absolutely necessary to be close to where she died."

In the service of ending the conversation as quickly as possible, I went for compromise. I said that it should be in between the two places. That was best. After they left, Rachel had raised her eyebrows at me. "It's a project," I explained. "For advanced English."

"God," she said. "If those are the kind of spooks you have to hang out with when you're smart, I'd rather be retarded."

I had agreed wholeheartedly, explaining how I never understood a word any of them said, how I was pretty sure I had only ended up in that class by a registration error. But now, as I walked along the water to the place we had agreed on, I tried to calculate how long a person might be able to stay alive after falling into the canal. The water moved quickly under its flat surface, sucking into pipes and grates, pulling under. She would have flailed, certainly. She would have fought. It was half a mile between the place where she'd fallen and the place where she'd been found. Probably, she had been dead for most of it.

They were already setting up, lighting candles and spreading a blanket on the ground beside the water. "You're late," Janice told me, and Sharon gave me a mistrustful look. I set the flowers down in the center of the blanket and pretended not to notice.

Janice looked down at the white roses, then sat back on her heels, nodding. "This is what she would have wanted," she said quietly, and I glanced at the other girls, waiting for them to remind Janice that she had not been friends with Polly, that she could not possibly know what she would have wanted. But the other girls said nothing. Somehow, Janice Reardon had become their leader.

We sat in a circle on the blanket with the roses spread between us. The wind stirred through our hair, sweeping out the candlelight, and Janice leaned forward, relighting it only to have it blow out again. She looked up at the sky and nodded then, as if receiving a silent message from the great beyond. "She wants it dark," Janice whispered and sat back down, tossing the matches into her backpack.

Janice instructed us to hold hands and close our eyes. I sat between Sharon and Colleen and their fingers were cold in mine as I touched my palms to theirs. "Now," Janice whispered, once we were all holding hands. "Really concentrate. *Think* about her. Reach out to her with your minds."

The air was chilled and the canal water gurgled alongside us. But I tried to concentrate. I squeezed my eyes shut and flexed my whole body with concentration. *Polly Cain, Polly Cain, Polly Cain.* I pictured her in my mind, leaning over the instruction manual in shop class, squinting at the pieces and brushing her brown hair behind her ears with her fingers. "Polly Cain," Janice whispered, and the sound of her voice made me jump inside my skin. "We're here, we're waiting. Come to us now and tell us what you want to say."

Polly Cain, Polly Cain, Polly Cain.

"I can feel her," Janice whispered. "She's here."

The silence sliced through me and I waited, waited to feel anything aside from the wind and the chill rising off the water. And then I did. Beside me, I felt a shudder, a small, silent heave as Colleen Murphy began to cry. She didn't make a sound, but her arm shivered against mine and her hand moved in my fingers so that I was holding on to her wrist. The pads of my fingers slipped around the knob of Colleen's wrist bone, the tender, veiny flesh at the base of her palm. And I felt them, the small slivered divots of scar tissue, the invisible evidence that she had wanted to die.

Polly Cain didn't come to us that night, didn't speak or appear blue-lipped, hair streaked with the broken bodies of mayflies. We gathered our things, folded the blanket, and loaded the candles back into Janice's backpack. Colleen wiped her eyes with the backs of her hands and no one said a word. I was the only one who knew that she had cried.

We said good night. The four of them headed one way, back to Janice's house to spend the night. And I headed the other. I waited until the sound of their voices had disappeared into the darkness, then tossed the white roses into the canal. A gust of air swept across my face, blowing my hair into my eyes, and the clouds parted, revealing a sliver of moonlight. The roses bobbed in the low canal water, their heads reflecting in the slender slip of moonlight like dying lightbulbs before they sank beneath the surface and disappeared.

At home, the barn was dark. Jerry and Nona had gone inside to bed and the house stared down at me with the dark windows of its eyes. I crept up the porch steps and eased the back door open, slipping inside. I started up the stairs, then stopped. At the top, there was a flicker of white and my breath turned to ice inside my lungs. Janice Reardon had felt her, had said she was there. And now she stood, wavering in the darkness, dark hair spilling down. She had followed me. She had come to take back the things that were hers.

"Baby."

"Mom?" I asked.

"Where have you been?"

My mother was standing in her nightgown, holding on to the

railing, and I climbed the stairs to her. "Nowhere," I told her. "Just outside."

She reached out, smoothing my hair with her fingers. "You left so long ago," she said. "I've been worried."

Behind her, the door to her bedroom was open, the blue light flickering from her silent television. Her lower lip was trembling and I reached for her elbow, guiding her into her room. I pulled back her quilt and smoothed her sheets while she stood behind me, then stepped back to let her slide between them. But instead of moving toward the bed, my mother reached her hands out, circling her fingers around my wrists. "He was falling in love with her," she whispered.

I tried to step back, but my mother tightened her hands around mine. "I don't know what you're talking about," I said.

"You do," she told me.

All the events of the day slammed together inside my head, the white roses and inky blood, the water, the gun, the spongy scar tissue on the inside of Colleen Murphy's wrist, my father's voice, flat and empty, when he spoke to me on the porch: *She's in good hands.* I closed my eyes, trying to separate one thought from another, trying to remember where I was.

"Tell the truth," my mother told me, moving her hands up my arms, pulling me closer so that I could feel the damp of her breath on my neck. "Was he going to leave us?"

The night that Polly Cain did not come back from the dead, I left my mother alone in the blue TV light, standing beside her bed like it was a grave. In my room, I looked around at all the pieces of my life, neat and tidy on their little shelves, my clothes and books and telephone, my shoes and hair barrettes, and tried to care about them. *Mine, mine, mine.* But they were only things, things that could have belonged to anyone. I fell asleep in my clothes, thinking about ghosts and lies and silence, about all the truths that would never be told, all the questions without answers.

fourteen

THIS IS THE TRUTH about things: If you take something that isn't yours, it will never belong to you. You can try to hold on to it, but somehow, it will slip through your fingers. If something wasn't meant to be yours, it won't be. No matter what you do to keep it, you will lose it.

A few days after Patty's accident, I spilled grape soda on my leather backpack. I dabbed it with a damp paper towel, but the mark remained, stained and sticky. After I went to her séance, Janice Reardon considered us friends. She called out to me in the hallways and lingered around my table at lunch. I could feel the cheerleaders disapproving, wondering why I tolerated Janice in her tiaras and fairy wings. But there was no point in snubbing her for their benefit. I was never going to be a cheerleader. Already, my hair was beginning to look shaggy at the ends. Soon, I would outgrow my expensive clothes, and without anyone to buy me new ones, I would slip back to who I had been before: a regular girl with regular hair who couldn't do a cartwheel.

The Catfish had yet to return to the barn, and with Sheila at rehearsals, the afternoons were long and silent. When my father was not driving the bus, he stayed inside the house. Jerry cleaned stalls, then worked with King in the round pen while my sister and I wandered through the barn, trying to guess what would happen to all the horses that didn't belong to us and how we would make money if they were gone. "It's only temporary," I told my sister. The Catfish were probably taking turns up at the hospital. Once things calmed down, they would come back. They loved their horses, I said, loved their afternoons of riding and gossip. "They're not going anywhere."

But the days passed and they did not return. No one came and no one went. So when we heard the sound of tires on gravel, Nona, Jerry, and I came out of the barn to see who it was.

The car was black, the windows tinted. I could only make out the shape of a person behind the steering wheel, but Nona turned to Jerry and said, "Dr. Patty Jo."

He got out of the car and stood for a second, blinking over the rims of his sunglasses. His eyes rested on the school bus and his head cocked slightly, his mouth flattening into a line. "Better grab your pop," Jerry told me, but when I turned to the house, my father was already making his way down the porch steps.

My father leaned onto his cane, extending one arm to shake hands, but the doctor held up one finger, indicating that my father should wait as he squinted up at the sky, then sneezed into his shoulder. "So this is the place where the women come when they run away from home," he said, and my father dropped his hand. "I'm here about the horse."

I waited for my father to say that the horse was Patty's, that she could call him herself, that he would deal only with her. But he lowered his eyes, nodding at the ground. "The horse is in the barn."

"How is Patty?" Nona asked, and the doctor glanced down at his watch.

"She had her face smashed to pieces," he said. "How do you think she is?"

"Whatever you need done," my father said, "we can take care of for you."

"You've done enough already," the doctor told him.

My father's face reddened and his breath came faster in his chest. This was the moment in a movie when a gun would be pulled, a punch thrown. I looked back and forth between them, wondering who would win if it came to blows. My father had a bad leg, but the doctor's hands were soft and smooth. He had never lifted anything heavy, never smelled like sweat. He had never been in a fight. But the doctor looked at my father long and hard and I felt the rest of us shrinking around him, small and insignificant. He would win any fight he entered.

"What's going to happen to Toy Boy?" I asked.

The doctor glanced sideways at me, and I could see the twin forms of myself, oblong and disproportional, in the lenses of his sunglasses. "He'll have to find a new home," he said. "She doesn't ever want to see him again."

My father limped forward on his cane. "She's upset," he said. "She needs time to get over the shock."

But the doctor held up one hand, and my father fell silent. "Nothing my wife was doing out here was ever going to last," he said. "This was just a hobby, Mr. Winston. And now it's over."

He pulled out his wallet, peeling off bills that he rolled into my father's palm. "That should cover things until I get him sold." My father folded the bills into his pocket without looking to see how much was there.

The doctor turned to leave, then paused, letting his glasses tip forward on his nose to look at me over the rims. "That's a real nice jacket you're wearing, kid. I hope you take good care of it."

After that, Toy Boy was left alone in his stall. No one rode or groomed him or paid him any sort of special attention. We ran out of sawdust and my father did not go out for more. So Jerry forked straw into Toy Boy's stall, like he was any other horse.

The night of Sheila's play, I stood uncomfortably on the porch steps, watching my father and sister smoke in silence. "Are we gonna go see Sheila's thing?" I asked. "The play?" Neither of them answered and I turned and scuffed into the barn.

Jerry was in the round pen, setting a saddle pad on King's back and holding him steady so that he couldn't throw it off. "I have this thing I'm supposed to go to," I told him. "This play thing that Sheila's in. It's tonight and I said I'd go. I can't find anyone to take me."

Jerry watched me for a moment, then spat sideways onto the ground. "They don't sing, do they?"

"No," I lied. "I don't think so."

"I could take you, I guess."

Mr. and Mrs. Altman were getting out of their car when we pulled into the parking lot. Mrs. Altman waved to us, and a shadow moved across her face, her fingers lifting to brush across her lips. "Have you heard anything about Patty?" she asked. Beside her, Mr. Altman stiffened.

I shook my head and Mrs. Altman reached out to touch my hair. "Sheila will be so happy you came," she told me. "You should sit with us." Jerry shuffled his feet on the pavement, glancing down at his dirty jeans and scuffed boots. Mr. Altman was wearing a tie and a sports jacket; Mrs. Altman had on high heels.

In the auditorium, I sat between Jerry and Mr. Altman. An orchestra was tuning their instruments in front of the stage and Jerry gave me a sideways glance. "No singing, huh?"

Throughout the play, Jerry shifted in his seat and Mr. Altman checked his watch. At the end, we all stood and clapped and Mrs. Altman leaned forward around her husband as the lights came up in the theater. Her cheeks were wet with tears and she reached out to squeeze my hand. "What did you think?"

"It was really good," I told her, and she beamed.

"Yeah," Jerry added. "It must have been a lot of work learning all those songs."

"It was." Mrs. Altman nodded. "Poor Sheila's been working herself into a frenzy."

"Well, it's over now," Mr. Altman said, moving toward the door. Mrs. Altman's face darkened as her eyes met his, and he held up his hands. "I just think Sheila could use a rest," he added quickly.

We waited with the Altmans in the lobby, and when Sheila finally came out, her face was bright and garish with makeup, her cheeks painted red, her eyes lined with thick black pencil. She threw her arms around me and I could feel the flutter of her heartbeat through the damp fabric of her costume.

"It's *crazy* backstage," Sheila panted. "Maria and the nuns are doing shots!"

"Good heavens," Mrs. Altman said.

Back in the truck, Jerry started the ignition and then sat with his hands on the steering wheel. He turned to look at me and shook his head without speaking. "I think I might need a beer after that," he said.

"Okay," I told him.

Jerry bought a six-pack at a gas station, then pulled off on one of the country roads. The air was chilled, and he pulled a blanket out of the backseat, wrapping it around my shoulders as we climbed onto the hood of his truck. "That might have been the strangest thing I've ever seen in my life," Jerry said after a moment.

"It *was* pretty weird," I agreed. "Like the nuns? The nuns were weird."

"Elvis's movies were musicals," he said, cracking open a beer and handing it to me. "But not like that."

"What?" I asked. "No nuns?" I waited for Jerry to laugh, but his face was serious.

"There was one with nuns," he told me. "This nun falls in love with Elvis and at the end, she has to choose whether to stay a nun or go be in love."

I choked in midswallow, leaning sideways to spit a mouthful of beer onto the ground. "She has to choose between Jesus and Elvis?"

"Yeah." He smiled. "Heavy, right?"

"Who does she pick?"

"They end the movie without saying."

"Oh." I looked up at the sky, clear and cold, sparkling with stars, and thought about the cowboy, the one whose death had ended Jerry's career. "Do you miss the rodeo?" I asked.

Jerry stretched his legs out in front of him, crossing them at the ankles so that the heels of his boots scraped against the hood of the truck. "Been doing it since I was fifteen," he said. I turned, waiting for the real answer. "Yeah," he said finally. "I miss it."

"But you gave it up," I told him. "For her."

"Nothing lasts forever," he said. Jerry was quiet for a moment, sipping his beer. "Do you know what happened to Priscilla?" he asked.

"I know she's still alive," I said.

"She left him," Jerry told me. "That's what happened. The only woman he ever loved. And she left."

"I'm in love," I said softly. I waited for Jerry to tell me that I was too young, that it was impossible for me to feel anything close to what he, himself, felt for my sister. But he looked down at his beer, the can frosty between his fingers.

"Mind-fuck, isn't it?"

I thought of Mr. Delmar, starving and flunking out of college, losing the woman by the waterfall to another man. *It killed me,* he'd said. *And I was dead.* I thought of my mother, waiting her life away in her bedroom, watching from the window while my father fell in love with someone else. "Why did Priscilla leave him?" I asked.

Jerry was quiet, and I could feel his mind searching for the answer, thinking back through all the books he'd read, the movies he'd seen, the tours he'd taken of Elvis's home. "Things fall apart," he said finally. "Sometimes we never know why."

The next day, I walked into advanced English to find a nervous blond woman with red fingernails and too much lipstick standing in Mr. Delmar's place. Her voice was high and pinched when she took roll, the attendance sheet trembling in her fingers. "Where's Mr. Delmar?" I asked without raising my hand, and she blinked at me through the clumps of her mascara.

"He's not here?" she said. I squinted, unsure if she was asking or telling me. "He, um, couldn't come in today? So they called me?" She turned to the rest of the class and the corners of her mouth wrenched back into a pained smile. "I know we're going to have a lot of fun together."

As soon as class was over, I ran downstairs to the pay phone and dialed his number. It rang and rang. He was sick—a bug or something. He was sleeping. Of course he wouldn't answer the phone. I called again at lunch and again when the final bell rang. Then I ran home along the canal and called from my bedroom: 3:00. 4:00. 5:00. It rang and rang and rang. During the night, I tossed in my bed, reaching for the phone and dialing his number in the dark, drifting in and out of restless sleep as the phone rang against my ear.

Four days passed and I convinced myself that it was a family emergency, someone was very ill or had died, a distant uncle or a third cousin, someone he wasn't terribly close to but had to show up for all the same. He'd been called back to Michigan. And of course he would not have gotten in touch with me. He didn't have my phone number. All this time, I had always been the one who called him.

On the fifth day, our principal came into advanced English and stood beside the substitute, clearing his throat to get our attention. "Miss Lee is going to be staying on with you awhile," he said. "Mr. Delmar won't be coming back this year." My heart shrank to a husk inside my chest.

"Why?" Janice Reardon asked.

"Something has come up," the principal said. "Mr. Delmar is moving back to Michigan."

It was her, the woman by the waterfall. She had called him, she had taken him back. He would have answered the phone, thinking, maybe, that it was me. And then she would have begun crying. *I've made the biggest mistake of my life,* she would have said. *You're the only thing that matters, the only thing that has ever mattered.* And now, he would go to her. He was at home this very moment, packing boxes. In college, he had starved for her. And now, he would walk away from his job, his home, his life. He would walk away from me.

At home, I waited outside for my father to return from his bus route. The air was cool, the sky the color of a bruise, and I shivered in my suede jacket, curling my fingers inside the cuffs. "I need a ride," I told him when he pulled the bus into the driveway. He looked at me for a moment, then reached out and swung the bus door open. I climbed the stairs and sat behind him, my first time inside since he had brought it home.

I knew the directions by heart, had traced the route from my house to his, running my finger along the squiggly lines on the map in the phone book until I felt as though I had walked it every day of my life. My father stopped the bus in front of the house, and I crossed the aisle to the opposite side, peering out the window. The curtains were drawn, but a car was parked in the driveway, small and rusty with age, the car he'd been inside when Janice Reardon saw him crying. "You don't have to wait," I said, but my father turned off the ignition.

There was no noise from the other side of the door when I knocked, so I knocked harder. The door opened and Mr. Delmar stood before me, pale and thin. His hair was greasy, his shirt untucked. I walked past him without being invited in.

The house was dark and shadowy, the walls blank, the hallway filled with half-empty boxes. I stood for a moment, staring. How many times had I imagined his home, tried to envision the world around him as he spoke to me on the phone? I had pictured him living in a house filled with books, with artwork on the walls and dark, polished furniture. But Mr. Delmar's sofa was worn and sagging, his carpet patchy with stains. I curled my toes inside my shoes and stared at the floor.

"I'm glad you came," he said. "I wanted to say good-bye to you."

"You could answer your phone," I told him. "When your phone rings, you could answer it."

He pointed across the room where the phone sat, wrapped in its cord, disconnected from the wall. In the deepest center of my core, I felt like I was falling. He was really going away. He hadn't even thought of me.

"You're leaving," I whispered. "And you weren't going to say anything."

"I'm sorry," he said.

My lip was beginning to tremble and I covered my mouth with my hand, speaking through my fingers. "Our substitute is awful," I told him. "She told us that people who read *Catcher in the Rye* too many times turn into serial killers." He smiled and I felt a flutter of hope, a slender beam of opportunity. I had caught him in time. I could save him from the choice he was about to make, the life he was about to give away. No blond woman beside a waterfall would ever care about him like I did. Never, when she looked at him, would she see what I saw. She didn't, couldn't, need him as much as I needed him.

"This is a mistake," I whispered. "I *know* it is."

"It's done," he told me. "I'm packed. I'm leaving. It's done."

"You could unpack," I said, the tears beginning to burn behind my eyes.

"Alice," he said softly.

"You could change your mind."

"No," he told me. "I can't."

I could feel the sobs rising like waves through my chest, the walls shrinking around me, the whole world running wet. "I'm in love with you," I whispered, and he dropped his chin to his chest.

"You're not." His eyes opened and they were kind, soft, filled with gentleness. "Alice, that was never what this was."

And there it was, at last: the truth. Nothing anywhere was as I thought it was.

My chest was closing in, my vision blurring. "You have so many good things ahead of you," he told me. "A whole life." He reached out to touch my hair, his fingers slipping through the ends, holding it for a moment. His hand was close to my face and I could smell his skin, like wet grass and cigarette smoke. All I had to do was tilt my head and we would have touched.

Instead, I turned. The top of my head felt light and empty, as though every substantial part of myself had suddenly evaporated into steam. There was no place for me here. There never had been.

I wiped my eyes with the cuffs of the suede jacket and crossed to the door. "Is that a school bus?" he asked.

"It's my father," I said. "He drives a bus."

I could have told him the rest. I wasn't Polly's best friend, wasn't her friend at all. I didn't know a thing about her. *It's all been a lie. From the very first moment.* But there was too much truth already, spinning around me, swelling through my mind. Any more, and I would have drowned in it.

A few days later, Mr. Delmar was gone. He left without saying good-bye. I never saw him again.

It got cold. The ground frosted over and the sky turned a blank slate of gray. He was gone and there was nothing I could do about it, no one I could tell. The pain screamed through me, tearing at me from the inside out like something with teeth and claws. But my body did not break or bleed. There was no bruising, no limp, no scar tissue. I walked through the days—breakfast-lunch-dinner—with my insides raw and shredded, my whole body scraped and gutted. No one noticed a thing.

"I can't remember the last time it was this cold," Nona told me as she fiddled with the thermostat in the living room. "Can you?"

I shrugged. Weather was weather. I couldn't make myself care enough to remember.

"Jerry and I saw an ice storm in Illinois last winter," she went on when I didn't answer. "Everything turned slick and silver—the streets and sidewalks, even the trees. It was amazing."

My homework was spread across the table and I sat staring at it without feeling the slightest interest or obligation to begin. "If it was so amazing," I said, "maybe you should have stayed there."

Nona whirled around to face me. "What's your fucking problem, Alice? Are you *looking* for a fight?" Her eyes were tight, her mouth drawn, and I felt an icy thrill stir in the pit of my stomach—a fight. I wanted to scream and slap and bite. I wanted to make her cry, make her yell. Maybe I could make her mad enough to hurt me. Maybe I could make her mad enough to kill me.

"You act like your life is so hard," I told her, "like you have things so bad. Everything's so *easy* for you. It always has been."

Nona stood, blinking at me. "Are you serious?"

"Jerry left his whole life," I said, "just because you asked him to. Dad treats you like you own the sun. You've spent your entire life getting everything you want, and all you do is complain about it."

My sister's face was sheet white, her hands balled at her sides. For a moment, I thought she might rush forward to shake me, might wrap her hands around my throat and squeeze until the last trickle of air had left my body. I'm right here, I thought. Come and get me. But Nona turned, crossing the room to the little drawer where my father kept his white envelopes. She bent over, shuffling through until she found the one she was looking for. Then she held it out to me, stepping closer so that I could read the writing my father had scrawled across the back: *Alice—college.*

"You think I have one of these?" she asked. "You think there was ever one of these with *my* name on it?"

I stared at the envelope, waiting to feel something: happiness, surprise, excitement. But I looked at the worn paper, the fold he must have touched so many times, and I felt nothing. "How much is there?" I asked, and Nona flipped through, counting silently.

"Four hundred."

"That isn't anywhere near enough," I told her. "Not even for a crappy college."

Her head dipped forward, and for a moment, I thought she was laughing. But when she lifted her eyes to look at me, her face was glazed with tears. "I forgive you," she whispered. "You're my sister, and I forgive you for all the things you don't understand."

Nona went upstairs, shutting herself inside her room while I sat alone at the table. My father was gone with the bus and Jerry had taken the pickup to buy straw. When Sheila Altman arrived for her afternoon lesson, I was the only one there to greet her. She climbed out of her mother's car eating a nectarine, and the wind whipped her yellow hair around her face. She reached back with one hand, catching her hair at the base of her neck while holding the fruit between her teeth, to knot it into a messy bun. "Where is everyone?" she asked.

"Everyone's gone," I told her. "It's just us now."

Sheila saddled Cap and I saddled Darling. "Shouldn't we wait for Nona?" she asked when I mounted Darling in the driveway and started toward the road.

"Wait if you want," I said. "She isn't coming."

Darling was nervous on the road, prancing sideways onto the pavement, scraping my knees into fence rails and mailboxes. Sheila kept Cap several feet back, watching over her shoulder for cars. "We should go back," she said every time that Darling balked or shied.

When we reached the canal, the bed was dry, the floor soft and sandy. I nudged Darling down the bank and Sheila gasped behind me. "What if the water comes?"

"From where?" I asked. "It's winter."

Sheila looked uncertain, but she nudged Cap after me, clinging to the saddle horn with one hand.

"I'll race you," I told her.

"I don't want to," she said.

"Ready?"

"I said *I don't want to.*"

I touched my heels to Darling's sides and she sprang beneath me. It didn't matter whether Sheila was going to try or not—she would never be able to keep up. Around us, the world passed in blurs of sand and gray, the dull shades of winter stirring together above the canal bank. I let the reins slide through my fingers, giving Darling her head, letting her go, and I felt her body extend beneath me, the pure, pulsating desire for speed. The sandy road of the canal bed rolled beneath us, bending and curving. We turned, and the bridge appeared ahead of us, the place where the canal disappeared into a rusty metal tunnel to pass beneath the highway.

I tried to gather the reins in my hands, pulling them toward my shoulders and sinking back on my heels. Darling's weight shifted beneath me, sliding through the sandy floor. The weight of a semi truck screamed on the highway above us, and Darling's knees buckled, backing away from the tunnel, the place where the canal left the town behind and stretched out to the river, the mountains, the world beyond. At a different time of year, we would have been underwater. We would have been dead.

"Oh, my God," Sheila said, and I turned in my saddle. She trotted Cap up beside me and reached sideways, touching my shoulder. "Are you okay?"

"We won," I said.

Sheila peered through the rusty tunnel, then up at the highway. "I'm going back now," she said. "I don't care if you come or not."

We walked our horses along the canal without speaking. Darling's coat was lathered with sweat and my breath was fast and thick in my chest. I kept glancing sideways at Sheila, waiting for her to laugh or smile, to be okay. But her jaw was tensed, her eyes locked on the road ahead. "I'm going to tell your father," she said.

When we got home, my father wasn't there. Sheila and I slid off our saddles in the driveway, and she stood a moment, waiting for someone to come from the barn and demand to know where we had been. "Everyone out here's gone crazy," she said finally.

"It's because of the weather," I told her.

"It's because of Patty Jo," she said.

"Patty Jo will be just fine," I promised. "She's in good hands."

"That's not what I meant." Sheila squared her shoulders. "Your father spent too much time with her," she said, her voice prim and knowing. "He crossed a line. And now this place is falling apart. *Everyone* saw it coming."

"You're one to talk," I said, and she blinked at me. "How many times a week does your dad have *night labs*?"

Her face froze in a blank half smile. "What are you talking about?" she asked.

From someplace far away, I could see myself, could hear the words I was about to say. And I wanted to stop. Really, I did. "Your father's not in love with your mother," I said. "He's cheating on her."

"You're a liar."

Her voice was thin, barely a whisper. She stared down at the ground with her chin cocked and her forehead creased. When she lifted her eyes to mine, the cords of her neck were rigid, her mouth wrenched back. Inside her head, she was putting things together, all the moments I hadn't seen, all the little encounters I didn't know about. And in that instant, I saw it in her eyes: what I'd said was true. And it was too late to take it back.

Her body went rigid, and I stood, waiting for her to cry or scream, to slap me, bite me, pull my hair. But her eyes were dry, her face blank. She took a few stumbling steps backward, then dropped Cap's reins and walked away.

I started to follow after her, then reached for Cap. Sheila sat down in front of the barn with her eyes on the road, and I led the horses past her, tying them at the hitching post. I took my time removing Cap's saddle and putting his blanket on, waiting for Sheila to rise, to chase me away from her horse, to do it herself. But she only sat, staring at the road. I led Cap into his stall, then went outside and sat beside her. An hour passed and then another. The sky darkened, and the air turned cold. But Sheila did not move, did not speak, did not glance in my direction. When her mother's minivan pulled into the driveway, she climbed into the front seat and fastened her seat belt. And they drove away.

One by one, the stalls emptied in our barn. The Catfish did not come for their horses themselves. They sent handlers with trailers. Heathcliff was the first to go, sold, the handler told me as he paused to light a cigarette, to people in Vermont. "You shouldn't smoke around him," I said. "He has really sensitive sinuses." A few days later, another trailer took Sierra—this one bound for Texas. Toy Boy was the last to go. They came for him while I was at school, and when I got home, his stall was empty. No one told me where he was sent.

My father spent more and more time inside the house. The weather was cold and sharp with the energy of an oncoming storm, and my father felt the shift in his knee, wincing in pain with every step he took. He didn't seem to notice the parade of expensive trailers as the boarders' horses disappeared from the barn. He didn't notice that Sheila Altman had stopped coming to ride. Cap was the only horse left in the barn, and he paced and nickered in his stall. "No one's coming for you," I told him. "No one loves you."

With the boarders gone, Jerry moved Darling and King into the barn. "Did you ask Dad first?" Nona asked, and Jerry nodded toward the sky.

"It's gonna snow soon."

"This is the desert," Nona told him. "It doesn't snow."

But Jerry was doing all the work, and so he made the decisions, looking after the barn as if it were his own. In the afternoons, he worked with King while I rode Darling in the arena. Day after day, I raced her down the length of the arena, trying to find the release, trying to find the fear.

"What the hell are you doing out there?" Jerry asked.

"Practicing," I told him.

"You're being reckless," he said. "You'll get hurt if you keep riding like that."

I closed my eyes when Darling ran, dropped my stirrups, spurred her toward the fence, but she never crashed and I never fell. I couldn't get hurt if I tried.

"I mean it!" Jerry said, shaking me by the arm when I came out of the arena. "You're out of control."

But I didn't feel out of control. I didn't feel anything.

"You'll ruin that horse and she'll never train right," Jerry said. "She'll never sell."

"So?"

"So what do you think happens to horses no one buys? They're beasts of burden, Alice—more of them than there are good people to love them. So what happens to the rest?"

I felt a shiver, ten thousand insect wings upon my skin, and I wanted to show him that I knew about darkness and cruelty, knew about pain. He was trying to scare me, but I could not be scared. "They starve," I said. "They get beaten half to death or turned into dog food or left in the desert to die alone."

Jerry grabbed me by the shoulders, bending forward so that I could feel the heat of his breath on my face. His jaw was clenched, his eyes tight and angry, but I did not look away. I wanted him to know that I was not some dewy nincompoop, not some little girl. I wanted to reach out and claw him, scratch his skin wide open with my fingernails, to make him bleed, to make him hurt. Instead, I kissed him.

I pressed my mouth against his and slipped my tongue between his lips until it met the spongy tip of his own. His hands fell from my shoulders and his body surged backward, stumbling away from me. "Why did you do that?" Jerry touched his fingers to his lips, his face a sheet of whiteness against the backdrop of darkening sky.

"Because I could."

He didn't tell my sister. It was a mistake, he said, pure and simple. Everyone made mistakes. But before he walked away, Jerry pointed his index finger at me and lowered his voice. "Never again," he told me. "Never."

After that, Jerry encouraged Nona to spend more time in the barn. He asked her advice about feed or tack, calling her back each time she started for the house. The day he saddled King for the first time, he told my sister that it was an important occasion and it would mean a lot to him if she would stay and watch.

Jerry brought King into the arena and I stopped Darling in the center, watching as my sister climbed onto the fence and lit a cigarette. "Let's get this show on the road," she sighed.

Jerry had been practicing with a pad and saddle for days, setting them on King's back to let him adjust to the weight without tightening the girth strap. But now he reached beneath the horse's belly, pulling the strap up to buckle it. King's ears flickered, and his nostrils widened, but he stood, letting Jerry pat his neck. "How about that?" Jerry called to my sister.

"Impressive," she said, then hopped off the fence, turning for the barn.

"Wait," he told her. "Do you want to mount him?"

Nona laughed. "Don't be stupid," she said. "He's too small."

"Not to ride him," Jerry said. "Just to let him feel the weight. I'm too heavy, but you'd be okay."

Nona shook her head. "Forget it."

"I'll ride him," I said, and they both looked at me.

"Alice, you will not," Nona told me.

I slid off Darling and led her toward Jerry while my sister climbed the fence into the arena, stepping between us. "I'll tell Daddy," she said.

"I'll tell Daddy," I mimicked, and my sister looked nervously at Jerry.

"Jerry, don't let her," she whispered.

"Jerry, don't let her."

Nona whirled around at me. "Okay, fine," she said and held out her arm. "Break your fucking neck, Alice. Just be my most special guest."

Jerry would never have let me mount the horse. He would have changed his mind, made an excuse, said no. But before he had the chance, we heard the creak of the arena gate and when we turned to look, my father was standing behind us.

"What's going on out here?" His face was white, his knuckles clenched on the handle of his cane.

"Daddy," Nona started, relieved by his interruption.

My father limped toward Jerry. "Were you going to put my daughter on that horse?" he asked.

"No," Jerry told him, but my father wasn't listening. He yanked the reins from Jerry's hand, pulling King away from him.

"What's my rule about studs?" my father asked, his face reddening.

"I was just getting him used to a saddle," Jerry explained. "No one was going to ride him."

"I was going to ride him," I said, and my father looked at me. I wanted him to be angry, to yell at me, to see that it was all my fault. But he turned to Nona.

"What's gotten into you?" he shouted. "You used to take care of your sister!"

"It's not my fault," Nona snapped. "Alice is acting crazy. She's all stupid with love for some boy at school."

"He isn't a boy," I said. "He's a teacher. And it doesn't matter anymore because he's gone."

The air went still and all three of them turned to me. The sky was darkening above us, low and thick with clouds. "What have you been doing, Alice?" my father asked, and I could see his frosted breath curling like smoke around him.

"Nothing," I said.

"Is this the English teacher?" he asked. "Is that where I drove you? To that jackass's house?"

My sister's eyes were red and she wiped her nose with the back of her wrist as she listened. "He was a good teacher," I whispered.

"He was a drunk," my father said. "He plowed his car into a telephone pole, then tried to run from the police. Hank on the posse knows the whole story. They found a quart of scotch rolling around inside the guy's desk. They fired him."

Everything was coming undone, my joints loosening like wax, the entire world breaking into pieces beneath me. "You don't know anything," I said. "You drive a school bus."

"Alice," Jerry breathed, but it was too late. Something had come apart. Something was open and I couldn't make it close.

"You can't even pay the bills."

My father had never hit me before. Once, I had seen him slap Nona across the face and the look on his face at that moment was the same as it was now. Frantic. Uncontrollable. His whole body seemed to swell on its frame, making him larger than he really was. Everything inside myself went cold and empty. *Do it.*

And he would have. But before he could take a step in my direction, King poked his nose forward and bit my father on the shoulder. It wasn't hard, just a playful nip, a colt begging for a sugar cube. Surprised, my sister laughed. And in the instant before the world came apart, her hands rose to her mouth, trying to push the sound back in.

But it was too late. My father turned and his hand moved like a flash of lightning, cracking the shaft of his cane across King's chest. The noise split the air and I felt a tear of fire across my palm as Darling reared away from the sound, ripping the reins from my hand.

King crossed one front leg over the other, a move so graceful that it might have been a bow, but as he fell to the ground, we all heard the second crack, unmistakable, as the bone of the front leg splintered, and the earth shook beneath his weight. The sound of screaming came from every corner of the dying world. From my sister. From my center.

He tried to stand, but his leg quivered at strange angles and he fell forward onto his shoulder, his face colliding with dust, his back legs digging at the earth, frantic to rise. My father let go of the reins, backing away. Still, the horse tried to stand, bone popping from the joint of the shoulder, poking through the flesh of the knee. My father stood motionless. The air was screaming. And Jerry was there with the gun.

Nona rushed to stop him, clinging to his arm, pulling the gun sideways. For a moment, he let her, but then the foal screamed, glass scraping metal, his mouth wrenched open, his nostrils clogging with dirt as he dragged himself on the ground. The front leg bent beneath him like a broken straw. Jerry shook my sister away and she fell to the ground, covering her face with her hands. The very first snowflakes were beginning to fall as Jerry lifted the gun. Beneath him, the horse was scraping himself along the ground, dirt catching in the foam of his mouth, sweat steaming from his body in the chilly air. Jerry cocked the gun and the foal lifted his head. With his last earthly breath, he was trying to stand.

I didn't look away when it happened. In the moment that the noise split the earth, the foal's body jerked for the last time, one violent, heaving shudder. The blood poured beneath his head as the world went still. Then the ground fell away beneath me. And there was nothing.

fifteen

AND THE SNOW FELL. It covered the blue mountains to the east, the red mountains to the west, until there was nothing left to distinguish one side of the valley from the other, until the whole world was buried in white silence.

It was Jerry who made the phone call that night, who gave directions to our house and spoke a skeleton of details into the receiver: accident, break, gun. When he hung up the phone, he repeated what had been told to him: It was too late for anything to be done that night. They would come for the body the next morning.

And the snow fell.

The driveway filled. The roof sagged under the weight. Desert Valley was not equipped to handle winter weather. There were no plows, no sanders. No one owned a snow shovel. The next morning, the roads were closed, the schools out of session. No one came for him. No one could. For the eight days that he lay dead in our arena, no one came and no one went.

Years later, my sister would still maintain that the leg might have been mended. The foal was young, after all, with strong bones and good resilience. Something might have been done. And if not, a veterinarian could have made a medical decision. Someone whom she did not know could have said the words and done the deed. A needle, she said. It could have ended with a pinprick.

Yes, I would tell her when she said this. Because it could have.

After Jerry pulled the trigger, my sister would not share her bed with him. She couldn't bear the feel of his body against hers, the scent of his skin on her bedsheets, the low, murmuring whispers he made in his sleep. She could not look at him. The night the foal died, my sister slept in my bed. And the night after that. And the night after that.

Three weeks later, Jerry would be gone. The sun would be shining, shrinking the snow to crusty patches, turning the ground loose and soggy beneath it. For a second time, I would stand in the driveway while Jerry loaded boxes into the back of his truck. Again, I would watch while he climbed inside and drove away. But this time, he would load only his own things. This time, when he left, he wouldn't ever come back.

Time, they say, is the healer of all wounds. Forgive and forget. What's done is done. But days would pass into weeks, then months, then years, and still people would talk about the blizzard. "Lord almighty," men would exclaim in the Co-op, "I've lived my whole life in this desert and I've never seen snow like that." They would call it a fluke, a wonder, a miracle, recalling how children made lopsided snowmen and used garbage bags for sleds. "That's the desert for you," they would say, giving it over to nature, to God, to the imperfect world and all its unexpected possibilities.

My father would go the rest of his life without ever speaking of the storm, the cold, the night that death fell from the sky, hiding the world beneath it. My sister and I, when we finally spoke of it, would not talk about wonders or miracles. We would not talk about God. Instead, we would talk about winter, about trees breaking under the weight of snow and water freezing in pipes. We would say that time had clouded our memories, dimmed the details and blurred the events so that we could not quite separate one moment from another, could not remember who had said what. Blame, we would tell each other, was irrelevant. What was done was done.

Here now, for once, is the truth: My memory is not clouded. The details are not blurred. My father struck the blow. Jerry fired the gun. But I alone killed him. And a life, whole and perfect, ended before my eyes. Blame is, in fact, irrelevant, if only because it changes nothing.

The night he died, I lay in bed with my sister's body warm against mine. In the darkness, I felt a raw, throbbing ache across my palm, and I lifted my arm above the sheets, confused by the pain. Slowly, the memory rebuilt itself inside my mind, the crack of beech wood on bone, the first movement of his fall, one slender leg crossing in front of the other as he dipped toward the ground. And then I remembered the sear of leather across my palm, the mare rearing away from the sound, ripping the reins through my hand. Until that moment, I had not thought of her. None of us had. We had left her out there. With him.

Outside, it didn't look like night, like day, like anything that had ever been before. The snow was falling in thick, cottony clumps, filling in my footsteps behind me. The sky was tinted orange. By the time I reached the arena, the foal was nothing more than a white mound in the center.

The mare stood at the far end of the ring with her knees locked and her head low. I looked into her mismatched eyes and the cold moved through my body like a wind. She had endured days tied beneath the brutal glare of the sun, weeks of beatings by the broodmares, but the hours she had passed in the darkness and snow had done what no man or beast could do.

Within a few months, the mare would be sold, bought by a nice family with two nice children. They would pay three times what my father had paid at the auction, complimenting him on her exceptional training and sweet disposition. "This mare is rock solid," my father would tell them. "You could fire a cannon off her head and she wouldn't even blink." And then she would be gone, taken to another life, a life where she was precious and perfect, a life where no one knew that she had once loved to run, that she had once been unbreakable.

What is *sorry*? What is regret? I went back for her, but it was too late. She had spent the night breathing the scents of his blood and fear, the sticky-sweet panic rising like steam in the cold air as he tried to lift himself. She had heard bone snap and flesh tear, the frantic, tinny screams that wrenched from his wide-open mouth. And she had seen us walk away, leaving his broken body to the night, the cold, the deep, unknowable silence of the earth disappearing beneath snow. By the time I went for her, her eyes were empty, her breath slow. I reached for the reins and she turned to follow me, passive, obedient, a perfect pet.

And the snow fell.

Like in a dream, it distorted shapes and colors, hiding everything that was familiar, burying everything that was real. Somewhere in the distance was the barn, the house, the world of my childhood. But the snow swirled like a million white insects around me, and I could see none of it.

And then, through the blizzard, a shimmer of movement appeared in the open gate. A white shadow, it shifted through the snow toward the center of the arena. As it moved closer, I could make out an outline—narrow shoulders, thin arms, dark hair flecked with white. I went still and the mare stopped beside me. The reins were stiff with cold in my fingers and I closed my eyes. This was a dream—all of it. Like the water that filled my bedroom before it, the snow would be gone when I opened my eyes. The sun would be shining. Nothing had been done that could not be undone.

But unlike in the world of my dreams, I could feel the cold air moving around me, the snow burning on my cheeks, seeping through my boots, dampening my socks and deadening my feet. And when I opened my eyes, she was still there, a pale slip of a girl amid the swirling white. She stopped beside the foal's body, looking down over the silver mound. Less than a month before, we had tried to call her back from the dead, and she had not answered. I had forked my path across the one that should have belonged to her, lied my way into her memories, stolen the life she would never live. I had entered a world that was never intended for me, and now that world was broken. So of course, she would come now. Of course, it would be her ghost that guarded him.

She did not look in my direction, did not seem to notice or care that I was with her, that I was responsible. I wanted to speak to her, to apologize, to explain, but when I tried to form the words inside my throat, there was nothing. What is sorry? What is regret? He was gone. No words could ever explain why.

And then, through the whirl of blinding snow, I heard a whisper: "Marian."

Her head lifted at the sound of my father's voice. As soon as the name was spoken, the spell broke around me and I saw her as she really was. It was not—had never been—the drowned girl.

My father crossed the arena in slow, small steps, his limp worsened by the cold. He had dropped his cane to the ground after striking it across the foal's chest and it lay, like everything else, lost beneath the blanket of snow. They stood for a moment without touching, without speaking. My father's head dipped, his eyes closing, and my mother turned, looking up into his face through the snow. She lifted one hand, moving his hair off his forehead with her fingertips. He opened his eyes and she leaned into him, wrapping her arms around his neck, letting him lift her. Her bare feet were pink with cold, her nightgown damp, revealing the rail of her body beneath—hips, nipples, shoulders, ribs. He turned back toward the gate, his steps slow and shaking as he carried her away from the body, away from the death and cold, through the barn, back to the house where she belonged.

This is the part of the story that I have never told my sister, the part I have never told anyone. This part of the story, I have kept for myself—the way they stood together over the body, sharing for a moment the huge unnameable grief of all the things that had come to pass, all the choices made, all the words unspoken. And in that moment, I saw them not as my mother and father, but as the people they were to each other after so many years of life intertwined, the people they had become: the woman who would forever be a child, the man who would forever carry her.

After Jerry was gone, my father would return to the barn. Horses had to be fed and exercised, things that broke had to be repaired. There would always be work, and someone would always have to do it.

Sheila Altman would return to the barn and my father would continue teaching her, continue encouraging her to bring her friends. The first time she appeared in the barn after the snowfall, I thought it might be to collect her things, but she climbed out of her mother's minivan and headed toward Cap's stall like it was any other day. "You came back," I said.

"Show season's coming." She lifted her saddle and paused, brushing her hair from her face with her shoulder. "And I think I'm getting better."

"You are," I told her.

Only a few weeks had passed since I'd seen her, but she looked older, long-legged and easy in her clothes. She shifted her weight, balancing the saddle on one hip. And in that moment, she looked like any seasoned show girl, like she'd been doing it forever. "Plus," she said, "what would Cap do without me?" She gave me a half smile, lifting her eyes to the ceiling to make fun of herself.

"He would be really lonely."

Sheila glanced over her shoulder, looking through the barn to the arena, clean and damp from the melted snow. "It's quiet out here," she said.

"Jerry left."

Sheila nodded, neither saddened nor surprised. "I suppose there's more to the story than that."

"There is."

We watched each other for a second and I felt a wave of sorrow rise in my chest—all the things I wanted to say to her. But before I could begin to find the words, she slid one foot forward, touching the toe of her boot to the toe of mine. "You don't have to tell me." Her voice was soft, her eyes deep with understanding. "That's what we do for the people we love."

"What?" I whispered.

"We keep their secrets."

Of all the things I have done in my life, what I did to Sheila still stands as the worst, the only one that came from a place of pure cruelty. And still, she forgave me. Just like that, she did. She would continue to ride at our barn, continue to invite me to every slumber party she threw. She would never ask about Jerry or the empty round pen where we had once kept Ginger's foal. I would never ask about her father. Three years later, Sheila and her mother would move back to California. They would take Cap with them. For a while, Sheila would send letters, telling us about her new house and new school, enclosing pictures of herself riding Cap on the beach.

"Jesus Christ," Nona would say when she saw them. "I wish she would have bought *me.*"

Though my sister had once told me that she would die without Jerry, she would eventually move on to other men. The night she slept with both Pope twins, she climbed into my bed after dark to give me all the details.

"At the same time?" I asked.

"Don't be ridiculous," she told me. "It was, like, *hours* apart. I think one of them might have been a virgin."

"Which one?"

"I can never tell them apart," she said. "Which one has the chipped tooth?"

"Zach."

"Yeah, him," she said. "*Anyway,* it was great. They both just looked at me like lovesick dogs the whole time. They were so *grateful.* I'm only sleeping with younger men from now on."

By the time Nona had her sights set on husband number two and tried, at last, to get a divorce from Jerry, it ended up being completely unnecessary. My sister had been seventeen when she got married in that courthouse, which turned out to be illegal in the state of Kansas. She had lied about her age, making herself nineteen. The marriage had been unofficial from the beginning, the contract null and void.

Husband number two was a marine, and after he proposed, my sister twirled through the barn with her hands above her head. He had lived everywhere, she told us, and was going to take her to California, Hawaii, *New York City.* "Do you think it will last?" I asked my father.

"I hate to be the one to tell you this," he said, "but your sister's kind of a birdbrain." His mouth was twisted in a wry half smile, but when he turned to look at me, his face softened. "I hope so," he said. "Really, I do."

I was seventeen, the age my sister had been when Jerry first approached her at the rodeo to tell her that she was the reincarnation of Priscilla Presley. Before she left with her marine, Nona kissed me on both cheeks and told me not to give up, that my ticket would come. One day, someone would take me away too. "Try being less hostile," she suggested. "And maybe wear your hair up."

A few weeks after Nona left with the marine, my ticket came not in the form of a man, but in an envelope addressed to my father. He opened it, then stood staring, his mouth opening and closing soundlessly. "It's for you," he said finally, holding the slip of paper between his thumb and forefinger so that I could see.

The check was made out to me, and the ground turned to liquid beneath my feet as I counted the number of zeros. "It's a mistake," I whispered.

"I don't think so," he said, then pointed to the signature— *Patricia Johansson.*

"Patty Jo?" I asked. My father nodded. "Why would she do that?"

He turned the check over in his hand, brushing his fingers across the amount and then the signature before folding it into my palm. "I guess she thought you might be able to use it."

"Did she send a letter?" I asked, and my father shoved his hands into his pockets, turning his back to look out the window.

"No."

I stood beside him, staring out at the front pasture. Over the years, we had lost the broodmares one by one to old age. After the foal's death, my father never bought another stud; even if we'd had the money to replace the mares, we had no need. Now the front pasture was empty, overgrown with grass and weeds. I curled my hand around the folded check, waiting for it to dissolve like ash between my fingers. "Do you still think about her?" I whispered, and my father's Adam's apple trembled in his throat.

"Sometimes."

My father had once flushed pink every time he made her laugh across the dinner table, had beamed each time she took a jump. It was something he had given her, that feeling of flying, that freedom. "She never meant to hurt you," I said, and beside me, my father smiled.

"Everyone gets hurt," he told me. "Meaning's got nothing to do with it."

I looked down at the check and pictured Patty Jo's hand writing out the amount, signing her name at the bottom. She was out there, somewhere in the wide world. She had left us, but she had not forgotten. "This is a lot of money, Dad."

"It's a lot of money to you," he said. "To her, it's just the price of a horse."

"We could have the barn painted," I told him. "We could go to an auction."

But my father turned away from me, limping toward the back door. "She wanted you to have it. It's *yours.*"

Maybe this was Patty Jo's way of apologizing, her way of making amends for mixing her messy life into ours, for never saying goodbye. Or maybe she really loved my father. Maybe he had told her about the little white envelope with my name on it, the money he would never have to fill it. Maybe, when she could not save my father, she could at least believe that she'd saved me.

And so I took it. Of course I did. I took the money, and I left.

Every time I went home, the valley would look less and less like I remembered. The money spread from east to west and the land around our house began to fill with expensive homes and sprinkler systems, restaurants and shopping malls. Eventually, my father would lose the battle and sell the barn. His leg hurt him more each year. The work was too hard, he said, and the money he was offered for the land was too good to turn down. He'd spent his whole life laboring, only to watch it slip away in pieces. Retiring, he told me, was not the same as surrendering. It was not weakness; it was merely acceptance.

Childhood is never over, not really. The new owners would tear down the house, leveling the barn and dividing the land into plots. But the places we come from don't leave us as easily as we leave them. Desert is land that cannot be owned, cannot be controlled, cannot be forgotten, a place so unique unto itself that, still, so many years later, I can sometimes feel it pulling.

An evening breeze will shift, soft and warm, like the desert in autumn, and for a moment it will all seem so near: those evenings when the barn glowed beneath the rosy light of sunset and my father and I made our rounds through the pens, throwing hay to the horses and filling buckets with grain. In the back pasture, the Old Men would lift their heads at the sound of my father's approach, clopping toward him on their creaking ankles. They would gather around him, closing their eyes and groaning in little breaths of perfect pleasure as my father scratched their ears and necks, whispering to them beneath his breath. In those days, when he still regarded me as an extension of himself, my father would sometimes let me stand beside him as he told me their stories, pointing out their strengths, explaining what each one might have been: the show horse, the barrel racer, the cutting horse, the jumper. And it is in these moments that I remember him clearly, the sound of his voice as he spoke their names, the gentleness of his touch, and the way that he loved, truly loved, every one of them: each of those broken promises, all those dreams that never came true.

acknowledgments

My sincerest thanks to the University of Montana, the Rona Jaffe Foundation, the Millay Colony for the Arts, the MacDowell Colony, and C. Michael Curtis and *The Atlantic Monthly* for the guidance and assistance they provided while I was writing this book. I have also been enormously fortunate to see my book in the hands of Denise Shannon, Sarah McGrath, and Nan Graham, who have each at different stages taken such good care of it. Lastly, I owe the deepest gratitude to Jen Kocher and Diana Spechler for their friendship and advice, to my family for their years of unwavering support, and to Kevin, without whom this book would likely not exist.

about the author

ARYN KYLE is a graduate of the University of Montana writing program. Her first published short story, "Foaling Season," now the first chapter of *The God of Animals,* won *The Atlantic Monthly* a National Magazine Award for Fiction. Other stories by her have appeared in *The Georgia Review, Alaska Quarterly Review, Best New American Voices 2005,* and *Ploughshares.* In 2005 she was awarded the Rona Jaffe Foundation Writers' Award, which is given to women writers at an early stage in their careers who demonstrate exceptional talent and promise. She was born in Illinois, but spent most of her childhood in Grand Junction, Colorado, and now lives in Missoula, Montana.

A SCRIBNER
READING GROUP GUIDE

THE GOD OF ANIMALS

QUESTIONS FOR DISCUSSION

1. Aryn Kyle chose to tell her story through the eyes of Alice, a twelve-year-old girl just learning about the adult world. What do you think of that choice? Does Alice's youth and inexperience make her vision clearer? More vivid?

2. What is the significance of the title? Who or what is the god of animals? What do the characters' interactions with horses demonstrate about human nature, power, and the natural world?

3. Alice struggles to make sense of her family and her world, and the Winstons' tendency to keep secrets and withhold the truth doesn't make it easy for her. What does she learn about her family and, in turn, about herself as the novel progresses? What did you think was most revelatory?

4. Alice fixates on her dead classmate, Polly Cain, and invents a friendship with her that never existed. Why do you think she seeks entrance into the life Polly left behind? What conclusion does Alice reach about what happened to Polly?

5. "My mother had spent nearly my whole life in her bedroom" (page 3). Discuss how this affects the Winston family dynamic. Why do you think Marian chooses to live this way? Is it fair? Do you think her family accepts her or enables her? Or neither?

6. Joe Winston's plans for the ranch often don't come to fruition, yet he stays hopeful that his fortune will change. How would you describe Joe? What ties him to the ranch? What does Alice see that he doesn't?

7. What draws Alice to Mr. Delmar? She keeps calling him, though she acknowledges that "in some way I could not name, we weren't playing by the rules. Eventually, there would have to be a price" (page 185). What is the price? Does their relationship do Alice harm or good?

8. Patty Jo separates herself from the Catfish. Why is she different? How do she and Joe help, but also hurt, each other? How does she affect Alice?

9. Alice surprises everyone, most of all herself, when she rides Darling at the horse show. What does she discover in "that moment of connection" (page 194) that she had never understood before? Is she better able to understand her father's and Nona's connection with horses? Why do you think she's unable to replicate that moment with Darling again?

10. Patty Jo states, "Marriage is the most expensive ticket to nowhere" (page 262). Does her bleak characterization of marriage hold true for the other married couples in the novel? Consider the marriages of Joe and Marian, Nona and Jerry, and Mr. and Mrs. Altman.

11. At the end of the novel, Alice says, "The places we come from don't leave us as easily as we leave them" (page 304). For which character is this most true? What hold does the ranch have on each of the sisters?

12. Over the course of the summer, the lifestyles of the Altmans, Patty Jo, and the Catfish come into sharp contrast. What does Alice observe about what wealth and class can provide, and what they can't? What happens when some of the characters reach for something beyond what they are accustomed to?

13. Discuss the role of violence and cruelty in the novel. Is there something about the harshness of life on a ranch, or working with animals, that brings them closer to the surface? How does Alice deal with her father's and grandfather's brutal acts? How might her own actions ultimately figure in to her feelings? Does she forgive them? Does she forgive herself? Why?

14. Horses play a part in some of the novel's most moving scenes. Take, for instance, when Alice retrieves Yellow Cap, Patty Jo's accident, and the weaning of the foals. Which were the most powerful? What did you learn about the characters in those scenes?

15. Kyle uses the changing seasons to give a loose structure to the novel, and the extremes of the climate and Colorado setting often coincide with pivotal events. How does Kyle use imagery and

descriptions of the conditions to enhance the plot? Did you find this effective?

16. *The God of Animals* may be considered a coming-of-age novel in that many of its events force Alice to leave the innocence of childhood behind. Was there one event that stood out? Does Kyle succeed in her portrayal of a girl on the brink of adulthood? What part of her portrayal felt most authentic to you?

AUTHOR Q&A

Your short story "Foaling Season," the first chapter of *The God of Animals,* won a National Magazine Award for Fiction for *The Atlantic Monthly.* Did you have the idea for your book at the time you wrote the short story, or did the novel develop over time?

Three years passed between the time that I finished the short story and the time I returned to expand it into a novel. I was always interested in the characters and in the town in which the story takes place, but after the story was published, I assumed I was done with them. In the aftermath of graduate school and a failed attempt at another novel, I found myself living back in my hometown of Grand Junction, Colorado, the town that Desert Valley is loosely based upon. More and more, I caught myself thinking about Alice again. I was interested in how the town had changed over the years, in the way that a tide of money and commercial culture was displacing the old families and the old ways. But mostly, I was interested in Alice's family, and in Alice's struggle to make a place for herself in a world that seems to have no place for her. The short story ended before she could really make any headway. I became curious as to where she might go and who she might become if the events of the story continued into the wider space of a novel. The story of *The God of Animals* starts with chapter one, but I've always felt that the novel really starts with the second chapter.

How did you think of the title? What are your own ideas about how animals can teach us lessons of spirituality?

The title didn't come to me until I'd finished the book. I was starting to panic a bit, figuring that no one would be too interested in publishing a book called *Novel,* which is what I'd named the file on my computer. So I did the only thing I could think of—I frantically thumbed through the pages of the draft, waiting for something to pop out at me. I reread the scene between Alice and Mr. Delmar where they discuss God and spirituality. Something about that scene seemed to encapsulate some of the greater themes of the novel, the uncertainty Alice has about the world, her desire to believe in something larger than herself, her fears regarding isolation and loneliness.

I'm by no means an expert on spirituality. At twenty-nine, I'm still trying to sort out what I believe about the greater workings of the world. But as a person who has spent a lot of time looking for answers, I think that paying attention to nature is a pretty good place to start: there is no good, no bad, no right, wrong, *fair.* The lines between beauty and brutality can at times be hard to locate. Alice wants to believe that there's something out there in the universe that *cares.* But in the end, she cares. And I think that, maybe, that's enough.

Although you have been published in several literary magazines, *The God of Animals* is your first novel. How has publishing a novel changed your writing career and what do you look forward to the most?

My *writing career.* That still sounds strange. I spent so much time working jobs I didn't like (and, frankly, wasn't very good at), staying up all night writing in my sweatpants and having anxiety attacks because I had no idea how I was going to pay rent, buy groceries, and, in general, be a functional member of society. When *The God of Animals* sold, I had thirty dollars in my checking account, owed $25,000 in student loans, and had just left my car on the side of the road after it sputtered smoke from underneath its hood and, promptly, died.

So what has changed? I got my car fixed—it just died again, though, so it might be time to trade up. I have yet to pay off my student loans—I nearly have a heart attack each time I imagine that money just vanishing from my bank account. ("It isn't *vanishing*," my mother keeps telling me. "It's paying for your *education*!") I still write in sweatpants, and I still have anxiety attacks. But in the midst of all this, it hits me once in a while: The publication of this book has made it possible for me to keep writing. It's the only thing I've ever wanted to do with my life. Some days it's working. Some days it's not. Still, there are times I literally have to pinch myself: Every day, I get to wake up and do the thing I most love doing. And what (really, *what?*) could be more amazing than that?

What happens to Marian, Alice's mother, at the end of the book?

The short answer: nothing.

The long, and perhaps more interesting answer: Of all the characters in the novel, Marian is probably the most all-knowing when it comes to the goings-on in the barn. She sees everything from her window, hears everyone's secrets through the walls of her bedroom. But her knowledge/view of the world comes from the fact that she has all but dropped out of it. She sees everything, but has given up all her power or influence by retreating to her room. In the last chapter, she is coaxed outside by the death of King. Presumably, she witnessed the acts that led up to his death from her window and when she ventures into the snowstorm to see the body up close, it seems like it might be a first step toward her returning to the world. But when Joe approaches her, she can't resist the old groove she has carved for herself.

Ultimately, I think of the book as being about choices. Marian has not found herself in the position she's in because of one grandiose choice made years ago, but because she made the same small choices again and again. Likewise, Joe has made the same small concessions again and again: His wife falls down and he picks her up. The scene in the snowstorm is not "the moment" of choice between them. It's only one of many. The thing that sets it apart is that it's a moment witnessed by Alice. She has spent most of the novel dissatisfied with her home life. But in the end, she understands that if her life is going to change, it won't be because her parents make different choices; it will be because she does.

As a graduate of the University of Montana writing program, what do you believe are the benefits of studying creative writing? What did you learn that you could share with aspiring writers?

There are plenty of successful writers who never attended a creative writing program. For me, though, the experience was invaluable. Looking back, I'm not sure I could really dissect the process into particulars. The creative writing workshop is a pretty mysterious beast. But the combination of deadlines, instruction, and just the permission to devote a couple of years to writing somehow really worked for me. Overall, being able to live in a community of other writers was hugely important. I was really lucky to go through the program with a group of students who were writing really well, and, as much as I learned from the instructors, I learned way more from the other people who were in my workshops. But as far as advice for other writers, I suppose the most important thing I learned (and it seems pretty obvious) is that if you want to be a writer, you have to write. You have to carve the time out of your day to sit in front of your computer, even on the days when nothing is happening. There are plenty of days that I spend writing a sentence, deleting a sentence, then playing solitaire. But showing up seems to be the key, even if you're just staring at a blank screen. Whatever happens, it starts with sitting down in the chair.

What are you reading now? Who are your favorite authors? What types of books appeal to you most?

I've been reading a lot of short stories lately. Joy Williams is perhaps my all-time favorite short story writer. She has three collections: *Escapes, Taking Care,* and *Honored Guest.* If you haven't read them, do it now. Seriously. Run, don't walk. I also love Lorrie Moore, George

Saunders, Antonya Nelson, Alice Munro; the list goes on and on. Kevin Canty is another of my favorites. I might be slightly biased on this one, as I live with him. But I don't think so. Check out *A Stranger in This World* or *Honeymoon* and tell me that the writing doesn't devastate you—in a good way.

As far as novels go, here's a short list of my favorites, both recent and long-standing: *Housekeeping* by Marilynne Robinson, *That Night* by Alice McDermott, *Middlesex* by Jeffrey Eugenides, *Catch-22* by Joseph Heller, *Bel Canto* by Ann Patchett, *Emma* by Jane Austen, *To the Lighthouse* by Virginia Woolf, *The Secret History* by Donna Tartt. Anything by Margaret Atwood—I would pay to read a grocery list written by her.

My list is pretty varied, I guess. I'm not sure I can accurately describe a "type" of book that appeals to me. Mostly, I'll read anything that surprises or engages me, anything that includes characters I care about or am interested in. They don't have to be good people—they just have to seem real.

How much of your adolescence and personal experience are incorporated into your novel? Like Alice, did you ride horses growing up in Colorado? Why did you choose a child to be the main character?

Lots? None? This is a tricky question to answer. As far as lifestyle and experience, my own adolescence could not have been more different from Alice's. I didn't grow up on a ranch; didn't have a sister; my mother got out of bed and went to work every day. But adolescence is adolescence. Like Alice, I certainly know about loneliness, about longing, about regret, and about the confusion of trying to live in the world without really understanding it. Though, if I were going to be perfectly honest, I would have to admit that these are all things I found myself working through in my twenties, rather than in my teens.

I did take riding lessons when I was about Alice's age, and I competed in a few local horse shows. It was such a different world from the one I'd grown up in, and though I gave it up when I started high school, I guess it made a pretty big impression on me.

I don't feel much like I *chose* to write from the point of view of a child. I just thought the character was interesting, and her problems felt important to me. Maybe, because the character was young, I felt like I had more permission to let her make mistakes. And the more she screwed up, the more invested I was in her, and in finding out what happened to her.

You have spent time in writers' colonies to finish your work. Do you prefer to work in isolation? When and where do you do your best writing?

I definitely prefer to work in isolation, mostly because I talk to myself and pace around a lot, and I don't much like to look insane in front of other people. Even when I'm at home, I tend to work during the night, just because I like the quiet and the feeling of solitude. This can make it tricky at times to have a "real life." But this is an area I'm still negotiating.

You have an uncanny ability to create highly accessible and relatable characters. What is the key to your character development and do you base them on people in your life?

I don't really base my characters on people I know, though I'm sure that there are people in my life who could look at certain characters and see some similarities to themselves. Mostly, I think that the writing process is pretty mysterious, and I feel like it's sort of bad luck to spend too much time trying to understand it. As far as characters go, I guess the best explanation I have is that I write about people I care about. I try to give them room to make their mistakes, to be thoughtless and cruel as well as just and compassionate, basically, to let them be human.

Do you have another novel in the works? Where do your ideas and inspirations come from?

Lately, I've been working mainly on short stories. It's kind of hard for me to spend so much time working on one project, then dive into another. I've needed the time to get Alice's voice out of my head before I commit to another novel. But I do have a second novel under way—I'm superstitious, though, and it seems like bad luck to talk about something while it's still in the works. Mostly, my writing starts with the characters, with understanding their flaws and their desires. Plot, for me, seems to come later, after I know what my characters want, and what they're willing to sacrifice to get it.

ENHANCE YOUR BOOK CLUB

1. Aryn Kyle's fiction has appeared in numerous literary journals. Visit www.pshares.org, www.theatlantic.com, or check out *Best New American Voices 2005* to find her short stories. Discuss them at your next book club meeting!
2. Get in the Western spirit and find a heart-stopping rodeo near you. Click on www.rodeo.com for links to everything from rodeo tickets and DVDs to horse decals and cowboy T-shirts.
3. Take your book club on the road and spend a weekend on a working horse farm. To find a ranch near you, visit www.horseproperties.net.